Greig Beck grew up a  in
Sydney, Australia. His k-
ing, and reading science nt
on to study computer science, immerse himself in the finan-
cial software industry, and later received an MBA. Today,
Greig spends his days writing, but still finds time to surf at his
beloved Bondi Beach. He lives in Sydney, with his wife, son,
and an enormous German shepherd.

If you would like to contact Greig, his email address is
greig@greigbeck.com, and you can find him on social media
and the web at www.greigbeck.com.

Also by Greig Beck

The Alex Hunter series
Arcadian Genesis
Beneath the Dark Ice
Dark Rising
This Green Hell
Black Mountain
Gorgon
Hammer of God
Kraken Rising
From Hell
The Dark Side
The Well of Hell

The Matt Kearns series
The First Bird
Book of the Dead
The Immortality Curse
Extinction Plague

The Valkeryn Chronicles
Return of the Ancients
The Dark Lands

The Fathomless series
Fathomless
Abyss – Fathomless II

LEVIATHAN

FATHOMLESS III

GREIG BECK

momentum

Pan Macmillan acknowledges the Traditional Custodians of country throughout Australia and their connections to lands, waters and communities. We pay our respect to Elders past and present and extend that respect to all Aboriginal and Torres Strait Islander peoples today. We honour more than sixty thousand years of storytelling, art and culture.

First published 2023 in Momentum by Pan Macmillan Australia Pty Ltd
1 Market Street, Sydney, New South Wales, Australia, 2000

NATIONAL LIBRARY OF AUSTRALIA

A catalogue record for this book is available from the National Library of Australia

Leviathan: Fathomless III

EPUB format: 9781761267796
Print on Demand format: 9781761267413
Original cover design: AJ Swarthout
Cover images: Shutterstock

Macmillan Digital Australia: www.macmillandigital.com.au
To report a typographical error, please visit www.panmacmillan.com.au/contact-us/

Visit www.panmacmillan.com.au/ to read more about all our books and to buy books online. You will also find features, author interviews and news of any author events.

To my dad, Barry, a man of the sea, and his little boat the Nellie. *Fishing in heaven now, and hopefully saving me a seat. Still miss you, big guy.*

"When the gates of hell open,
the first beast through will be the Leviathan."

The Mysterious Super Predator

Scientists have been tagging great white sharks for decades to study these ancient creatures' feeding, mating, and migration patterns. But in 2003 something occurred that baffled them.

A research team tagged a nine-foot female great white shark off Australia's South Australian coast and followed its movements for days. And then the animal vanished.

As later reported in the *National Geographic* in 2014, the tracking tag eventually washed up on a beach miles from where it and the shark had vanished, and the information revealed something confounding. It recorded the animal's position, depth in the water, and the ambient water temperature with data they expected – the shark was cruising in about 500 feet of water – when suddenly it plummeted to around 2000 feet below the surface. And, alarmingly, the recorded temperature spiked dramatically from 46°F to 78°F.

It was concluded that a temperature at that depth could only come from the female great white's tag being inside another sea creature, a creature big enough to kill and eat a nine-foot predatorial shark.

To this day, suspicion falls on a super predator, with a monster great white being the prime suspect. Searches have been undertaken for this colossal creature, but nothing has been found.

At least not yet.

PROLOGUE

The Southern Ocean, 180 miles beyond the tip of what would one day be South America, 2 million years ago

The male Carcharodon Megalodon glided through the dark waters after leaving behind the last landmass a day ago.

It continued to travel southward, rising to a depth of just on 100 feet, where the weak sunshine rippled across its pale upper body, giving it a faint tiger-like striping. It was a rarity in that its hue was more clay colored than the usual gray to black of its kin. This meant it avoided the shallows during the day and preferred to haunt the depths, only rising to feed at night.

The fifty-five-foot creature was just on sixty tons and not the largest of its kind. But the mass of its body meant it needed a lot of fuel. And after not eating for several weeks, it was now underweight, and starving.

The cooling waters and climate meant more glaciers and ice shelves locked up more of the sea, cutting off breeding estuaries and seaways and disrupting ocean currents. The great cetaceans it had dined upon in its early days had vanished and their telltale squeaks and clicks were just a dim memory.

Outside of the warm sea corridor it was swimming within, there was nothing but a cold and empty darkness. But this strange near-tropical current it navigated now was like a highway, and it held a promise – the scent of food, and of its own kind.

The Megalodon's snout had a bank of nerves that were sensitive enough to detect a single drop of blood in sea currents even many miles wide, and on each side of the ten-foot-wide head were two nostril-like nares that drew water in and over the olfactory lamellae, a huge sensitive area that registered smells and then sent directional signals into the brain. Those stimuli were now like a blaring siren compelling it onward.

It detected the new landmass many miles before it was close to it. The waters here were dark and deep, and it increased its speed. It feared nothing, as there were few creatures other than its own kind that could challenge it.

It approached the landmass, but found not rock or shallows, but an opening in the rock face. From within, it sensed its own kind, and an abundance of life.

It swam inside and emerged into a warm sea with a blue light shining above. The Megalodon shark immediately began to hunt.

CHAPTER 01

The South Coral Sea, last voyage of the *Pequod*, 1842

"*Thar she blows*," Ahab pointed the tip of his harpoon, his eyes round and white with wild fury. He turned. "Row, row, you dogs. The gold doubloon awaits he who puts their barb into the beast's eye. Now row, damn you, *row-www*!" Ahab's voice boomed like the thunder exploding all around them.

The waves smashed into the whaling boats and the six oarsmen pulled with every ounce of strength they had, stretching their backs and chafing hands that were already hardened like beaten leather.

It was just mid-morning, but the storm stained the day with a gloomy darkness, and it was made even more ominous by the screaming winds and churning foam on the iron-gray ocean.

Another crack of lightning, and their world was momentarily lit like white-hot flame, with Ahab standing firm at the bow of the boat, teeth bared, and pointing the tip of his spear as he sighted his quarry.

Coming up behind them, like a great wall of wood and canvas, was the *Pequod*, unbelievably in full sail even into the teeth of the storm. A reckless act, but Ahab's soul was tied to that of the beast he pursued, and he'd send them all to hell if it meant taking the monster with him.

In the next boat, Ishmael was more frightened than he had ever been in his life. All the men were. But not one of them would dare stand up to Ahab. His resolve and fury were like a physical force, greater than the storm, greater than the churning sea, and matched only by the monstrous white creature they pursued.

"There." Ahab pointed.

In the distance, they saw the rise and fall of the whales' backs as the pod breached, blew air, and then went down again.

"It follows the whales. The white devil always follows the whales." Ahab's eyes seemed to glow in the storm's murky shadows. His grin made his head look like a mad skull.

Ishmael sighted the back of the monster again through the driving rain and whip of the salty spray – never had he seen or even heard of a beast this size. All the men agreed it was twice the size of anything they knew, and being so close now they could smell its stink, like an island exposed at low tide, giving off a rank odor of rotting barnacles and age-old things that wriggled in the depths and waited to feed on men's bones when they sunk down to the slimy sea bottom too many fathoms below them to count.

But there was something else that filled him with doubt and fear – the creature they chased didn't swim like a whale. And though mighty sperm whales had fins on their backs, the white fin cutting the water far ahead of them rose as high as a barn roof.

But they were gaining on it now. The beast seemed to be slowing, allowing them to catch yards on it. *Did it want them to come closer?* Ishmael wondered.

In the lead whaler, Ahab balanced on his one good leg, his other familiar peg-leg carved from the rib bone of a long dead whale. According to Ahab, the missing leg was inside the beast they chased.

The men pulled and pulled again on their oars, drawing ever closer while Ahab urged them on, his screamed words and spittle merging with the chaotic fury of the storm. And then they were beside it. Rather than wait until they had the beast between their boats, Ahab drew his arm back, and launched his harpoon.

It flew straight and swift and penetrated the white hide, taking the trawl rope attached to the barbed lance with it. The mighty creature arched at the pinprick and rolled. Other harpoons flew, some hitting their targets and others missing.

As the white monster surged, the boats whose harpooners had struck their target were pulled forward by the trawl ropes tied off to the prow spike.

And in that one brief second of thinking they might triumph over Ahab's nemesis, their world turned to hell.

The beast dived. Those tied off were immediately dragged down. Of the two boats and their sixteen men that went down, only a few heads bobbed back above the frothing waves. And none of them were Ahab.

Two boats were gone, and two more were on the surface. Then, it was as if the storm held its breath, and even the wind eased back.

"Where are they?" yelled a man in the water who swam to one of the boats.

"Taken straight ta hell," an oarsman replied from behind Ishmael.

There were just three survivors in the water, and the two boats came together as the men watched the sea. But it was desolate, iron gray, as deep and cold as the devil's home, and it refused to reveal what hid below.

Then the beast breached underneath the two boats, exploding upward and catching one boat in a mouth lined with gigantic, triangular teeth as long as Ishmael's arm. The boat was turned to splinters.

The beast rose into the air like a mountain of white muscle. Two thirds of its body left the water, and hung there, impossibly, for a second or two. It was as if the laws of the natural world were cancelled out by this hellish creature.

But in those seconds it hung in the air, a fork of lightning illuminated it. The remaining men saw it was no whale, it was a shark, white, filling the sky, and its massive black eyes were as dark and soulless as death itself.

Just before it hit the water, Ishmael saw that the ragged remains of the bottom half of one of the men was caught in the beast's teeth. A man with one good leg, and one pegged stump. It seemed Ahab had finally met his monster. And the monster had prevailed.

As the tower of white muscle and teeth came crashing down, the remaining men screamed and dived overboard. It landed on their whaleboat, creating a wave fifty feet high.

Ishmael swum toward the *Pequod* and tried to shut out the sounds of the men being picked off and eaten by the monster. Whales didn't do that to people. Sharks did. But he would not let it happen to him, and he never looked back.

The lights of the *Pequod* drew him toward it in the darkness of the storm. It was his one chance of rescue in the maelstrom of wind and rain and monster. But then Ishmael felt the surge wave pass beneath him, and he was lifted high. He realized the mighty beast's fury was not yet spent – it had one more act of revenge to execute on Ahab.

In those last few seconds where he still had hopes of rescue, he saw the creature come up – its huge fin cutting the water as it accelerated and struck the *Pequod*'s midship with a sound like a titan beating a drum. Masts collapsed, men screamed, and rigging fell to the deck. Round and round the white monster circled the boat. Their stricken ship now sitting low in the water, as its hull beams surely had been cracked.

Faster and faster the massive shark's corpse-white body moved until the *Pequod* began to turn. Then spin. Around and around, quicker and quicker, and while Ishmael tread water he could only watch as a vortex began, as the creature used its massive tail to circle the ship, creating a sucking hole in the center of the sea.

The vortex sunk lower, and the *Pequod* was its eye. Lower and lower the ship went until he saw the final standing mast fall below sea level, and he heard the last scream of a doomed man. Then the monster shark also dived into the vortex, chasing down the morsels of meat.

And then it was over. The vortex closed and the monster vanished. Perhaps it was sated, its fury spent.

Ishmael was alone, and he knew he was all that remained of a brave crew, a fateful ship, and a driven man who took on the devil. And lost.

A few broken remnants of the ship bobbed back to the surface. One of them being the empty coffin of his friend, Queequeg. He clung to the carved box and drifted. And prayed.

Ishmael remembered a priest's sermon telling them that when the gates of hell opened, the first beast through would be the leviathan. The devil's pet.

Today was that day.

CHAPTER 02

Nick's Cove, Marin County, California, present day

Cate Granger leaned on the railing of Jack Monroe's boat, the *Heceta*, and watched the line of bubbles pop to the surface.

It was mid-afternoon, the wind had fallen away, and the sun was caressing her face. She closed one eye against the glare from the shimmering bay's surface and inhaled the soft scents of clean salt water, suntan cream, and warming deck wood.

The sixty-two-foot motor yacht was their home now, and the beautiful mix of original teak planking over a white oak frame was their private fortress and their getaway machine. It was like being on holiday every day.

Cate drew in a deep breath as the tiniest of ripples made the boat rock gently and told her something was coming up.

She opened both eyes and, after another moment, she spotted the dark shadow, and then Jack's head in snorkel and dive mask appeared. He pushed it up onto his slicked down hair.

"How is it?" she asked.

"Quite a bit of growth on the hull, a few barnacles, and the paint is flaking. About time she was hauled up and had her ass scraped."

She smiled and rested her chin on her forearms. "I love it when you talk dirty."

He laughed, the sound rolling over the still bay, and his handsome face with the sea blue eyes suddenly took on a wicked glint. "Plenty more where that came from, beautiful."

Jack swam to the stern platform and climbed up. Cate followed and he threw a hand up to her. She leaned out and grabbed it and he stepped over the transom.

He grabbed a towel, rubbed his face and hair, and then sat on the waterproof cushions on the rear seats. He tilted his face to the sun, shut his eyes and let out a long sigh. "I love this life."

"Me too." She shared a smile that was like pure sunshine.

"Only one thing could improve it." He turned to her. "Cate Granger, will you be my wife?"

She laughed and came into his arms. "What is that, three times now?"

He kissed the tip of her nose. "And I'll keep asking you until you say yes."

"Yes, but not yet," she replied. "I love this life too. And you make it perfect. Let's enjoy this for now, and leave the serious stuff for another day, hmm?"

"Okay." He shrugged. "But I'm a pretty good catch – looks, brains, and money."

She scoffed and sat opposite him, lifting her newspaper. "You're lucky Sonya Borashev funded you."

He opened one eye. "What else is a Russian girl to do with a few billion dollars after Valery left her his empire?" He shut his eyes again. "And the money has nearly run out. This boat eats hundred-dollar bills for breakfast."

"We already know what else she's doing." Cate threw both legs up on the long plastic seat cushion. "Still chasing her sea monsters."

Jack sat forward. "I don't blame her. They took the love of her life."

He turned to look over the side at the calm bay's waters. The sun sparkled on its surface and there was only one other yacht half a mile away that seemed becalmed.

She turned from the newspaper to the water, following his gaze and guessing what he was thinking. "Do you think they're still out there?"

"Out there, down there, somewhere?" He bobbed his head from side to side. "Maybe, maybe not. But if they are, then that's where I hope they stay."

"Yeah, me too." She turned a page of the paper and read some more. An article caught her eye. "Have you seen this? A massive glacier sheet broke away in Antarctica. They think it might have exposed a cave beneath the ice shelf. A bi-*iiig* cave."

He shrugged. "Doesn't mean anything to us."

"What if I told you, its name was the Doomsday Glacier." She smiled.

He chuckled. "Now I'm interested. Because if you give something an awesome, scary name then that's certainly going to make me pay attention." He turned away, smiling. "From now on to get more of my attention, Cate Granger will be known as Cate Danger."

She grinned. "I don't need a scary name to make you pay attention." She reached behind her neck to undo the bikini top knot, and let it drop.

Jack immediately got to his feet. "Oh yeah, that works too."

CHAPTER 03

Pine Island Bay, the Amundsen Sea, Antarctica

"We are green on launch." Phil Silvers, head geomorphologist aboard the privately funded research ship, the *SeaTayshun*, quickly ran his eyes over the instruments, seeing the all-green on the launch panel for their miniature submersible, the *Krill-1*, or *K1* for short.

Aboard the submersible, the pilot, Andy Hanson, and his engineer copilot, Heather Banks, confirmed their dive status.

"We are good to go, *SeaTayshun*." Andy gripped the joystick and turned to nod to Heather.

"Confirming, all green across the board," she replied.

The *K1* was basically a streamlined tube with a large acrylic glass dome at front and a pair of extendable arms ending in either a clasping claw or multiple tools depending on the task. It was a little like an underwater Swiss army knife with seats and a camera.

The *K1* was small, compact, and lightweight, and designed more for speed than deep dives. But it was packed with sensitive instrumentation and still capable of attaining fifteen knots in open water.

"Flooding bay area." Silvers spoke like he was part of the machinery as the freezing Antarctic water rose around the vessel. "Opening doors," he said, as the sub launch doors in the hull slowly swung open.

The heaters were working overtime to keep the cold out.

If, in a worst-case scenario, *K1* suffered a total power loss far from its support ship, it would take just three minutes for the small steel and glass tube to drop below zero. Andy and Heather had warm clothing and several thermal pads that could be initiated to supply a burst of heat for up to fifteen more minutes. But any longer than a few hours, and they'd be blocks of ice before they were brought home.

"Initiating . . . *and* launching." Andy calmly and professionally worked the instruments and as soon as the cradle arms retracted, he launched *K1* from its cradle and maneuvered it toward the edge of the ice pack.

"Whoa, frosty." Andy could already feel the cold radiating from the thick window against his knuckles as he gripped the u-shaped wheel. The forward camera was relaying images, but he spoke into his microphone to deliver a supplemental record of what he was seeing.

"Visibility is excellent, water temperature is a balmy twenty-eight degrees, or minus one point eight Celsius for any of our Aussie or European friends listening."

"For our Discovery Channel members that's lower than the freezing point of fish blood, which is about thirty point four degrees." Heather grinned into her mic. "Snap question: why aren't the local fish all turned into fish-cicles?"

"I'm guessing magic." Onboard the *SeaTayshun*, Phil Silvers chuckled.

"Might as well be," Heather answered. "The local fish have a frost protection protein in their blood that is far better than any household antifreeze we've ever invented. But no one really knows how it works."

"Thank you, Heather. Next time I play Trivial Pursuit, you're definitely on my team," Silver replied.

"Too late, Phil, she's part of the *Krill* team." Andy gently pushed the wheel forward. "Approaching the shelf. Taking us down to fifty feet."

"Roger that, *K1*," Silver replied, now all business.

The submersible glided down through the pristine waters. The *SeaTayshun* was sitting on the surface about half a mile from the massive glacier ice wall and would pull back now that the craft was away. What they were doing was high risk – if a huge chunk of ice calved from the edge of the glacier, it could crush the submersible, but also send a wave that would swamp their support boat. A double whammy that nobody might survive.

At around two hundred feet, the waters here weren't that deep, but Silver hoped his team could get under the edge of the shelf and see what was creating the inexplicable huge ice cavern beneath the massive glacier.

And then there were also the baffling sonar pings that never bounced back. The theory was that the glacial cavity had exposed an even deeper cave that had been locked away by the ice sheets. This one burrowing deep below the icy continent itself. And that's what their sponsor wanted to find out.

The light faded as *K1* passed under the ice overhang and the weak rays of Antarctic sunshine were left behind.

"This is one mother of a cavity, boss. Hundreds of feet across and high," Andy said into his mic and looked upward. "I'm betting there's an air pocket up there." As the small craft passed under the edge of the glacier sheet the light became muted. "Switching on lamps."

He flipped a small switch, and a bank of high-brightness LEDs came on – the new generation light-emitting diodes were powerful, their light held together over long distances, and weren't affected by cold or pressure like standard lamps.

In the strong, white beams billions of flecks like floating dust were illuminated.

"Lots of krill and algae," Heather remarked.

"There shouldn't be," Silvers replied. "Other than being freezing, the water should have a high fresh water content from the melt. Not good for the local sea life."

"Yeah, that's not the only anomaly," Heather said. "The temperature is going up."

"What?" Andy frowned and leaned across to look at Heather's screen. "How?"

"Not sure, but it's jumped from twenty-eight to thirty-two degrees. Not much, but it might give us our first clue why we've got such a big melt-cavern forming." She half turned. "Geothermal?"

Andy nodded. "Yeah, that's my guess. They've already ruled out climate change and freak sea current distortion. Maybe that inner cave theory is no theory. Right, Phil?" He worked the controls. "I'm going to take her down a little more, to give us more room in case anything breaks from the cavern roof and falls."

"Visibility is still good," Heather said.

"Taking her down another hundred feet to skim the bottom, over," Andy said into his mic.

"Roger that. Everything okay down there?" Silvers asked.

Andy knew that they were getting the same image and feeds so probably already knew what they were encountering.

"Yeah, Phil, just playing it safe," Andy replied as he saw the sea bottom coming up. "You see the temperature?"

"We sure did. We're thinking a thermal vent in there somewhere."

"Yeah, that's what we think. It's normal Antarctic temperature outside, but only going up in here. The heat has got to be coming from somewhere further in." He looked down at the temperature gauge. "And it's still climbing."

"Okay, take it slow, *K1*," Silvers replied.

Andy reached up to unzip a few inches of his coveralls as the submersible moved along the bottom.

Andy and Heather pointed out things of interest to their audience back onboard the *SeaTayshun*. The exposed bedrock had been gouged by the millions of tons of glacial ice as it slid toward the sea. But now it had been hollowed out by the venting warm water.

"Tube worms," Andy said.

"Not like any tube worms I've seen before," Heather replied. "Those guys have got to be eight feet tall."

"Maybe growing bigger on the warm, nutrient rich water coming from inside the cavern." Andy nodded. "Must be it."

"They don't look right." Heather sat back. "Simple design. More ancient looking."

"Maybe some throwbacks," Andy said. "Hey Phil, *National Geographic* is gonna love this."

"*I* love this," Phil replied.

"Depth of water is around two hundred feet inside the cave. But cavern roof is about fifty feet high." Heather laughed softly. "We could have taken a rowboat inside here. Hell, if the tide was lower, maybe you guys could have sailed right in. Hold up." Her voice became serious. "Pan left, twenty degrees."

"On it." Andy hovered the submersible and used the starboard propellor to turn them slowly, so their bubble capsule was pointed to where Heather indicated.

"You see that?" she asked.

"I do, but not sure what I'm looking at." His eyes narrowed. "Let's take it in a little closer."

Andy gently touched the drives, and the aft prop increased its rotations to gently glide them in.

He squinted. "Is that a tail? Or what's left of one."

"If I didn't know better, I'd say that's an orca tail," Heather said. "A big one. Or it was. Taking some shots now."

Heather took dozens of rapid, high-resolution images with the forward camera while Andy kept the fragment of flesh in the strong beam of the lights as they inched nearer.

When they were closer, they could see tiny crustaceans working on the ragged flesh.

"Fresh kill." Andy sat back, frowning. "What could do that to an orca? They're the biggest, baddest carnivores on Earth."

Heather shrugged. "Maybe another orca. They're quite common in the subpolar seas."

"They're not usually cannibals, are they?"

"Some are. They can take on other orca packs. We think it might be territorial," Heather replied. "When they're done beating up trespassers they make a free meal out of them."

Andy touched his mic. "Phil, do we have any signs of orcas in the area?"

"Nope, nada, no orca packs in the vicinity," Silvers replied. "Nothing down there but you guys."

"Do you think they might have gone further in?" Heather asked. "Attracted by the warmer water?"

"Why don't we find out?" Andy moved away from the tail of the killer whale and continued along the bottom.

They continued for another five minutes, and Heather began to slowly shake her head. "Water here has a higher salinity content than we expected. And another thing, look up."

Andy saw the shimmer of something like the water's surface just above them. "Air?" he asked.

"No, that layer is only twenty feet above our head, but sonar says it's exactly fifty-two feet more water to the ceiling. She smiled. "I think it's a major halocline."

He snorted. "A fresh water layer on top of a salt water layer."

"Yep, salt water is heavier so it sinks. We end up with warm salt water down here and cold fresh water up there, obviously from the glacier melt."

"Let's take her up for a quick check." Andy eased back on the stick and the submersible slowly rose.

Seconds later they broke through to the surface, which was like a shimmering layer of oil. There was little difference in the water clarity, but they immediately felt a wave of cold come in at them.

"Yeah, freezing up here." He bobbed his head. "I'm betting that's why the glacier hasn't totally collapsed. This is keeping it insulated."

Andy pushed the wheel forward and dived again. "How long until we hit the Antarctic continental wall?"

Heather checked her instruments. "At this speed should be in five minutes." She clicked her tongue in her cheek. "But just like the initial sonar readings from the remote, I'm not getting a return ping."

"Could there be a glitch?"

"Not sure, but unlikely. On the sonar, I can see the walls either side of us, the sea bottom, and even the ceiling above us – everywhere but up ahead. There's just nothing coming back." She pressed more switches, bringing up different data feeds. "Even if there's no glacial ice left down here, we've gotta hit bedrock soon."

"Okay, we'll give it another few hundred feet." He pressed his mic button. "Phil, we're getting the same screwy data you picked up. Our sonar is not finding the continental wall either. The melt might be bigger than we expected. We don't want to run aground, but this suggests a void. And a big one."

"Roger that. Exactly what the drone told us a month ago. And one of the reasons you guys are there. Proceed, and describe what you see."

Andy glanced across to Heather who shrugged. "Can do," he replied. "Proceeding at four knots." He increased the propellor rotations and they scooted forward.

17

Andy leaned forward to switch the mic off for a moment. "You know what? I kinda get the feeling Phil knows more than he's telling us."

"About the void on the sonar?" Heather asked.

"Yeah, I feel we're just confirming what he, or our mysterious benefactor, already knows."

She hiked her shoulders. "Doesn't matter. We're first in, so let's see what they think is in there."

"Copy that." Andy switched the mic back on.

The submersible continued for another few minutes, passing more bones and pieces of whale. Not just orca this time but humpback and some smaller varieties.

"This is a kill zone," Heather whispered. "What's going on here?"

Now that they were deep inside, it was a black void with their lights illuminating about twenty feet of the water ahead of them.

"Let's slow it down a little," Heather suggested.

"Yep." Andy's lips pressed into a line. "Easing us back to two knots."

The *Krill-1* slowed, and Andy counted down the feet and seconds until they reached the position that was supposed to be the continental cliff wall.

"One twenty feet, one ten, one hundred," Andy announced. "We should see it any second."

"Take it slow." Phil Silvers' voice sounded close to the microphone as though he were sitting on the edge of his chair.

Andy's eyes were wide and fixed on the darkness ahead. "Forty feet, thirty, twenty, land border visual coming up in ten, nine, eight . . ."

Every inch meant more of the cave was revealed to the lights, but then they reached the end.

"All stop." Andy slowly sat back and exhaled.

"Ho-*leeey* crap," Heather whispered.

"Phil?" Andy asked.

"I'm here."

"Are you seeing this?" Andy swallowed. His throat was dry.

"Yeah, yeah, we see it, *Krill-1*. And it's unbelievable." Silvers sounded like he was out of breath. "This could be exactly what she is looking for."

"*She*," Heather murmured. "Our secret benefactor is a woman."

"She who buys all this cool stuff and pays our wages," Andy replied. "And if she wants to stay a silent, but fully funding, partner, then that's A-OK with me."

Before them in the rock cliff face, was an enormous cave, nearly as wide as the massive ice cave they had been traveling through. And it looked as old as time itself.

"I think we found the source of our warm water," Heather said. "Thermal sensors indicate it's seventy-two degrees in there." She shook her head in disbelief. "That's near tropical."

"*SeaTayshun*, what do you advise?" Andy asked.

"Hold your position, Andy. We're concerned we may lose radio contact with you if you enter the cave."

"Holding position." Andy allowed the submersible to hover and went back to staring at the massive, dark hole before them.

Heather reached forward to flick on the additional lights, and they illuminated another forty feet into the cave. But they still had no hope of pushing back the impenetrable darkness inside the huge void.

"I would love to know what's in there." She slowly turned to Andy. "Wouldn't you?"

"Yeah. If only we had a drone to send in first."

Heather leaned closer to him. "Guess what? We do have one, and we're sitting in it."

"What do you want to do?" Andy asked.

"I want to go in. I mean, this cave has probably been sealed for however long the glacier has been here."

"That might have been millions and millions of years."

"Exactly." She nodded. "It's been sealed for millions of years. We could be – no, we *would be* – the first human beings to see what secrets it's been keeping all this time."

"It might not be that long though," Andy replied. "There have been warming periods in the past that might have exposed the cave for months, years, or decades. Back in the early to mid eighteen hundreds –"

"Okay." She cut him off. "Then maybe we'll be the first modern humans to see inside."

Andy slowly nodded. Heather's eyes were near luminous with excitement. He turned back to the dark cave.

"I think we should wait." He shrugged. "Let's see what Phil wants us to do."

"Aww." She slumped back into her seat.

The pair sat silently for another few minutes and Heather sighed, theatrically loud. "What's he doing up there?" she asked.

Andy hiked his shoulder. "He can see all our data and read our sensors. Plus, they've got the *SeaTayshun* scanners, which are more powerful than ours. I bet they're trying to work out the risks involved in us proceeding or whether they want to launch an unmanned drone to take over from us."

"Well, they're taking too damn long." Heather opened the mic. "Phil, what's going on?"

There was silence for a moment before Phil Silvers came back online. "Hold fire, you two, we're getting some strange readings on deep sonar here."

Andy frowned. "What do you mean by *strange*, Phil?"

"We're picking up movement. From inside the cave."

Heather and Andy glanced at each other, and then looked back into the darkness of the huge cave.

"Movement," Heather said softly as if testing the word in her mouth.

Andy's brows knitted. "*SeaTayshun*, can you please clarify? What type of movement are you reading? We are seeing some strong tidal flow, is that what you mean?"

"Maybe it's those cannibal orcas returning," Heather said hopefully.

Andy looked down at their scanners and saw the blip appearing on their sonar. "Hold the phone, Phil, I think I'm seeing it now."

"Still coming," Phil Silvers said. "Range at approximately eight hundred feet." He whistled. "That's some cave. It must extend –"

"All the way under the continent," Andy suggested. His eyes burned as he watched the cave mouth. He glanced down and could see the blip was closing in on them.

"This thing is bigger than we are," Heather said. "Wait, there's two of them. I think we should –"

Andy nodded. "Move out of the way. Yeah, on it." He moved the joystick and gave them some thrust. "Phil, moving *Krill-1* out of the mouth of the cave."

"Good idea, Andy. Not sure what these things are, but the first is around forty feet, followed by another that could be around –" Silvers whistled. "– sixty-five to seventy feet. And there are no metallic signatures. They're probably biological, and both traveling at around twenty knots."

Andy stared straight ahead. "Phil, they're coming at us like freight trains, and they both have significant mass. I think we should evac."

"No." Heather reached over to grab his arm. "I think we're about to find out what secrets this cave has been hiding."

"Hold it, hold it," Phil said. "Signatures are four hundred feet out but are merging." Seconds later, he added, "And merged."

Over the external microphone Andy and Heather heard a thump. It created a small shock wave that was big enough to push the submersible in the water.

"They've stopped," Phil said.

"Whatever those things were, when they hit it was like a bomb going off," Andy whispered as he checked the sonar. "No forward motion. They stopped inside the cave at –" He checked. "– three hundred feet." He looked up. "Jesus, they're just in there beyond our light."

"I don't think it's *they* anymore," Heather said. "I think the big, fast guy caught up with the slower, little guy."

"By little you mean forty feet," Andy said. "That's nearly as big as a humpback whale."

"Something interesting is going on in that cave." Heather folded her arms and then turned to him. "We should go in. Just to get some images. Besides, whatever's going on in there between object A and object B, I think they're more preoccupied with each other."

From over the external microphone, they heard some crunching noises. Andy turned his head slightly. "Hear that?" He listened for a few more moments.

"Yeah," Heather replied. "Like, ripping and tearing." She half turned. "Or maybe feeding."

"This is not good."

"We've got to see," Heather urged. She tilted her head to the console. "I can't hear anything anymore. We're going to lose them. We've got to hurry."

"Okay, okay, maybe just a peek." Andy switched on the mic. "*SeaTayshun*, permission to take us in a hundred feet – be good to get some footage."

"Negative, *Krill-1*," Phil Silvers replied. "This might be more complex than we expected."

Andy shrugged and sat back, but Heather craned forward. "Do you see what I'm seeing?"

The warm current from the cave was drifting by them. But now it contained something other than 72-degree seawater. The clear current water was tinged with red. Then fragments of flesh started to drift by.

"Something in there just got its ass handed to it." Heather sighed. "Shit, I've gotta see what's going on in there. The curiosity is going to kill me."

"It might indeed." Andy let out a gentle laugh. "Something forty feet long, and way bigger than *Krill-1*, just got toasted. I'm not sure we want to be around when that big badass finishes its snack."

Heather continued to stare at the red tinged water. She spoke without turning. "This is blood, so we now know it's a biological entity – one was approximately forty feet, and the other around seventy." She shook her head slowly. "Just what the hell is in there? It ain't no orca pack."

The image slowly receded on their sonar.

"Going, going . . . gone." Heather sat back and then threw her hands up. "What a missed opportunity! Probably the biggest missed opportunity in the history of missed opportunities." She turned; her arms now pressed tightly over her body. "Fuck it, Andy, I didn't spend four years studying marine biology and sign up with the Mironov Marine Research Group to study krill populations. I want to push the ocean's boundaries, find something unique, make a difference."

He nodded his head. *So do I.*

He switched off the communications link to the *Sea-Tayshun*. "Some mysterious questions were just posed to us and I think we owe the world some answers." He turned to her. "So why don't we just take a little looksee. Just a few hundred feet further in. Who's gonna know, right?"

Heather grinned from ear to ear. "I won't tell." She crossed her chest. "Promise."

Andy turned back. "Okay. Let's take her in, nice and slow. And let's stay close to the wall and be invisible."

* * *

"The hell? What just happened?" Phil Silvers frowned at his screen. "Is the *Krill-1* advancing? Who gave them authority for that?"

He opened the mic. "*Krill-1*, this is *SeaTayshun* command, please respond." He waited a few seconds. "*Krill-1*, return to your position immediately, that is an order. *Krill-1*, please acknowledge." He swore under his breath. "Come on, Andy, this is not a joke."

Benny Harmon seated just across from him spoke. "I'm betting they're doing what you would have done if you were down there – gone ahead to investigate." He turned back to his screen. "And they didn't want Daddy to overrule them."

"This is dangerous, Benny," Silvers growled. "Tell me we're at least still receiving data from the submersible."

Benny nodded. "Oh yeah, we're getting everything. We just can't talk to them." He grinned. "Kids gonna be kids."

"They're not teenagers." Silvers scowled. "And they can't do whatever they want in a sixty-million-dollar submersible. I'll kick their asses when they get back on deck." He leaned toward the monitor screens. "But I am interested in what they find."

The small team in the *SeaTayshun* control room watched as the video feeds from the bow of the small submersible fed the data back to them. It measured everything from chemical analysis, thermal, and a range of light spectrums. Phil would have liked the audio on so he could pose questions, but he expected that Andy was recording his observations for future analysis. Or at least he'd better be.

The team sat in silence, watching the silent film roll on, and monitoring the plethora of new data. Benny pushed his seat back.

"You know, that cave's been covered up ever since the glacier grew over the top of it. Given, the glacier has been around for fifteen million or so years, that means whatever is in there has been sealed off from the outside world for that long too."

"Yeah, I get it, Benny. I'm interested to see what's in there as well. But we are not currently set up for anything above scooping up brine shrimp and small crustacean samples." Phil raised a single eyebrow. "You saw the size of the signatures just before, right?"

"I wonder what they were," Benny said thoughtfully. "We should take bets. My money is on some sort of monster kraken."

Silvers snorted. "You've been reading too much fiction." He turned back to his screen. "So far the only thing they've discovered from all the buried lakes they've drilled into across Antarctica are ancient algae, bacteria, and various species of blind copepods." He smiled. "But sure, be kinda cool if we were able to find something other than a basket of prehistoric shrimp."

"They've found something," Sotomeyer, who had been sitting with his back to them, said.

The group of marine research scientists immediately spun back to their screens and watched as the camera feed approached the underwater cave bottom. The water was still clouded with blood and fragments of flesh swirled around them, churned by the *K1*'s propulsion jets.

"Holy shit, is that a fish tail?" Benny asked. "Damn, I shoulda bet on a big fish."

"More like half a fish." Silvers took a still image and then accessed the satellite link to enter it into the marine database. He got an answer almost immediately.

"Shark."

"What sort?" Benny asked.

"Big one," he shot back. "Closest match is Carcharo-don carcharias. Weird, very pale. Almost an albino, but not quite." Silvers turned back to his screen. "We need something for scale."

"Is this the sucker that got attacked by something bigger?" Benny asked. "I mean, what could take on a shark that size?"

"A bigger shark?" Silvers shrugged. "Something we haven't met yet?" He pointed. "And don't say a kraken again." He leaned forward and then nodded. "Here comes our scale."

The submersible approached the tail-end of the shark. They saw the claw extend. It clamped onto the tail and lifted. The propulsion units strained. Even though the weight wasn't significant under the water, it was still a twenty-foot object that probably weighed as much as the mini submersible did, and the shape made it difficult to work with. As the claw dragged on it, more blood entered the surrounding water.

The *Krill-1* team were determined to bring it back though. And Phil Silvers was onboard with the idea.

Everyone in the room watched silently as the small craft continued to back out of the huge underwater cave with the tail.

Then Benny broke the silence.

"*Whoa, whoa, whoa!* We've got some big signatures, incoming – two thousand feet inside the cave and coming fast. I got two – no, three of them. The first two are giving me a sonar impression size at around fifty to fifty-five feet." He stared, his fingers flying over the keyboard. "Holy shit, third one is even bigger – maybe seventy feet plus. And they're doing thirty knots."

Sotomeyer spoke over his shoulder. "Maybe the big guy from before is coming back."

"That speed's impossible," Silvers replied.

"Nope, they're doing it. And they're on direct collision course with our guys. ETA in –" He turned. "Twelve seconds."

"*Shit.*" Silvers grabbed the mic. "*Krill-1,* come back! *Krill-1!*" he yelled as if his loud words would be heard over the dead communications. "This is an emergency!" He swore and one of his hands curled into a fist. "Come on, Andy and Heather, turn your damn mic on."

"Do you think they've seen it?" Benny asked.

"How could they miss it?" Silvers seethed. "At least drop the damn chunk of meat."

He turned about, desperate to do something. He could think of only one thing. He hit the internal mic to the wheel-house. "John, bring us in closer to the glacier. If they surface, then I want –"

"There's something there!" Benny shouted.

Silvers swung back to the *Krill-1* image feed, just in time to see the lead two objects explode out of the darkness. They shot past the *Krill-1* so fast it was impossible to make them out. But they were big, clay-colored, and the turbulence they created buffeted the small submersible and pulled it away from the wall.

The objects, or creatures, kept going out into the freezing sea where they peeled off, one going one way, the other in a different direction.

"Whatever they were, they were scared shitless," Benny said. "Hold the phone, here comes the last one. Here comes big daddy." Benny's voice was high.

And then the thing filled their world. Unfortunately this time *Krill-1* wasn't hovering safely out of the way.

On the screen, something that might have been a mouth opened and then the camera simply whited out.

Phil Silvers shot to his feet. He just stared, his mouth working uselessly for a moment. After a few more seconds he pointed at the screen. "What happened? *What just happened?*" He reached forward and his hands flew over the multiple keyboards.

"Lost camera, lost forward and aft sensors, lost sonar images. Oh god. No signature." Benny turned, his eyes wide. "They're not there anymore."

Silvers felt like his brain was short-circuiting. He stared at his own screen, not wanting to believe what it was telling him.

Benny turned slowly. "Did they just get eaten?"

Silvers rounded on him. "*Don't you dare even fucking think that*," he yelled. "It was – it was a cave-in." Silvers frowned. "That's what happened. That's what she'd want us to say. Until we know more and analyze our data, we keep this under wraps. It's too important to share with the world, just yet."

The ships alarms blared, and Silvers cringed from the sudden excruciating noise. "Jesus, what is that?"

"The big one. It's coming back," Benny said. "Those first two signatures are still out in the open ocean too. They're all out here. With us." His fingers were a blur over the keyboard.

Silvers paced, trying to think. He folded then unfolded his arms, and then turned to Benny. "Where is it? The big one?"

Benny grimaced. "It's, ah, it's circling us."

"Oh Jesus." Silvers breathed. "She's got to be told what's happening." He turned back to his keyboard and opened a direct link to the head of Mironov Marine Group. He rapidly composed a message and linked in all the data, film images, and sensor information from *Krill-1*, and then sent it.

"Still circling," Benny said, and then spoke through fear-clamped teeth. "Boss, are we in trouble?'

"I don't . . ." Silvers straightened from his screens. "Fuck it, we're out of here." He touched the mic button. "Engine room –" He began.

"Oh no." Benny grabbed his head. "It's stopped circling. And it's turned. Toward us." He let out a sound that might have been a sob. "It's going to ram us. If we go in the water here, we're dead. Fucking dead," Benny shrieked.

It won't be the cold that kills us, Silvers thought. "Hold it together, man," he said. "We'll be fine. This ship is double hulled and made from toughened steel to break ice packs. Nothing is going to damage us."

Silvers flicked on all the external underwater cameras and instructed their programming to send their images over the open communication's link back to home base as well.

"*Here it comes, here it comes, here it comes*," Benny's voice was so high it was almost a shriek.

The seventy-five-foot creature accelerated, bearing down on the equal-sized boat. Silvers knew that, even though the *SeaTayshun* was made of hardened steel, it was primarily hollow. What was bearing down on them was probably a solid mass of bone and muscle. Plus, all the ship's reinforcement was in the bow, not the sides.

And that's where it struck – the collision to the starboard side was like a bomb going off. Everything inside the boat was thrown to the port side at such high velocity that the men's bodies were crushed, and everything else shattered beyond recognition.

The *SeaTayshun* broke in half. There were sparks of electricity, a few fires and secondary explosions, and a shower of debris that rose a hundred feet into the air. But then the vessel sank quickly.

The last image sent back to the Mironov Marine Group was of the thing at the moment of impact. After that, the frozen sea returned to being as cold and silent as the grave.

CHAPTER 04

Edge of the Southern Ocean, aboard the fishing
vessel, the *Boris Yeltsin*

Yuri Zagreb had the binoculars to his eyes and scanned the
smooth waters of the Southern Ocean. He knew they were
coming up on the Antarctic Exclusion Zone, a no fishing
border, and so far they had caught nothing. It was as if the
ocean had sent out a warning to stay clear of his fishing boat.

He lowered the glasses. "Are we that fearsome?" he exhaled
through a large and weather-beaten nose above a salt and
pepper whiskered lower face. "We only want a little."

At eighty-seven feet, steel hulled, with two net cranes, and
rising forty feet from hull to wheelhouse cabin top, the *Boris
Yeltsin* was thirsty and drank a lot of oil. Even sitting idle, she
burned through fuel as the engines needed to run continually
to heat them when in the frozen south.

And the cost of fuel was criminally high right now, so if they
went home with nothing, Yuri knew he would be dripping in
red ink. Possibly drowning in it. It would be a dour voyage
knowing that the next trip wasn't for profit, but to pay debts.
Or worse, just to accrue more.

He sighed. They needed something. Anything.

And then the fish gods answered.

"Whale song," Belsky, his sonar operator, said while holding the earpiece tighter against his head.

Yuri turned. "Single animal or pod?"

"I think it's a single animal. Sonar image says it's perhaps forty to forty-two feet, and only moving at four knots." He fiddled with a keyboard and then let a computer system analyze the noise. "Got it. Cetacean database says it's a female humpback."

"Good size, and slow moving." Yuri turned back to the window, scratching his chin as he thought. He spoke without turning. "Where is it?"

The sonar operator checked and then slowly shook his head. "Unfortunately, it is within the Antarctic Exclusion Zone."

Yuri nodded, and let his mind run. They had zero catch and were burning fuel with no return on his investment. He needed something to sell when he got back. Whale meat still had a few markets he could sell into. He made a snap decision.

"Turn off the transponder," he said evenly.

"But, that would –"

"Turn it off." Yuri's voice was low and had an edge.

Without the transponder, his ship would vanish from the international satellite database. If there was ever an investigation, the rationale for it would be obvious. But by the time anyone noticed something was wrong, he'd be back out of the exclusion zone. With his prize.

He turned to his second in charge. "Mr. Chekov, plot me an intercept course with that whale."

"Yes, sir." Chekov grinned at him.

"Good man." Yuri nodded. He knew Chekov understood his pressures, that's why he liked and trusted him.

Belsky whistled. "Moving fast now – sixteen knots."

"Maybe it knows what's on our minds." Chekov said.

"It's doing sixteen knots?" Yuri bobbed his head from side to side. That was odd as humpbacks usually only did around five. This big *mahmochkah* was in a hurry. "Then we better do twenty. But don't worry, it'll tire soon."

Yuri lifted the mic to get the attention of one of his most trusted and experienced crewmen. It was time to reassemble a piece of technology they hadn't used in years.

"Mr. Agmanov, please gather a team and ready the harpoon gun. Stand by for orders." He clicked off the mic and turned to the still concerned looking sonar operator. "Looks like a whale has strayed into international water." He shrugged. "We'll take it. For research purpose only."

Beside him Chekov threw his head back and laughed.

* * *

The *Boris Yeltsin* moved further into the freezing Antarctic waters, and the sea around them was still a slate gray and calm as a sheet of polished glass. Yuri wanted to take the whale, haul it in, and then be out of the restricted waters before anyone asked any questions.

He knew that fifty tons of whale meat wasn't a lot, but it was better than going back with an empty hold. And maybe on the way back they'd catch something else – after all, luck brought luck.

He let Chekov direct them on an intercept course with the cetacean as he watched Agmanov and his team assemble the harpoon gun. It was an older model, a Foyn's harpoon cannon. He couldn't exactly go and buy a new one, as the red tape involved would have smothered him, especially as he didn't have a license for whale hunting.

He smiled as he saw the device come together – it was more than adequate as a forward-mounted, muzzle-loading gun. It fired a heavy harpoon that would bend without breaking, the head of which was equipped with a time-delay grenade to damage vital organs or cause massive bleeding when detonated.

Humpbacks needed to be reeled in quickly as they had a tendency to sink, and fifty tons of dead weight was a considerable job to haul in when using just the net winches.

"On approach." Chekov's voice was all professional now. "Ten degrees to starboard, five hundred feet." He pointed. "*Breach*."

Sure enough the back of the whale came to the surface, a geyser of air and water was ejected, and the whale continued, not slowing at all.

"Slow down, you *svolach*, you're getting me to burn too much fuel," Yuri complained.

Yuri put the glasses to his eyes and watched the massive creature as it surged ahead of them. The humpback whale was a baleen whale, and one of the largest members of the rorqual family. But they were basically like giant cows – docile, and rarely fought even after being speared.

He hoped Agmanov struck well with the harpoon – if he delivered a good strike and entered near the brain or heart and detonated the grenade, then the whale would die instantly. But if he caught the flank or near the tail, then they'd be in for a sled ride.

He watched his crew finish assembling the gun. The red-tipped arrow head with the collar of explosives was loaded into the barrel. Agmanov manned the control and ran through a quick check. He then turned and gave the thumbs up to the wheelhouse.

"Good," Yuri said. "Get us in close. Careful now, I don't want it getting spooked and diving."

"I think it is already spooked." Chekov frowned. "Why is it still moving so fast? I don't think it is running from us."

"Must be us," Yuri replied. "What else?"

"It was running before we even got close." Chekov gave the engine a little surge and they quickly bore down on the huge animal.

"Steady. Steady," Yuri said, as they came into range. His eyes widened. "Come on, Agmanov, take the shot."

And then he did. They heard and felt the explosive discharge of the cannon even up in the wheelhouse. The harpoon and its cable ran out in a looping spiral and struck the whale toward its front end. In seconds there was a pop and a discharge of blood.

Immediately the animal slowed.

"A hit." Yuri thumped the cabin window edge with his fist. "Very good." He lifted the mic to speak to the crew. "Good shooting. Quickly now. Attach the winches and haul it in."

Yuri checked the radar and saw no other ships in the vicinity. *Good.* It would still take them an hour to get the whale closer, hauled up onboard, and then more time to cut it up and get it into the freezers below deck.

But he'd begin sailing out of the exclusion zone while the whale meat, blubber, and even skin was still being cut up.

He rubbed his chin as he thought through his tasks – he'd order the deck hosed down, and then as soon as they'd crossed into international fishing waters he'd turn the transponder back on. And report he'd had an equipment malfunction. If he could do all that in a few hours, he'd be very satisfied.

He smiled. Something is always better than nothing. And today, something was fifty tons of whale meat.

He watched as the twin net winches dragged the massive cetacean toward the *Boris Yeltsin*. It was slow work and the machines strained under the enormous weight.

The dead whale began to sit lower in the water as the gas escaped its lungs. Professional whalers had special injector spikes that they used to pump the carcass full of air to keep it afloat. But he'd have to rely on luck and timing.

Plus, he hoped the harpoon spike held. If not, the weight of the deflated animal would pull it free, and it'd sink to the bottom. Then he would have burned the extra fuel, risked having his license confiscated for fishing in an exclusion zone, and go home with nothing but a bad mood, debts, and a ferocious vodka hangover.

Yuri cursed. He couldn't risk losing the whale, so while the men were still dismantling the harpoon cannon, he decided he had a priority job for them.

"Mr. Agmanov, take a boat and secure a line to its tail. If the harpoon pulls out we'll lose everything."

The man looked up at the wheelhouse then to the whale. Yuri could almost hear his mind work – the water was freezing, and he'd need to go in. But to his credit, the crewman saw the problem and nodded.

Yuri wished he had a few more like Agmanov as he watched him professionally organize three other men, change his clothing, and then take a large tow rope while they began to lower one of the rubber dinghies.

In just minutes the men raced across the glassy gray water to meet the rapidly sinking whale. They trailed the thick rope, which had been tied to one of the large, iron deck bollards. Poor Agmanov sat in the boat in a thick wetsuit. Even the cold-water suits never kept out the bone-chilling bite of the Antarctic water.

Yuri would give the man an extra ration of vodka when he returned to get some heat back into his belly.

A few minutes later, the small boat reached the whale, and they had the winches shut off so the men could work. Agmanov pulled a mask down over his face and then went over the side. He grabbed the end of the rope, dragged in one huge, deep breath, and then dived under.

"Better him than me," Chekov said.

"He's a good man," Yuri said. "Crazy, but good." He could almost feel the bite of the icy water. He lifted his mug of steaming tea and sipped as if to warm his own bones.

"We have contact," Belsky said.

"More whale?" Yuri turned, his brows slightly raised. "Another boat?" He knew he'd be in the shit if it was.

"No, non-metallic signature." Belsky listened a little more and stared intensely at the computer as it tried to resolve the sonar impression. "Maybe another whale. Big one. Bigger than the humpback."

Yuri snorted, relieved. "Maybe husband. Too late, Mr. Humpback, your wife already dead."

"No whale song. And much, much bigger than a humpback – maybe seventy to seventy-five feet. It's mid-water and coming fast." Belsky turned. "Not at us. At the whale."

Yuri frowned. "It's heading to the dead whale?" He turned back and lifted his binoculars. He couldn't contact his men, unless he had someone go on deck with a loudhailer.

He thought about it and then discarded the idea; too much trouble, and he needed them to finish their task. They'd be back soon anyway.

"It's gone deep," Belsky said.

Yuri nodded. "And that's the end of that."

"I don't think so," Chekov murmured. He faced Yuri. "I think we should wait before we –"

"*No.*"

They had seen Agmanov dive, and then just a few minutes later he came back to the surface and gave a thumbs up. The rope attached to the ship went tight.

"See, it's done." Yuri sipped his tea again. It was already cold. *Nothing stays warm here*, he thought. "Now we have two lines and, even if the harpoon is pulled free, we will still have hold of it."

"This is strange." Belsky spun in his chair, looking confused as he faced Yuri and Chekov. "That thing is coming up fast, right underneath the whale." The warning noise from his console pulled him back to his instruments. "*Contact*," he said.

Yuri turned back to the freezing sea in time to see the whale carcass lift from the water in a geyser of foam, blood, and fragments of flesh. There was something huge and off-white within that explosion of chaos.

The Russian captain's mouth dropped open and he could only stare. The small inflatable dinghy beside the whale was flipped aside, and the men catapulted out. Many immediately started swimming back to the thankfully not swamped raft. But there was no sign of Agmanov.

The remaining men clambered back in the raft and started the engine to then speed back to the ship.

Yuri stared hard at the water behind them – it was still boiling as if there was frantic agitation going on beneath the surface. He watched as a slick of bloody foam and chunks of whale flesh was spreading out over a hundred feet.

"What happened? What was that?" Yuri turned to Belsky, and the young man just shook his head.

"Shark," Chekov said.

"*Horse shit.*" Yuri rounded on him. "Are you mad?"

Chekov shook his head slowly. "I've seen this before. In South Africa there is a bay where the seal colonies live. The water is deep, and the sharks wait for them down in the depths." He turned. "They take the seals from underneath, just like this."

Yuri's eyes bulged. "That was a whale, not a seal pup. What shark could lift a whale from the water like that?" He snorted his disdain. "And the water is freezing here. No sharks."

Chekov just stood at attention, and Yuri rested his hands flat on the window ledge. He shook his head. "Everything, gone. Agmanov, gone."

"Captain, it went back down. But it's not gone." Belsky looked up. "Just heading away."

"Back to the deep," Chekov said.

Yuri exhaled. "Yes, with half my whale. Enjoy your free meal, you bastard."

"We still have the whale. Or what's left of it," Chekov announced.

"What?" Yuri's head came up.

"The harpoon has been dislodged, but we still have the rope attached." Chekov shared a flat smile. "We should haul in what we have left."

"Yes, yes, do that." Yuri straightened.

Chekov gave the order, and the tow rope was attached to the winch and hauled in. It came in quickly, indicating there wasn't a fifty-ton cetacean attached to it anymore.

In minutes it was beside the boat, and then hauled up the port side and hung over the fish catch platform.

Yuri could only stare. Only the tail and last third of the animal was remaining. Above the rear dorsal fin, there was just a massive, ragged stump. It was still dripping oily blood to the deck. Of the forty- to fifty-ton cetacean there remained about eight tons.

Yuri sighed as he watched a few of the men congregate around it. Gobbets of loose flesh fell free, and a slight movement of the deck caused a few other items to be jarred loose.

One man ran in under the remains of the beast and picked something up. He held it aloft and Yuri squinted, and then motioned for the crewman to bring it up.

The man took off his bloody slicker and raced up the metal steps to the wheelhouse cabin. Inside, he held the object out to his captain.

Chekov grunted. "You see?"

Yuri held the object on his open palm – it was a tooth, triangular, serrated, and gleaming white. It was broken off from its root, but the piece was still about eight inches in length.

"Shark tooth," Chekov announced.

"It's too big. And what shark can take two thirds of a whale in a single bite?" Yuri lifted his head to look out at the now calm waters.

"One we haven't met before," Chekov replied. "A monster."

"It was white. A rare monster." Yuri turned to Belsky. "Do you still have it on sonar?"

He nodded. "Yes, moving at depth, but toward the edge of the glacier and into shallower water."

"Moving toward the continent? Interesting." Yuri checked their position and found they were still in the exclusion zone. "I have had a stomach full of this accursed cold place." He turned. "But I want to know what it is that stole our catch. Perhaps we might find something of great importance. And of great value."

"You want to go deeper into the exclusion zone?" Chekov raised his eyebrows.

"Yes," Yuri stated. "Something there attacked us, and in my opinion it poses a risk to global shipping. I think it is our duty to find out what it is." He laughed, and then nodded toward the wheelhouse window.

"Cut up and store that meat. And clean off the deck." Yuri's eyes narrowed. "Then full speed ahead, Mr. Chekov. We have a new target."

* * *

The *Boris Yeltsin* stopped in the water, and Yuri held the glasses to his eyes.

"Thwaites Glacier," Chekov said and looked down at the online charts. "Big, and very old."

"And melting," Yuri said without taking the glasses from his eyes. "Our monster shark swam toward it." He lowered the glasses. "Not just toward it but under it, and then it kept going. What does that tell you, Mr. Chekov?"

"That it's hollow," Chekov replied.

Yuri nodded and turned to Belsky "Update?"

"Yes, sir, it was still traveling at a consistent eleven knots.

Entered the glacier zone without slowing. Then vanished from the sonar."

Yuri's mouth curved into an upside down smile as he looked at the glacier. "That's new ice melt. A cave. And I think a big one."

"You're not thinking of getting any closer, captain?" Chekov asked. "If that sheet calves, it'll sink us."

"I am, and I will." Yuri scratched at his chin. "The fish went closer, and so can we."

Chekov groaned. "We should at least dynamite the lip. That will dislodge any ice that is about to fall."

Yuri slowly shook his head. "No, the entrance looks small from the waterline and will be impossible to see via overhead satellite. I also think it is newly formed." He turned and grinned. "So that means we are first to see it." He turned back. "And first to claim what we find."

Chekov threw his hands up. "You can't claim anything you find in Antarctica. It's internationally protected, under the United Nations –"

Yuri waved him away. "No one knows. And no one will tell them." Yuri gazed at the blue-tinted glacier. He'd already decided.

"We go. We take two inflatables, harpoons, ropes, guns." He nodded. "Plus we will take the portable winch and some heavy fishing tackle. I think today might end up being more profitable than we expected."

CHAPTER 05

Valery Mironov Enterprises, New York City

Sonya Borashev sat at the huge desk flanked by multiple computer screens that painted her stony visage in cold hues of blue and white. She watched the footage sent to her, the benefactor of the expedition, by her now missing ship, the *SeaTayshun*.

She watched it again, and again. And then slowed it down until it was frame by frame on the images of the mini submersible, the *Krill-1*. She stopped the footage at the moment the huge maw came into view.

She sat staring at if for many minutes, feeling her fury rise. She had suspected something strange was emanating from down there but didn't know for sure. This creature was huge though, and it was white, or a clay color. Was she wrong?

"Could it be something else?" she whispered.

Finally she sat back, closed her eyes and steepled her fingers, thinking about the lost lives. Had she sent them all to their deaths? Had she adequately warned them?

Sonya closed her eyes for a moment. No, she had suspected but hadn't known for sure. All they were supposed to do was gather evidence. It seemed the crew of *Krill-1* had exceeded their instructions.

Her gaze was drawn again to the screen and the huge mouth. Sonya's eyes narrowed. "Is that where the last of you have been hiding, all these millions of years?" Her voice resonated in the huge room.

Sonya turned to look out the impressive row of windows and over the nighttime New York skyline. She didn't see the skyscrapers touching the dark sky, or the shadowy streets and laneways; instead her mind conjured the peaks of underwater mountains, the stars became dots of bioluminescent creatures out in the dark void, and the streets became the abyssal valleys as she navigated the depths in the submarine with Valery.

She blinked several times and turned away from the view, feeling the pang of loss that never went away. Sonya exhaled and turned to face the floor-to-ceiling fish tank stocked with a pair of rare dinosaur eels both now in their dens, their heads hanging out, mouths gaped open and displaying near transparent needle-like teeth. Their cold and emotionless eyes were on her. Always on her, as if biding their time until they could get hold of her soft flesh and tear chunks from it.

She hated them. But they were Valery's pets, and they, and everything about the mysteries of the deep sea, were his passion. They were a small but remaining connection to him.

Valery had been killed in the sea, and many would have said he died doing what he loved. But that wasn't true at all. Because the truth was, he was eaten by a monster. And he died saving her and his crew.

The great man had always planned ahead as if he could see the future. And in the last trip he had seen his own death, and so made plans to transfer the multi-billion dollar construction and investment company to her. He had loved her, and in turn she had adored and loved him with the intensity of a white-hot fire.

Sonya had been Valery's lover, and bodyguard. She had been trained in the Mossad Special Forces camps to be a lethal weapon. He had said she was his perfect woman. But she knew she had flaws. She was not merciful and kind-hearted like Valery was. Instead, she held violence and vengeance in her heart, and a fury that would never let it go.

She would track Valery's killers across the seas until the end of time. If they showed up, she would spend whatever it took to destroy them as they had destroyed her love.

She sat staring at nothing for several more minutes before she exhaled and watched the footage again. This time she started the film where the small submersible entered the cavern beneath the glacial ice sheet, and then journeyed on into a cave. A cave that shouldn't be there.

She watched when the *Krill-1* was attacked, and then continued watching from the *SeaTayshun*'s underwater cameras as the ship itself was set upon. And destroyed. What could do that to an eighty-foot ship with reinforced hull? Not a Megalodon. Unless it was a different sort of Megalodon.

There was a knock on the door and Sonya checked the external camera – she had made many enemies over the years and security was her friend now. Satisfied, she pressed a button on her desk to unlock the thick oak double doors.

The short Spanish-looking woman approached the desk, her heels clicking on the hardwood floor. She had a pleasant face that right now was all business, and her large intelligent brown eyes were unblinking as she bore down on Sonya.

Meena Delgado slid a report in front of Sonya, keeping her hand on it for a moment. "No survivors. Plenty of debris on the surface, but the bulk of the ship went to the bottom. The submersible has completely vanished. No wreckage."

Sonya nodded slowly. "Dead men tell no tales." She looked up. "How many families?"

Meena didn't need to consult her notes. "Twenty-two wives, husbands, and partners, and thirteen children, ranging in ages –"

Sonya held up a hand. "That's enough." She sighed. "Send them each one – no, five million dollars."

"I already have." Meena smiled.

Sonya smiled sadly. "You know me too well, Meena."

"One more thing," Meena said. "The *Krill-1*'s transponder was still working for around ten minutes after the attack. It showed the submersible went deeper into the glacial cave."

"How much deeper?" Sonya looked up.

"Half a mile before it stopped working."

Sonya grunted her acknowledgment, already guessing that's where the thing had come from and went back to.

"A territorial attack." She turned one of her screens around to face Meena. "What do you make of this?"

Meena leaned forward and narrowed her eyes at the last images taken by the *Krill-1* submersible – the maw. "Massive, serrated, triangular-shaped teeth – undoubtedly Otodontidae." She straightened. "But the color? Megalodon or a new species?"

"I don't know." Sonya turned the screen back around. "But nothing we know of could do that to an eighty-five-foot ship."

"Nothing we know of *today*," Meena added.

Sonya tilted her head. "That's right."

"A giant, white sea creature that sinks ships." Meena held out the package she had. "I'm guessing that's why you wanted this?"

Sonya took the bound bundle and carefully unwrapped the paper from it. She then lay it gently on her desk and looked down at the pristine 1851 first edition of Herman Melville's *Moby Dick*.

"Interesting," Meena said.

"Research," Sonya replied.

"Of course it is." Meena smiled, nodded once, and then departed the room.

Sonya went back to the screens and turned to scroll through the alerts she had set up globally across the internet, in internal marine message boards, and coast guard radio frequencies. Anything related to unexplained sightings, sinkings, or attacks by unusually large predators would be scooped up and listed in a file for her.

Ever since the glacier melted and opened a large ice cavern revealing an even deeper cave, a door beneath the dark ice, then things had been going crazy.

There were messages about giant fins cutting the water, and sharks longer than ferry boats patrolling the edge of the deep-sea shelf. There were reports of fishermen disappearing in the night in Western Australia, and huge shark sightings. But she knew they always had big great whites haunting the shallows over there.

Everything would be collated, and she would dispatch teams to check them out. Every one of them. But there were also sightings of huge white things just below the surface that were only seen at dusk and dawn – they also intrigued her.

She sat back and drew the antiquarian book toward her, her fingers drumming on it for a moment. She flipped it open and began to read.

In two hours she had devoured it entirely and sat staring straight ahead with her vision turned inward. Then she sprang forward, her fingers dancing across the keyboard as she searched the internet for supplementary data on Herman Melville. She also looked for information on the whaleship the *Essex*, the supposed source of inspiration for the story, which in November 1820 was attacked and sunk by a giant white whale off the coast of South America – close to the freezing southern waters.

She had found out that in the early 1800s there was a brief warming period, and that meant that possibly the Thwaites Glacier might have receded just enough to open the way to the cave. Could some great beast have escaped at that time as well – a great sea beast so big it was mistaken for a whale?

And now the glacier had retreated again. Once more opening the cave to the Southern Ocean. She needed to act quickly before the monsters got out. Or rather, even *more* got out.

There was so much more she needed to know. And best to do her investigation at the source.

She needed to get to Nantucket, about forty miles from Rhode Island, and just ten from Martha's Vineyard. Sonya checked her watch; from where she was in New York, she could be there in a few hours.

She headed for the door, calling out to Meena as she went.

CHAPTER 06

Four miles out, Safety Bay, Rockingham, Western Australia

Duncan Shira looked toward the western sky; the sun was dropping to the horizon and laying down a pathway of gold on the seemingly endless sea, and he knew that its usual shimmering blue would soon turn impenetrably black.

He checked his watch – only 6 pm, and the fish were biting. He'd hate to pull the pick now and head in. Some days he could sit out here for hours and not get a nibble. But today, they were definitely *on*.

With the sun gone he took off his hat and threw it onto the back seat of his fifteen-foot Quintrex coast runner with the new fifty-horsepower four-stroke engine.

He ran a hand through his once thick red hair, now gone gray. Duncan was weather-beaten by the years and elements but still had good strength in his shoulders and back.

He loved two things above all others – three if he counted cold beer – and they were fishing, and Angela, his wife, who said he was a grumpy bastard. But then who wouldn't be these days with all the bills, taxes, politics, and everything coming at him like a magpie continually pecking the top of his head.

But not out here – out here it all went away. He inhaled the sea salt, taking it deep into his lungs and then letting it out slowly. He closed his eyes and smiled as he listened to the gentle lap of the waves against the tin hull.

He wanted to keep doing this until the day he died. He remembered his dad telling him once that every minute a man spent fishing was a minute that was added to the end of his life. He guessed if that were true, then he'd probably live to be a hundred and fifty.

The fish had gone quiet, so he dipped the old pineapple tin into the burley bucket which was a soup of fish guts, old prawn heads, and bloody water, and flicked it over the side. It'd take a while to sink, and if that didn't bring them back, he'd call it a day.

Duncan sat a while longer, enjoying his own thoughts and memories, and when he inhaled again, oddly, this time the smell of clean salt air had been replaced by something else – something unpleasant: the smell of dead things, drying barnacles on rocks, and rotting fish washed up on the tide.

"What the hell is that?" he muttered and reached forward to lift one of his caught fish closer to his nose.

Nope, wasn't that.

He turned about, but the sun had dropped to the horizon leaving just an orange line far away in the distance. He could still see the flat ocean, but this time it wasn't all flat.

Duncan's brows came together. There was a lump there. A big freaking lump. And it was an off-white color. Was it the bow of a sunken boat coming to the surface? he wondered. That might account for the smell and color.

He continued to watch. It hung there, not moving. It was about 200 feet from his boat and rose close to ten feet above the water. It was now too dark to make it out clearly, and his first thought was to start the engine and go and check it out. He could make a claim on it if it was a lost boat.

But an instinct told him to not even think about getting any closer to it. He was a man of the sea and had seen whales stuck on sandbanks, schools of porpoises shooting the waves, sea turtles, dugongs, manta rays as big as his front garden, and grouper that could swallow you whole. But this thing reminded him of something else.

"No. That is *not* a shark," he told himself. "Nope, no way."

The orange glow on the western horizon was vanishing and he knew that in about five minutes the only glow would come from his luminous wristwatch.

"Fuck that." He had no idea what the thing was, but it wasn't there before, and he didn't want to be just a few hundred feet from it when the lights went out completely.

He began to haul his line in, his hand shaking slightly. Then he changed his mind and picked up the boat knife and just cut it through. He started to drag in the anchor, the metal pick and sandbag taking its time coming to the surface. It strained his shoulders and back, but he moved like a machine, hand over hand, coiling the rope in the front of the boat until the clank of the steel against his hull told him he had it all.

He looked around – the sun was nearly gone but so was the weird white thing. He turned one way, then the other, but there was nothing. It didn't matter, he was outta here.

Duncan moved to the back of the small tin boat and tugged on the pull cord. Blessedly, the new engine started like a dream.

"Atta boy," he whispered and put it in forward drive. He twisted the handle, putting the propellor in high rotation, and then moved the handle again to swing the nose of the boat toward shore.

It'd take him a good forty minutes to reach the first of the sandbanks, but every second put him further away from this spot. And that was fine with him.

For some reason, Angela's face flashed into his mind, and he couldn't wait to see her again. He'd tell her about the weird thing in the water. And they'd both laugh at his nervousness.

"I deserve a cold beer tonight." He grinned. "Make it two, Ange."

The impact was so explosive, Duncan was twenty feet in the air before he even registered what had happened.

He came down with an almighty splash, and his boat landed forty feet from him with the propellor still spinning. Bait, burley, fish, lines, and all his equipment rained down around him.

"*Jesus Christ!*" He spluttered salt water.

On the opposite horizon the huge moon had risen, throwing down a silvery glow onto the water's surface.

Something hit you, his mind screamed. *It was that big fucking thing in the water.*

It's not a shark, it's not a shark, he tried to tell himself. "No shark is that big."

But his mind knew better.

Swim.

Don't splash.

Get out of the chum cloud.

He knew he'd be in the water for hours, but it was warm here. He could do it.

From somewhere behind him in the darkness, he heard the smashing impact as the thing hit his boat again. It was followed by the sound of crushing steel so loud it would surely have carried for miles. The propellor kept spinning, but the sound of it was getting farther away and muffled as if it had been taken below the water.

I hope someone heard that. He prayed. But there was no one for miles.

Don't look back, just swim.

He focused, and started swimming breaststroke, slowly but surely putting a yard distance in with every stroke. Look to the moon, his experience told him; it was rising in the east, and that's where the land is. That's where home is.

He stroked and stroked a dozen, a hundred times. And stroked some more.

Follow the moon. Duncan kept his eyes on it. Its beautiful silver glow. Its promise of land, and warmth, of safety and life.

Then the thing passed in front of the moon.

This time Duncan saw the unmistakable fin shape. Except it was big, huge, so much bigger than anything he had ever seen or heard of in his life. And its white color cast a ghostly glow.

How tall was the fin? Ten feet? Twelve? That can't be right.

Duncan felt a tingle run all the way to his toes and fingertips. He needed to piss, but there was no way he was putting urine into the sea now. He'd hold it forever.

He saw the fin sink, slowly, but just before the tip went fully under, he saw it begin to curve in the water. It was coming around.

Duncan began to sob.

No, no, no.

Humans have a sixth sense. Something that comes to you in the moments of your greatest fear, or when death appears to stand silently at your shoulder.

Duncan knew the beast was coming up. From below, fast. That big ole tooth-ringed mouth larger than the double doors on a barn and gaping wide open.

"*Angela!*" He screamed.

The Megalodon shark took him, and as he was lifted in the air, the beast bit down, sinking eight-inch, shovel-shaped, serrated teeth right through his mid-section.

Mercifully, his mind had shut off all his pain receptors, and as the creature began to fall back to the black water, Duncan finally saw it was the biggest thing in the world.

And then his mind would finally admit it. *It was a shark.*

CHAPTER 07

Thirty miles south of Cape Cod, Nantucket Island, Massachusetts

On the flight down Sonya made several calls, quickly found out the information she needed and then made an instant seven figure donation to the church restoration fund there.

As she expected, she was there in just on two hours and went from the chopper pad directly to the downtown area on main street.

The once thriving whaling town was still a beautiful little village-like area with pretty, well-kept houses, manicured gardens, and cafés with tall, long-limbed people sporting golden tans and blinding white teeth.

She headed for the First Congregational Church in Nantucket. She knew from her research that its oldest building, the Old North Vestry, was constructed nearly three hundred years ago, and still in use today. But it was decaying. And that was her opening.

Father Andrew Merrick met her at the door. "Ms. Borashev, it is a real pleasure." His small hand delivered a surprisingly firm shake. "It's not often we have a new patron, and one who arrives within the same hour as their donation for a private tour."

Sonya nodded, looking down on the diminutive, portly man. "I'm impulsive, Father." She looked around. "And I've always loved places that are built on peace and beauty. And all in the center of this beautiful little town."

"We like it." He clasped his fingers together proudly. "Now, how can I help you? Would you like a tour of the vestry? It was built in the early seventeen hundreds and had a lot of –"

"No, thank you, Father. But I would like to see your records. I had some old friends and relatives here that the family lost track of, and it would be interesting to see what happened to them."

"Any particular dates we can use to track them down?"

"Around the mid eighteen hundreds, I think," Sonya replied.

"Then those would be in new sanctuary. It was built in 1834." He paused. "But I'm afraid anything before the 1960s is not digitized, so I hope you're not allergic to dusty old records."

Sonya laughed. "I'll just hold my breath."

He took her along the front of the ancient building. Just as she thought, it needed work. She knew how much it took to stop old buildings from trying to return to the sand and gravel from whence they came. Her money would be put to good use.

Father Merrick entered via a small gate and headed to the new building. For a new structure, it was also in need of work, and unfortunately in among the magnificently well-kept small houses just down the street it was becoming an eyesore.

"This way, this way." Merrick took her inside and through the chapel, then down a set of steep steps until they came to a solid oak door. He turned briefly to smile and then unlocked it. He reached in to flick on lights that blinked a few times as if coming awake after a long nap.

"Watch your step," he whispered over his shoulder.

Sonya followed him in and started down the stone steps to the basement. It smelled of old papers, dust, and something that might have been cleaning polish. But at least it was cool and dry.

"You have air-conditioning down here?" she asked.

"Yes, installed in the sixties and updated every decade. Nothing eats old records faster than mold and rising damp," Father Merrick replied.

He crossed to an old oak bench table with a light over it. "Now, tell me who exactly you're looking for." He waited.

She smiled. "All records and information on Ishmael Jonah Bartholomew."

His brows slowly came together. "Really?"

"Yes, really." Sonya's gaze was direct as she studied his response. *He knows something. Good*, she thought.

"Call me Ishmael," Father Merrick said softly. "Not many people know he had a full name." He pursed his lips. "But you do know that he was just a fictional character created by Herman Melville?"

"No, he wasn't. We both know that don't we, Andrew?" She dropped the formality on purpose, her gaze pinning him.

He licked his lips, and then he smiled almost sadly. "My dear, *Moby Dick* was a work of fiction." He lifted a finger, waggling it in the air as though searching his memory. "But there is a kernel of truth in it. Some say that the author, Melville, was inspired by the true life story of the whaling ship, the *Essex*, which sailed from right here in Nantucket in 1819. It met its doom in the middle of the Pacific in 1820, when a sperm whale attacked and sunk it."

"I know all that. I know all about the *Essex*. And I agree there is a relationship. But the *Pequod* was no work of fiction; it was a real ship, and the creature that attacked it was also very real. The animal was territorial, aggressive, and overly large." Sonya leaned forward on the table. "I need to know more about what Ishmael saw. What he *really* saw."

The father's brows were still slightly knitted. "Are you an author or a journalist?"

"Neither. I am a seeker of truth," Sonya replied. "And an impatient one."

Father Andrew Merrick stared at her for a moment. "I see no value in chasing old ghosts."

"Humor me, Father." Sonya held her ground.

He nodded slowly, still examining her before seeming to come to a decision. "Around 1842, you say?"

"*From* 1842. That was when the *Pequod* was sunk, and Ishmael Jonah Bartholomew was rescued by the ship, the *Rachel*. And brought home. Here to Nantucket. I don't know what happened to him after that. He might have lived for another year or fifty. I want to know more about him, his thoughts, and if he spoke to anyone about his ordeal."

Merrick sighed. "The cataloguing wasn't ideal. And there was never any funding for reorganizing it. This will take some time."

"I don't have *some* time." Sonya shared her steeliest gaze with him. "I have just donated one million dollars to your church. I don't want anything in return other than for you to perform an accelerated search, with my help."

Sonya saw the look in his eyes and decided to add one more carrot. "And there'll be a million dollars more if we satisfactorily conclude our search today. That should take care of your cataloguing problems."

After a second or two Father Merrick's face broke into a broad grin. "Indeed it will."

The basement area under the new vestry was huge, almost warehouse sized. Father Merrick led Sonya to long rows of filing cabinets. The first were made of aluminum, but as he progressed, they turned to wood, then old wood, then cupboards, and finally, ancient sea chests.

"As you can expect, as the age increases, the quality progressively degrades." He shrugged.

"Then we will see if fate has been kind to us." She looked along the huge volume of information. "Alphabetical?"

"No, it's organized via date range. There will be birth and death notices, newspaper clippings, personal works and reference to the works and the people by others." He walked along a line of cupboards and stopped at one. At least it had a date range drawn on it: 1840–1850.

He lay a hand on it. "And so we begin."

They each took a pile of folders and papers back to the huge table and began to sort through them. The folders were bound with cloth ribbon, and needed to be perused, page by page. Minute by minute. Hour by hour.

Five hours later, Sonya was alone. Father Merrick had left her with a small bottle of water and the door key while he attended to other duties.

Many times she needed to walk away to clear her mind. She'd stretch her back, and blink her bleary eyes back to clarity. She knew if she allowed her mind to wander she might miss something.

When she hit 1869, she was beginning to think Ishmael Jonah Bartholomew had simply vanished from the pages of history.

And then she found him.

Ishmael had been married, and was working as the owner of one of the local taverns known as the Benbow Inn. He wasn't blessed with children, and sadly he had lost his wife to pneumonia.

He had been invited to write a piece for the local newspaper, the *Nantucket Inquirer*, to coincide with the sailing of the *Bark Oak*, which was set to be the last whaleship to depart from Nantucket, marking an end to nearly two centuries of whale fishing.

Ishmael's column was the first time he had ever laid down in print his recollections and thoughts following the fateful last day of the *Pequod*. History had probably missed the article because he had penned it under the name of I. J. Bartholomew. Thankfully, it had been added to his historical record here.

Sonya read it slowly, taking in every word. It showed that, even twenty-seven years after Ishmael Jonah Bartholomew's ordeal, he was still deeply scarred by the incident. He started from the beginning, excited by the sense of adventure he'd felt as a young man setting off on his first whaling trip. He also talked of the strange characters he met, and the camaraderie among the crew. And then of the cruel and dominating sea captain, driven by a merciless hatred of a monster that had taken his leg years before.

His words grew dark as he wrote of the *Pequod* finding the great white beast and then their very one-sided battle at sea.

Sonya already knew that the whaling ships of the mid-1800s that were intended for lengthy voyages were up to 150 feet in length, twenty-five feet wide, and anywhere from 250 to 400 tons, depending on cargo and whale oil storage.

Sperm whales could grow to be sixty feet, a third of that was the head, and weigh up to fifty tons. They were a uniform dark gray color.

But Ishmael said this creature was white to gray, and was two thirds the length of their whaler, putting it close to a hundred feet. It also ate the crewmen.

Sonya exhaled slowly. She knew large sperm whales might be able to do that, but more than likely wouldn't. However, she knew something else that would.

She turned the brittle page and felt a tingle across her scalp as she stared down at the image. It was hand-drawn by Ishmael and hadn't been used in his article for the newspaper. Perhaps they had asked him to recreate the whale based on his recollection and were disappointed that his drawing didn't fit with their expectations.

She couldn't take her eyes away from the image – it was a shark, shaded white, and towering from the water with a small boat being splintered in its mouth. The bodies of men fell from the craft, and some even into the tooth-lined maw.

It might have been a rogue, she thought. An outlier. There were plenty of them. Examples were found everywhere in nature and even among the human population – an average man was five feet nine inches tall, however, there were some basketballers well over seven feet.

But she knew it was something else. Something that had been released into their ocean from a place where it had been locked away for millions of years. A place where there were other ancient species that were thriving, and she bet they too were released when conditions allowed.

Of course the *Pequod* found it as the ship always stayed close to the whale pods and that's what the monster was feeding on.

She quickly scanned the next decade of papers and found nothing until 1882, where there was a single paragraph that was Ishmael's death notice. And then Ishmael Jonah Bartholomew would have passed from history, if not for a book that immortalized his encounter with a true horror from the deep.

Sonya flipped back to the man's article in the *Nantucket Inquirer*. She briefly glanced over her shoulder before taking the page and the drawing, folding them, and slipping them into her pocket. Ten minutes later she was in the air and on her way back to New York.

* * *

Sonya got straight back into her research on return. She had resources well beyond those of the normal public or even most organizations. Many were legal experts, tech consultants, and data centers, but she also had connections into the darker avenues in life.

She was sure now that a huge form of Otodontidae Megalodon, or several of them, had been released from the cave beneath the dark ice of Thwaites Glacier.

There was one new piece of information that intrigued her: a report written in 2009 by a paleolinguist by the name of Professor Matthew Kearns. It was about a world he and a support team of military specialists had discovered deep beneath the Antarctic ice.

The report was fragmented and incomplete, and it was hidden in a series of backup vaults in the bowels of a military facility, but her technical research team had found it. It told of a place Kearns found with landmasses and an enormous sea. She was familiar with the established research on the buried lakes below the ice in the polar caps, and the collective wisdom from the investigating scientists had been that they were populated by albino shrimp, algae, and some species of blind fish.

But Kearns had reported that he and the team were nearly decimated by creatures that were enormous, carnivorous, and relentless. He had also written about an ancient underworld god. In several places was a word: *Qwotoan*. And then he posed a question: *Qwotoan* is *Croatoan*.

She had no idea what that meant, but a quick internet search had shown her that it might have referenced the missing colony of Roanoke Island in 1590. The only clue left behind from the vanished 121 colonists was the word, "Croatoan" that was carved into a tree.

If that wasn't eerie enough, Kearns' report read like horror fiction, but interestingly, it had been pulled from the open internet by the US military, marked as highly classified, and now only existed well off the standard research avenues.

Sonya sat back. A theory had formed in her mind, and she was already planning her next steps.

She looked again at the images of the last moments of the tiny submersible, the *Krill-1*, and the blurred picture of a massive mouth opening. She knew it had gone all the way over them. And then they were gone.

She reopened Kearns' report, feeling a prickle of apprehension move up her spine. The report was in fragments across several databases and trash centers. But her experts had reassembled the data jigsaw for her – she read it with interest, especially the section on an accompanying secretive military force called the HAWCs.

She folded her arms. That name pricked at her memory. Several years ago she had been being visited by a brutal and efficient-looking military colonel named Hammerson, who had demanded Valery's plans for his prototype high-speed submarine engines. Hammerson brought with him a tall soldier who never spoke, but whose eyes seemed to glow silver in the dark.

When a few of Valery's security specialists tried to eject them, this unidentified soldier had put both the highly trained Mironov security men down in seconds. She had never witnessed such efficiency, and such a display of speed and raw power. The unnamed soldier seemed to have the strength of ten men.

Sonya had taken on many adversaries in her time, but this was one guy she did not want to get in front of. In the end, Hammerson left with the submarine propulsion plans and a promise of future goodwill from the military. They had never heard from them again.

Sonya had used the CCTV footage of the two men to run a search. Of the tall young man there was nothing. But she had got a hit on the older guy – Colonel Jack Hammerson of a specialized team of soldiers called the HAWCs. He reported to just two people: a four-star general called Chilton, and the Commander in Chief. That was it.

She also found that Matt Kearns existed and was well respected. He was real, Hammerson was real, the HAWCs were real, and she bet his report was real.

Sonya narrowed her eyes as she stared at the screen. There was something beneath the dark Antarctic ice. Of that she was now sure. A wound had been opened, or rather reopened, and that wound was allowing an infection to spread. If the Megalodon monsters were there, trapped, then she had a chance to finish them.

"Clean the infection, close the wound," she said. "For good."

* * *

Sonya pushed her chair back. She had access to the best weaponry, technology, and underwater equipment in the world. And money was no object to her. But what she had learned from past mission dives and explorations was that tech provided little advantage without the best minds behind it. So she needed the best people.

She opened another screen and looked at a database she had compiled over the years. It listed the names, pictures, and bios of hundreds of people. She went through it slowly, already having an idea of who she needed.

She dropped them all into a mission folder. There were two high priority candidates she marked as mandatory, and she studied their faces for many minutes. They would resist, but even though their wills would be like a brick wall, her resolve was an iron battering ram.

Finally she stood. "Sorry, old friends, but I need you. And this is important." She pressed the button on her intercom. "Meena, ready the chopper. I need to travel to Marin County."

CHAPTER 08

Nick's Cove, Marin County, California

Jack Monroe dipped the rag into the small tub of Nevr-Dull and applied some of the thick cream to the cleat. He hummed as he smoothed it on, ensuring he had covered *all* of the brass fixture, then stood back to let it dry a little in the afternoon sunshine.

Cate was below, and he was alone on deck, the boat barely moving on the smooth blue water. Sunshine dappled on its surface making him squint even with his sunglasses on.

He briefly looked down at one of his shoulders, feeling the slight burn. He had on a tank top and his already tanned and muscular arms hung free. He grinned – suns out, guns out – but today the old guns were starting to fry.

He began to polish off the brass cleaner, humming again and very satisfied with the gleam he was getting back from the cleat. There was nothing like salt and sunshine to strip, discolor, and corrode anything anytime. Living on the water had costs. He straightened. But they were small ones.

He heard footsteps coming down the long wharf. There were a few boats in, and his was right at the end. If he heard them coming, it meant they were coming to see him, or Cate.

He looked up. And smiled. "Hello, stranger." He quickly half turned. "Cate, we got a visitor."

"Who is it?" she yelled back.

"A ghost from the past." He walked down toward the stern of his boat and held out a hand, but Sonya Borashev lightly jumped down to the deck beside him.

She was as striking as ever – close to six feet tall, long silver-blonde hair and intense blue eyes. Sort of attractive, but with a hint of hardness around her eyes, plus an athletic physique that told of someone who liked to keep in shape. Very in shape.

He held out his hand again and this time she took it, gripping it hard. She shook it up and down twice before releasing it. She had a folder under one arm.

"Long time no see, Jack." Her voice had the familiar hint of a Russian accent. She looked over his shoulder. "Cate." She crossed to her and shook her hand as well. "I missed you guys."

Jack could see the look on Cate's face – surprise, confusion, and a little caution. He understood why; Sonya represented a time in their life that was traumatic to say the least.

"Why are you ..." Cate began, but then it was like her frozen expression thawed and she smiled. "It's great to see you, Sonya. We missed you too." She turned to him. "Jack, get her a drink."

"Beer, water, soda?"

"Vodka?" Sonya grinned.

Jack shook his head. "Bourbon's the only spirit onboard I'm afraid."

"I thought all sailors at least had rum hidden somewhere." Sonya smiled widely. "Then just a catch-up will do." She sat down, watching them. "You both look well. Fit, tanned, relaxed." She nodded, still appraising them. "Still teaching, Cate?"

Cate bobbed her head and sat down opposite the Russian woman. "I write a few papers for the university. And do some guest lectures now and then."

"On what?" Sonya sat forward.

"Things that take my fancy. Like raw or invasive marine species."

"Good, good." Sonya clasped her hands together. "I have a confession – I've read them. All of them. You're a brilliant woman, and I agree with your hypotheses about species overlay. If a more aggressive, new species enters an environment, it can spell doom for many other species." She tilted her head. "We need to keep our guard up at all times."

Cate nodded slowly. "Sounds like you're keeping tabs."

Sonya waved a hand. "No, no. But you know we have similar interests. I read widely, and your work is always well researched and reasoned. I'd be a fool to ignore it."

Now it was Cate's turn to smile. Jack could read the hint of wariness that was still in the corners of her eyes though. He watched the two women talking back and forth, feeling like he was watching a game of chess.

Cate sat back. "It's always nice to see you, Sonya. But now that the pleasantries are concluded, why are you *really* here?"

There was a small table between them; with Sonya and Cate seated opposite each other, and Jack standing with his back to the stern. Sonya placed the folder on the table and then flipped it open. She found a picture and turned it around.

"This was taken two days ago, down in the Antarctic."

Cate sat forward. It was an underwater photograph of a ragged stump of a shark's tail. But it was impossible to tell its size without something for scale.

Jack leaned over the table to see better. "Looks like a shark. And the crescent-shaped tail makes me think it's probably Carcharodon carcharias, the great white." He looked up. "But that's unlikely in Antarctic waters. They can tolerate extreme cold, even frozen waters, but they don't like it enough to hang out there."

Sonya smiled sympathetically. "Jack, you know it's not a great white. And that tail is far bigger than a normal shark's."

"Here we go." Cate sat back.

"There's more. Or rather something else." Sonya flipped through more of the images until she came to the one she was looking for and turned it around. She sat back, watching them.

Cate and Jack stared at the picture for several moments.

"I see," Jack finally said.

"What do you see?" Sonya asked.

It was the image of the massive shark's maw as it was about to envelop the camera.

"It's white," Cate remarked. "Why is that?"

"Maybe it's something else, something new. Or something old." Sonya put the pictures side by side – the image of the torn shark's tail, and the huge maw. She sighed, looking down on them.

"But this tells a story. Representative analysis of the shark tail infers that the remaining portion was around twenty feet. And something tore that fish in half." She put a finger on the picture of the giant maw. "*This*, tore it in half."

Cate opened her hands. "Well then, that problem's solved, isn't it?"

"Not quite." Sonya kept her finger on the maw. "This thing also attacked and ate the submersible. Swallowed it whole. There were two pilots onboard."

"Jesus," Jack whispered and looked at Cate, who had visibly blanched.

"Then it came after the support vessel, and sunk it. Everyone aboard, *everyone*, was lost. Thirty-two good men and women all went to the bottom."

"No. Nope." Cate shook her head. "Not a chance, Sonya. I know where this is going. We are not diving to the bottom of the ocean to seek out this thing, or another Megalodon, or anything else you might have seen or heard of. We are out of the game. Period."

Jack was intrigued, but the growing knot in his stomach told him his own nerves probably couldn't deal with it again either. They'd seen things in the ocean that would bring most people to madness. He'd witnessed bodies crushed, shredded, and eaten whole. He was not inclined to see any of that ever again.

"She's right, Sonya. We can't be doing that anymore. We're too old and too sane now."

Sonya nodded, and then turned to face Cate. "I understand. But your papers tell me otherwise. Surely you must be intrigued, and you know the threat these species pose – the Megalodons, or whatever the hell this thing is. These monsters kill people, *have* killed people. I know in your heart you want to help."

Jack leaned forward to pick up the image of the massive, toothed mouth. He stared as though mesmerized.

Cate began to shake her head again. "Intriguing, sure, but still no. There's no way in hell I'm going to the bottom of the ocean again. I just can't."

"You wouldn't have to. I'm preparing a mission to investigate the Antarctic. No diving involved." Sonya smiled. "Aren't you a little interested?"

"Of course we are, but –" Jack began.

"But no." Cate glared up at him.

"No," Jack quickly agreed.

Sonya didn't move. "A week's work, ten million dollars. Each."

"Not for fifty million," Cate said quickly.

Sonya shrugged. "Okay, fifty-one million. Each."

Jack coughed and looked away.

"*No.*" Cate got to her feet. "I'm sorry that you came all the way out here for nothing, Sonya. But we are not interested in any amount of money. You can't put a price on our lives now."

Sonya also rose. Cate was a tall woman, but at five foot eleven Sonya looked down on her. "I need you, Cate. You and Jack. No one else on Earth has seen and faced what you two have." She sighed. "I've got a team of experts that will be better and safer having you two with them."

Cate shook her head. "We'd be of no use. That type of stuff already burned us out." She held out a hand. "Just talking about it makes me feel ill."

Sonya turned to Jack, who was looking down at the ground. "Jack?"

Cate stood in front of him. "He says no as well." She folded her arms.

Sonya held her arms wide. "Okay, okay. You can't blame me for trying." She scooped up the images, but then changed her mind, and left the folder where it was.

Sonya stood looking at each of them, the tension still hanging in the air.

Jack cleared his throat. "Okay. Good luck Sonya." He pulled out his phone. "One for the road." And moved next to Cate and took a picture of the three of them.

As he looked at it, Sonya held out her hand. "No hard feelings."

Cate smiled tightly and shook the offered hand.

"Of course not." Cate continued to hold onto the Russian woman's hand. "Personally, I hope you don't go. Because if the Megalodons *are* down there, *in* there, you know what they're like. They're the devil made flesh, and your luck will run out one day." Her expression soured. "Like Valery's."

Sonya's face dropped at the name of her lost love. She let go of Cate's hand and turned to Jack. She nodded mechanically. "Jack, good to see you again."

She was about to leave but paused. "And you're right, Jack, Megalodons do not like cold water. So once they're out of that cavern the first thing they'll do is try to get somewhere warmer." Her gaze was level. "Somewhere like here."

With that she leaped onto the gunwale and then stepped up onto the wharf. She walked down the weather-beaten planking without once looking back. They heard a helicopter start up.

"Well, that was intense," Jack said.

Cate sat back down and dragged in a deep breath. She held up one of her hands; it was shaking. "You said you had bourbon?"

Jack nodded.

She exhaled. "Make mine a double."

* * *

Sonya climbed into the helicopter and placed the headphones over her head. The pilot lifted off and at about a hundred feet began to veer away from the picturesque little fishing village.

Sonya connected through to her security team. "Initiate plan B."

She sat back and watched the *Heceta* at the end of the dock get smaller and smaller.

She sighed. *Looks like we do it the hard way.* She closed her eyes.

CHAPTER 09

Thwaites Glacier, Antarctica

Yuri was in the lead boat and Chekov in the second. Each inflatable had six men, mostly fishermen although some had military backgrounds. Even though Yuri had opened the weapons cabinet, few were permitted to be armed with guns. But all the men carried long knives, and one man brought an old speargun.

The men knew how to fight and had been called upon to do so many times. When they fished in northern waters near Africa, pirates sometimes made the bad decision to try to storm their ship. Yuri never called for help, or took prisoners, he simply shot every raider that stepped onboard his vessel and then dumped the bodies back over the side. Then he chased and raided their boats and took all their belongings. He was always surprised at how much money, weapons, and drugs, they carried – it seemed pirating paid better than fishing.

As their boats approached the ice shelf he turned off the outboard motors and had the men take to the oars. They gently rowed underneath the thick shelf of ice, which dripped freezing water down on them. Looking up, he saw the ice was a dark blue indicating it was old. Very old.

He reached out to put a hand over the side. The water felt cold, but he had a feeling in his bones that they were heading toward something unique. Something no one had ever seen before. For the first time in Yuri's life he felt an almost boyish excitement at the promise of something big coming to him.

The thicker the ice, the darker it got inside the ice cavern, and he had his men switch on lanterns. It took them another ten minutes to find the huge cave in the rock. Yuri stopped his oarsmen and turned to shine his flashlight on the other boat.

"What say you now, Mr. Chekov?"

"I say I am still nervous," his second in command replied.

Yuri scoffed. "Let me know if you need me to hold your hand." He motioned for them to proceed. But slowly.

They entered the cave, and he felt a rush of warm air on his face. The Russian captain inhaled. "Do you smell that?"

The crewmen looked about, and a few who had flashlights shone them on the walls and water.

Only Chekov responded. "I do," he whispered. "Land."

CHAPTER 10

Nick's Cove, Marin County, California

It was a beautiful warm evening, and Jack had bought a large lobster that afternoon at the markets. He hummed as he grilled, dribbling melted butter over the plump white meat in the split tail, and then moving the lobster around on the heat.

Cate was on deck, waiting. When he detected the char smell of the flesh, telling him it was done, he drew the crustacean out and inhaled the magnificent fragrance.

"Oh yeah."

He placed half on each plate, added a little of the salad he'd made, and then finished by dribbling more melted butter over the tails, a sprinkle of salt, a grind of black pepper, and he was done.

"Not bad if I do say so myself." His mouth watered in anticipation.

Upstairs he had a cooler of beer, and with the sun just on the horizon, the warm still evening was going to be perfect.

"Here it comes." He pushed open the galley doors and saw Cate in her chair. "Hope you're hungry."

"Always." She reached forward to the cooler and pulled out a beer and popped the cap for him.

He slid the plate in front of her, and saw that she had lit a candle.

"Is it my birthday?" He grinned and placed his own plate down.

"Every day is your birthday." She laughed and then leaned forward to look over every inch of his cooking. "This looks magnificent."

He had to admit it looked and smelled delicious, and as it was freshly caught he knew it would taste as good as it presented.

They ate, making small talk, enjoying the food and each other's company. Afterward they sat back, now side by side with their feet up on the table. They sipped beers and looked up at the black velvet sky with stars so bright they seemed to twinkle in metallic shades of silver, gold, and titian red.

Cate let out a big sigh, and he turned to her. "Sonya?"

"Yeah." She leaned forward. "What if what she said was true, and the monsters are out there again? She's right – people will die."

He reached out and took her hand, letting her talk it out.

"I mean, could there be a hidden place where these creatures have been living undisturbed for millions of years? Another place?" She tilted her head back against the cushions.

"You know what they say . . ." He began. "We know more about the surface of the moon than we do about the bottom of the oceans. But inside some sort of hidden cave? I don't know about that." He faced her. "I'm sure she can deal with it without us."

"Maybe. But she was right, we *are* the experts. The only experts." Cate groaned. "I think we should have taken her up on her offer. I mean, she came all the way out here and I blew her off like she was nothing." She turned to him. "She saved our lives."

He nodded. "Fifty million bucks apiece would have been handy as well." He shrugged. "So, what do you want to do?"

Cate looked out over the dark water. "Monsters are real. And all we have to do is face them again." Her eyes were dull as she stared out over the smooth bay. "We know they exist. There could be one below us right now, looking up at us, and we'd never know it until . . ."

He snorted. "Those sort of sharks don't need to be under the water to stare up at us. They have eyes that allow them to see just as well above the water as below it."

She turned to him, frowning, and he took that as a sign of interest.

"A shark's retinas have a unique reflective layer. It's the same thing that makes cats' eyes appear to glow in the dark. It allows them to see in murky water or the dimness of the deep ocean. Plus, the great white species, and their relatives . . ." He looked meaningfully at her. "The Megalodon."

"Shut up, Mr. Boring Scientist. Just shut up." She smiled at him. "Bottom line, you're telling me that if one of those big bastards was out there, it could be above the water? Maybe, even looking *down* on us."

"Nah. Too shallow here." He sipped again. "Nothing's out there, we're safe."

"And that's why I like it here. No more monsters." She put the bottle to her lips, but then her eyes went wide and she froze.

The bottle fell from her hand and her head slumped back against the chair.

Jack turned to her. Was this some sort of joke?

"Very funny." He leaned across her.

He drew in a breath. Her eyes were rolled back in her head and her mouth open – she was out cold.

"What the fuck?"

Another small hypodermic dart then struck him in the neck. There had been no sound, and it was like the sting of a bee. He reached up to the dart, his teeth bared as his jaws automatically clamped shut.

Then everything went black.

* * *

"Two down. Recovery inbound." The man dressed in black with the long rifle stood from where he had been lying on the wharf. He waved and another team dressed in black ran down the wharf as a boat sped toward them.

In under a minute both Cate and Jack's unconscious bodies were handed over the side. The food and even the plates went into the water. And then they were gone.

CHAPTER 11

Whittle Rock, False Bay, South Africa

The huge bay near Cape Town at the extreme tip of South Africa had been prized by divers, sailors, and fishing enthusiasts for over a century.

There were several golden sandy beaches and the shallows were a gently sloping sea bottom to about 200 feet for the rest of the bay. For shipping and sailors, there were hazards to watch for in the form of multiple small rocky islands, with many only just breaking the surface at high tide.

These rocky upthrustings were home to seal colonies numbering in the many hundreds. And where there were seals, there were predators. Big predators.

This day, the sun beat down with its usual midday ferocity, and the steel blue water tempted the seals with an offer of cooling comfort and, potentially, food.

Few went in as the older animals knew that a strongly lit sky meant anything on the surface became an easy-to-spot target for the giant razor-lined mouths that lurked in the dark depths.

Most heeded the warning. But not all. One cape fur seal pup was only eight months old, large enough to free swim now, but still inexperienced in all the bay's potential dangers.

Wheeling gulls not more than a quarter mile away suggested baitfish on the surface, and the cool water also promised soothing relief against the harsh sunlight that the pup's skin had not yet toughened up against.

The pup glanced briefly at its kin, who either dozed or watched with large, doe-like eyes. It hesitated only for a moment, but hunger and the heat forced it in.

The pup dived and swam straight and fast toward the gulls. It knew that if there were larger fish below they would chop up the smaller fish and he might be able to grab a free meal of sweet fish bits floating on the surface.

Halfway to its goal, the pup swerved around a small wave, causing it to thread a fraction off its course – and at that second the sea exploded from beneath it.

The eighteen-foot, 3800-pound shark rose in the air, massive tooth-lined maw gaped open.

The pup screamed in fright, but because it was fractionally off its course the shark's charge had been misjudged by bare inches, and instead of taking the seal all the way into its mouth, the pup bounced off the jaws and tumbled through the air.

The shark landed in an explosion of water. The pup came down, and immediately headed like a dark bullet back to the safety of the rocks.

It knew that the killer would be coming again. The big tooth was unlikely to miss a second time.

As the seal pup skipped along the top of the water, threading itself in and out of the waves, it saw its kin on the rocks in the distance. All now had their heads up and were watching.

The great white shark came up again. And the pup screamed its terror. But this time when the shark breached it wasn't underneath the small pup, but beside it. And the nearly two-ton beast was in the mouth of something even bigger.

The colossus had the eighteen-foot shark around its midsection, and the seal pup glanced back, hearing the cartilage crackle and be crushed with a noise that bounced right across the bay.

When this huge creature hit the water, it created a towering wave that the pup surfed all the way back to its small rocky island.

Like a dark spear it shot from the sea and didn't stop until it was at the center of the colony. Only then did it drop, panting, on the rocks.

The other seals continued to stare, not at the pup, but back out at the water. Something ominous had arrived in their bay.

CHAPTER 12

Aboard the *Sea Princess*, 50 miles north of
Thwaites Glacier, Antarctica

"Ooh." Cate sat up and immediately put a hand to her throbbing head.

She blinked open crusted eyes and looked about. Thankfully she saw Jack lying on the bunk next to her, mouth open and snoring.

"What happened?" She slid forward on the bunk bed and put her feet down. Her shoes were missing, and her eyes widened as she felt the gentle movement of the floor that told her they were at sea.

"Jack." She stood and crossed to shake him. "Wake up."

He groaned.

"Wake. Up." She tugged on his arm, and he opened his eyes.

"What time is it?" he said sleepily.

"Time to get up." She dragged him now. "We're at sea."

"I know, I know." He sat up. "The *Heceta* . ."

"No, not on the *Heceta*. Somewhere else." She continued to drag him. "And I don't know where," she said. "What's the last thing you remember?"

"Eating . . ." He frowned. ". . . lobster." He grimaced. "And I'm starving."

She looked at him incredulously, but then realized she was hungry as well. And then she noticed that he had a two- or three-day stubble coming in. No wonder they were both hungry.

"How long have we been out?" she asked.

Jack rubbed his face and then turned about. "No idea. But all our belongings are gone." He looked down at the pajamas he was wearing. "Who stripped us?"

"These must be ours." Cate found two piles of clothing – both outfits looked the same: white t-shirts under dark blue coveralls, and shoes like soft-soled hiking boots.

Jack grabbed his. "Well, I ain't barging out there looking for a fight in my pajamas."

They both dressed quickly, and then Jack put his ear to the door. He tested the handle and found it turned easily. He looked back at Cate and shrugged.

"I guess we're not prisoners." He gripped the handle. "On the count of three. One, two –" He pulled the door open and went out fast.

"Ah, Mr. Monroe, and Ms. Granger, good to see you're up." The woman smiled widely.

She was dressed in similar clothing to Cate and Jack, but her coveralls were a lighter blue with a small crest of a trident on the breast. She looked to be early thirties, perhaps Spanish, with dark haired pulled back, friendly looking, and with a disarming smile.

It obviously worked on Jack, as his anger seemed to short-circuit.

"Oh, I, we, were just, um . . ."

Cate made a sound in her throat and elbowed him aside. "Where the hell are we?" She pointed a finger in the woman's face. "We've been kidnapped, and I demand –"

The woman didn't even flinch. "Of course you do, Ms. Granger, and I am here to answer all your questions. But first let me show you around." She smiled even more broadly. "By the way, my name is Meena Delgado."

"But . . ." Cate began, but Meena had already turned away.

Jack hiked his shoulders and followed.

Meena took them through the engine room, displaying powerful and unbelievably clean machinery. A couple of men turned to wave and nod. Jack nodded in return.

"We're on a ship," Jack said.

"You are indeed. The *Sea Princess*. I'll show you more."

They went past the crew's quarters, and on past the gymnasium, plus hydro-pressure chamber for anyone who had depth sickness. Then onto a large area where they kept the diving equipment. Sitting in a cradle and attached to a hoist was a small, yellow, bean-shaped submersible.

Meena put a hand against its hull. "We call it the *Krill-2* – small but perfectly formed." She bobbed her head. "Two-seater, mainly for repairs and observation work as it's not that powerful. But it does have boosted propulsion, self-recharging batteries, and can get up to six knots when needed."

"Beautiful." Jack ran a hand down its smooth side. His stomach rumbled.

Meena heard it and clapped her hands together. "That reminds me, it's time to get you guys something to eat." She waved them on and spoke over her shoulder. "I'll brief you in the mess, and then when you're done I can inform the captain you're ready to meet."

"This has been fun, Meena," Cate said, "but I want to see the captain *right* now."

The woman's smile still didn't falter. "She's not available at the moment. But she's looking forward to catching up. We didn't know when you'd wake. But she won't be long, I assure you." She tilted her head. "While you wait, let's grab some food. Our chef is the best."

"I am hungry – starving actually." Jack shared a pleading look with Cate.

"Argh. Okay." Cate threw her hands up.

Meena raised a finger in the air. "Onward." She turned and led them toward the galley.

On the way they passed several other crew members who nodded and smiled at them. Meena addressed some in Spanish, some in German, some in French, and one in a language Cate thought might have been Russian or Ukrainian.

"You're a linguist," Cate surmised.

Meena half turned. "Yes, I can read and speak many languages. I studied math and music at university. And I guess the same part of my brain works with languages." She continued, "I can learn the basics of a new language in a few days. My brothers say it's spooky, but it helps in my work."

"I'll bet it does," Jack replied.

* * *

Aboard the Russian fishing vessel the *Boris Yeltsin*, the sonar operator, Seaman Belsky, stared hard at the small green screen and put a hand to the cup at his ear. The frown in the center of his forehead was as deep as an axe wound.

"There is another boat coming into the vicinity." He turned to the officer left in charge, Mellenov. "What do you want to do?"

"We are in protected waters. Fishing. We can't afford to be intercepted or even questioned." Mellenov stroked his bearded chin. "We can't contact the captain while they are inside the cavern, but if they exit they can radio us. For now we need to lay low."

"We should hide?" Belsky asked.

Mellenov shrugged. "Our transponder is disengaged so they can't identify us." He crossed to the wheel. "We'll pull back a mile and stay out of their way."

* * *

After close to forty minutes Jack was finally done eating. He had managed to eat a slice of grilled fish, a poached chicken breast, fresh asparagus spears with a mustard sauce, biscuits, and then finished with two types of donuts. Cate had shrimp pasta with crusty bread, and when she lay her fork down he nudged her.

"Do you think they're fattening us up to eat us?" He wiggled his eyebrows.

"Pfft. Doesn't take much to win you over, does it?" She elbowed him in the ribs in return. "Have you forgotten they drugged and kidnapped us?"

"No, I haven't, and I'm sure we'll find out by who and why now." He nodded toward Meena, who was approaching their table.

She collected them in her usual cheery manner and then escorted the pair toward the upper deck. They entered a small elevator, rose, and then they were on a huge floor in a room that looked like a combination of a high-tech data center and wheelhouse. At the front a large curving window surrounded them, and outside was a freezing, steel-blue sea.

Inside there were banks of instruments and three people working the wheel and other guidance equipment. Also standing there, and impossible to miss, was the tall and athletic form of Sonya Borashev.

She smiled and crossed to them.

But when she was in range Cate threw a right hook. "You bitch."

Sonya blocked it easily and pushed Cate back gently with one hand. The smile never left her face.

Two security guys who had been standing back stepped forward and Jack immediately muscled up, but Sonya almost imperceptibly shook her head, and they went back to standing silently.

Cate's fury hadn't abated, and she stood looking up at the tall Russian woman with fists balled. "You freaking kidnapped us. How dare you!"

"I did." Sonya's mouth turned down. "I had no choice. Sorry."

"Sorry?" Jack said. "You're not in Russia anymore. You're a resident of the United States of America. We don't do that shit here."

"Here?" She turned and lifted an arm to take in the vista. "Here is a long way from the USA." She sighed. "I want to tell you all about it. What we are doing. And why you were brought here." She stared at each of them. "It's critically important. Can you calm down enough to listen to me? Please."

"And if we don't like what we hear, you'll allow us to leave, right?" Jack asked.

"No." Sonya's smile flattened. "This is too important. That's why I needed to employ extreme measures to recruit you. Like I told you, I need you. Just for a few days." She turned and waved them to the front window. "Please."

"We won't be any part of this. You can't make us work for you." Cate stayed put.

"I know. And I hope I can change your mind." Sonya folded her arms. "If I had just told you what I knew, it would have seemed unbelievable. But if I show you then maybe you'll see how important it is. Important to us, to science, and perhaps to the safety of the world's seaways."

"Sounds ominous." Jack lifted his chin. "Do the payment terms still stand?"

"Jack?" Cate's mouth fell open.

"If we're going to be forced to stay here, at least we can walk away well compensated," he replied.

"Of course the terms still stand – fifty-one million dollars. Each," Sonya replied smoothly.

She waved them on, and this time Cate and Jack followed her. At the huge windows, she stared straight ahead and nodded at the vista. "What do you see?"

"Frozen sea and ice," Cate replied.

"*And*, a glacier," Sonya said. "Thwaites Glacier to be exact. One of the largest on the Antarctic continent." She sighed. "And it's being hollowed out."

"Climate change, huh?" Jack said.

"That's what many people think. And it's possible. But that's not the main cause here." She turned to them. "When our submersible and ship went missing we guessed it was because a doorway had been opened. But it took me a little time to find out exactly where. And why."

Her eyes narrowed as she stared at the ice. "And now I know." She turned to them. "The doorway is in there. And the beasts are now loose."

Cate and Jack looked back at the glacier. "There's an opening in there? Under there? And you're saying it's now been exposed?"

"When the gates of hell open, the first beast through will be the Leviathan." Sonya shared a crooked smile. "It sounds biblical, but it's not. It's more like a historical warning. And it's true. The beast is free now. Again."

"I don't like the sound of this," Jack said. "You mean a Megalodon shark is back out in the world's waters?"

"I believe there's more than one." Sonya turned to them. "I sent a research ship with a submersible, and what they found was extraordinary." She studied each of them.

"Yes, you told us," Cate said. "And you said they were both destroyed."

Sonya's face hardened. "Yes, I did."

"Then this is a suicide mission." Cate shook her head in disbelief. "Are you mad?"

"No, I'm scared," Sonya shot back.

Jack looked at Cate, then Sonya. "Well, so are we."

"This is important." Sonya took in a deep breath and then let it out slowly. "Time is against us. "If we don't investigate, someone else will." She turned to one of her technicians. "Is the Russian boat still there?"

"Yes, Ms. Borashev," the crewman replied. "Its transponder is switched off, but we can see them. They've pulled back a mile and are still sitting idle."

"They're waiting," Sonya said. "It's a fishing vessel in protected Antarctic waters. It should not be here."

"Neither should we," Jack replied. "I'm guessing that's why we can't report it."

"Very astute, Jack." She turned back to the glacier. "The other possibility is that they are waiting for their crew to get back from entering the glacier cavern. I don't like them being here."

"Sonya." Cate slowly turned to her. "Just what are *you* doing here?"

"I'm going in," she said confidently.

"And what are *we* doing here?" Cate asked.

Sonya tilted her head. "You're coming with me."

CHAPTER 13

Beneath Thwaites Glacier, Antarctica

"*Eto* . . ." Chekov's mouth hung open. ". . . *nevozmozhno.*"

Yuri shook his head slowly. "No, not impossible, my friend. Just unknown." His face was covered with a broad grin. "Until now."

Chekov had unzipped his thick jacket and wiped his brow. "It must be eighty degrees in here."

Yuri dipped his hand over the side. "It's the water. It's like a bath. No wonder the glacier was melting." He looked up, contemplating what was above them for several moments. Then he slowly reached out and switched his lantern off. "Everyone, lights off, now." He turned to the other boat following them. "*Lights off.*"

Everyone did as told, and the boats glided silently in the darkness on the inky warm water for a moment. Gradually, the men's eyes adjusted, and then they could see – shapes, then faces, and then more of their surroundings as the environment came to life under a soft blue light.

"Some sort of light. Maybe fireflies," Yuri postulated.

"It's bigger than I expected," Chekov whispered. "Much bigger."

"And it's ours. All ours." Yuri was still grinning.

They rowed on for another thirty minutes until further ahead in the twilight darkness something splashed, and all heads turned toward the sound.

"Remember, the beast that took half our whale is in here," Chekov whispered.

Many of the men gripped their weapons a little tighter, and turned about checking the water's surface.

"Is nothing," Yuri said.

He stared off into the darkness for a moment more before dipping a hand over the side and cupping the water to his mouth. He swilled it and then spat it out with a nod. "Probably the best fishing ground on Earth – clean seawater, untouched, no doubt fully stocked, and no one knows about it." He nodded. "Just waiting for us."

"There's land over there." Chekov pointed.

"Good. Here's what we will do. We make for the land and set up camp. One of the boats will return to the ship for more supplies, and the harpoon gun. We'll set up a fishing factory right here and part process our catch. That way no prying eyes will see us at work." Yuri scratched his chin. "We then transport them back to the cooler and keep going until our freezers are full."

He turned back to the water. "And if we find a good place to set up the winch then we can try to catch our big fish. If we have our harpoon gun, then that will make our job even easier." He pointed to the shoreline. "Row."

The men stroked to shore, and as soon as they came up against the shallows a few crew members at the front leaped out.

"Ach," one complained.

The shoreline underfoot was muddy, and they sank to their knees as they slid the boats up the bank. There were remnants of things that might have been plants, but they were twisted like mangrove roots and hung with shreds of slimy moss.

"This a dead place," Chekov observed. "There's a headland over there. I think there's more light the further in you travel."

"Then we will need to investigate. Maybe, in the near future we can set up some sort of permanent base." Yuri nodded, agreeing with his own logic.

He turned, hands on hips. There were twelve of them, and he had jobs for everyone. "Unload the boats. I want two men to head back and retrieve the extra supplies. Mr. Chekov, take three men and scout what's around that headland. If there's better campsite, then we can move." He wrinkled his nose. "Because this place stinks like a swamp."

The small boat set off with the two crewmen onboard, rowing slowly and carefully, almost as if they were worried about making noise. Yuri and his five remaining sailors set to organizing their supplies.

He wanted the catch boxes ready, and the nets checked. He'd trawl first in the shallows, and then they may set long lines, or even use both the boats to rig a dragnet between them and pull the fish in to the shallows.

He squinted out over the dark water and saw small ripples and movement indicating some sort of fish below the surface. He was feeling enormously confident. The Russian captain then turned to watch the small boat disappear into the gloom. He saw the lanterns at its bow light up. He didn't blame them. It got darker toward the mouth of the cave.

He faced the water again. Like any fisherman who found a new spot, he was excited to see what they'd catch in this place, and he wondered at the species, their size, and abundance.

He smiled. "Captain Yuri Zagreb, fisherman, explorer, discoverer."

Today will be a good day, he thought.

* * *

Milo Andropov and Andre Lemindov were the two crewmen tasked with returning to the *Boris Yeltsin*. They were well on their way to the cave exit when they finally decided to engage the outboard motor. They hated being in the dark cave, on unknown dark water, and with only long knives to use as weapons. The sooner they got back out into the freezing but open air, the better they'd feel.

Andropov turned to Lemindov who held the outboard handle. "I might get sick," he said, loud enough to be heard over the sound of the motor. "Maybe I have to stay in sickbay." He grinned, although he doubted his crewmate could see his face in the growing darkness.

"Yes, the captain likes those jokes," Lemindov replied. "He'll make you swim home. After a beating."

"I suddenly think I'm feeling better." Andropov turned. "But this place is bad – *plokhaya voda* – bad water."

Lemindov shrugged. "Then let's hope we catch a lot of fish and get a big quota bonus to make us all feel better."

"And quickly." Andropov turned back to the front of the boat.

The boat thumped against something and lifted a little as it ran over it.

"Careful," Andropov said and leaned out to stare over the side into the dark water. "You ran over something."

Lemindov slowed the boat. "That's your job, you whale-blubber head. You're supposed to be our lookout."

"I didn't see anything." Andropov spun his finger in the air. "Come on, full throttle. The quicker we're out of here the better."

Lemindov agreed and pushed the throttle forward to give maximum revolutions. In response the boat's nose lifted as they sped toward the mouth of the cave. The tiny engine screamed like an angry wasp as they cut the impenetrably dark water – so smooth it looked oily.

At the bow Andropov moved his flashlight back and forth over the water from port to starboard. He then shone it back behind them to check the water they'd just passed over to see if he could spot any snag, logs, or maybe a reef they'd bounced over before so they could avoid it on the way back.

Instead he saw what he thought was a surge wave coming at them.

"Hey." He frowned and focused his light on the anomaly. It was still there. He lifted his arm holding the flashlight, pointing it. "*Hey!*"

"What?" Lemindov turned to look over his shoulder as a white mountain rose behind them. The horrifying thing then surged forward, and jagged teeth clamped down on the entire back of the small boat, stopping it dead and then dragging it under.

Andropov in the front, was immediately catapulted into the air. In those seconds of chaos, when the spinning torchlight offered him glimpses of what had happened, his mind snap froze the images – the massive cave of hundreds of teeth, around nine feet wide, and surging over his shipmate. Then the mouth closed and Lemindov vanished inside, along with the outboard motor, and the entire back half of the boat.

Andropov remembered what happened to the whale carcass. The beast they had followed into the cave had been waiting for them.

He splashed down.

He didn't think they had been close to the shoreline, but underneath him was a ledge which he immediately clambered up on. Oddly, it didn't feel like rock beneath his hands even though he felt barnacles. Instead it was rough like coarse sandpaper.

And then it moved. The rock began to move – no, to *swim* – fast.

He was on the back of the beast.

He screamed and the monster accelerated, rolled, and then went down. The huge scythe of a tail that whipped from side to side as it glided past just missed Andropov.

He held the flashlight above the water – the creature was so big that, as it went past him, a vortex dragged him along for a few seconds.

Andropov turned in the water. "Help! He-*eeelp*!"

But he knew there would be no help. He began to swim, one way, then the other. His mind began to short-circuit from fear and indecision – should he try to swim out through the cave mouth to the boat? The cave was long, and then he would get to freezing water. What then?

Or should he try to swim back to the land? But it was further away and who knew what other monsters lived here.

Get out, just get out, his mind screamed at him. Better to die freezing than be eaten alive. He began to swim toward the cave mouth, cold be damned.

He swam with a one-armed stroke as he held up the light, swinging it back and forth, but the beam simply ended in a forbidding darkness.

There was just the lap of the water against him, and the odor of rocks exposed at low tide. He mustn't have been far from shore after all.

But then he felt the swoosh of a current beneath him. He prayed it was some sort of tidal drag from the cave mouth. But that notion was dispelled when he felt something heavy knock his boot.

Andropov spun in the water. Even though he was an atheist he began to pray to Jesus, Buddha, Gaia, and anyone else who might take pity on him.

He held the light up. Then whipped around, playing the beam over the water.

Then he held it beneath him, ducked his head under and opened his eyes. The torch only illuminated a few feet beneath the surface. But that was enough.

Hanging in the water below him was a monstrous head, ghostly white and over a dozen feet across. It was slightly turned to the side so one jet black, glass-like eye could regard him, just for a second or two.

No, no, no. Not me, Andropov pleaded as he began to swim backward.

His heart was hammering, and it was making him short of breath, but he sucked in air and ducked his head under again, just in time to see the monster give a flick of its tail, swing about, and then come at him.

Beneath the monster's white snout and eye, a mouth bigger than the world was beginning to open.

As the jaws clamped around him, Andropov lifted his head to scream so loud that he tasted blood in his throat.

And then he was gone.

* * *

Yuri turned. "Did you hear something?" he asked the man working next to him.

The man looked up, then glanced out to where Yuri was looking and slowly shook his head.

"Forget it," Yuri said. "Place is strange enough without inventing mysteries."

"*Captain.*"

Yuri turned.

Another of his crew pointed. "Mr. Chekov has found something. He needs you."

"Something good, I hope," Yuri said. "Take me there."

CHAPTER 14

"That's insane." Cate scowled at Sonya. "For a start the boat won't fit, and just getting close to a melting glacier is suicide. Have you ever heard of calving?"

"She's dead right, Sonya." Jack agreed. "We could be crushed, or if we somehow avoided a direct hit, we might be swamped instead. Either way, we end up in the sea and it will be deadly in these freezing waters."

"The tide falls fast here and has a huge sea-level difference between high and low," Sonya said. "It's getting to low tide now, and we know we can make clearance with a little tweaking." She folded her arms. "Also, the waters at the mouth of the glacier are seventy-two degrees. At least below the surface." She smiled flatly. "It would be like taking a warm bath."

"And what, we take our bath until someone arrives? When? I'm betting this isn't a formal sea voyage that's been logged anywhere," Cate said sharply.

"You're right. I've also turned off the transponder and we use a signal scrambler so we can't be tracked or even seen by satellite. The *Sea Princess* is a ghost ship as far as surveillance is concerned."

"Well, that's just great." Jack threw his hands up. "If something goes wrong, we're as good as dead."

"Don't worry, Jack, you know I plan well. I have significant backup resources if we get into any difficulty." She sighed. "Look, my plan is one of rescue and survival. If the Megalodon are in there, I kill as many as I can find, and therefore take out an apex predator class. Its potential prey will rejoice." She faced them squarely. "The creatures have been attacking and killing people all over the Southern Ocean since I last spoke to you, and now they're up into the Indian and Pacific oceans. They've got to go."

"We've done this before. People died. Leave it to the government this time," Cate urged.

Sonya rounded on her. "I'm aware people died. That's why I'm here." Cate bore the brunt of the Russian woman's furious gaze. When Cate took a step back, Sonya's expression softened.

"Cate, you know what governments are like. If we leave it to them, nothing will happen for months or years. Maybe never. More people will die while some bureaucrat shuffles their papers." She straightened. "But we're here now. We have the capabilities, the expertise, and weaponry, and we know what we're dealing with. Think of us as the exterminators."

Cate held a hand up. "Sonya, I think –"

"Enough talk. We must make the tide." Sonya turned to the helmsman. "Jorge, take us in. Meena, ready the deck laser."

"Deck laser?" Jack and Cate glanced at each other.

"We need to widen the external lip of the glacier ledge so we can take the ship in," Sonya said. "And also reduce the calving risk. It's that little tweaking, I mentioned."

"This is madness!" Cate walked away.

"Madness? No, this is our destiny." Sonya walked toward the wheel to stand by Jorge and stare out at the wall of ice with the dark hole they were rapidly approaching. After a moment she lifted a pair of binoculars to her eyes.

Jack sighed and followed her. "Okay, Sonya, seeing we're

along for the ride whether we like it or not, what are your plans once we're inside? *If* we make it inside."

She continued looking through the glasses, but he saw her mouth curve into a smile. "I like you, Jack. You're sensible, and not as hot-headed as . . . others." She lowered the glasses. "I'm not some mad person on an avenging crusade. But we both know what these massive killing machines are capable of. Evolution got rid of them for a reason. I just want to make sure they don't get a chance to repopulate in today's oceans. That would make Amity Beach look like a school picnic."

"*Jaws* was just a book and movie," he said evenly.

"So was *Moby Dick*." She turned to him.

"What?" he asked.

"Forget it." She waved it away. "I'm going to widen the hole. We then enter and I expect there to be a significant cave that will take us in and below the continent, and allow us access to an underground sea." She folded her arms. "And I suspect there will be things in that sea no one has ever seen. At least outside of a museum. Aren't you excited by that prospect?"

"Of course I am. But I was once excited to see a living Megalodon. I'm not anymore."

Sonya tilted her head. "Why not anymore? Because you know that once they enter our waters they're inimical to human life. They're a threat, and I know you know it."

Jack tilted his head back and exhaled loudly. He then faced her. "And if we can get inside, then what?"

Her gaze was unwavering. "We explore. We hunt." She drew in a deep breath, swelling her chest. "Either way, whether we kill or don't kill the beast, I'll be rigging enough explosives on a timed charge to seal off the cave to the outside. We'll lock them back in."

He frowned. "Why don't you simply start with that?"

"I'll tell you why." Cate stepped forward. "Because she *wants* to kill them. Her blood vengeance has not yet been sated." Cate returned to the window. "Isn't that right, Sonya?"

"Yes, I want to see them dead. I want to kill them a dozen times over." Sonya's face was devoid of emotion. "And then I will be satisfied."

Cate snorted. "You just mentioned *Moby Dick*. That's appropriate as I think your obsessive desire for revenge has twisted your thinking. You are Ahab now." Cate stared at Sonya who returned her gaze. "I don't think you'll ever be satisfied. Or find peace."

"Laser ready," came Meena's voice on the bridge.

"Stand by," Sonya replied, and then turned to Jack and Cate. "Don't worry, like I said, we'll have insurance." She hailed below decks. "Drop the communication buoy."

She received an affirmative and then turned back to the pair. "The buoy will establish contact with a temporary base we've set up in Tasmania, the southernmost state of Australia. If anything happens to the *Sea Princess*, then we only need to make it back here to call a spotter plane with emergency supplies, followed by a ship that will be on permanent standby."

"So all we need to do is swim back out here?" Cate rolled her eyes. "In the freezing Antarctic."

"We have rafts, wetsuits, and a miniature submersible. The plane would be here within two hours. We'll be fine." Sonya turned to Jorge. "Take us in close and then reverse thrust to hold our position."

Jorge nodded. "Steady as she goes." He gently pushed the double handle of the throttle forward and, without any sensation of movement, the large and sleek craft glided toward the blue-ice glacier.

"Nothing to worry about, just taking an eighty-foot craft in under a glacier overhang." Cate groaned. "And even if we don't get crushed and make it inside, you do remember what one of those full-sized megs did to your other craft?"

"Oh, I do. This time we'll be ready," Sonya replied. "For payback."

The *Sea Princess* glided to within 300 feet of the glacier rim. Up closer the glacier's physical mass was awe-inspiring and terrifying. It was like an enormous blue tidal wave of ice about to come crashing down on them.

"Jesus," Cate whispered.

"Hold position," Sonya said. And then, "Meena, make a hole."

On the foredeck, Meena, now in thick parka, and with a small team, worked something that looked like a telescope on a tripod. At its base was a powerful-looking generator, and Meena swiveled the thick round barrel end toward the rim.

Meena focused. "Commencing burn."

From the front of the laser a small pencil-thin beam of white light appeared.

"I didn't think lasers worked on ice," Jack said as he watched the woman move the beam over the glacier rim, slowly. And then, almost by magic, a ten-foot sliver of ice simply fell away into the water, with a significant splash.

"Standard lasers aren't very effective. Even green light lasers." Sonya half turned. "But we've found that CO_2 lasers work, and we learned this due to the new projects they're doing on ice drilling. We now power the CO_2 laser up to ten point six micrometers, that's a wavelength at which ice strongly absorbs light. It's not efficient but it does the job."

"Impressive." Jack continued to watch as Meena took the laser back to the start and then cut through another slice.

Jack could see what she was doing – paring the glacier back bit by bit, so as not to cause any surge waves, or risk the weight suddenly shifting and causing a hundred-foot chunk to be dislodged.

"How do you eat an elephant?" Cate asked, and then answered: "One slice at a time."

After just twenty minutes, Meena had widened the hole, and even targeted some of the larger chunks of ice in the water, cutting them into smaller portions.

"Well done," Sonya said. "Leave the laser in place." She turned to Jack and Cate. "Like I said, we'll be well prepared for whatever long-forgotten freaks of nature this cave can throw at us. If any large marine creature attacks us, I'll cut it in half with the laser."

"Normally that sort of talk would piss me off, but today it doesn't." Jack whistled. "Nice work."

"Jorge, take us in, slow and steady," Sonya commanded.

"All ahead, two knots." The young man's face was as calm as if he were taking a stroll down a quiet leafy street instead of maneuvering an eighty-foot vessel into an ice cave.

Everyone on the ship, above and below decks, seemed to hold their breath as the craft eased forward and passed under the huge lip of ice. Immediately blue shadows were thrown over them, and they each marveled at the ice wall and roof surrounding them.

"Hey, it's not melting." Jack craned upward. "I thought you said the water was seventy-two degrees?"

"It is, but deeper down. On top it's cold seawater – that's why the ice doesn't just collapse. As we enter the cave, it changes to near tropical," Sonya said.

"So much for swimming out and treading water for two hours," Cate said.

The filtered sunlight began to darken as the ice grew thicker inside the cave.

"Lights on," Sonya ordered.

Along the entire length of the ship lights came on, as well as huge spotlight beams at the bow. The illumination coverage was nearly complete and created a glowing halo surrounding the ship.

"You do know that anything in here that hunts by sight and is dark-adapted will regard these lights as ringing the dinner bell?" Jack said.

"Good. That will save me hunting them," Sonya replied evenly.

They continued along the ice cave, and though the ship rode high in the water, they still had a good twenty feet clearance above them, and more than that on either side.

"See that?" Jack pointed out one of the side windows. "That's tidal smoothing. I've seen it in Greenland. It happens when the tide rises against secured ice."

"That's correct," Sonya replied. "There are significant tidal extremes here. And why we needed to go now. It'll get a lot lower, and a lot higher, which might make clearance a problem."

"Just how high?" Jack asked.

"That's a good question," Cate said. "The tidal extremes might make for a tide surge that'll be like a rushing river. The Earth's average height variation in sea level from tides is three feet. But there's a place up in Canada called Wolfville, in Nova Scotia's Minas Basin, where the sea-level variation can be as much as fifty-three feet between high and low tide."

Sonya nodded. "It's not quite that here."

"Not quite?" Cate asked. "Because if it does get like that here, the cave could be totally submerged at high tide."

"Landfall coming up," Jorge said, keeping one eye on the bank of sensory equipment in front of him, and the other on the huge windows before them.

"The Antarctic continental landmass," Sonya added. "And, *yes*, there it is. What I was expecting."

The ice cave ended but did so at another opening. This one slightly smaller but made of rock.

"Holy shit." Cate stepped forward as if in a trance. "How far does it go?"

"At this time, that's still unknown." Sonya folded her arms. "Our sonar pings still aren't getting a bounce back, so your guess is as good as mine." She faced forward. "But considering the beast that came out of there, it's got to be a significant biosphere for a large animal to exist in."

"And breed in," Jack added. "For a population of colossal animals, I suspect it's got to be hundreds of miles of deep waterway."

"Going to be tight," Jorge said. "Good clearance below the hull, and we're at mid tide, so we're sitting high; might lose some paint. It should be better in a few hours when the water level drops a little more." He eased back. "Orders, ma'am."

Sonya didn't even blink. "Proceed."

"Proceeding at two knots." Jorge stared straight ahead, his expression stony as he steered the large boat into the hole in the rock wall.

"Threading the needle," Cate whispered.

The *Sea Princess* was a glowing ball of light as they passed through the cave, and Sonya turned to them. "No chance of ice fall here, so why don't you join me on deck?"

Jack looked at Cate, and then shrugged. "Don't see why not."

They left the wheelhouse and made their way along the side gangway to the front deck.

Jack inhaled. "Sea air, and warm. Absolutely not what you'd expect in the Antarctic."

"Not in the Antarctic, *under* the Antarctic." Sonya laughed and then lifted a radio to her mouth. "Jones, prepare to place package."

"On it," came the reply.

"Jorge, all stop," she added.

Jorge initiated a gentle reverse thrust and the boat slowly stopped in the center of the cave as a larger team assembled on deck. They had a mobile crane and ladder, and several dark plastic suitcases.

Jack and Cate watched with interest as, in a matter of seconds, the professional team assembled a device that Jack could see was packed with packets of C4 explosives.

"Your close-the-gate insurance?" Cate raised her eyebrows.

"You got it," Sonya replied.

The team scaled the ladder and used a drill to fix the package to the ceiling of the cave. On completion, Jack and Cate could see a red light blinking on it.

Sonya nodded her satisfaction. "Remote detonation. It should bring the roof down and close off the cave."

"Let's hope we're on the right side of it when it goes bang," Cate replied. "I assume you'll personally be detonating it. But what do we do if something happens to you?"

"We will be on the right side. And Meena is briefed on the procedure. I'm happy to show you two as well if that would make you feel more comfortable."

Jack slowly began to shake his head. "No, it's okay."

"Yes," Cate replied. "Show me."

Sonya smiled, and showed Cate the detonation device, switch, and fail-safes. And also where it would be kept.

After a moment, Cate nodded. "Okay, got it." She inhaled. "I smell tidal flats." She squinted into the darkness. "How long is the entrance cave?"

"A scan indicated a length of 800 feet. We should be emerging in around two minutes at a speed of three knots."

"Emerging into what?" Cate exhaled. "That's the question."

"You might be emerging into the history books." Sonya smiled. "If anyone knew about it."

"Yeah, see, that's not great if we run into trouble." Jack frowned. "We'll be marooned."

"We do our job, and then we exit. All done in a few days." Sonya walked forward to the bow.

Cate watched her for a moment, and then she called Jack aside. "I'm not sure we're getting the whole story here."

"Probably not. Let's hope she finds what she's looking for quickly. Best-case scenario is we leave and blow the cave. Everything back to normal."

"Normal?" Cate tested the word. "Yeah."

"I know, normal except we have a hundred million dollars between us." Jack held up his hand. "The breeze is near tropical. I think we're coming out of this rock cave."

"Exiting in forty feet," Jorge said over the deck intercom.

Meena reappeared with a case, and a sidearm strapped to her waist. She opened the case to display other guns and handed one to Sonya who placed it on her hip. Meena approached Cate and Jack.

"Sidearms." She smiled up at them. "Just for security, not mandatory."

Cate and Jack looked at each other and then nodded. "We'll take one each."

Jack saw they were a new full-sized SIG Sauer P226. But these were beefed up to a high capacity, double stack magazine. He checked the rounds: SIG .357s. This thing could take down a rhino.

"Taking no chances, are we?" Jack said.

Meena smiled. "Risk management is my middle name."

He and Cate threaded the holsters onto their belts. There were other notches and pouches in the clothing they wore, and Jack guessed there might be more equipment coming later.

"Exiting," Jorge intoned mechanically.

And then they were out.

At first it was just a general sensation of openness as the bounce back of noise they had been getting inside the cave vanished. The powerful front lights illuminated a vast expanse of water and, swiveling them, they saw cave walls that rose from rocky platforms and then coal-black, sandy, or muddy beaches.

They continued slowly for another few minutes before Sonya half turned. "All stop. Lights off."

Once again the craft glided to a stop, and then all the lights on and below the ship were extinguished. The impenetrable blackness was all encompassing, but only for a moment, as little by little pinpricks of a soft blue light appeared on the ceiling, high above them. Seconds later they could make out each others' faces, then the ship, and then their surroundings.

"Looks like we've arrived." Sonya's eyes narrowed as she stared out over the dark water. Her expression hardened. "And now your time is up."

CHAPTER 15

Yuri and a few of the *Boris Yeltsin* crew members walked along the dark shoreline and closed on where Chekov and his team stood at the base of a towering, flat rock face.

The cliff wall went from the water level all the way up to the blue-lit ceiling way above them, and it divided the land between where they stood and whatever was beyond the vertical sheet of rock.

"What is it?" Yuri called.

Chekov waved to him, and then pointed his light up at the wall. "Seems we are not the first after all."

There were drawings on the wall. Extremely old drawings. Most of them were faded, and other areas were encrusted with moss and lichen as if the paint or minerals had been particularly tasty to the tiny organisms in the dark, humid cave.

"So, cave men lived here? Or they came here to fish." Yuri grunted and turned to his crew. "Can anyone read it?"

All stayed silent.

Yuri nodded to one small man. "Mozgi?"

It was Yuri's nickname for one of their engineers; a small man named Moshev, but *Mozgi* meant brains in Russian, and as he was best onboard at trivia and crosswords, and just generally knew about anything and everything, the name seemed a good fit.

Mozgi looked along the drawings and strange symbols and then after a moment slowly shook his head.

Yuri sighed. "Then at least we can read the pictures." He walked to where he thought the fresco started and looked up at the coiled beast that had what might have been an eye at its center.

"It might be one of their gods." It didn't make sense to him. But he didn't like it. "Maybe next one."

But many of them were the same, and some showing two small figures crossing out of a labyrinth. He was about to give up when Chekov pointed to several more pictures at the end of the cave wall.

"The shark," he said.

Yuri stood in front of it. "Yes, yes."

There was a boat, and beside it the unmistakable rendition of a shark – a white one. The shark was three times as long as the boat.

"Our monster." Yuri laughed. "Even then they knew of it."

Chekov shook his head. "Not the same one." He turned to the dark water behind them. "But this is where the great beasts must thrive."

Yuri snapped his fingers. "Mozgi."

"Yes, sir." Mozgi stood to attention.

"When was Antarctic last with no ice?"

Mozgi scratched his chin. "It has always been iced over at the southern pole for millions of years. And, before that, it was always cold here. But there have been periods of little ice – every few hundred years – with the major one about thirty-five million years ago . . ."

Yuri waved a hand in his face. "No, no. When could people have lived here?"

"Oh, maybe during the last interglacial period," Mozgi replied. "That was about 12,000 to 15,000 years ago."

"Ah, yes." Yuri turned back to the wall. "This looks like the right time period."

The next image showed the shark smashing the boat and the men in the water.

Yuri snorted disdainfully. "This looks familiar."

"Did they hunt the sharks, or did the sharks hunt them?" Chekov asked.

Yuri looked at the pictures again. "I think the shark wins every time."

"Not every time. What's this?" Chekov stood in front of a last image. Something as big as, or bigger than, the shark was in front of it. This creature was fatter and did not have the same fin shape. "A whale?" Chekov asked. "Looks like a sperm whale."

Yuri shook his head. "Whales don't fight sharks. Maybe an orca or a pack of them."

"They did once," Mozgi interjected.

The men turned to him.

"Yes, it's true." Mozgi nodded vigorously. "Just a few million years ago there was a different species of whale. I found out about it when I was learning about the different types of animals we might be catching. I read a lot." He shrugged.

"What was it like?" Chekov asked.

Mozgi seemed to think on it for a moment as if his brain was accessing the memory files from deep storage. His eyes lit up as he found the correct information. "A little like the sperm whale but bigger, much bigger, and its jaws were more powerful, thicker, and stronger. Plus, each of its teeth was a foot and a half in length. It was the ocean's alpha predator. It even ate other whales."

Chekov brushed a few dangling bits of lichen from the image to show more of it. "Are they all gone now?"

"It was called Livyatan." Mozgi grinned broadly, this time showing a mouth full of gray teeth. "*Supposed* to be extinct. But no one knows why. All gone, all dead. Unless a few are hiding in here."

"Livyatan?" Yuri rubbed his chin. "Back from the dead or back from here?" He turned to Chekov. "Imagine bringing one of those monsters home."

"It would be . . . something." Chekov agreed.

Yuri walked down the black sand to the edge of the water and gazed out over its glass-smooth surface. *This is a place of wonder. Maybe the richest fishing ground in the world*, he thought. And right now, it all belonged to him.

He looked up. The blue glow from above was intensifying the further into the giant cave they ventured, and he had already learned that it seemed to switch on and off if there were loud noises.

Yuri took a few more steps until his toes were at the water. The sea before him was calm, just a few swirls indicating there might be something moving beneath the surface. But it was dark. Looking down at the shoreline, he saw the water was clear, but just a few feet in it turned to ink.

He turned and clicked his fingers at his crew. "Give me a stick." He held out a hand.

One of the men handed him a glow stick which Yuri snapped at its center and shook. It glowed a vibrant yellow, and he tossed it out a few dozen feet.

They all watched it sink with the water around the glowing stick crystal clear. It went down a dozen feet before coming to rest on a sandy sea bottom. Then it vanished.

"So, things that like to hunt by light and movement. We can use that." Yuri turned. "It's too shallow here. We need to find deeper water. We can try fishing for our monster from the shore, as I don't think an inflatable is a good place to reel a monster shark in on." Yuri laughed darkly and then waved his hand in the air. "Mr. Chekov find us a deep-water inlet. Move out."

"The boat?" His second-in-command asked.

Yuri glanced back at where they had pulled the inflatable ashore, thought about it, and then shook his head. "Leave it there. We'll just take the gear we need. I want the others to find our beachhead when they return." He bobbed his head, deciding. "But I will stand a guard."

He pointed at one of his men. "Belakov, stay and mind the boat. We'll be back in a few hours. If not, send out a search party."

The group then set off along the desolate shoreline. Yuri glanced upward, wondering how high the cavern rose above them. He continued to watch and, from time to time, he thought he saw something fly from one part of the cave ceiling to the other.

Just my imagination, he told himself. The shadows and darkness were distorting and shifting as if the biological light up there was moving in waves. He also observed that the light was cool, even though inside the cave it was a balmy high 70s and the water felt exactly the same temperature.

As Yuri, Chekov, and the seven crewmen walked along the shoreline, the captain observed something bobbing at the water's edge.

"Fetch me that," he said to one of his men.

The crewman quickly walked down to the water and crouched to lift out the long object. He brought it back.

"Driftwood." Yuri held it out.

"There are no trees on the Antarctic continent. And it's not plank wood." Chekov ran a hand along it. "Strange."

Yuri nodded. "Like you say, there are no trees *on* Antarctica. But below it?" He shrugged. "Who knows."

He let it drop, and the group continued. In another fifteen minutes they came to a river pouring from a low cave.

Mozgi bent at its edge and cupped his hand into it. He sniffed and then put it to his lips. He looked up. "Good news, we will not die of thirst here. Fresh water."

"Good. Maybe one day we can sell holidays down here." Yuri laughed loudly at his own joke, and the noise was enough that some of the overhead lights winked out for several seconds.

He looked up. "What, you don't like my jokes?"

The group waited as the lights slowly eased back on as if dawn was peaking over the horizon. The light's muted brilliance was the quality of light at late evening or early dawn – enough to see clearly, but it left many shadows.

The small river they stood before was only about knee-level deep, and the men crossed in single file. As Chekov was leaving the water he looked up at the mighty cave wall rising into the darkness beside them and stopped.

He walked closer. "This might be a problem. See this?" He pointed at something on the rock face just above his head height. "This is a tide line. It must be low tide now, and by the look of these barnacles, I'd say the tide comes in at least another six to seven feet. This small river would be too deep to cross at high tide, unless we swam."

Yuri shrugged. "It doesn't matter. We'll simply wait for the next tide."

They continued and rounded the next rocky outcrop. They came to a stretch of rock like a broad, flat ledge. Here the water looked deep and foreboding, and beyond was another beach.

Chekov lifted his binoculars to his eyes. "Looks like trees over there."

Yuri ignored him for a moment as he stared down into the dark water and then the flat rock shelf.

"We'll look at that later. Our priority is here." He waved an arm over the flat rocks. "This looks perfect. Deep water close to the edge." He looked about. "We rig up. First I want to catch a baitfish. Something big enough to tempt our monster."

Yuri ordered the heavy rigging set, while the men prepared some whale meat and threaded it on a fish hook the size of a man's finger. It also had a wicked barb on the end to ensure that once it was sunk into the flesh it would not come out. The hook was then attached to a line that was nylon but thick and had what was termed a break-and-strain of up to 500 pounds. It was usually used by tuna fishermen.

For now, they had set aside the big rig fishing equipment: a steel cable and twelve-inch-long meat hook. It was attached to the portable winch for when they had their bait. Once organized the crew would attach the winch to the rock platform, and then wait for their monster to come calling.

The men unwrapped the stinking whale meat and cut free a chunk about the size of a bowling ball and stuck it on the hook. Already the rank odor of the greasy, fatty meat was making the men gag.

"Ha, perfect to attract our fishy," Yuri said from a safe distance. He knew that oily fish sent out chemical trails on the currents, which brought in the predators.

Lemnov got the job of casting and holding the line – mainly because he was the only one who had brought his rod. It was a big game fishing tackle set, and the big man often trawled for tuna behind the boat when they were heading in and out of fishing grounds.

Lemnov's arms, chest, and back were like a gorilla's, and behind him for support was Dardov who had equal-sized shoulders, but a huge belly and would provide a good low center of gravity when acting as Lemnov's anchor.

The line flew out a good hundred feet before splashing down noisily and then quickly sinking. The ripples moved outward from the spot and then, after a few seconds, the surface settled back to its usual glass-like stillness.

"And now, we wait." Yuri folded his arms.

They didn't have to wait long. A hot *zizzing* noise came from the reel and Lemnov grunted. "Got something." He gripped the line. "It's heavy."

The fishing line went so taut it flicked the water off as spray. Lemnov began to work the reel, a two-speed shifting mechanism and a set of heavy-duty stainless steel gears. It also had harness lugs and he dropped the rear stub of the rod into the bucket harness at his groin.

Lemnov worked the gears like a racing driver, but whatever he had hooked wasn't budging.

"Not coming up." He groaned from the strain.

"Are you sure you haven't hooked the plug?" Chekov watched the water.

The big man grinned back, but his face began to redden, and the veins stood out on his neck. "There's good weight there, living weight. It doesn't know it's hooked yet."

Dardov was gripping Lemnov's harness from behind with his legs braced and was leaning back. He lifted his head. "Then why don't we let it know?"

Lemnov nodded, sucked in a deep breath, and lowered the rod toward the water. Then he heaved back with all his strength, dragging the line toward him.

It worked, as the line began to pay out.

"*Now*, it knows." Lemnov laughed heartily and began to work the unseen creature below the water.

Minutes went by. Then an hour passed. Then two.

In all that time, the line had barely been reeled in more than a dozen feet and Lemnov was looking fatigued.

Yuri felt his impatience peaking. "Enough. Pull this fish in or cut it loose," he growled.

The glance Lemnov shot his captain meant that there was no way a fisherman like him would ever cut loose a magnificent fish when he had it hooked and had been playing it for so long. Further, he was not going to lose a lot of his expensive high-strength line, as he knew there was no way the captain would reimburse him.

"Then we will pull it in." Lemnov turned to two more shipmates and bade them get behind Dardov and, on his word, get ready to pull.

"We may lose the hook. But we may also get a fish." He locked the reel and stopped any more line running either way. Now there were only two ways to go – the fish came in or broke the heavy-gauge line. "On the count of three, two, one . . . pu-*uuulll*."

The line of men dragged Lemnov backward and he held the line tight. The line came in, further and further.

"*Forward*." Lemnov yelled as he unlocked the reel and walked forward. Then he locked down again and ordered the same thing. Gradually, by repeating this process, they began to win their battle with the fish.

Chekov walked down the rock platform all the way to the waterline and held up his flashlight, pointing it at the line as it came in.

"I see something," he yelled over the sound of the grunting men. "Here it comes. Prepare the gaff hooks."

The two men behind Dardov grabbed up the long poles with wicked hooks bigger than their hands. They got down close to the water, braced themselves, and held them in both hands.

"I see it," one announced and then both men got each side of the line. "One more heave, Lemnov, it's coming up."

Lemnov did as asked, and then both men shot their gaff poles forward and dragged them back to sink the big hooks into the fish.

They tried to drag it up, but the fish was too big to get up and over the lip of the rock ledge.

Yuri saw the danger of the fish getting caught on the rocks and pointed at the other men standing around. "Everyone together." The entire group came to assist – holding the men, the line, or the gaff hook poles. They all strained and then, in one great surge, the massive fish came up and over the lip of the rock ledge.

The men continued to pull back, faster now, until the fish

was ten feet from the water. The huge purple-hued fish lay on its side gulping air.

"Now, *that* is one weird fish," Yuri said.

Amazingly, the fish grunted like a pig and then righted itself and began to use four lobed fins to try to walk-drag itself back to the water.

"What is this?" Yuri said. "You're not going anywhere." He held out his gun and shot the fish in the head.

The lights went out.

The loud report in the cave echoed for miles, as the men quickly switched on their lights.

They waited. And then the lights began to come back on. It was like a wave of blue luminescence approaching them as whatever creatures were creating the light gradually assumed the threat had gone, and lit themselves back up.

The group looked down at the fish. It was at least eight feet long and about 350 pounds if it was an ounce. It was covered in thick armor with each overlapping scale the size of a fist. The enormous thick-lipped mouth stayed open and they saw it was full of needle-like teeth.

Yuri crouched and grabbed one of the weird fleshy fins. He squeezed it. "It's like it's got finger bones in there." He looked up. "Mozgi, do you know what is this fish?"

The small man had been staring at the creature. "I think I've seen pictures of something like it. I think it's a *coelacanth*. They're nocturnal, so living in caves is what they like." He looked up. "Everyone thought they were extinct. They are a very ancient form of fish that might be 300 million years old."

He crouched and, like Yuri, grabbed one of the thick fins. "This line of fish is called a lobed-fin fish, you can see why. It might have been where walking animals evolved from." He looked along its length. "Some species still exist, but they don't get this big. This one seems more ancient." He shrugged. "It's different."

"I know what this one is." Yuri looked up.

"What?" Mozgi asked.

"Bait." Yuri guffawed, and then snapped his fingers. "Some for bait, and some as steaks for our dinner." He patted Lemnov on the shoulder. "Good fishing."

The crew began cutting up the fish. They set aside most of the thick fillets, which was around two hundred pounds of meat, for their meals. But the front end, which was a heavily armored head, gills, and weird hand-like fins, and still probably weighed 150 pounds, they fixed to the massive hook on the iron cables.

The tackle and bait were heavy and would tax even the winch wire, which was a double strand of high-tensile and flexible steel. If one strand broke, the other would hold long enough to get whatever the creature was they had hooked close to the boat. Or shoreline.

"I think we have a problem." Chekov stood looking down on the fish head with hands on his hips. "It's heavy. How do we get it out there? I mean, further than the edge of the rocks."

Yuri walked up to the huge lump of bleeding flesh and gave it a small kick. It didn't budge an inch.

"Good question." He looked from the bleeding lump of fish meat to the pitch black sea, and then walked a few paces down the rock shelf and stood watching the water for a moment.

"I think the tide is still going out, and that's a good thing." He snapped his fingers. "Old fisherman trick – we float it out."

Yuri ordered one of his men to run back to the boat and scavenge some of the old canvas, Styrofoam-filled life jackets tucked under the seats. It took the man thirty minutes, but he came jumping and jogging over the cracks and pools in the rock platform holding three stiff, red jackets.

Yuri had the men then tie them to the giant lure, and then he stood back surveying his work.

"This should allow it to stay above water. Or at least off the bottom."

Now, all he needed was for it to work long enough for the tide to drag it out to deeper water, so the scent trail was picked up on whatever currents operated out there and spread outward, up and down the coast.

"In it goes." He snapped his fingers and pointed to his men. Several of them lifted the huge chunk of bloody fish meat, dragged it to the water, and then on the count of three, heaved it in.

Sure enough it sunk, and Yuri held his breath for a moment. But then the red vests broke the surface, meaning the meat was suspended below them. Slowly it began to bob its way further out.

Yuri pointed to Lemnov. "Time to really test your fishing skills, Mr. Lemnov. Man the winch." He turned back to the impenetrably black sea. "And now we wait."

Lemnov and a few of the men stood by the winch. Its base was now bolted to the rock. The others stood around and smoked, talked, or laughed at some or other joke.

Yuri and Chekov stood close to the lip of the rock ledge and watched their bobbing makeshift float as it slowly moved away from them, taking the heavy cable, and huge, baited hook with it.

"Do you think we'll catch it?" Chekov asked.

"I think we will catch it or one of its kind. Or maybe some other huge thing that lives out there," Yuri said. "But we have several mountains to climb – the first and smallest is catching it. Then we try to reel it in without losing our winch and cable." He turned. "And then what do we do when we get it close to the rocks? If this thing is as big as we expect, I doubt we'll be able to pull it up onto dry land."

"I see." Chekov nodded. "Do you have a plan?"

"I always have a plan." Yuri smiled, supremely confident. "We get it close to the rocks, and we shoot the monster to death. Then we use the boat to drag its carcass back out through the cave."

Chekov turned. "Be easier if those bastards got back with our supplies. And their boat."

Yuri nodded. "If I find out they decided to even have a cup of coffee, I'll dock them a week's wages."

They stood in silence for a moment more. Chekov looked upward at the cavern's ceiling high above them. Yuri followed his gaze.

There were twinkling blue lights that seemed to be stars in a pitch-black night sky. But weren't.

"I wonder how big this place is," Chekov said.

Yuri continued to look up, and then frowned as he thought he saw something moving across the ceiling. It was just an outline as it passed over the sprinkling of lights, but he thought it looked a little like a man with long arms. Or maybe a giant bat with folded leathery wings.

"It seems to be a cavern of unimaginable size. There's life in here. Lots of it. And large animals that could only exist in an equally large place." He exhaled and looked back out at the ocean. "The Russian science department will be very interested in what we have found." He turned and half smiled. "After we have finished taking a few cold rooms full of fish and making some good money." He pointed to the plastic sheet under which they had stored the coelacanth meat. "We only need to catch a few dozen of those to have a good foundation catch."

Chekov nodded, but then tilted his head to look at his captain. "I would feel better if we had the *Boris Yeltsin* with us." He looked around. "In here, it feels like we are a long way from home."

"We are." Yuri snorted.

"No, I mean, a long way in time." Chekov exhaled slowly through his nose. "It is like this place is very ancient, and we modern creatures shouldn't be here."

Yuri scoffed. "High risk, high return. Sometimes it is the captain's duty to make those calls. And it will be the difference between the men getting a full catch bonus, and just minimum wages." He turned briefly. "Or nothing."

Chekov nodded but didn't reply.

Yuri watched the bobbing lure, which was now a good hundred feet from the rock ledge.

It is a strange sea, he thought. And why wouldn't it be? A sea hidden by a glacier that might have locked this place away for millions of years, only temporarily opening when there were warming periods. Or at least that's what Mozgi thought.

Yuri felt good, very good. "I think this place is going to give us everything we dreamed of."

* * *

Captain Yuri Zagreb squinted along the dark, rocky coastline. He was sure there were plants along there, tall odd-looking things that had to be trees, but they were just shadows in the gloom and might be nothing more than weird rock formations.

His curiosity urged him to explore, but he knew he had to stay focused and leave it for another time. Or perhaps another team.

From behind he heard Lemnov make a small sound in his throat. Yuri turned to look over his shoulder at the man, and saw him, staring dead straight out at the water, gaze unwavering, and his hand on the winch controls. The man then fractionally tilted his head as if listening to the wire.

Yuri turned back to the water and saw that their float was now about 150 feet out. Was it sitting lower than before?

And then the float went under, fast, and things started to happen all at once – Lemnov yelled, the heavy cable ran out with a whirring sound, and men scrambled.

Yuri watched as the line vanished into the dark water, and then it started to move down the coast. Lemnov yelled for them to get out of the way, as he swiveled the winch. It didn't have a lot of mobility other than simply up and down, left and right, but at least he could face the way the line was being dragged.

After a moment, he slapped the lock on. The cable wire went so taut that water flicked from it with the sound of a harp being plucked, and the toughened metal of the winch where it was fixed to the ground moaned and complained as it was put under enormous pressure.

"*Here we go!*" he yelled.

Lemnov's lips pressed together as he started to wind the crank handle on the winch. For now, he just tried to turn the beast, as it seemed to have swallowed their gift and was heading down the coast.

When the sound of the steel bending began to become ominous, Lemnov let out a little of the cable. But after a few more seconds, he snapped the lock back on, and began winding the cable back in.

About ten feet came back, and then five more.

"She's turning." Lemnov grinned. "She's turning."

He managed to reel in another ten feet, and Yuri estimated he had about another 150 to go from where he thought the float had been taken.

The Russian captain could feel his pulse rise as the cable slowly came in – the man was actually doing it.

Yuri turned. "Ready with the guns," he said and felt for his own pistol at his hip. "Try to shoot for the eyes. I want as little damage to the carcass as possible."

More line came in, and then it started to move, from the left where it had been dragged, to then change direction, as the fish started to swim back the other way.

"It knows it is hooked now," Chekov said.

"If it pokes its head up, it'll know it's been shot as well." Yuri drew his pistol.

The line came in a little slower now, and the toughened steel cable was increasing in its speed, back and forth, as the monster began to fight with them.

"How much more line is out?" Yuri yelled.

Lemnov, eyes wide with excitement, glanced down. "Another seventy feet. It's close now."

The men turned back to the water in time to see a head breach. It was enormous, and in the darkness the serrated triangular teeth shone white, and the massive black eye on one side stood out sharply in the corpse-pale head. It seemed to hang there momentarily, regarding them as a snake might regard a mouse.

Yuri lifted his gun arm and shot, the sound frighteningly loud. He hit it. But he had forgotten the effects of sound on the lights above them, and everything immediately went dark.

Men yelled and water thrashed, and just as the lights were coming back on, the monster surged, throwing up a geyser of water, and in that second the strengthened wires went tight, tighter, and it wasn't the winch that gave away, but the over-extended wires.

One of the strands snapped like the sound of a giant guitar string being plucked. The single cable wire whipped back to its home, passing by most of them and on its way back to the winch . . . and Lemnov.

Yuri turned and saw the big fisherman lifting his head just as the whipping wire reached him. The wire never slowed, or even deviated on its path, and it went right through his face – from his open mouth and out the back of his neck.

Yuri's jaw dropped open as Lemnov continued to work the winch even faster as the top of his head flicked away into the darkness.

It was a ghastly scene and Yuri wished the lights had remained out, as the upright body was still obeying the last orders from the man's brain and trying to reel the fish in.

Yuri wondered if, somewhere off in the darkness, the top half of the head was wondering why it was on the ground as its eyes blinked in confusion.

Men screamed and moved away, and then, after another second or two, Lemnov's body fell to the side, twitched a few times, and then lay still with the pump of thick dark blood slowing as his heart stopped.

The rest of the cable still had the shark hooked, but with another ferocious tug, the winch was pulled completely off its base by the remaining wire strands, and it lay flat on the rocks, with the wire still extending out into the water, but hanging limply. There was a splash from behind Yuri and he turned to the dark sea.

Several hundred feet further out in the dark water, the now sagging life vests rose, obviously still attached to the wire, but the shark was free. The massive conical white lump of the shark's head lifted from the water again. The snout was turned at an angle and the massive maw gaped open. One black eye as soulless and dark as polished obsidian stared at them, remembering them. Yuri had a cold thought: *It is marking us down for vengeance.*

It could have broken free any time it wanted. It's laughing at us.

Yuri lifted his gun again, but didn't fire, conscious of the fact he'd throw them all into darkness once more. After what had happened to Lemnov, he knew it would panic the men.

He lowered the gun. "Next time," he whispered.

The shark slid back beneath the water. He saw the huge fin rise, and further back the tip of the tail fin. He guessed it must have been around fifty feet separating the fins. A quick calculation to include the long snout put the beast at sixty-five feet, maybe seventy. A monster.

Yuri still had the crazy idea he could catch it. He had a spare hook back in the inflatable. Plus there was still plenty of cable on the winch, although it was broken from its base now. He bet if he could get the beast a little closer he could still kill it by shooting through its eye and into the brain.

He saw the fin rise again, this time going in the opposite direction.

Yuri snorted. "So, you think you are going to hunt us now?" He pointed his gun and mimed shooting. "I think we'll kill you before you kill us, dumb fishy."

He holstered his gun and turned, sighing heavily. "Collect our comrade's body. All of it. We will take him home."

"The winch?" Chekov asked.

Yuri shook his head. "Leave it. And leave the wire out there. Maybe we can repair and rerig it later. Perhaps we can have another chance at our monster tomorrow.

"We'll take our fish meat back to our base camp. Make some steaks for dinner. When the other boat gets back with our supplies, we can send Lemnov back in it for the freezer to be taken home." He shook his head. "Today, we lost. Tomorrow, we will win." He took one last look at the wire leading out toward the bobbing red life vests. He hoped the chunk of meat was still there, and he hoped the shark would choke on it.

* * *

It took the Russian crew another fifteen minutes before they could begin the trek back along the shoreline rock platform. They'd been fishing for hours and the tide had come in at least six feet. The shallow river they had previously crossed by wading was now a broad and dark expanse of water.

"Looks like we are stuck here," Chekov said.

"No, the boat will pick us up. We just need someone to go and get it." Yuri turned to the group. "Mr. Ivanoff, you are our best swimmer. Get across and get Belakov and our boat. Come back and pick us up."

121

Ivanoff looked at the inky black water for a moment and frowned. But then reluctantly he began to take off his clothing. He stripped down to his underwear, leaving his clothing in a pile on the rocks. He pointed to them and then one of the other crew members. "Bring those."

The man nodded.

Ivanoff stood at the river's edge, which was now a large inlet from the sea to the cliff wall. He waited there for a moment, staring across as if marking his position and deciding where he would emerge.

He waded in, and then dived. When he surfaced, he immediately began to stroke hard and fast. Within seconds he was already a third of the way across.

But that was as far as he got.

Surging in from the dark sea, the massive Megalodon came up into the shallow water like a steam train. One second the swimming Ivanoff was there, then he raised an arm as if to ward off the white predator. But he was a tiny morsel to the monster, whose massive jaws opened and went all the way over him.

"*Get him out, get him out!*" Yuri screamed and pulled his gun as he and the other men ran toward the water's edge.

Medvedev held up a gaff hook and actually stepped into the water. Yuri began to fire into the massive creature. But once again the lights went out, leaving him without a target. And worse: they now had no idea where the monster was.

In the pitch darkness there was the sound of thrashing, then a scream. But this time the throat it came from was not Ivanoff's.

"Get back from the water," Yuri called out. "Get back." And then. "Everyone. *Silence.*"

Yuri heard Chekov's heavy breathing beside him, as if the man had run a marathon. But that was all.

They waited, and slowly a patch of blue came back on.

Then another and another. In a few minutes the ceiling shone with its usual twilight glow.

"Where is Medvedev?" one of the men breathed.

Yuri turned to where he had seen the man step into the water. He was gone. There was no sign of him at all – no blood, no torn clothing. Nothing.

"It took him," he whispered. "Right from the shore. Just like it said it would."

"What did you say?" Chekov asked.

Yuri turned. "I could see it in its eyes. It wanted its revenge. And it took it."

Chekov glanced at his captain for a moment before turning back to the water. "It could see us, but we couldn't see it."

"Sharks can see in the dark," Mozgi said.

"Now you tell us." Yuri holstered his weapon. "I guess no one will be going for the boat. Looks like we are stuck here until the tide turns."

"I don't think so," Chekov replied. "Look at the cave walls."

Yuri did as requested. And then he saw. "The tidal zone." He felt a tingle of shock at his temples. "It is well above this rock platform."

"Yes it is," Chekov said. "So we will all be swimming soon." He turned to the dark water. "But not for long if that white demon is still out there."

"It is." Just a hundred feet from the rocky edge of the platform they were on the huge fin patrolled the dark water.

Already the water was lapping over the stone. As a captain, and one who had seen a lot of the world's oceans, Yuri had also seen the extreme high and low tides, and he knew they allowed the seaborne predators to come in closer to the shoreline.

Yuri sighed. A tide like that would be more than enough water for the monster to get at them.

"I think it would be best if we are not here when the water comes higher," Chekov said.

Yuri looked to the towering rear cave wall and saw few handholds. And to the left of him was the now surging river. To the far right, further down, was a rock fall, rising about a hundred feet, but it was potentially climbable.

He had no idea what was beyond that. But at the moment the unknown was better than the known – which was a gruesome death.

"We climb. Bring the equipment. We will see what is beyond that mountain of fallen rocks." He turned back momentarily to the water. He couldn't see the monster shark fin, but his gut told him it was out there. It would always be out there.

"We can return when the tide turns."

He had a depressing thought: he hadn't followed the beast in here to kill it; the beast had lured them into its world to eat them.

Yuri's face was greasy with sweat and he used a thumb and forefinger to press on his eyes momentarily. When he blinked them open, he saw that all the men were watching him. Their faces were filled with fear.

He raised an arm. "Onward. Let us explore a little while we wait for the tide to turn."

The men set off and he turned back to the now surging dark river. *Farewell valiant crewmen, Medvedev and Ivanoff,* he thought. *We will not be joining you.*

Yuri turned and followed the line of men as they had headed toward the small mountain of fallen rocks.

CHAPTER 16

Aboard the *Sea Princess*, beneath Thwaites Glacier, Antarctica

Meena stood on deck and filmed, turning slowly. Two crew members worked enormous high-intensity searchlights that they swiveled slowly on their stands. The beams reached out for hundreds of feet into the darkness.

Mostly there was nothing but water, but behind them was a towering cliff face, reaching up into nothingness, indicating the cavern they were in was beyond anything they had ever imagined.

"The Son Doong," Cate whispered. "It's a cave in Vietnam – 650 feet high. Its main cave alone is large enough to house an entire New York City block." She turned to Jack. "It even has its own lakes, rivers, and beaches."

"This is beyond a cave," Jack replied. "This is an entire world."

The ship moved ahead slowly, and Cate drew in a deep breath through her nose. She smelled the brine of warm seawater, the dankness of the cave that was like rocks at low tide, and something else – soil, plants, and maybe something like wet animal.

"Time to put your shark expert hat on, Jack – find me that Megalodon." Sonya said.

"Megs were once in every bay, sea, and ocean around the world. Deep water or shallow, cold or warm, it didn't matter." Jack walked to the railing. "But their preferred breeding and hunting grounds were shallow seas, under 200 feet deep."

"Good." Sonya touched her ear mic. "Jorge, patrol the coast, remain in water under 200 feet deep. We'll do a sweep and then zigzag back."

"We've got a signature on sonar," Jorge said. And then, "Whoa, we've got two now. Separate signatures. One small, close by, and the other big, real big. Around a hundred feet, but in deeper water and quite a few miles out."

She lifted her head. "Cate, Jack, we've picked up something – one big signature at around a hundred feet. The other much smaller."

"A hundred feet?" Jack frowned. "That's bigger than a meg. Don't tell me we've got something even more formidable down there."

"Picking up something on hydrophone from the direction of the large object," Jorge said.

"Put it on speaker." Sonya folded her arms, her eyes staring into the distance.

Over the speakers came staccato pops, squeaks, and squeals. Jack tilted his head. "Whale song?"

"Identified?" Sonya asked.

"If it's a whale," Jorge replied, "then the cetacean database can't find it. Getting an unknown classification."

Sonya touched the earbud again. "Are they moving?"

"Big one is moving away from us. Now at ten miles out, traveling at around eight knots. The other is staying put. Not huge, possibly under twenty feet. But it's an interesting shape."

"Okay, set us a direction there. I want to see what it is." Sonya turned. "We've got something."

"Contact already?" Cate asked.

Sonya continued to stare out over the water. "Maybe, maybe not. Could just be debris. But worth checking out, and it's on our way."

"That larger object was close to a hundred feet," Jack said. "Remember something sunk your first ship. Are you sure we're ready for this?"

Sonya briefly glanced at Jack before turning away and walking to where Meena stood, still filming. "Meena."

The woman turned.

"Set up the deck cannon," Sonya requested.

"The what?" Jack frowned.

Meena nodded and quickly headed to something still under a cover. She whipped the plastic sheet off, revealing a deck-mounted gun.

Cate and Jack recognized it as being like the one Sonya had used to great effect on the Megalodons before.

"Mark thirty-eight machine gun system. Manually operated. Got it from a friend in the navy," Sonya told them. "Range with high accuracy, 8200 feet. One inch caliber shells, with explosive tip."

Cate shook her head. "When you come ready for war, then war you will make."

"There's already a war. And these things threw the first stone. We'll throw the last." Sonya half smiled. "Just want to get everyone home safe, Cate."

"Coming up on signature," Jorge said. "Fifteen degrees, starboard side, closing at 300 feet. Just on or below the surface."

"Got it." She pointed. "Floodlights on." She repeated the direction for the operators. The beams flicked on and walked across the water to where Sonya had indicated.

The *Sea Princess* slowed, and the beams waved back and forth over the dark water's surface.

"One hundred feet," Sonya said. "Slowing to two knots."

The big ship glided gracefully on the water. On deck there was absolute silence as Cate, Jack, and Sonya, plus many of the crew, all stared at the sea surface.

"There." Meena pointed, and the lights flicked to the object.

The ship altered its direction just a fraction. "All stop," Sonya said.

Many went to the railing and looked down at the thing in the water. It took a few moments to determine what it was, and it was Sonya who recognized it.

"Life raft. Older-style Russian model."

Jack and Cate stared down at the raft. Even though the water seemed an inky black, it was clear, and they could now clearly see the shredded inflatable.

"What happened here?" Meena asked.

"Isn't it obvious?" Cate turned to her, and then Sonya. "Seems they found your Megalodon first."

"No, I think it found them." Meena cursed under her breath.

Sonya turned. "Scan the water's surface for survivors. But I'm not hopeful."

"That Russian fishing vessel we saw outside on the radar." Meena walked closer to Sonya. "This craft must have come from there."

Sonya nodded. "Yes." She rested her hands on the railing and stared out over the dark water.

"Do you think it was the only one?" Meena asked.

"If it wasn't the only one, then where are the others?" Cate asked.

"Probably dead as well." Sonya's mouth turned down.

"What the hell were they doing in here? In just a damn inflatable." Jack shook his head. "The fools."

"Chasing a fishing catch. If they thought they had found an unknown and well-stocked fishing area, it would have been irresistible to a commercial fishing vessel." Sonya shrugged. "Maybe they wanted to catch a Megalodon. And they paid a high price." She turned to them. "Now do you see why we must act?"

"They can't have known what they were up against." Cate shook her head. "Now they do."

"Should we recover it?" Jack asked.

"Why?" Sonya replied.

"Oh, I don't know, we could look at bite patterning, other clues to confirm what it was that attacked them."

Sonya shook her head. "I know what it was." She walked a few paces from the railing, turned to the wheelhouse and touched her earbud. "Send out a pulse."

She turned back to Jack and Cate. "A little something else we brought along to improve our search time."

Jorge's voice drifted from the overhead speaker. "Echo pulsing in three-two-one . . . *pulse*."

There was a brief sensation of pain between Cate's eyes, and she was left with a slight ringing in her hears. She touched one of them.

"Don't worry about that, it'll stop in a few seconds." Sonya smiled. "Just another project Valery had started working on. That I completed. It's like a cross between whale echo location and bat sonar. We send out a signal pulse in 360 degrees. It can travel for a hundred miles, and when it reaches a hard object, it bounces back. The computer then reads the performance shape of the signal, diagnoses it, and then paints a picture based on what it thinks it has found."

"Ingenious." Jack nodded. "The ultimate fish finder."

Sonya smiled in return. "I knew you'd appreciate it, Jack." Cate rolled her eyes.

Sonya folded her arms. "It shouldn't take long."

"We have an impression. Three miles to port, close to the

shoreline," Jorge said. "Computer image extrapolation says it's the right size and shape for a Megalodon target."

Sonya turned and nodded. "Excellent. Set course and take us there, eight knots." She faced Cate and Jack. "And now we have our target."

CHAPTER 17

Belakov paced, glancing at the water. The tide was coming in rapidly, and though he still had plenty of dry land, he had never seen a tide come in this high, this fast. He had needed to pull the inflatable further up by himself, twice.

The crew had been gone around eight hours. Did the captain mean it when he said to send out a search party? Because he was the damn search party.

If they were in trouble or trapped, there'd be hell to pay if he didn't go and get them. And if he went, and they didn't need him? Well, he would burn a little fuel, and say he had concerns for them – so no real downside.

He glanced at the rising water again. "No choice."

He quickly filled the boat with the remaining supplies, turned it around and dragged it back to the water. Once there, he leaped in and started the motor. It caught immediately and he steered the inflatable down along the shadowy coastline.

Belakov still found it hard to believe they were in a huge cave. He also found it hard to believe the captain thought he was going to catch something in here. But if anyone could sniff out a school of fish, seal pack, or lonely whale, it was Captain Yuri Zagreb.

He stayed close to the rocks, keeping his speed down to about three knots. The shoreline moved between a beach of black sand, tumbled rocks, and then sheer cliff face. So far, he had seen nothing of his crewmates.

Belakov came to a river, a wide and surging torrent that emptied from somewhere deep within the cliff wall and surged on a tidal swell. He slowed the boat, and rode in a circle looking back over his shoulder. How could they have crossed that? It was a good hundred feet wide and looked dark and deep.

He took the inflatable in a bit closer. He then turned back the way he had come for a while, but he still had no clue where his crew was. He could only guess that the tide had been so much lower earlier that it had allowed them to cross. In that case, they had to be further along the coast.

Belakov opened the throttle and powered along the shoreline, staying about a hundred feet out now that the blue light seemed to be increasing and he could see the rocks clearly.

After another ten minutes he thought he began to hear voices – faint – but he was sure if it. Then shouting. And then he saw them.

"Hey." He raised an arm to wave at them. Or some of them. They were all on top of a huge pile of tumbled boulders. They were yelling something and pointing.

He waved one more time and sped toward them – it looked like they wanted something.

Belakov opened the throttle further, the nose of the craft lifting, and the growl of the powerful outboard engine kicking up its revolutions.

* * *

The remaining crew with Yuri numbered six, four crewmen including Mozgi, plus Chekov and Yuri. As they neared the top of the hill of tumbled boulders they heard the familiar whine of a propellor.

"Oh no." Chekov groaned.

"That idiot, Belakov," Yuri hissed. "Our last boat."

He stood. "*Go back. Go back.*" He waved his arms furiously, but the man in the boat returned the wave and kept coming.

The others also began to shout and wave, but all it did was encourage Belakov to increase his speed and veer directly for them.

Yuri lowered his arms. "Maybe he'll be oka–"

Like a breaching submarine, the ghostly shark exploded from the dark water directly underneath the inflatable. The items in the boat fanned out in the air, including Belakov whose body, arms, and legs spread, spun like a Catherine wheel.

The inflatable hit the water with its nose, bounced and landed upside down. Belakov came spluttering back to the surface, moving groggily, and looking stunned. He coughed, the sound carrying over the now still water.

Chekov got on his toes. "Swim. *Swi-iiim!*" he roared with every breath in his body, and waved the man in.

"*No.*" Yuri shook his head and then cupped his mouth. "Get the boat. *Save the boat.*"

Belakov threw one arm over the other, but only got about half-a-dozen feet before the monstrous white shark returned. It eased out of the water next to him, and then casually turned its head to grab him in its huge jaws. But it didn't take him down. Instead it held him in the side of its mouth as Belakov let out a scream so blood-curdling, so long and loud, that Yuri saw one of the men put his hands over his ears and turn away.

The body hanging there gave Yuri scale – the shark looked as large as a bus, and its black eyes coldly regarded the group on the shoreline: challenging them. And maybe promising them what was to come for each and every one of them.

Belakov's scream continued, but then the shark must have

bit down as the man's cry turned to a moan of agony.

"It's torturing him," Chekov whispered.

"It's not smart enough to do that," Yuri said, but he knew that was exactly what the shark was doing. The bullets he'd fired into the shark had hurt it. And now it was going to make them pay. All of them. One by one.

The Megalodon shark bit down harder, and Belakov's voice was silenced. Even across the hundred feet of water, they could hear the cartilage and bones crack along with a meaty squashing noise.

The shark then eased back below the water, leaving a swirling whirlpool on top that dragged some debris from inside the boat toward it.

No one spoke. They only stared at where their shipmate had been tormented, killed, and then eaten. And Yuri knew they were all imagining how it would feel when the same thing happened to them.

But there was a single glimmer of hope – the tide was still ebbing in, and the upside-down inflatable wasn't that far from shore. Perhaps the last few feet of tide coming in would push it toward them. Maybe even beach it, because no one, even if ordered under pain of death would dare set foot in the water.

Yuri stared at the boat. "I think –"

And then his hopes were dashed, as the pale snout of the shark came up beside the boat, opened its train-tunnel-sized maw and clamped down on the toughened plastic and canvas boat with the aluminum ribbing. It shook its head from side to side several times and the twelve-foot inflatable was shredded.

It let go and the boat sank, but the shark didn't. Once again it hung there, watching them.

"It's the devil," Chekov whispered.

Behind them, one of the men began to sob.

"Shut up." Yuri rounded on him. "Shut up, you coward." He sat down and put his hands to his head. "Shut up and let me think."

The group was silent, probably all lost in their own gloom-filled thoughts. Yuri's head came up.

"We need to get back to where we came ashore." He looked about. "Either our other boat will return with supplies, or our ship will eventually know we are late and surely come looking for us. We need to make it easy for them to find us."

"How will they find us?" Chekov asked.

Yuri snapped his fingers. "The driftwood. We collect more of it, dry it out and start a bonfire. It will light this place for miles."

He stood. "And I believe our shark friend, after living so long in this cave, will find the illumination of a fire a little unbearable, yes?"

Chekov nodded. "It is a plan I like."

"We have time before the tide retreats. We can gather our wood." Yuri looked toward the top of the pile of boulders they had been climbing.

"Brains."

Mozgi lifted his head. "Yes, sir."

"Climb to the top and tell me what you see. I want to know if there is any driftwood, or anything worth collecting over the other side." Yuri turned back to gaze out over the dark water.

He wondered whether the shark was there, gliding just beneath the surface, patrolling the shoreline like a giant watchdog. Waiting for one of them to make the mistake of entering the water. Or even getting too close to it.

In a few more minutes Mozgi had climbed to the top of the boulders. He stood there, just looking over the top.

"Well?"

"It's, it's . . ." The man just stood there with his mouth open, pointing.

"Are you a fool?" Yuri clambered up after him, and several

of the others followed.

At the top he dragged in a huge breath from the exertion. Though the light was still just a twilight glow, they were treated to a view that took in nearly a mile of the dark land-scape below.

Chekov snorted. "I think there will be enough wood for our fire."

Yuri turned, slowly taking it all in. "I don't believe it." He straightened and put a hand into the small of his aching back. "It's a forest."

"What's it doing here?" Chekov asked. "How can it grow?"

The men stood in awe and stared. There was a thick forest leading back into a valley that was lost in the twilight gloom. At its center there might have been a river, and Yuri was sure he saw something moving through one of the mossy or grass areas.

"Enough wood for our fire?" Yuri grinned. "There's enough wood in there to build an entire boat."

* * *

The seventy-foot Megalodon shark glided closer to the surface and lifted one side of its head. Its specialized eyes allowed it excellent vision in light, dark, heat, cold, depths, and shallows. And they also allowed it vision out of the water.

It saw the group clambering over the rocks. It had tasted several of them already and, though small, they were soft and warm. The taste and smell of their blood excited it.

It slowly sunk back below the water and followed the small two-legged creatures. It was a big animal, but it knew there were bigger in its world. Bigger ones of its own kind, and other creatures that would hunt and attack it. For now, it was alone and had the small herd of animals to itself.

But on the periphery of its senses, it detected the thrum of something new. It was not another animal and more like the buzzing things that had floated on the water. Except this one seemed larger, and bigger.

It didn't need to change its course to investigate – it could continue to follow the bipeds on shore – because the sound was drawing closer. Whatever it was, it was coming to it.

CHAPTER 18

Sonya was back in the wheelhouse, and Cate and Jack remained out on the foredeck. Meena stayed with them. The small woman had her arms folded as she watched the dark water. The air was sultry and warm, and Jack felt slick perspiration on his brow.

"This is amazing." Meena turned to them. "How many times in your life do you get to do something like this?"

"Believe it or not," Jack said, "this is not our first rodeo."

Cate walked to the railing. "But this *is* something else. If this really is the last place where the Megalodon are holding out. It should be left as a sanctuary." She turned. "Don't misunderstand me, I hate them as much as she does, and I never want to see them in our waters again. But I'd prefer to simply wall them in and leave them alone."

Meena nodded. "I know you two have a lot of history with the creatures. Mostly bad –"

"All bad." Cate injected.

Meena nodded. "And that is true of Sonya as well. But she is obsessed with finding the creature that killed Valery. She feels she never finished it off. And maybe this is where it came from or went." She turned away. "Until she gets her blood, she will chase them to the ends of the Earth." She turned back. "Or beneath it."

"Well, five days is what she told us. We'll hold her to that." Jack's voice had an edge to it.

Meena nodded. "Sorry, figure of speech. Sonya is a woman of her word. She'll complete her voyage within the timeframe she promised."

"Let's hope so." Cate half smiled. "Otherwise, we're hostages."

Meena smiled. "Not a chance. Don't worry, Cate. She's a good person at heart who is very passionate. I know you know that."

"It's like there are two Sonyas – one who is warm and passionate, and the other who is so focused, she might end up running over the top of everything and everyone to get what she wants," Jack said.

Around them, teams were working to set up the deck-mounted cannon, and also the laser on the tripod.

Jack motioned toward them. "Which one is yours?"

Meena glanced at them and then turned back. "I get the laser. Its condensed light beam will even penetrate seawater without losing intensity. All we need to do is locate our target, and then we can cut it to pieces." She shrugged. "I'd prefer to go for disable, rather than kill." She looked up at them from under her brows. "But Ms. Borashev wants the head."

"Just like Valery did." Cate sighed. "And that didn't end well."

"Coming up on target," Sonya said from over the deck speaker. "Everyone to their stations."

"We're up," Meena said. "You two had better head up to the viewing area in the wheelhouse."

"Good idea," Jack said and he and Cate climbed the metal stairs to the upper deck.

It was blessedly cool inside from the air-conditioning.

"What have you got?" Jack asked.

"Our fish," Sonya said. "We're taking the *Sea Princess* in closer to the shoreline."

"Isn't that a risk?" Cate asked.

"Everything is a risk down here," Sonya replied. "But we can see that the water is deep in most places, and our sonar is smart enough to warn us if we come across any shallows. Plus, the hull is strengthened for moderate icebreaking. We'll be fine.

"Concentrate lights on the shoreline," she told Jorge. "But turn off the underwater illumination. Our guy might be light sensitive, and I want to get nice and close."

The huge beams swung toward the shoreline, and they slowly passed by what looked like a river surging from inside the cliff wall.

"I'm betting that's ice meltwater. Fresh," Cate observed.

They continued along the coastline, not more than one hundred feet from the rocks. Cate and Jack looked from the dark water to the rocks, and back again.

"Target is half a mile further along the coast. And moving away." Jorge said as he steered. "Hundred feet of water below us; plenty of room."

They watched the water as all of them expected to see a fin breaking the surface soon, but it was Cate who instead spotted something on the shoreline.

"Up ahead. On the rocks." She pointed.

"Biological?" Sonya asked without turning. Her eyes were unblinking and moving from the sonar to the dark sea surface ahead.

"No, it looks like . . . machinery." Cate frowned and leaned forward. "Move the light over there as we pass by it."

The light operator did as asked, just as they were coming up beside it.

"What the hell is that?" Jack asked. "It's new. Or at least not old." He snatched up a pair of binoculars from the console top in front of him and focused them.

They were just moving past the object. "I've seen something like that before. When I was onboard a coast guard ship that was interrupting an illegal whaling operation – it was on their deck and looked just like that – an old style crank-winch."

"A winch?" Cate frowned. "Down here?"

"And . . . *shit!*" Jack's eyes widened. "It's still rigged. *And the cable's out . . .*"

Sonya turned at his raised voice. "What is it?"

"The winch cable!" he yelled. "*Stop! Stop!*"

It was too late. They heard grating and scraping coming from under the hull and then the sickening noise of grinding as the propellor became enmeshed. On the shoreline, the winch mechanism was hauled across the rock platform with a clattering sound that echoed in the huge cavern, as their propellor chewed up the cable and it wound tight around the propellor shaft.

But then the winch jammed itself into a rock crevice and held tight, the cable lifting from the water and pointing in a direct line to their ship. The *Sea Princess* stopped dead, now effectively anchored to the shoreline.

"All stop," Sonya yelled.

Jorge had already pulled back on the throttle as warning lights blinked on the control panel.

After another second or two he shut it all down. He turned slowly. "We're snagged on something."

"We're snagged on a wire cable. Around the prop shaft," Jack said. "Whoever left that winch there also left a cable snaking out on the water. We just found it."

There was another tug as the ship pulled on the now tightly secured cable.

"Well, that's just great." Jack put his hands on his hips and exhaled. "That damned winch is acting like a ship-to-shore anchor. We're not going anywhere."

Sonya folded her arms and paced for a moment, her head down as she looked to be thinking it through.

"Can you use one of the guns or laser to cut through it?" Cate asked.

"Yes, we can," Sonya said. "But freeing us from the winch still leaves the cable wrapped around us. And without power, we are without control over the ship. We could end up on the rocks. Then it's all over."

Sonya continued to pace for a moment more. She stopped and turned. "We have no choice, we need to unsnag it." She went to the onboard comm system. "Prepare a dive team. With cutting tools."

"You're joking," Cate said in disbelief. "You'll send divers down when you know there's a Megalodon in the area? That's a death warrant." She jabbed a finger at Sonya. "It'd be murder."

"And slow suicide if we stay here drifting and unable to start our engines." Sonya's eyes were half lidded. "We have multiple sensory tools to keep an eye on the underwater landscape, and our divers' equipment is rigged with an inbuilt comm system so we can warn them of any danger long before it arrives."

"You could be sending them to their deaths. You need to inform the divers of the risks," Jack said. "And I mean the *big* risks."

"My divers are the best in the world. And I wouldn't ask anyone to do something I wouldn't do myself." Sonya smiled. "That's why I'm going down as well."

* * *

Sonya left the deck to change into a wetsuit and Meena and Jorge were in control of deck operations. But there was little to do while the boat was hooked on the cable.

Cate pulled Jack's arm. "We can't let them go down. It'll be suicide."

"Do we have a choice?" Jack asked. He lifted his head. "Jorge, is the sonar still clear?"

The young man checked his instruments, and then nodded. "Nothing here but us. Clear for bow, stern, starboard, and at the port side we have the cliffs." He turned and nodded. "It should be safe to enter the water."

Sonya reappeared, looking like a superhero in her wetsuit. She had a tall, athletic figure, and the suit was a mix of neoprene and toughened rubber over some areas for protection. There was a small, flat tank on her back, and she held her swim fins and dive mask.

Behind her came a man and woman who Jack and Cate had seen before in the submersible room, and they were dressed similarly. The man carried cutting tools with a small gas mixture tank, and the woman had some sort of large speargun and a quiver over her shoulder with several more bolts in it. Each one had a red stubby dart on the end.

Sonya turned to the man with the cutting tools. "Miguel, equipment check?"

Miguel nodded. "All tested and working fine. Good to go."

Sonya then checked the woman's gear, all strapped and belted over a brilliant yellow wetsuit, and stopped at the huge darts at her shoulder. "High explosive tip," she explained to Jack. "The gun can fire it up to fifty feet, and then detonate on impact. It'll blow a hole the size of a truck tire in anything it hits." She patted the woman on the shoulder. "And Alina doesn't miss."

"That won't kill it," Jack said. "That'll just piss it off."

"I know," she replied. "But we just need to deter it if it shows up." She made a show of crossing herself. "And I'll pray it doesn't." She smiled.

Cate shook her head. "We'll all be praying. I don't know whether you're brave or just stupid."

"Both," Sonya replied. "Jack, if it does arrive, what can I expect? You've been in the water with them."

"Aggressive confidence. It'll come at you like a great white shark ambush attack, except on the scale of a locomotive."

He rubbed his chin. "The thing I remember was the size. When you first see one in the water with you, it freaks you out." He looked up. "A little like the lion's roar, the shock is meant to stun its prey into immobility for a split second. Seeing the shark did that to us."

"Thanks," Sonya said, meaning it. She went to turn away.

"Oh, and one more thing," Jack said. "It's fast, unbelievably fast for a creature that size." He hiked his shoulders. "For some reason, you expect it to be a lumbering behemoth like a whale. But it's not."

She nodded. "Light on or off?"

"I'd turn them on," Cate said. "That will assist you in your work. It's going to be pitch dark down there and you want to get your job done and back out of the water as quickly as you can."

"She's right," Jack agreed. "The shark has more senses than its eyesight. That's the last sense it needs or uses." He sighed. "If it's around, the noise you make will attract it far more than the lights will. Try to keep the noise level to a minimum. That includes any vibrations."

"Good suggestions." Sonya shared a broken smile with them. "I didn't really want to be working in the dark anyway." She gave them a little salute. "See you both soon."

Sonya turned away and clapped her hands together once. "Okay, everyone, let's get this done. In, cut the cable, and out. Drinks are on me when we are back on deck."

Jack watched them go and exhaled through pressed lips. "Shit, I'm nervous just thinking about her going down there."

Cate nodded, and then turned to Meena who had just joined them.

"They'll be okay." Meena said confidently.

"Have you ever seen a living Megalodon?" Cate asked.

Meena lifted her chin. "I've seen all the footage shot over the years – yours, Valery's, and Sonya's." She shook her head.

"But I've never seen a living one, in the flesh. They must be *terrifying*."

"Oh, they are," Cate said. "The footage will never prepare you for seeing one in the wild. And it could never allow you to appreciate the horror of seeing one while you're in the water."

"Think of a great white shark, except weighing in at about eighty tons, around fifty, sixty, or even seventy-five feet," Jack added. "Highly aggressive, territorial, and constantly hungry. And with the speed and strength of a freight train."

"I hope they'll be okay." Meena stammered.

"Jorge," Cate said sharply, and the man turned to her. "You keep every sensor you have focused on the surrounding ocean. And Meena, I want you to have someone on every deck gun, cannon, and laser you have. If this thing shows up while the team is in the water, I want them out before it gets anywhere near them. And if it does I want you to rain hell down on it to let it know it's not welcome."

Meena opened her mouth, obviously knowing she was supposed to be in charge, but not finding fault with Cate's suggestions. Her mouth snapped shut and she nodded. "We're on it." She went to the internal comms system and began to issue those orders.

Cate walked toward Jorge. "Where are they up to?"

"We have a waterline bay door. They're at that and preparing to drop."

"Yeah," Jack said, "into hell."

"Can they hear us?" Cate asked.

Jorge nodded. "We have direct comms with all three of them." He flicked a switch on the console. "Testing link. Ms. Borashev, do you read?"

"Loud and clear, Jorge," Sonya replied.

"Miguel, Alina?" he asked.

"Good comms, online," Alina replied.

"Reading you loud and clear," Miguel also replied.

"Ready to jump. All clear on scans?" Sonya asked.

"Confirm all clear. Nothing but us for miles," Jorge replied.

Cate heard Sonya breathing heavily, almost hyperventilating, and imagined her heart racing a mile a minute.

"Okay, let's do this," Sonya said.

There was a sound of splashing water, and then the three divers dropped into the black water.

* * *

Sonya pulled the full-facemask down. It covered her forehead to her chin, allowing excellent uninterrupted vision, breathing, and vocal send and receive.

She hesitated for only a second or two before stepping forward and then easing herself into the water, rather than leaping or even rolling backward from the open bay door.

Her team followed her lead. They also followed Jack's instructions to stay as quiet as possible. When the work began, they would not be able to avoid noise, but they'd at least give themselves a head start until then.

There was now a halo of light from the underwater lamps all around the huge boat, but beyond that was just a wall of impenetrable darkness.

A few fish scooted by Sonya – some she might have recognized and others with bony plating over their heads she could only guess at.

She led the team to the rear of the ship. She knew she wasn't really needed, but the work was critical to them completing the mission, or perhaps even to their survival. It had to be done, and done right. And she knew her being there and leading by example would stiffen the spines of her crew.

"Coming up on the propellor," she said.

"Roger that," Jorge said. "Scans are all clear."

Good, let them stay that way, she thought.

In seconds they came to the huge shaft and propellor. They could see the cable wrapped around the few feet of shaft and also strangling the actual blades. In addition, there was the dark line of thick cable stretching off toward the shore, which Sonya knew was attached to the winch and acting as their anchor.

They needed to deal with that first to free them. Then they needed to pick which loops to cut so they could unthread their propulsion system.

"Miguel, cut the line anchoring us first," she said.

He swam toward the propellor and grabbed the cable stretching off into the darkness. He tested it.

"Old but high-tensile wire. Gonna take a few minutes to burn through."

He ignited the torch. There was a pop of brilliant light, and a stream of bubbles. Sonya could hear the hiss of the ignited gas as he adjusted the burn rate.

Miguel pulled a darkened visor down over his facemask and adjusted the flame a little more. When he was satisfied, he brought it close to the first cable wire. Thankfully, it began to glow immediately.

On the other side of Miguel, Alina had the speargun weapon held in two hands. She hovered with neutral buoyancy and faced outward.

Sonya sighed into her breathing equipment. She knew it was a near-impossible task. The wall of darkness was only a hundred feet from them. If the monster shark burst from that wall and was coming fast, there would be little time to aim and shoot.

Sonya half smiled. Perhaps she was only there to provide them all with a sense of security, false as it was. But a more honest and brutal reason was it was also to lessen the odds of each of them being taken. She wondered if Alina knew that.

"Keep talking to me, Jorge," Sonya said.

"Still clear on all scanners," Jorge immediately replied.

Sonya squinted into the light of the cutting work on the wire. She was just in time to see a piece of molten steel drip away. It quickly cooled and vanished as it fell toward the sea bottom, around seventy feet below them.

Sonya rotated slowly in the water, staring out into an utter nothingness so black it was like the void of space. Though the water was near to tropical temperature, she felt cold. It was fear. She had been in near-death situations before, and this is what it felt like. Every time.

She turned back, and saw that Miguel was still cutting. *Come on, come* on, she urged.

"Ah, Ms. Borashev." Jorge's voice was cautious. "I think . . . I think we've got something coming in on the outer reaches of the sonar."

* * *

Ping.

Jack turned.

Ping.

"Oh shit." He rushed to the front console, with Cate at his shoulder. Meena walked in quickly from the opposite side of the bridge.

"What is it?" she asked.

"Something big just appeared about two miles down the coast." Jorge looked up and out at the twilight darkness. "Straight ahead."

"Inform Sonya," Meena ordered.

Jorge opened the comms link. "Ah, Ms. Borashev." His voice was cautious. "I think . . . I think we've got something coming in and out on the outer reaches of the sonar."

"Distance, bearing?" Sonya replied in her cool, business-like tone.

"Coming directly along the coast from our bow. Range is two point one miles, and traveling at around five knots."

"We have time. Keep us informed," Sonya replied.

"That woman is ice cool," Jack said.

"She has no choice," Cate replied. "If they bail out now, we might not get the chance to re-enter the water, and if the meg stays close to us while we're stranded . . ." She shook her head. "Damn, if we drift onto the rocks, we're staying."

"Jesus." Jack paced away but then spun and came back. He reached around Jorge to open the mic to Sonya. "How's the cut progressing, Sonya?"

"Good progress," Sonya replied, now sounding like she was breathing heavily. "Finishing on the anchor cable in a few more seconds. Then we'll start on the prop. Stay cool, Jack, we're all good down here."

Over the comms came a sound like a giant guitar string breaking.

"Okay, stage one complete. We are now free of the cable anchoring us to the shoreline," Sonya said.

"The noise," Jack said.

"Bogy has increased speed, now coming at us doing nine point five knots," Jorge intoned.

Jack closed his eyes. "It heard us."

* * *

Sonya thought she'd get more time than this. She mentally calculated the distance and how long it would take the Megalodon shark to get to them – if it stayed doing around ten knots over two miles, it'd be with them in about twelve minutes.

Dammit, they'd be cutting it fine.

They needed at least two minutes to get back to the bay doors and get out of the water.

"Miguel, we have ten minutes, tops," she said.

"There are several loops around the shaft and over the props. Cutting one just won't do it," he said without turning from his task. "Gonna be close."

"Which direction is this big asshole coming from?" Alina asked.

Sonya pointed. "Along the coast from the bow line."

Alina nodded, and then swam to put herself between Sonya and Miguel, and the potential shark arrival point.

Sonya reached down and felt for the only weapon she had – a diving knife strapped to her thigh. A pitiful tiny silver tooth against a fast-moving colossus of teeth and muscle.

She had to focus. It wasn't the shark that was her problem, but the cable, and the rapidly dwindling time they had until the beast arrived.

She swam closer, but the torchlight was so bright she couldn't see what Miguel was doing or how much more he had to do. That was something else; the spot of light was so brilliant it could probably be seen for half a mile. It'd be a beacon drawing the beast right to them.

"Sonya . . ." Jack began.

Sonya swore under her breath. "Jack, you're not helping. Unless you've got important –"

Jack cut in on her. "It's speeding up. Now coming at you at fourteen knots. We estimate it'll be here in seven minutes."

"*Bastard.*" She turned. "Miguel, we're going to have to wrap this up for now."

"Almost done with this one," he said.

With a loud *clonk*, a piece of cable sprung upward, its glowing end quickly cooling in the water.

"Three more minutes – five max." He held the flame to another cable.

"One more, and we do the other one later," she urged.

Miguel kept at his task, but now everything seemed to be happening in slow motion as the adrenaline in her system began to spike.

"Speak to me, Jorge."

"Under a mile. Estimated intersection in five minutes and thirty-two seconds," he replied quickly.

Intersection! She almost laughed out loud. That was professional speak for monster arrival. And anyone still in the water would end up dead.

"Count me down, ten second intervals," she said. "At two minutes, we're returning." She sighed. "We will not be finished."

"Five minutes, ten seconds," Jorge said steadily.

"Miguel?" she asked.

"Nearly done on this one. Maybe I can make a start on the last. Weaken it enough so we can just break it," he said.

"Four minutes, thirty seconds," Jorge intoned, and then: "Oh no." He breathed.

It was exactly what she didn't want to hear.

"Signature is increasing speed again. Estimated time of arrival is now three minutes. Closing fast," he said quickly.

Sonya made up her mind. "That's it, we're done."

"Not yet. Not yet," Miguel replied.

There was a loud *clunk*, and he immediately focused the flame on another cable around the propellor blade. "If I can just weaken this."

"Two minutes twenty," Jorge almost shouted.

"Forget it, we're done." Sonya swam toward Miguel, prepared to drag him away.

"Get out, get out now!" It was Jack this time, and the tone in his voice scared the hell out of her. "It's just increased to twenty knots. *It sees you! It sees you.*"

"Move it, mister," Sonya yelled at her crewman.

Miguel switched off the torch and began to swim toward her.

"Hurry." Sonya began to swim, her legs feeling like rubber as the adrenaline was making the muscles feel strange, and her entire body tingled.

Alina still hung in the water, her yellow wetsuit brilliant in the ship's sphere of illumination. She stayed about twenty feet out from them, acting as an aquatic bodyguard.

"Fall back, Alina, we're done here," Sonya said.

The woman began to slowly stroke back to them, still facing the darkness.

"It's here," Jack said softly.

* * *

Sonya felt her scalp prickle under her wetsuit's rubber hood. They only had about another twenty feet to travel underneath the keel of the boat. Miguel hadn't finished the cut, but perhaps he'd done enough that once they restarted the prop it would chop through the remaining strands and release them.

She let Miguel pass her as he had equipment to haul back into the bay door. She was right on the tip of his fins, and Alina was just a little out from them, keeping up her bodyguard duties.

Sonya looked over her shoulder – the surrounding halo of illumination from the hull lights was comforting but beyond it the curtain of darkness remained.

Then something changed.

A current washed past them. Sonya guessed what it was before Jack even spoke into her ear.

"It's just gone past, but it's circling back," he said softly.

"It's taking a look at us," Sonya replied.

"Yep, and it's a big one – around seventy feet."

"Got it." Sonya could barely get her head around a shark that big. Instead she tried to focus on getting to the door. And they were nearly there. "Get your ass in there, Miguel. Alina, back here, *now*."

The surge wave passed again, and this time it buffeted them, causing Miguel's welding bottle to clank against the hull.

Sonya turned in time to see a vision from hell – out of the curtain of blackness the massive pale head of the shark loomed, coming right at them.

Alina fired a bolt, but the monster's sudden appearance, and at such close range, meant she could not get the speargun around properly. Or maybe the shock made her hands shake just that fraction, meaning the bolt skimmed the top of the shark but struck and detonated on the ten-foot dorsal fin, blowing away about three feet of the tip.

It worked. The shark swerved away and Alina hurriedly reloaded another bolt.

Sonya was at the hull hatch. She screamed into her face-mask. "Alina! Get your ass –"

But the wall of darkness was broken again as the Megalodon came right at the smaller woman. She didn't have a chance to fire. She just looked up as the maw opened and she went into it. But not before her terror caused her body to tighten up, and her fingers flexed on the trigger just as the mouth closed on the unfortunate woman.

Sonya could still hear Alina's screams as she vanished behind the huge row of serrated teeth. But the explosive bolt flew. Backward. At the ship.

"Oh no," Sonya whispered, still hanging in the water.

The high-explosive-tipped projectile struck the hull door where Miguel was finishing his climb in and dragging his bottle of the hydrogen cutting mix with him. Whether the dart hit the tank or not, the detonation was a brilliant orange flash that blinded her for a second. The last thing she remembered was Miguel's body, or rather his legs, being flung away.

Then the percussion wave hit her like a thousand hammers, and everything went dark.

* * *

The Carcharodon Megalodon felt the hot sting against its ten-foot dorsal fin just before it took one of the small creatures that was floating in the water. Then came the impact of the blast wave, which shocked it enough to cause it to veer away into the darkness.

The taste of the small, soft thing was like the calves of the great warm bloods. It relished it – and craved more. Hunger still flared in its belly; that, and an evolutionary drive to protect its territory from all intruders. And the large thing on the surface was an intruder.

It had faced bigger creatures in the sea of the caves. Some it conquered, and devoured. Some it had needed to flee from. And there were others in the stygian darkness it had avoided completely as it knew they were too deadly to even approach.

Whether the large floating thing was birthing the small warm bloods or was feeding on them itself, it had entered the Megalodon's hunting grounds, and there was no room for two of them.

It rounded again but was cautious, staying a half mile away. It would wait until its damaged senses settled. Its huge, pale, muscular body veered away again, but its agitation was increasing.

* * *

"What just happened?" Cate sprang forward at the sonar screen. "What the hell just happened down there?"

Jack spun to her. "*Explosion.*"

It wasn't just the sonar and sensors alerting them to anomalies, but right across the control console warning lights were screaming at them. Jorge's hands flew over the controls as he tried to understand what had happened.

"Water-tight compartments, three, four, five, all shutting down. Engaged." He shook his head. "Some sort of detonation – torpedo, I don't know. But it blew a hole in the hull. We're taking on water, fast." He cursed. "And we're still flooding."

"Where's Sonya, Alina, or Miguel?" Jack yelled. "Are they still down there?"

"Not responding." Meena had a mic pressed to her ear and talked rapidly into it, trying to reach any of the three divers.

Jack leaned closer to Jorge. "Where the hell is that damn shark?"

Jorge looked over the sensors. "It's there, but half a mile out. The explosion scared it off." He turned, his expression hopeful. "Maybe it's hurt."

Cate shook her head. "That's too much to hope for."

Jack stared down at the sensor screens. "Can we see the others? Anywhere?"

"Alina's comms are still active." Jorge grimaced. "But the trackers are all wrong; they're telling me she's with the shark."

"Oh god, no." Cate put a hand over her chin and mouth.

"She's not with the shark, dammit, she's *in* the shark," Jack roared, and then regretted shouting at the already panicked man, as everyone in the wheelhouse turned to them.

"No, no – she can't be. *She can't be.*" Jorge shook his head furiously, fear making his eyes round enough to show all their whites.

"Sorry, we all need to calm down." Jack leaned closer to him. "We need to find the others. Where are they?" he asked Jorge.

"I can't find Miguel. He's just . . . gone." He stared at the screen. "Ms. Borashev is still online, but not responding."

"Where?" Jack looked down at the screen.

Jorge was pointing at a sensor image. "She's about forty feet down, hanging mid-water. Maybe she's looking for Miguel."

"No, neutral buoyancy. I'm betting the explosion's percussive force knocked her cold," Jack said. "That's why she's not moving or responding."

Cate paced away for a moment and then came straight back. "We need to get her."

"Problem." Meena spoke up. "Everyone onboard can swim, but Miguel, Alina, and Sonya are the only ones with scuba diving experience."

"I can dive," Jack said.

Cate grabbed him and turned him to her. She shook her head.

He put his hand over hers. "If it was you down there?"

She let him go. Then she rounded on Meena. "Get Jack into a suit. Then get up on deck and man those guns. Anything comes within two hundred feet of the boat, you turn it to dog meat." She faced Jorge. "Jorge, where's the meg now?"

"Still a half mile out, down the coastline. Just cruising," he replied.

Jack nodded. "Forty feet of water down to Sonya. There and back is about five minutes. Piece of cake."

"Um, one complication," Meena said. "We have no bay area, as the watertight compartments have shut it off. We're working to manually open some of them without compromising the ship's ability to stay afloat. You'll need to go over the side."

"Rig a sling," Jack ordered. "If I get to the side with an unconscious Sonya, I'm not going to be able to climb quickly." He laughed but knew it sounded high and nervous. "And I do not want to be in that water longer than I need to."

"On it," Meena said, but then grimaced. "There's something else."

"Something else?" He turned slowly.

"The leak I mentioned; we're taking on water." Meena's face was pale. "The pumps seem to be maintaining an equalization between water in and out, for now. But I think the hull is cracked."

"And here we are again." Cate tilted her head back for a moment before sighing and looking back at Meena. "Okay, but you said the pumps can deal with it, right?"

"For now," Meena replied cautiously.

"For days, for hours, what?" Cate frowned.

Meena just hiked her shoulders.

"But you're *not* confident we'll remain seaworthy?" Jack asked.

She shook her head. "No, I'm not. If we lose power, or enter turbulence, or even push it to top speed, then the pumps won't be able to keep up. And then . . ."

"And then we're all swimming." Jack sighed. "Okay, one problem at a time. First, I need to get Sonya."

Cate grabbed his arm. "I don't want you to do this."

"I don't want to do this either." He swallowed down a lump of fear rising in his throat.

"I understand why." She half smiled back. "Just promise me this. Sonya is important to this vessel. But you are more important to me than Sonya, this vessel, the shark, or anything. If you get into trouble, you abandon everything and come straight back."

"I promise." He held up a hand. "Scout's honor."

She punched him softly in the stomach. "And no hero shit. Promise me."

"Me?" He pointed at his chest. "Nobody in here but us chickens."

Meena reappeared with a wetsuit and kit. Plus, another speargun. Jack took the wetsuit from her and began to strip down immediately.

"Forget the speargun – it'll just get in the way. I am *definitely* going for speed." He took a large flashlight instead and then began to pull the wetsuit up over his legs. He dragged it over his shoulders and left the hood hanging down his back for now. He decided to take a knife, which he strapped to his leg.

He grabbed the fins and mask, and he and Cate headed out on deck with Meena following.

Once there, he saw that there were crew members on the cannon, as well as the laser that had a bank of lights running down the barrel, indicating it was fully charged and ready to go. Everyone nodded to him as he went past, acknowledging his bravery. Or madness.

On the port side of the *Sea Princess*, they'd rigged a portable winch that had been secured in place by bolts. There was rope trailing from it, and a metal platform.

"Will the winch hold?" Cate asked Meena.

The woman exhaled. "Yes." She smiled flatly. "But only for one person."

"Of course it only holds one person." Jack laughed and then sucked in a huge breath. He looked up to the wheelhouse.

Jorge gave him a thumbs-up and then reached for the mic. "Bogy still half a mile away. All clear on sensors." He tapped his ear.

Jack nodded, and sure enough he heard the sound test, and gave the man a thumbs-up.

"I'm online," he said to Cate.

"Do you need a minute to center yourself?" Meena asked.

Jack shook his head. "Sonya doesn't have a minute." He pulled the rubber hood over his head and placed the mask on his forehead. "Besides, the more I wait, the more I think this is a dumb idea and I shouldn't be doing it." He walked toward the winch platform.

He looked over the side – he estimated it'd only take him a few minutes to dive down to Sonya, locate her, grab her, and bring her back. But the winch cage travel time up and down would more than double that.

He stepped over the railing and placed one foot on the metal floor of the cage. It wobbled precariously.

"Easy, fella. Just there and back, okay?" He waited for it to stop moving. "You can do that for me, can't you?"

He put both feet on it, sucked up his courage, and then

turned to nod. "Let's go. I want to be back on deck with Sonya in under fifteen minutes."

Cate reached over the railing and grabbed him, pulling his head closer so she could kiss him. "I'll be with you the entire time."

He nodded and pointed to the wheelhouse. "Get up to the scanners. If that big bastard out there so much as sneezes, I want to know."

"Count on it," she said.

Jack spun a finger in the air and the winch started to lower. He liked that it was a smooth and near noiseless drop. He hated that it was so slow, and knew that once he put Sonya in it, he'd be in the water by himself waiting for his turn. And that scared him.

* * *

Jack reached the water and the platform stopped lowering and then waited at sea level for his return.

He slid off and immediately flipped over and began to dive. The huge swim fins powered him down quickly, and he had to slow himself as fear made his adrenaline flood his muscles and urged him to kick faster. But he knew he'd need that energy later.

"Jorge, come back," he said into his visor mic.

"I read you, Jack, loud and clear."

There was the sound of muttering, and he smiled.

Cate came on the line. "We're right here with you, Jack. How's visibility?"

"Clear, but dark water, of course," he replied. "What's my proximity to Sonya. Any change?"

"She's now at forty-two feet, still hanging there, and still no movement," Cate replied. "Almost directly below you. You're at twenty-five feet. You should see her soon."

Jack passed out of the comforting sphere of the ship's lights, and he switched on his powerful flashlight. It was a column of white in the darkness, but it made him even more nervous about what was outside the beam. And, what else could see it.

Jack pointed the beam downward and followed it down.

He stopped and repressurized his eardrums. Getting down to forty feet didn't seem far, but every foot down you traveled the pressure rose enormously. If Sonya slid down anymore, it might become impossible for a diver to reach her.

Jack started as something like a long eel materialized out of the gloom to check him out, but when he swung the light toward it, it acted like it had been scalded and shot away into the blackness.

"How's my big buddy?" he asked Jorge.

"Still at half a mile. Seems to be staying there for now."

"Good," Jack said. "Nearly there."

He continued down a little more. He waved the light around him, but there was nothing but blackness and tiny specks floating in the light beam.

"Ah, Jack." Jorge said hesitantly.

Shit, he thought, guessing what was coming.

"What is it?"

"It's gone."

"Cate?" he asked

"It's weird," Cate said. "The Megalodon has vanished from the sensors. It seemed to speed up, then went down, and suddenly, it was just, gone."

Jack thought for a moment. He still had time.

"Okay, as long as it's not heading this way, no problem. I must be . . . *yes*, I see her, there she is."

Hanging in the water, arms and legs spread out in her aqua blue wetsuit, was the unconscious Sonya. He sped up, reached her, and drew her to him.

He quickly checked her over and saw no rips or tears in her suit. More importantly, her visor was still full of air and she was breathing.

"Got her. She's alive," he said.

Over the mic, he could hear cheers in the background.

"Bringing her up."

Her neutral buoyancy made her body easy to maneuver in the water, and he simply grabbed her around the waist and with strong kicks propelled himself back to the surface. He had to be mindful of his speed, as even from this fairly shallow depth, he could make them both very sick if he went too fast.

On the way back up, Jack had an ominous thought. "Jorge, what's the seabed topography up ahead? Where the shark was before it vanished, I mean."

"On it, Jack, checking sonar extrapolation of the bathymetry now. Okay, got it. No gradual slope in that region. But a lot of peaks and crevasses. Also, there's a shelf leading to a big drop off into deeper water – over 500 feet."

Jack shut his eyes for a moment as he swam up to the huge ball of illumination above him.

He had a nagging thought that wouldn't let go. "Listen, could the Megalodon have dived over the edge of the shelf and moved into a sonar shadow?" he asked. "Couldn't possibly use the shelf to –"

"Oh god, oh god, *yes*. It could. It *did*," Cate said. "It's just reappeared, just under 1000 feet off the starboard side, the opposite side to you. Get up, get up here now."

"That clever bastard." Jack powered up, using one arm to stroke and kicking his legs furiously.

"Move it, Jack, move it," Cate urged.

"I can make it." He was feeling slightly nauseous now, from either the strain of rocketing up too fast, or more likely the fear making his heart race and his stomach flutter inside his wetsuit.

Jack entered the large halo of light around the hull of the ship and surfaced a few feet from the winch cage. Now that he was on the surface, Sonya's weight bore down on him, and he sluggishly maneuvered her toward the platform.

It took him several moments to get her onto the wire floor and use a strap to secure her in place – and he was forced to take his time – as the last thing he wanted was for her to fall back down into the water. The splash alone would give him a heart attack.

He paddled back a few feet and lifted an arm, thumbs-up. "*Go, go.*"

Sonya immediately began to rise from the water. But slow. So damn slow.

Jack looked back down below him, but beyond the glow of the lights there was nothing now but inky blackness.

Then the ship rocked slightly, and waves slapped against the hull.

He grimaced, feeling his heart rate beating now like a drum. It was beginning to make him short of breath. *Nothing to fear but fear itself*, he told himself. *Yeah, bullshit.*

"Speak to me, people." He put his back against the hull and gently moved his legs to keep his head above the waterline.

"It's out there, Jack, about 300 feet away and just outside the illumination sphere. It's circling the boat," Jorge said. "Moving slow."

"Yep, well, now would be a really good time to use that laser or deck cannon." He started to shiver, even in the bath-warm water.

"Jack, it's staying too deep," Cate replied. "It's down at about fifty feet. Little chance of hitting it. If it surfaces, we'll cut that bastard in half."

Damn, he thought. A huge Megalodon could rise fifty feet in two seconds. He looked up. Sonya was nearing the deck railing. *Not long now*, he promised himself. But in the water, with the monster shark circling them, it felt like time was standing still.

"Okay, stay cool, Jack, but just letting you know it's circled around to your side of the ship now." Jorge spoke softly, almost conspiratorially, as if he thought the shark might hear him.

And maybe it could hear or sense the electronic vibrations through the water. Jack knew sharks extremely well, and he knew the carcharodon species could detect minuscule volts of electricity, and even microscopic drops of blood. Everything evolution had gifted the creature was designed for hunting, killing, and eating. It was nature's greatest predatorial accomplishment, and in a species like the Megalodon it was enlarged to the size of a school bus.

"Going past you now. Still at fifty feet. Not changing behavior or direction," Jorge whispered.

"Keep going, keep going," Jack prayed as he stared out over the dark water.

"Damn it," Jorge said, "hold on, it's stopped. Now circling. Coming back around."

"It's found me." Jack gasped.

He looked up and saw Sonya being pulled from the platform and dragged over the side. In the crew's haste, the metal platform banged against the hull. He felt the vibration run through the steel, and he could imagine it emanating like waves out into the water.

"Goddamnit, guys, you're ringing the damn dinner bell on me." Jack turned back to the water.

It was out there. Somewhere. And it probably saw him – his small, soft body standing out starkly against the white hull of the ship. He hoped the illumination sphere caused it to be wary, but he knew that was too much to hope for.

"Jack . . . oh god, it's close." Cate's words sounded like they came from between her clamped teeth. "It's coming up."

Jack felt the electric shock run right though his body. Small pops of light started to go off behind his eyes. He felt like he was going to black out. He swallowed. "Guys, feel free to lay down some shielding fire anytime now," he whispered.

"It's. Right . . ." Cate's words were little more than a breath now. ". . . Below you."

"Oh fu-*uuuck*." Jack tilted his head to look down. The halo of light extended around the *Sea Princess* for about fifty feet and normally beyond that was a nothingness of dark velvet. But just at the edge of that darkness, just out from him, he could see a massive pale lump, just hanging in the water.

It was motionless, but seeing it there so close, he could appreciate its size for the first time. It was bigger than he'd ever imagined. Some acidic bile shot up into his mouth, and he swallowed it down rather than spit it out into the water in case the monster could smell it. And taste his fear in it.

Thankfully the shark wasn't directly below him, but about twenty feet further along toward the bow. But the way the monster was angled meant it was probably looking right at him. He wondered what it was doing. What it was thinking.

Jack looked up. "Guys, can we hurry that platform up a little? I'd really like to be out of the water now."

"Jorge tells me they have some depth charges," Cate said. "We can deploy –"

"No, you're liable to take me out. Or the blast will knock me unconscious like Sonya." He sighed. "And if I sink, no one is coming to get me."

"I would," Cate shot back.

"I know you would." He laughed. "You and all your hero shit."

The platform was dropping again. He glanced down and thought that the huge shadow had edged forward a few feet. *What are you waiting for?* he wondered. *Fine, then just give me a few more minutes. Or even just one minute,* he wished.

"Going to try something." Jack took off his slim scuba tank. He also took one of the weighted disks from his dive belt and attached it to the tank.

"Here goes." He opened the valve on the tank, so it began to hiss oxygen, and then he let it drop. He watched it sink, spinning slightly as the gas made it run a little like a Catherine wheel.

It headed down past the glowing ball of light surrounding them and entered the gloom. The huge shadow slowly dropped as it eased back behind the curtain of darkness to follow it.

Yes, he thought. He lifted his head from the water and looked up to see the platform just five feet above him now and coming down smoothly.

Gonna make it, he thought, his spirits exploding. He reached a hand up.

Come faster, he begged, as his arm and fingertips stretched.

"Ready all guns," came the urgent, shouted order.

Jack turned back to the darkness momentarily. "What's happening?"

"Here it comes. Get on the platform, Jack, *now*," Cate almost screamed into his ear.

I'm not gonna look, Jack thought as he gritted his teeth and stretched his arm.

The platform just touched his hand, and he kicked, using the powerful fins to surge upward. He grabbed the metal platform and yanked himself up into it.

But it was still coming down.

"Up, up," he yelled.

As it stopped dead, the metal platform banged against the hull again. Then, at an almost glacial speed, it began to be hauled back up.

Around him gunfire exploded, and huge tracer rounds created a fiery trail as they smashed into the water. The beam of the laser touched on the now surging water and penetrated down into the depths.

Jack could see where they were targeting but as yet couldn't see the monster he knew must have been just below the surface – all he knew was it was too damn close.

"*Come on,*" he yelled, his legs dangling over the edge of the platform as he was slowly lifted away from the dark water.

He felt exposed, so he got up to crouch on the shaking wire platform. He then quickly reached down to lay a hand on his knife. But then changed his mind.

Forget it, he thought. *If I'm using that, I'm already dead.*

Then, with a shuddering boom, something struck the ship, moving the huge vessel in the water. And, of course, making the platform swing wildly.

Jack's eyes almost bulged as he clung to the guide wires waiting for the platform to settle.

"We just got hit," Jorge said.

"No shit." Jack clung on tight but noticed the firing had stopped. "Did you get it?"

"Maybe, we don't know. There's no blood in the water," Jorge replied. "It's gone under the ship."

The sound of the gunfire started up again, this time from the other side of the *Sea Princess*. Jack didn't mind that at all. It bought him time, and he only needed a few dozen more seconds. He looked up, knowing that as soon as he got close, he was going to leap the fuck over the railing himself. He took off the pair of large fins in anticipation.

The firing stopped again, and now he was close enough to hear the voices of the crew on deck.

"It's gone under," he heard. And that was the most frightening thing he had experienced in years, until –

From below him the monstrous Megalodon shark surged upward. The other side of the ship must have been a feint to draw their fire – was it that smart? He bet it was – as the massive mouth, like a colossal tooth-rimmed cave, came up at him.

Jack couldn't help screaming.

By now he was a good twenty feet up from the water, with just another ten to go. But the head of the beast alone was around ten feet wide and came up directly under him.

"*Fuck off.*" He flung the fins down, and stood on the wire grating, ready to leap up, down – anywhere – to ensure he didn't go into the gaping mouth.

He couldn't help but look down again at that pale face of horror – the massive teeth, big as white shovels. Between a few of them was the ragged shreds of a wetsuit – brilliant yellow – the color that Alina had been wearing. And he smelled it then, the stink of a carnivore, and the briny smell of the ocean depths, all lifting from the stomach of the beast.

His fins disappeared into the maw, but the Megalodon kept coming. He knew then that it was going to raise to the level of his platform, and sure enough its speed and strength allowed it to easily rise the last few feet.

The jaws came together on the wire platform, but Jack wound one of the wire tracers around his hand, and leaped high, swinging his legs upward like a gymnast.

The metal platform was crushed like a soda can and the guide wires pulled from its edges, making sounds like a guitar being plucked and leaving Jack dangling by one hand.

The wire bit into him and the resultant pain was excruciating. He wished he'd donned diving gloves, but, regardless of the wounds and pain, he'd hang on, because the alternative was to fall into that cavernous mouth.

The shark reached its peak and fell back down, sliding into the dark water. The head turned just a fraction as it went and that basketball-sized, black, soulless eye regarded Jack for a second before it was gone.

It will remember me, Jack thought.

With pain-gritted teeth, Jack looked up. Faces stared down at him.

"Get me out of here," he yelled through his grimace.

"Winch is broken," someone yelled from above.

But then another rope came over the side, hanging close to him, and he reached for it. This one was a soft, elasticized rope that was able to take more of his weight, and therefore take pressure off his hand and wrist with the wire coiled around it.

In seconds, he reached the railing, was grabbed, and dragged over the gunwale to flop to the deck, eyes closed, and gasping like a landed fish.

Cate was by his side in an instant. She cradled his head for a moment, but then grabbed his hand, seeing the deep cuts, and began yelling orders for the ship's medical officer.

He looked up at her. "That went well, I thought." He grinned.

She shook her head. "I could kill you myself. And I *will* if you ever do something like that again."

Jack nodded through his pain. "How's Sonya?"

"Sedated and sleeping peacefully. She'll probably have a mild concussion, but other than a whopping headache, she'll be fine." She bobbed her head. "If she wakes."

"I hope she does." He groaned as he sat up.

Cate helped him, and then rubbed his back as she looked deep into his face. Her own was ripped with worry.

Jack turned away to sit with his head down, elbows resting on his knees. He sighed deeply. "We only just got here and we've already lost two people." He looked up. "Please tell me that the propellor is clear."

Meena was crouching behind him and stood. "We haven't tested it yet."

"What are you waiting on?" Cate frowned.

Meena's face was composed. "Ms. Borashev should be awake for that."

Jack shook his head. "Test it *now*, see if we're free. And if we are, then we turn around and get the hell out of here." He lifted his gaze to her. "If we get hit again, we'll sink."

"We'll test it." Meena spun away and jogged toward the wheelhouse.

Jack looked at Cate. "Whether Sonya is awake or not, if we can move, we head out. Or this place is going to kill us all."

CHAPTER 19

"Did you hear that?" Chekov turned back to the dark sea.

"An explosion? And there's more." Yuri walked a few paces toward the water's edge and stared out over the water.

"Could it have been our inflatable returning? Maybe with grenades?" Chekov said.

"No, I heard heavy gunfire too. There's someone else in here." Yuri cursed. "We might have competition."

"No, we might have a way home." Chekov reminded him.

Yuri nodded. "Yes, that would sure beat trying to dig our way out." He grinned.

"Provided they take us."

"Pfft." Yuri waved Chekov's words away. "They'll take us. Or we'll take their boat." He looked along the shoreline as he scratched his silver whiskered cheek. "It sounded close by but further down the coast. Let's send a scout back and then we can understand what it is we need to deal with."

Yuri snapped his fingers to get the crew's attention. "Gentlemen, another party might have arrived by ship."

The group cheered.

"But we need to ensure they take us as passengers." He stuck his thumbs in his belt. "And they *will* take us, I promise you that. But first we need someone to return along the rocks at high speed and scout for us."

No one said a word, so he pointed. "Thank you, Mr. Zimchenko, very kind of you to offer your services."

The other men roared with laughter and slapped the man's skinny back. None more than a large and bearded bear-like man.

Yuri picked him out. "And because you find it such a joke, you can go too, Mr. Petrov."

The big man swore and looked murderously at Yuri, and then Zimchenko.

"You will leave now. Run like the devil is after you. Tell me everything you see." Yuri thumbed over his shoulder. "Go."

The small, older crewman turned to the dark rocks, and then began to jog. Petrov was content to lumber at his heel.

"*Faster*," Yuri yelled after them.

The men began to pick up their pace.

* * *

Zimchenko slowed as soon as he was out of sight of Yuri. He had no flashlight, and the overhead illumination was like being in a dark room with a dim blue light bulb that desperately needed changing. He could make out shapes but the last thing he wanted was to put a foot in a tidal pool and snap an ankle. He doubted anyone would carry him.

"Can't see a thing," Petrov grumbled from behind him. "How we supposed to see a boat?"

"The captain asked us to tell him what we can see." Zimchenko grinned. "That might be nothing."

The pair scaled the hill of tumbled boulders, and fast walked across the rock shelf.

At the river cutting the shelf, they stopped and Zimchenko walked along its edge, trying to see any shallow spots, rock islands, or anything else they could use to cross. After seeing what had happened to Ivanoff earlier, he knew there was no way either of them was setting foot in the water.

After another few moments, he looked at the cliff face, examining it for a while before marching up to it to tear away some of the hanging weed. He then saw the deep crevices and turned to grin.

"We can't swim across, and we can't fly over." He pointed to the cracks in the rock. "But we can climb."

The smaller Russian went first, moving carefully, hand over hand. Petrov then followed. It took them twenty minutes, but they could finally leap back down to the rock shelf.

They continued along the broad ledge and the smaller man slowed to look out at the dark water. It was like a sheet of oil. However, now and then, there were small bubbles popping here and there, and ripples rose to move in V-shapes one way then the other.

"There's fish out there," Zimchenko observed. Wish we'd brought a net."

Petrov grunted. "You can fish, I'll be staying back from the water. I don't want that monster snatching me from the rocks like it did to Medvedev."

That memory caused Zimchenko to move back to the cliff wall. He stumbled a little and reached out a hand to help him regain his balance. He placed it against the slick rock face, but then quickly snatched it back and looked at his fingers – they were covered in a sticky substance.

"*Yebat*!" He cursed, and shook his hand, hard, but then resorted to wiping it on his already grimy pants.

"What is it?" Petrov frowned.

"Some sort of . . ." He lifted his hand and sniffed it. "Sticky moss, I think." He wiped his hand a little more vigorously.

The pair set off again, crisscrossing the rocks, avoiding pools of water that held things like barnacles the size of dinner plates, and growths like wet potatoes that squirted water at them as they passed by. It was in another twenty minutes that Zimchenko raised a hand. They both stopped, hunkered down behind a boulder, and peered over.

It was a gleaming white ship and it seemed to be anchored just a few hundred feet from the shoreline. Its lights blazed and its sleek modern design was incongruous inside the massive cavern.

"It looks like a pleasure cruiser." Petrov sneered.

"A pleasure cruiser with some sort of deck cannon mounted at its bow? I don't think so. They came prepared . . . for something." Zimchenko turned to his big crewmate. "Maybe they are hunting the same things we are."

"What can you see?" Petrov asked as he squinted.

Zimchenko turned his sharp eyes back to study the ship. "People on deck. But no engine sounds. They're staying put for now." He smiled and nodded. "Not far out. If we can get to it, then I'm sure the captain can persuade them to offer us safe passage out to the *Boris Yeltsin*."

Petrov's laugh was a deep rumble. "*Persuade*. Yes."

Zimchenko frowned. "I wonder what they're doing." He scratched at his graying beard.

"Or what they were shooting at before," Petrov added.

"I think we can guess what they were shooting at. I just hope they hit the white demon." Zimchenko backed up. "We've seen enough. Let's get back."

The two men jogged back the way they had come. As with before, they stayed close to the cliff wall. It was Petrov who stumbled on a knob of rock this time and placed his hand in the substance against the wall. It was a bigger blob this time and his hand stuck.

He tugged, but his palm was glued flat. "This shit is like flypaper."

"Hurry up." Zimchenko was a dozen paces ahead. "I don't like it here."

Petrov tugged harder. He was a big man, but even though the substance on the wall stretched a little it held. He leaned his entire body away from it, but all that did was make the skin on his palm begin to rip.

"Fucking hurts! It's ripping my hand." He reached down with his free hand to pull his blade out.

The big Russian then jammed his blade in beside his hand and tried to cut the substance. But the blade began to stick and wouldn't saw.

"I need help," he called to Zimchenko.

"Idiot," Zimchenko growled, turning back. "Only you could get yourself into this mess." He reached into his pocket for his matches. "I'll try to burn it."

"Don't burn my hand," Petrov pleaded.

"Oh, shut up." As the smaller man approached his huge crewmate, he detected movement from the corner of his eye. His head jerked up, and then his mouth dropped open.

"*Ga –*" He backed up. "*Gaaa.*"

Petrov stared at him. "What's the matter with you? Get back here."

But Zimchenko continued to back away, his eyes like twin moons. And they weren't on Petrov.

He could see now what the substance on the wall was. And Petrov saying it was like flypaper was probably more accurate than he could ever have imagined – because *he* was the fly.

As the big man continued to try to tug or cut his hand free of the sticky material, slowly lowering itself down the wall was the most revolting creature Zimchenko had ever seen. It looked like a cross between a centipede and a long spider. Its body was elongated like a giant loaf of bread with many sharp-tipped legs spaced all the way down the side.

And it was huge, easily the size of a Russian mountain dog, and those canines got to be 220 pounds. But the worst aspect of the thing was the crowd of eyes – like black, glass bulbs on the front of its face. And just below the eyes were a pair of downward curving fangs that looked wickedly sharp.

Zimchenko pulled his knife again but was not inclined to approach or even attempt to save his big colleague. Instead, he continued to put distance between himself and the horror.

It was only then that Petrov saw that Zimchenko wasn't looking at him, but something above him and his head jerked upward.

In that single moment of revelation, his eyes shot wide, and he screamed. The spiderpede then dropped the last half dozen feet in a blink, and its face burrowed in on Petrov.

The big man howled his agony, and he finally managed to rip his hand free.

But by then the front legs of the thing held him tight and began to turn him, turn him, turn him, all the time exuding more of the sticky substance to cover his upper body.

Petrov's mouth was still open, and perhaps his eyes too, but it was hard to tell as he began to vanish into something like a cocoon.

The man only whimpered now. "Help me," he said, but his gruff voice was now little more than a mewl.

"I will. I will." Zimchenko was now forty feet from him. "I'll get help." He turned to sprint away.

* * *

A hundred feet from the rock ledge shoreline, the huge, pale snout of the Megalodon shark stayed suspended above the water. It watched the small biped creature run across the rocks, the movement attracting it. It had a taste for the soft animals now and wanted more of them.

It slid back below the water and glided down along the coast to follow him.

* * *

Zimchenko never slowed his entire way back and sprinted the last few hundred feet back to the group. Yuri turned to stand

175

with fists on hips watching, and even Chekov and his team, who had been cutting down some tree-like plants, stopped their duties.

Yuri looked past him. "Where is Petrov?"

Zimchenko arrived and bent over, hands on knees, breathing hard. He looked up and shook his head. "He didn't make it."

"He didn't what?" Yuri scowled, furious that he had lost another man, on what he thought was a simple task. He bent closer. "*What happened, fool?* Did you go swimming?" he bellowed.

"No, no." Zimchenko straightened but still sucked in breaths. "A big spider got him."

"He died of a spider bite?" Chekov's head tilted with curiosity as he approached.

"No, not just a bite. The spider was a giant. It ate him. Came out of the wall." The small man shook his head and held his palms up. "I couldn't do anything."

"Except run." Chekov snorted with disgust.

"I tried to help, but it was too big." He held his arms wide. "Big as a man."

"*Svolach!*" Yuri threw the piece of wood he had in his hands down onto the ground, causing it to bounce away. He drew his long blade and turned to point it at the smaller man's face. "You left him, didn't you?"

"No, no, it was as I said. The thing came so quickly, I could do nothing. *No one* could have done anything." Zimchenko pleaded as he began to back up. He stopped. "It was just after we saw the ship."

Yuri's furious expression dropped. "The ship?"

"Yes, a big modern ship." Zimchenko nodded furiously. "About an hour along the coast and anchored close in. It was nearly as big as the *Boris Yeltsin*, but expensive looking. All its lights were on." He nodded. "I think it might be American."

Chekov's eyes slide to Yuri. "This is our way out."

"Exactly how far from shore?" Yuri asked.

"Not far. Maybe 100 to 150 feet. There are few guards on deck." Zimchenko's confidence began to return. "We can take it."

"If we can get to it," Chekov added.

"Any sign of the fish?" Yuri asked.

"No, the water was all quiet."

"Then our plan is unchanged," Yuri announced. "We finish our boat, take it back along the rocks and launch it. A hundred feet to freedom. We can do this."

The Russian captain spoke confidently, but he knew that a hundred feet of water might end up being the last hundred of someone's life. And it certainly wouldn't be his.

"Everyone, back to work. We don't know how long they'll be there. We want to be on that ship before they leave." He clicked his fingers. "I want our boat done in the next two hours. *Hurry.*"

* * *

Five hundred feet from shore the conical lump hung in the water, watching, and waiting.

CHAPTER 20

The hidden sea beneath the Antarctic ice, 50 miles south of the *Sea Princess* position

The female Megalodon still hadn't reached adulthood, and though she was already thirty-five feet, she still had plenty more growing to do.

She was learning where she fit in the food chain and the predator hierarchy in this warm, twilight world. Basically, she had learned that everything smaller than her was food. Everything bigger was more than likely to be deadly.

Though she had hundreds of square miles of underwater seascape, the larger denizens were territorial. The big Megalodons could patrol for dozens of miles in every direction of their territory, chasing down and eating anything they could, and fighting everything of equal size for dominance, mating, and defense of their piece of the sea.

But there were other things, things far bigger than the biggest Megalodon; things that came up from the dark, warm depths and could pulverize and shred even the biggest of them.

The mid-sized female had never encountered one of them. But with all her sensory organs she had detected them. And as soon as she did, she left the area.

She was now crossing one of the deeper chasms on her way to a far shoreline. There was a river mouth there, and some of the smaller warm bloods often tried to cross it. They'd usually be successful. Unless a meg happened to be waiting for them to be pushed into deeper water.

The meg swam with its mouth hanging open, picking up and "tasting" the scent trails. A small flick of its powerful tail propelled it forward in a silent glide. As the water passed over its snout, extremely sensitive receptors there, called the *ampullae of Lorenzini,* could detect a single drop of blood or even the faintest of electrical fields, as it gathered information about its environment. It could already taste the fresh water from the river mouth, still several miles way.

Its body was a mass of power, being little more than a huge pipe of muscle with an enormous mouth filled with serrated, razor-sharp teeth. She could move at up to thirty knots, with even greater bursts of speed when needed.

The mid-sized female meg's senses went into overdrive – she felt the minuscule vibrational pressure of auditory *clicks*, *pops*, and *squeaks*. These odd signals were something she had never experienced before. But somewhere in her brain an ancient species memory set off clear alarms.

The meg accelerated, her muscular flanks now pumping her ahead at around thirty-five knots. Her only vulnerability was her belly because it was softer skinned than the rest of her pale body, and exposed to whatever was below.

And that was where the attack came from.

Bursting up from the impenetrable dark depths of a sea-bottom crevasse the monstrous carnivore came in a bow wave of ferocious speed and power.

The hundred-ton Livyatan whale was a remnant species from a time when it and the Megalodon battled in the world's oceans for dominance.

To the Megalodon shark, the monstrous cetacean was a specter of death, and its jaws were larger and more powerful than a modern sperm whale. They also contained tusk-like teeth, each measuring over a foot in length – the largest teeth of any known carnivorous animal to have ever lived – and they enabled it to crush and tear even the toughest creatures to pieces.

The young Megalodon's body was brutalized from the impact, and the whale's bite force of 40,000 pounds per square inch crushed the meg's backbone and forced the shark's stomach to extrude from its gaping mouth.

The Livyatan whale dived, increasing the bite pressure until the tough skin of the giant shark tore. One shake of the whale's bulbous head and the shark's body separated into two pieces.

The smaller half containing the head of the Megalodon shark still opened and closed its mouth as if trying to gulp water. Already smaller fish were following in the stream of trailing blood and flesh fragments.

The monstrous whale continued into the depths to consume its meal in peace as the head of the shark slowly headed down into the crevasses of the dark, hidden sea.

CHAPTER 21

Meena shook her head. "We've got power, but the propellor is still not turning. Engine room is worried if we keep trying to engage the rotors we'll either buckle the shaft or burn out the engines."

"So, we failed." Jack threw his head back and exhaled loudly. "Well, that's just great."

"Miguel and Alina died for nothing." Cate lowered her head. She tried to quickly think through their options.

"There's something else." Meena sighed. "The last of the tidal surge is pushing us toward the rocks."

"Drop the anchor," Cate shot back.

"If we were in shallower water, we could. But it's around 175 feet deep in this area and that exceeds the chain length. Without any anchor we could – *we will* – run aground."

"Then that'll be it for us." Jack scratched his chin.

"We'll use the mini submersible." Cate looked up. "Could we send someone out from under the cave lip to get a message out? Bring in some help."

Meena nodded. "Could be done. You could simply initiate the beacon or communicate via the buoy we dropped. Once out the satellites will pick up the signal. A spotter plane would be overhead in hours. And a rescue ship within twenty-four hours from then. Maybe."

"Maybe." Jack snorted. "It will still take hours and the *Sea Princess* will be on the rocks by then." He looked up. "We could use the submersible to nudge the boat around. But with the cable still fouling the propellor shaft, it's only a temporary save."

Cate folded her arms. "So, what we really need is two submersibles – one to exit the cave and send an SOS. And another to keep us from washing ashore. Or at least until the tide turns again."

"Then just like before; the priority is to cut that cable," Jack said. "It can still be done."

Cate turned to him, but Jack folded his arms and stared down at the deck, not meeting her eyes.

"That's a death wish," she replied softly.

He looked up and hiked his shoulders. "We can't lose the ship. It's got everything we need from armaments to supplies." He winced. "Bottom line: we need to free it."

"That cable must be nearly cut through by now," Meena said. "I think the team only needed a few more minutes before –"

"Before the Megalodon shark turned up." Cate frowned. "The shark that's still out there somewhere." She turned to Meena. "I thought you said that this type of submersible didn't have the fixtures for industrial work. Could it even do the cutting?"

Meena bobbed her head from side to side. "Not really. It has no real working components and was only designed for observational work. We might be able to rig something a little more useful. But it'll be primitive."

"Then do it," Cate urged. "If we hit the rocks, this hellhole will be home."

Jack sighed. "I think we'd be faster diving than in a submersible. After all, the tiny sub would be just as vulnerable to the meg. I know I can do it. And do it fast. This time I don't need to swim down to grab an unconscious woman – it'll take me minutes." Jack held up his hands at the horrified look Cate threw him. "I don't want to do it, but I'm the best diver we have. And I know these creatures."

"Jack . . ." Cate gave him a warning look and folded her arms. "Anyone goes, they go in the sub. End of story."

"It'll be slower for me, but fine." Jack shrugged.

"And sorry, buster, you went down solo last time and nearly got killed. You're not diving alone." Cate closed her eyes for a moment. "Because I'm coming with you."

"No, you're not." Jack put his hands on her shoulders and bent forward to look into her face. "I need you up top, looking out for me."

"We're going in the submersible." She gave him a fragile smile. "If we go down, we go down together." She looked up at him, her eyes resolute. "We also rig some sort of distraction this time." She turned to Meena. "So you can draw the shark away if it shows up on the sonar."

"Okay, okay." Meena nodded. "Yeah, we can use one of the life rafts. Rig something to start making a noise when it's half a mile from the ship."

Jack looked at Cate with weary eyes. "Well . . ."

"Well . . ." She half smiled. "The sooner we're in, the sooner we're out." She gazed at him. "And the sooner we're home, drinking cold beers on the *Heceta*, right?"

"I can almost taste them." Jack grinned.

Cate began issuing orders. "I want the distraction raft prepared to go. I want the submersible rigged with some sort of cutting or burning apparatus that can be operated from inside the cabin. And I want all hands on deck operating guns, lasers, and even freaking slingshots if we've got them."

"On it." Meena scooted off without any pushback.

Jack saluted her. "It seems we have a new captain."

Cate rolled her eyes. "Nope, just trying to ensure we get the job done and return safely."

They headed down to the bay. The hull was damaged, but the submersible was untouched and still hanging in its hoist. The external bay door was jammed open, and there was a gaping hole from the explosion beside it.

The pumps had worked overtime, allowing the bulkhead doors to be manually opened, but there was still six inches of water over the floor. It was actually a good sign though – it meant the pumps were doing their job and keeping the outflow just above the inflow.

Cate walked around the small submersible craft. It was canary yellow, sleek, and with an oval bubble of toughened Plexi-glass material over the top. At the front, technicians worked on fitting the small, skeletal-looking arms. When not in use they would fold underneath the nose, a little like a praying mantis.

Jack poked his head inside the cabin and quickly did a sight check.

"Any weapons?" Cate asked.

He shook his head. "No weapons, sluggish maneuverability, and top speed of only six knots. We can't fight back, or run away, or even hide." He grinned. "Still want to come?"

"Nope. Yep." She saw Meena return and she pointed at her chest. "You make sure you tell Sonya when she wakes that we deserve a bonus."

"Double bonuses," Meena said brightly. But then she crossed herself. "And you have my prayers."

The technicians rapped on the hull indicting they had finished their work.

"Good enough." Jack climbed the detachable ladder propped against the hull and looked deeper inside – there were two seats, one behind the other. The front one was for the main pilot and had the majority of the controls. The one behind had a subset of the controls. Behind them both was a ballast area that contained some life jackets, med packs,

184

a flare-gun case, water bottles, and a package that looked like it might have been a basic raft with an extendable plastic oar.

Jack then climbed into the front seat to practice working the controls and check the other instruments.

Cate was half up the ladder but paused and turned to Meena. "The distraction raft?"

Meena lifted her chin. "It's ready to go. We'll lower it and put it on silent running for a mile. Once it achieves its designated position, we'll initiate a signal that will turn on a music player – the sound and vibrations will penetrate the water for miles."

Jack looked up from the controls. "That should work."

Cate finished her climb and sat down behind him. There were a few instruments on her console, and a secondary joystick in the event the front ones became disabled. Or the pilot did.

Jack ran through the test and got all green lights. "We are good to go."

"Good luck." Meena saluted and began to back up. "Clear the bay area. Prepare to lift," she yelled.

The hoist whined to life and the twelve-foot-long craft moved sideways on its crane to the doorway. The left few feet of the rails had to be straightened after the explosion, but except for a few bumps they worked well, and soon the sub was hanging on the outside of the ship.

Meena opened the mic. "Jack, Cate, all sensors clear, no unfriendlies. Good luck and keep us posted." She nodded to the engineer. "Lowering. Now."

The submersible eased into the bath-warm water to rest on the surface without a ripple. Then the harness disengaged.

Jack switched on the motors, did one last check, and then half turned to look over his shoulder. "All good?"

"Ready to go," Cate replied.

"Taking her down." Jack pushed the u-shaped wheel forward and the small craft submerged and then began to glide forward.

CHAPTER 22

Yuri put the field glasses to his eyes and looked along the length of the gleaming ship.

He grunted his approval. "It is a beautiful ship. And expensive. But I think it has sustained some damage."

Chekov pointed. "Big hole at the waterline. Maybe an onboard explosion."

"We won't know until we ask them." Yuri momentarily took his eyes away from the glasses.

Behind him and Chekov the three remaining men stood around the boat they had built, waiting. It was little more than a raft with a few large paddles. And it looked to only be able to take three to four passengers. But it only had one job – to get enough of them to the ship. And in that, it would do.

Yuri scanned the deck of the ship a little longer and then finally lowered the glasses. "Mr. Chekov, time for a little trip. But don't fear. I'll be coming with you."

* * *

The men carefully brought the raft to the water along the rocks. Yuri selected Dardov, who was strong of arm and he needed his rowing prowess, but also his strength for when they arrived onboard. And Moshev could fix anything.

Yuri's plan was to quickly seize control of the ship. To him it looked like a pleasure cruiser, even with the deck gun. More than likely it was a fat and rich research boat, with perhaps a few crewmen who might be ex-navy and potentially could put up a struggle. But they would be overpaid, out of condition, and would have no real stomach for a prolonged fight.

In turn, Yuri was prepared to kill to get what he wanted. The rules of law and order didn't apply when it came to his survival. Also his crew's survival. But primarily his.

Chekov and the two chosen sailors waited on the raft as Zimchenko held it. Yuri stepped out, and felt it wobble under his feet. It floated barely above the water's surface, and he looked down into the briny depths. It was like he had just stepped onto a sea of oil. But Yuri knew that, below them, the water was clear, and contained things that would delight in dining on them.

He looked one last time at Zimchenko, the only man left on shore, safe, and a small voice asked him if he knew what he was doing.

Yuri looked at the distance between their raft and the ship – though it was little more than a few hundred feet, it was over open water. His men had already been attacked and eaten in shallower water, and closer in.

The blue, twilight illumination above meant the shadows ruled, but the thing below didn't need light as it could hunt in total darkness. Was the monster out there now, he wondered, watching, and waiting for them? Was it still wanting them all as revenge for the bullets he had shot into it?

No shark is that smart, he told himself.

As he stared, for the first time in his life he felt scared by the sea. And it was another few moments before he was able to tear his eyes away from the dark water.

He looked up at Zimchenko, standing silently on the rocks. His face looked ghostly pale in the soft, blue twilight. He saluted the man. "Stay silent and keep watch. We'll be back soon."

Zimchenko just stared, and he thought the bedraggled and whiskered sailor with bad teeth looked like a frightened schoolboy.

I will lose no more men, Yuri promised himself.

He turned away, trying to look more courageous than he felt. "Mr. Chekov."

Chekov turned to Dardov and Moshev. "Silently now, pull."

The men worked the oars and the raft slowly moved away from the rock ledge.

Yuri had his legs spread wide to maintain his balance. To their credit, the men paddling dipped their oars in and gently moved them along the raft to drag the water back and glide them forward.

Their destination ship was well lit, and Yuri could now clearly see the gaping hole in one side – that would be their destination – they wouldn't even need to climb to the deck, they could just step up and inside.

As long as there were no sealed bulkhead doors, they'd be onboard and heading up to the command deck in under five minutes.

He felt the pistol at his belt. He was ready.

* * *

Meena and several of the *Sea Princess* crew were on the bridge and the small woman paced, feeling nervous. She stopped and turned to Jorge. "Anything on the scanners?" she asked, probably for the tenth time.

Jorge checked, starting with the longer range, and then bringing the investigation in closer in concentric rings. He shook his head. "All clear, all quadrants. Half a mile out our decoy raft is still heading away and will reach its initiation position shortly."

He looked in closer, frowned, then craned even closer to one of the screens that showed a small object at the side of their boat. "Okay, I've got a small signature close by that must be Jack and Cate in the submersible. Other than that, looks nice and clear on sonar, radar, and all long-range scanners."

"Okay." Meena exhaled and nodded. "Then why do I still feel nervous?"

Jorge grinned. "Because that's your job."

* * *

Chekov held the raft up tight against the side of the boat as Yuri, Dardov, and Moshev climbed in. He then tied it off to a piece of bent and jutting steel and followed them in.

With weapons drawn, they moved fast and silently toward the bridge.

* * *

Cate and Jack slowly let the submersible drop a few feet in the water. Jack held it in place for a few seconds, checking all the seals. Only when he was satisfied did he begin to power it gently toward the rear of the ship.

He tried to keep it as close to the hull as he could manage without scraping it. He wanted to make them as invisible as possible.

Soon they were at the propellor and could see the strands still circling the shaft and blades. Though they looked thin, he knew the high-tensile wire was strong enough to hold the huge ship in place and was not to be underestimated.

The good news was that the work Sonya and her crew had done was almost complete, and it looked like they had needed only another few minutes to finish the task. Poor Miguel never got that time.

"Okay, bringing her around." Jack was laser-focused on the controls as he guided the small submersible's nose in toward the huge propellor. "Get ready."

"Anytime," Cate replied and reached forward to gently stroke his neck.

"Stop distracting me." Jack smiled and then spoke over his shoulder. "Okay, I want you to take control of the craft while I use the arms."

"On it." She gripped the auxiliary steering and propulsion units that Jack had switched back to her control now. "Just going to keep you in, nice and close." She watched as he reached out with the clamp arm to grip the remaining half-cut cables.

He then ignited the small torch which bubbled furiously and glowed like a miniature sun – they could hear it even through the thick Plexiglass canopy, and Jack had to squint as he had no shield goggles.

Cate switched on the mic. "How's it going topside, Meena?"

She watched Jack begin to cut. The torch was small, all the engineers could scrape up quickly, so it would take a few minutes to cut through each of the remaining cables, but at least it was better than trying to sever them with bolt cutters.

She frowned and switched on the mic again. "Hello, Meena, how's it going? Over."

Cate waited a few more seconds. "What's going on?"

"Problem?" Jack asked while staying focused on his task.

"Not sure." She lifted the mic again.

They heard the engines start up right through the ship's hull.

"What the hell?" Jack straightened in his seat. "*Shut 'em off, shut 'em off,*" he yelled.

"Meena, Jorge, anybody? What's going on? Come back." Cate heard the engine grow louder. "Oh no."

The huge propellor began to turn.

Luckily, or unluckily for their small submersible, Jack had nearly completed his work so the huge propellor broke the remaining strands of the cable that had been snaring it.

"*Release, release!*" Cate yelled.

The propellor's rotations began to pick up speed. The first thing it did was chop right through the attached gripping arm of their mini-sub.

"Forget it – *back up* – just get us out of here before we're sucked into those blades," Jack yelled.

The huge propellor began in earnest and Cate put the submersible into reverse.

"Take it." She switched the controls back to the front pilot seat.

Jack immediately put them into a starboard-side dive, veering away at full power. Already he had to fight the turbulence being created by the huge propellor.

In seconds he had cleared some distance and he hovered the submersible as the *Sea Princess* moved forward. The pair could only watch in confusion.

"Taking her up." Jack pulled the stick back and the submersible headed to the surface. They breached, and he lifted the buoyancy to keep them floating there. He popped the canopy and retracted it back along the craft. Warm air rushed in at them.

"Meena, Jorge, anyone, come in." Cate spoke rapidly into the microphone. "Meena, Jorge –"

"Hey! *He-eeey!*" Jack cupped his mouth and yelled into the warm, humid air, but his voice was drowned out by the engines.

"What just happened?" Cate asked as she watched the ship move away.

"What just happened?" Jack frowned in disbelief. "We just got marooned."

* * *

The small raft Meena had set up reached its designated point of operation just on three quarters of a mile from the ship. The timer initiated and the sound pulses entered the water as planned. The noise and vibrational waves emanated outward – a few feet, a hundred yards, a half a mile, and then kept traveling out in concentric rings.

The Megalodon shark quickly sensed the rhythmic sound and found it irresistible. It knew an animal in distress could make similar noises on the surface, and that meant a slow-moving feast. It swung around and accelerated rapidly up to around thirty knots.

The sound continued. It swam at its fast cruising speed for another ten minutes, and then, when it entered deeper water, it went down in preparation for its usual ambush attack from below.

The sound above it continued and when it was directly below what it thought was the floundering animal, it swam in a large circle. It was the first predator on the scene, but there would soon be more.

The monstrous, seventy-five-foot Megalodon turned upward. This time its acceleration was to its top attack speed of forty-five knots. Just like its smaller cousin, the great white shark, it had honed the depths-to-shallows attack until it was its greatest feeding weapon.

The shark exploded from the depths of the warm dark sea, launching itself thirty feet from the water to take the raft in its jaws. The massive seven-inch triangular serrated blades came together with a bite force of tens of thousands of pounds per square inch, pulverizing and shredding the small craft.

The pale shark fell back. It didn't detect meat or any edible substance in its mouth.

The now deflated raft was shaken free, and the monster shark swam through the debris cloud that was spreading through the water. But there was no blood and no other scent trail.

With a flick of its huge scythe-like tail it surged away, furious, and now hungry as the attack had stimulated its gastric juices. They needed to be sated.

In the once again still water it detected the rhythmic sound it had heard many hours back. The large thing on the surface that had birthed the small meat things was moving.

The Megalodon shark swung around and headed back, accelerating, and ignoring the burn of the gastric juices that had risen in its gullet.

CHAPTER 23

Yuri had his gun to the back of Jorge's head. Several of the other control room crew stood back against the wall with their hands up. Meena had her hands balled into fists and down by her sides. She refused to raise her hands.

"Take us in closer to pick up my crew member," Yuri said. His confident grin matched his buoyant demeanor as he saw the man half turn to the small woman for instruction.

"We have people still in the water," Meena said. "You can't leave them behind." She went to take a step forward but the huge form of Dardov pushed her in the chest back to her position. So, instead, she pointed to the side window. "You know what's out there? In the water."

Yuri's mouth turned down in mock sympathy. "I know what's out there. The beast. It's already killed several of my brave and faithful crew and made more simply disappear. But I can guess where." Yuri pointed to his open mouth.

He laughed for a moment but then his expression grew serious. "My priority is to get my men to safety. We pick the last one up then you take us out of this big cave, and back to our ship. Then –"

Moshev reappeared and pushed another of the crew members toward the group. "They've got a deck cannon, and this man here tells me they have a laser. This ship is better equipped than one of our navy's destroyers."

Yuri nodded, thinking it through. "For hunting big game, I think."

He rubbed his chin; his safety and escape were now assured. But if he left now, he would have nothing to show for his whole trip, except mountains of paperwork to explain what happened to his missing sailors.

His eyes slid to Chekov. "What do you think?'

Chekov shook his head. "I think we head straight back to our ship and return home. This has been a disaster."

"I see." Yuri paced for a moment. "We return to our ship, and sail home. With empty pockets. Or . . ." He turned. "We now use the magnificent facilities provided to us to complete our task." His eyes were level. "And capture this monster shark."

"And a big bonus." Dardov grinned.

"I like your thinking." Yuri returned his huge crewman's grin, and then turned to Chekov. "Not yours."

Chekov sighed and looked down at the ground.

"The hell you will." Meena barged forward. Even though she only came up to the huge Dardov's shoulder, she ducked under his arm. "You will be civil onboard our ship. We will give you safe passage, but we need to rescue our own people." She pointed into Yuri's face. "Or we will ensure on our return you are charged with international piracy. Even Russia is a signatory to the international banning of piracy."

Yuri's eyes narrowed in displeasure, but Meena pressed on.

"You'll lose your boat, be subject to huge fines, and more than likely spend time in prison." She folded her arms. "I promise you."

Yuri pointed the gun right between her eyes. "Do you know where you are, little pest?"

Meena dropped her arms and stared into the barrel. She nodded. "I do."

"No, I think you do not." Yuri walked closer so the gun was a few inches from her face. "You think you are under the Antarctic.

But you should not be here any more than we should," he said. "In fact, these waters do not exist. People who go missing in here will stay missing." He leaned forward. "Forever."

Meena licked her lips nervously. "You wouldn't dare."

"Oh." Yuri nodded. "You think I am not serious." He scratched his chin for a moment as he walked toward the other assembled *Sea Princess* crew members.

He looked along their fearful faces. "Okay, I must show you."

"*Captain.*" Chekov warned.

Yuri stopped and pointed with his gun at one of the young men. "What is your name?"

The man visibly paled for a moment. "I'm, ah, my name, is Carlos Rodriguez."

"Nice to meet you, Mr. Carlos Rodriguez." Yuri nodded. "And what do you do onboard this fine ship?"

"Deckhand." Rodriguez replied, moon-eyed. "And –"

Yuri shook his head. "No, we don't need to know." He half turned. "Mr. Dardov, throw this man overboard."

Dardov strode forward to grab the man by the collar. The other crew rebelled, and Yuri fired a round into the deck, eliciting a few shrieks and shouts, but it then succeeded in scaring everyone into frozen silence.

The pair exited, and following a scream, Dardov soon reappeared. The man grinned with brown teeth. "Swimming home."

Meena's eyes blazed. "I swear, you will pay for this."

"Really?" Yuri looked at the crew. "Does anyone else want to swim home or should this pest keep her mouth closed?"

There was silence. After a moment he nodded.

"We have a list of jobs to do. We pick up my crew member. Then we track this big shark. If you all do your jobs and behave, you will survive." He lifted the gun. "Do we have understanding?"

They all understood.

* * *

Jack and Cate watched the ship move away, frozen in disbelief. But only for a moment or two.

"Let's get 'em," Cate said.

"Oh yeah." Jack's fingers were a blur over the controls. "Close hatch."

"On it." Cate worked the controls and slid the clear canopy forward, locking it down with a hiss of air. The cool, canned atmosphere quickly filled the capsule.

"Ejecting arms," he added.

"Are you sure?" Cate asked. "They're the closest thing we've got to a weapon."

"If we're close enough to a seventy-plus foot meg to use a burner, we'll probably already be inside it." Jack disengaged the arms and they fell away into the darkness.

"Stay on the surface," Cate added. "Lights off."

Jack dimmed the internal lighting and covered the console. From the ship, they'd be invisible to anyone watching. And he hoped their small sonar signature would be too insignificant to bother checking out.

"They're doing the same speed as us for now, but if they open it up, we'll never catch them." Jack shook his head and sighed. "What the hell are they doing?"

"Should I hail them again?" Cate asked.

"Not for now. Let's go radio silent. Something happened onboard that changed everything. The ship is fully operational now, so I think that change occurred at the leadership level."

"Sonya wouldn't . . . would she?" Cate asked.

"I don't think so. But . . ." Jack half turned. "She's different to us."

"Something's happening." Cate pointed to the starboard side of the ship.

Jack craned forward. The pair watched intently as two people appeared on the highly lit deck, went to the rail guard where there was a brief struggle, before one went over the side.

"Holy shit." Cate's mouth dropped open. "Someone just got thrown overboard."

"They were still alive," Jack said. "Let's find them."

He steered the submersible to where he thought the person had entered the dark sea, and in a few minutes they saw a man treading water.

They retracted the hatch as they came alongside.

"Nice day for a swim." Jack slowed the sub so it glided up to the man. He swam toward them. Fast. "Rodriguez, isn't it?"

"Yes, Carlos Rodriguez." He grabbed onto the side of the submersible and coughed water.

He grinned up at them, but his face told them he was clearly still shaken. "Room for one more?"

"We'll make room." Jack looked around to Cate. "Toss out the life vests, and anything else you don't think we need."

Cate tossed out a few excess items, creating a small space behind the pilots' seats. "You're up, Carlos." She reached over the side and grabbed his collar, and the man climbed in past her, showering them both with warm water.

"Thank you. Thank you." Carlos tilted his head back as he folded himself into the rear and moaned with relief. He then rested his head against the side of the craft. "I thought I was dead. Or soon would be when the monster found me." He coughed again and then croaked up some of the seawater.

"What the hell happened up there? Why did you leave us? Who threw you overboard?" Cate fired at him.

"Pirates." He wiped his wet face with his hands and pushed his hair back. "Russian pirates. It seems they came inside the glacier a day before us."

"That ship that was outside the glacier," Cate said.

"Yes, they were attacked by the shark. A few of them paddled out from the rocks and took over the *Sea Princess*."

"How many?" Cate asked.

"Four. But they are planning to retrieve the rest of their crew now," Carlos replied.

"Did they have weapons?" Jack asked.

"Yes, I think a handgun, a machete, and a club. They took us by surprise." He rubbed his eyes.

"A gun, not good." Jack turned. "At least they didn't shoot you."

Carlos half smiled. "They said they would kill someone if they didn't get their way. To prove they meant it, they threw me over."

"Upside is that two of them having only clubs and knives means they don't have that many other guns." Jack snorted. "That's why they sent you swimming and didn't shoot you – saving ammunition."

"Yes, I think I am lucky then." Carlos began to laugh but it quickly turned into more coughing. "Me being thrown overboard was a little motivation to get everyone to obey their orders. I hope they will leave the rest of my friends alone now."

"Unlikely." Jack shook his head. "The captain will know that, in many countries, piracy is punished by long-term imprisonment, or even the death penalty. And throwing you to what they thought was your death will also put a rope around their necks."

"They are bad people," Carlos agreed.

"No, much worse than that." Cate picked up from Jack. "The likelihood of them killing again, or killing everyone, is high. They're already murderers so they have nothing to lose now. And the only people who are witnesses are not going to be kept alive."

"Dead men tell no tales." Jack sped the submersible up and began to follow the ship. The submersible was a little more sluggish in the water with the extra weight, but he got it up to four knots quickly.

"Will we try to retake the ship?" Carlos asked.

"They have us outgunned and out-muscled," Jack replied, "but we can't take the do-nothing option, as I think they're about to turn the *Sea Princess* into a slaughterhouse."

"Where are they going?" Cate asked. "The entrance we came through is miles behind us. But they're going deeper into the cave."

"They haven't finished their hunt," Carlos informed them. "They plan to pick up their crewman and then use our ship's big weapons to hunt the shark."

"Oh good grief." Cate lowered her head to run both hands up through her hair. "Is no one in here sane? They're just like –" She shot upright. "What happened to Sonya?"

"She was still in a coma." Carlos lowered his head. "Perhaps that is a good thing for her."

"She needs to wake up," Cate said. "She's the only person who could make a difference right now."

"We'll get closer. See what happens," Jack said, as the trio tailed the huge ship through the twilight cave.

* * *

Yuri and Chekov toured the ship, opening doors into private cabins, the galley, and stores, and then checking out the damaged bay area, noting the water around their ankles and the ever-present sound of the pumps.

"Damaged, but pumps doing their job," Chekov observed.

On the way back the Russian captain grunted his approval. "Yes, and plenty of space. The men will enjoy the soft beds." He turned to his second-in-command. "Maybe we can keep the ship. Repaint it."

Chekov's eyes momentarily slid to the Russian captain, but he remained silent.

Yuri came to the *Sea Princess*'s captain's cabin. "This must be mine." He put his hand on the door handle, but Meena came at him shaking her head.

"No, it's off limits. Sickbay."

"Nothing is off limits to us now," Yuri growled as he pushed her back and forced open the door. He frowned at what he saw, and then entered slowly.

There was a woman on the bed. Tall, attractive, perhaps late thirties or early forties. She had a drip hooked up to her arm and a heart rate monitor attached to her.

"Who's this? What's wrong with her?" he asked.

Meena went and stood between Sonya and the men. "That's our captain. She was caught in the blast while trying to free the ship." She gently touched the comatose woman's forehead with the back of her hand. "She hasn't woken from it."

"So, she's a vegetable." Yuri leaned over her, and slowly lifted the sheet to peer at her near naked body. "A shame, she looks like fun."

He reached under to grab her breast. Meena charged at him, but he elbowed the smaller woman in the chin, causing her to fall to the floor.

"Don't do stupid things. You'll get hurt." Yuri scowled and then let the sheet drop. "I'm going to need her bed. But seeing you love her so much, you can put her somewhere else. Otherwise I'll keep her in here with me." He leered at Meena until he was sure the small woman knew what he meant.

"You'll pay for this," Meena seethed.

"Probably." Yuri shrugged. "But not today."

* * *

On the way back to the wheelhouse, Yuri noticed Chekov looked troubled.

"Problem?" he asked.

"There's too many of them. We can't watch them all."

"Pfft." Yuri turned. "We can just throw a few more of the major troublemakers overboard. The rest will behave."

"No." Chekov turned his half-lidded gaze on his captain. "Please, I did not sign up to be a mass killer of anything other than fish. I won't be part of this. Your own crew will not support it."

Yuri thought on it for a moment. He would bet that most of his crew *would* support any actions that got them home, especially home rich. But maybe some would not, and the last thing he wanted was conflict within the ranks. Or someone who would run to the newspapers or authorities when they got back. He'd spend his life in prison. Or worse: getting his neck stretched.

He spoke as he walked. "We need our crew, but we don't want *their* crew." He clicked his fingers. "We swap them. When we pick up our man from the rocks we drop off all unnecessary personnel. Let them spend some time in this hellish cave."

"I still don't like it." Chekov bobbed his head from side to side with his mouth turned deeply down. "But at least it gives them a fighting chance."

"That's the spirit." Yuri slapped the man on the shoulder. "Now, let's get the rest of our crew. And maybe break out the vodka stores."

The pair appeared on the command deck to be greeted with sullen looks from some of the operational crew. Yuri pointed to Dardov.

"I want you to get the names and duties of everyone aboard this ship, no exceptions. Some we may retain to do their jobs, and others we'll confine to their quarters." He turned to conspiratorially leer at Chekov.

He went and stood next to Jorge. "Take us in closer. When I say stop all engines, we'll drop a raft."

He turned to Meena, who was now hovering close by with

an expression like thunder. "I want a volunteer to transport my crewman from the shore." He turned away. "I don't care who it is."

Yuri waited a second or two, and then spun back. "Get the boat ready. *Now!*"

Meena's jaws clenched and she muttered something that sounded Spanish through gritted teeth as she headed up on deck.

Yuri had the strongest spotlights trained on the shoreline as they approached.

"Water is good," Jorge replied as he looked from the controls. "Seventy feet, twelve fathoms, all the way to the rock shelf."

"Take us in closer," Yuri replied.

"For safety, no more than fifty feet," Jorge replied. "The tidal surge in here is extreme. We scrape the rocks with an already damaged hull –"

Yuri raised his gun. "If I order you to run this piece of shit aground, you'll do it. Understand?"

Jorge just stared back.

The Russian snorted. "But fifty feet will be close enough." And then. "There." Yuri pointed.

Just as they moved past a huge tumble of boulders on the shoreline they could see a bonfire with a man jumping up and down, waving, and then coming down to the water's edge.

"A good day for a barbecue, yes?" He laughed. "Stop next to him but do not drop anchor. Maintain position and ready the inflatable."

Chekov leaned closer to Yuri as they headed for the doorway. He lowered his voice. "We have selected several of the *Sea Princess* crew who will not be needed further. Do you want them assembled?"

"Not yet. It might cause an extreme reaction. I don't want to start a fight unless I can finish it quickly. Wait until we have our extra man onboard."

Chekov nodded, and the two men headed out to the deck.

The hoist was already whining to life, and a single *Sea Princess* crewman was seated in the rear of the twelve-foot inflatable. He looked up, his eyes round with nerves.

Yuri pointed. "Bring him back. Be quick." He smirked. "I hear it's dangerous on the water."

The man nodded, started the outboard, and scooted away from the side of the ship. Regardless of Yuri's orders he kept the speed down and also the noise. But he still crossed the short expanse of water in minutes.

Yuri turned to Chekov. "Make sure our current crew members are behaving. Soon some of them will be taking a little Black Sea holiday on the rocks." He laughed at his own joke as Chekov headed inside.

* * *

Chekov went below decks in time to see Meena and another crew member carrying Sonya down the corridor. They stopped, startled for a moment.

But Chekov came and lent a hand, grabbing hold of her shoulders. "Where to?"

Meena pointed and they took Sonya to Meena's cabin and laid her gently on the bed.

"Thank you," Meena said suspiciously.

"How is she?" Chekov asked.

"Unchanged," Meena replied, curtly. "She really needs proper medical care. We need to get her home."

Chekov nodded and then sighed deeply. "I'm sorry this is happening. Things are spinning out of control."

"Then stop it."

"The captain is my captain. And he has the bulk of the men on his side." He spoke wearily. "All I can do is try to shield you from some of his worst inclinations."

"I see." She looked up at him from under her brows. "He wants to kill us, doesn't he?"

Chekov backed out of the room. "Not all of you." He turned and vanished.

* * *

As the small raft approached the shelf, Zimchenko moved closer to the rock's edge and quickly jumped in. The inflatable immediately started heading back.

On the wheelhouse deck Jorge frowned down at the sonar. "*Contact, contact.*" He seemed unsure of who exactly he should be reporting it to. He then opened the mic to the foredeck. "We have contact, signature indicates a seventy-five-foot marine entity, running at a depth of a hundred feet, speed fifteen knots, bearing one hundred and ten degrees. Interception in forty-five seconds."

* * *

Yuri cursed loudly and turned from the speaker to the railing just as Chekov arrived.

"*It's coming*," he said.

Both men looked down at the inflatable raft coming back slowly across the dark water.

Yuri cupped his mouth. "*Hurry up!*" he yelled. He banged a fist on the railing. "I should have made that bastard get us closer to the shore. We have plenty of water beneath us."

"Now I wish we didn't," Chekov replied ominously.

The raft got closer, and Yuri leaned over, watching the raft and watching the water. The searchlights were all moving over the surface, but Jorge had concentrated the main one forward.

Ahead of the *Sea Princess* the water was still dark and calm, but below they all knew something was bearing down on them.

"Four hundred feet, veering toward our port side." Jorge's words became rushed. "Increasing speed."

"Of course it is." Chekov exhaled. "It's coming for the raft."

Yuri turned to the crew member on the deck gun. "Fire, fire."

The man swung the huge cannon-like weapon around, but as yet he had no target.

"It's gone past us." Jorge exhaled loudly.

Yuri had his hands on the railing and slowly leaned forward to rest his forehead on the back of hands. They gripped the railing so hard they were white. "Thank you, thank you," he whispered.

CHAPTER 24

After what Carlos had told them, Cate and Jack had submerged to a depth of about fifty feet and approached the ship from the stern. They couldn't take the chance of being spotted, and some asshole taking potshots at them.

"Should we come up?" Cate asked. "Take a quick look?"

"Not yet," Jack said. "I can see the glimmer of the ship's lights, but that's about it. I want to ease us alongside where the breach in the hull is. Maybe we can climb in undetected." He grimaced. "Problem is, we have few sensor instruments on this toy. Just some proximity acoustics that'll warn us if we're going to run into something close by."

"For night dives I guess," Cate said. "Don't hit the dock."

In the back Carlos coughed up the last of the seawater in his lungs and then shifted a little. "We must hurry. We need to stop them throwing any more of our people over."

"We'll do our best. But we have to play it cool, as we don't want to walk right into their arms. Otherwise, we'll end up in the sea as well. Without a sub." Jack pushed the small u-shaped wheel forward, accelerating just a little.

On the control panel a light began to blink. Cate saw the same warning. "We've got an approximation warning. Something in the water, off our port side. No idea of size or shape."

"Port side?" Jack asked, frowning down at the annoying light. He tapped it, then shook his head and sighed at the few bits of data. "Come on, little fella, help me out here with a bit more information." He sat back. "Switching on all external lights. Maybe those assholes onboard are throwing debris over the side."

Jack switched on all the external lights. And time seemed to stop as the three humans beheld the monster.

Carlos put both hands over his mouth to stifle his scream. Cate sucked in a breath and Jack felt his testicles shrivel in his pants.

"No. Body. Move. A muscle," he whispered. "Shutting off engines." He flicked switches and the craft glided to a slow stop.

All three of them stared out at the monstrous, pale shark hanging in the water. It was so close they could see inside its dark maw.

The black and glassy truck tire-sized eye closest to them swiveled, but it was hard to tell if it was looking at them, seeing them inside the small craft, and examining each of them, or if it just saw the small yellow object floating in front of it.

Jack bet the Megalodon saw them. But he hoped that the steel shell they huddled within masked their scent and might have telegraphed an impression of being non-living or inedible.

Time stretched and, for the first time, they were able to see the full size of the creature. Jack had studied sharks all his life and had seen live Megalodons before. And up close. But he'd never been so near to one that he felt he could almost reach out and touch it.

He licked his dry lips. He felt it was like seeing death itself suddenly appear at your shoulder.

"What's it doing?" Cate breathed.

"Listening. Smelling. Sensing for electrical impulses," Jack replied from the corner of his mouth.

"The dorsal fin." Jack whispered.

They saw the notch of missing flesh from the massive fin. It was still red.

"Maybe where Alina hit it," he said softly.

The massive Megalodon shark began to ease backward in the dark water.

Jack watched the monster carefully. "Everyone stay still and –"

Carlos coughed.

The Megalodon shark stopped retreating. Carlos clamped his hands even tighter over his mouth and Cate and Jack sat frozen, watching the huge creature glide closer again.

And then even closer.

The snout nudged them. Luckily there were no loose objects, and the only effect was that the submersible was bumped backward a few feet and started to roll in the water.

The shark stayed where it was, probably observing the bright yellow bulb as it tumbled slowly.

"That's right," Cate whispered. "We're just a lump of debris. Nothing to eat here."

The submersible did a full tumble in the water, and then when they came around again, the sea was empty.

"I think it's gone." Cate slumped. "I feel sick."

Jack half turned in his seat. "Carlos, please don't get thrown out of two vessels in one day, will you?"

The *Sea Princess* crew member hiked his shoulders to his ears. "I'm sorry, I cough when I'm nervous."

"Why did it leave?" Cate asked.

"Powering up." Jack turned on a few of the instruments and stabilized the rolling craft. When it was leveled off he tilted his head. "Maybe that – listen."

Just faintly in the background they could hear what might have been an outboard motor.

* * *

Jorge kept watch on the sonar. So far all he saw was the inflatable coming in toward the side of the *Sea Princess* where the gaping hole opened at the water level. He also saw the small shape of the submersible that he had kept from the Russians.

But the sonar must have been playing up as the submersible signature kept changing sizes – from small to big to small. Thankfully, it was back to normal now.

He was just relieved that Cate and Jack were alive and were following them. He didn't know what they might be able to do but it gave him some small hope knowing there was someone else out there on their side.

"Oh god."

His mouth dropped open. Seemingly out of nowhere, the monster shark appeared. It was coming, at the raft, like a missile – all seventy-five feet and probably seventy tons of it.

He had no time to do anything other than hit the alarm. Over the ship the klaxon horn blared. Yuri and his men turned one way and then the other but everyone else onboard knew the drill – move to emergency positions and brace for danger.

* * *

Yuri turned from staring up at the control room back to the dark water.

"The shark," was all Chekov said.

Yuri gripped the railing. "This monster torments us."

The inflatable was slowing as it came in closer to the ripped-open bay door. Then Yuri saw the massive pale head of the creature rise from the depths.

It happened almost in slow motion; Yuri uselessly raised an arm to point, but he had no time to even shout a warning. One second the water was dark and empty, and then the ghostly leviathan breached. Its snout left the water and the mouth opened wide, then wider and the huge, serrated teeth in the jaws seemed to telescope forward.

Zimchenko and the *Sea Princess* crewman screamed and jumped over the side.

The boat went inside the monster's jaws which clamped down, and the massive, heavily muscled creature kept up its forward movement and struck the side of the ship.

It was like a massive gong being sounded and vibrations from the impact went right through the *Sea Princess*'s super-structure. On the foredeck, Yuri and Chekov heard things being thrown around below them.

Chekov clung tight to the railing as the monster attacked their ship, and Yuri was thrown backward to skid along the decking.

* * *

Warning sirens now screamed all over the ship, even drowning out the mournful klaxon horn that still blared out its cry.

The ship might have only suffered minor damage if it was in perfect condition. But the cracks it already had suffered in its hull were now widened. The trickle of incoming water, which had been managed by the pumps, became a torrent.

In the control room, Jorge went from instrument to instrument. "No, no, no! This can't be happening."

He looked up, disbelief turning to fear on his face. "We're sinking."

* * *

Below decks Meena was thrown to the floor, smashing her head against the metal bunk edge. Sonya was also thrown from her bed. But as Meena struggled back to her knees Sonya groaned.

Meena rushed to her, sitting her up.

The Russian woman blinked open sticky eyes. "What . . . happened?"

Multiple alarms still sounded, and Meena put an arm around Sonya's shoulders to support her. "Ms. Borashev, Sonya, are you okay?"

Sonya looked down at her arm. The drip needle was still in it. She made a guttural sound in her throat and pulled it out. She winced. "I've got a headache like a jackhammer." She rubbed her face and used the edge of the bed to push herself to her feet. She swayed a little.

"Careful, you've been unconscious for over 24 hours." Meena held onto her arm and steadied her, even though Sonya was a head taller.

Sonya blinked again and her vision cleared. She looked around. "Why am I in here?" She frowned. "And the *Sea Princess* is tilting."

She headed for the door, but Meena grabbed her and held her in place. "Not yet. We've been taken over by pirates."

"*What?*" Sonya scowled and turned to the smaller woman. "What the hell has happened? How?"

"So much." Meena exhaled. "When the cable snagged us and held us in place, it gave some stranded Russian sailors a chance to sneak onboard. They had weapons and took us over. Threw Carlos overboard."

Sonya growled in her chest. "Is everyone else okay?" she asked.

"Jack and Cate went out in the submersible to cut the remaining strands around the propellor. But Yuri, the Russian captain, started up the *Sea Princess* and left them behind. One of the pirates just helped us though. He may be an ally."

"I see." Sonya's eyes narrowed. "And why are we tilting?"

"I'm not sure. But there was another explosion just now. Or something hit us." Meena sighed. "It must have opened the crack in the hull wider. I think we're taking on water. And faster than we can pump it out."

"This is not a good place to sink," Sonya said. "We need to leave."

"What about Cate and Jack?" Meena asked.

"We secure the ship first. Then we rescue our people." Sonya staggered for a moment and shook her head to clear it.

She spotted Meena's plastic bottle of water and snatched it up, opening it and draining it all.

"You need to rest some more." Meena tried to take her arm.

Sonya smiled down at her. "If I rest any more we'll all end up drowned, or as shark food." She placed a hand on the shorter woman's shoulder. "Get to the bridge and tell them to be ready. I'm going to retake my ship."

Meena beamed at her captain, nodded, and headed for the door. But Sonya quickly shot out an arm and grabbed her shoulder.

"Wait. Someone comes."

***

Yuri had been thrown backward from the impact but scrambled to his feet and staggered back to the railing, holding an elbow.

"Ach." He gripped the railing with both hands as he stared, his eyes almost bulging.

The inflatable boat was gone, but thankfully he spotted the men. One swam to the bow, and one to the stern. The one swimming to the bow had a *Sea Princess* uniform on and, as Yuri watched, a huge corpse-white head rose up, turned sideways, and like Jonah entering the mouth of the whale, the crew member vanished inside the massive tooth-lined maw, screaming as he went.

Yuri put his hands over his ears as he swore he could still hear the man in the monster's gullet as it went back under the water.

"Swim back, swim back here!" Chekov yelled to Zimchenko at the stern and pointed to the ripped open bay door. But like a piece of bread thrown onto a pond's surface for goldfish, he too was overtaken. Instead of a fast kill, the massive shark almost gently took Zimchenko and bit down, perhaps wanting to savor the salty blood before he was swallowed.

This time the man's shrill scream only lasted a second or two, before he and the beast went under. Yuri placed his forehead on the railing and pounded it with a fist.

Chekov put a hand on his captain's shoulder. "Yuri, we're sinking."

Yuri moaned and then looked up. "This accursed fish." He straightened and turned to the wheelhouse. He could make out the form of Jorge standing there watching them.

Yuri swiveled his hand in the air, but the man simply continued to stare so he went to a ship's intercom post against the foredeck wall. He opened it, hailing the bridge.

"Turn us around. We are –"

There was a sound like a groaning animal, and the lights flickered. Then the sound began to die away, taking the lights with it.

"And so it begins." Chekov walked back to the gunwale railing and stared down. "The engine room must be flooded." He turned back. "The ship is already riding lower, and the sea is pouring into the bay area."

Yuri nodded. "And of course that means the pumps have stopped working." He came and also leaned over the side. "And if we are forced to take to the lifeboats, what do you think will happen?" He laughed at his own predicament.

Yuri paced away for a moment, before turning. He called to the hulking form of Dardov to come closer, along with Moshev. When they were near he spoke in a soft, conspiratorial tone. "The boat is sinking. If we go into the water, then some or all of us will die."

"But then what?" Chekov asked. "Even if we make it to the rocks, we are still stranded in this hellhole. We need to get back to the *Boris Yeltsin*."

"The shark will not let us." Yuri continued to stare out into the twilight darkness for a moment. But then he held up a finger. "Unless the shark is occupied."

The small group stared at him intently.

"If we all go in the water, then most will undoubtedly die. Even if we take to the remaining life rafts and move at top speed – as we just saw, these too are vulnerable to attack." He smiled. "But if there were a lot of bodies swimming at the same time, and only one raft, then I think the shark will be preoccupied."

"It is a risk," Chekov said but bobbed his head. "But there is a chance of survival. In the water we are as good as dead. And on the land we will also die, but just a little more slowly."

"Then we are agreed?" Yuri's lips curved into a cruel smile.

"Maybe we can give them the other raft. Give the innocent ones a fighting chance of survival?" Chekov asked.

"But if they survive and escape, it might mean that we do not." Yuri shook his head. "For this to work – and for the four of us to get all the way to the cave opening that leads outside – then we need a lot of people in the water all at once." He shrugged. "Then it is up to fate whether they live or die."

After a few seconds Chekov sighed and nodded.

"Good." Yuri turned to his two remaining crew members. "Round the *Sea Princess* crew up quickly, and bring them up on deck. Swimming lessons are about to begin."

Yuri handed Dardov one of his guns. "No need to be gentle. After all, dead and bleeding bodies will be just as attractive to our big friend in the water."

Chekov looked pale, but Yuri laughed as the two Russian crew members headed down below decks.

CHAPTER 25

"They're sinking," Cate said. "What do we do?"

"We can't take on more survivors. Perhaps they could cling to the outside of the submersible, and we could ferry them to shore. But we'd be slow and more vulnerable to attack," Jack said.

"The Russian crew may be more desperate, and dangerous now," Carlos said.

"I agree, and they may think they need to even up the odds," Jack turned in his seat. "How many lifeboats remain?"

"Two. And that's not enough for the entire crew," Carlos replied.

"You can bet the Russians will take one. But that leaves all of the *Sea Princess* crew and they cannot fit into just one." Carlos groaned. "When the boat sinks they will have to swim."

"And I doubt the Russians will be breaking their backs to help." Jack leaned forward to look along the deck railing. "Whatever happens, I'm betting those pirates will do everything they can to improve the odds for themselves."

"Do you really think they may do something stupid?" Cate asked. "We can't let them."

"I agree. They have weapons, but we have the numbers. For now. Plus they don't seem to know we're down here,"

Jack said. "I'm going to bring us alongside the bay area." He turned in his seat. "Up for a fight, Carlos?"

"I'm not a very good fighter." The crewman hiked his bony shoulders. "But I will fight for my friends."

"Good man," Jack replied. "Just remember, the element of surprise is as good as a howitzer."

"Who said that?" Cate asked.

"I did." He turned and grinned. "I hope it's true."

They maneuvered alongside the ship and Jack retracted the clear canopy. Carlos used some rope to tie off the small craft to the ship, which now hung three feet lower in the water.

Inside it was dark and silent.

"Sinking fast," Jack said. "I give it another hour until the water reaches the top deck. And then it's anyone's guess how long until she goes to the bottom." He reached out and gripped the bent steel. "Are we ready?"

"Three bad-ass howitzers, incoming," Cate said and was first to climb inside the *Sea Princess*.

* * *

"Wait. Someone's coming." Sonya heard the bellowing of two Russians as they went from cabin to cabin, into the galley areas and even the storage rooms.

"They're rounding up the crew," Meena said. "They'll be here soon."

"But not both at once." Sonya's eyes were half lidded. "Get behind me."

The heavy footsteps and the loud voice of one of the Russians sounded in the hallway outside and Sonya quickly looked one way then the other for some sort of weapon she could use. There was nothing obvious, except some clean towels folded on a benchtop. She snatched one up and held it in one hand as she turned back to the door, waiting.

The door burst inward, and a Russian man stood in the doorway. He began to shout, but then he saw Sonya and his mouth snapped shut in momentary surprise.

He looked at the towel in Sonya's hand. "You about to take a shower?"

Moshev's face became serious, and he motioned with his hand. "Come. Up on deck, quickly."

Sonya stood, her arms down beside her body, and stared straight back at him.

"Don't make me hurt you," Moshev growled.

"Try," Sonya said in warning.

Moshev snorted and walked forward. "Your choice." He extended his hand, expecting to take her by the upper arm.

Sonya pirouetted out of his way, and suddenly the towel was held in both her hands, and she flicked it into his face. Moshev shut his eyes, just for a second, but in that time Sonya had ducked under his arms, got behind him, and had wrapped the towel over his face.

She jerked his head back and the Russian was taken by surprise. "*Don't make me hurt you,*" she said in Russian. And with that she used her bodyweight to swing his face into the left-side cabin wall. Then she swung his face into the right-side cabin wall. The white towel had a growing stain of blood on its front.

Moshev's fingers scrabbled at the towel, trying to pull it off, but Sonya held on tight and used their combined bodyweight to pinball him into more walls, tables, and bunkbed edges.

Meena crowded herself into a corner as the maelstrom of violence wrecked her cabin.

The Russian man's movements were growing slower and the next vicious swing into the wall ended with a crunch of bone, and his hands dropped to his sides. Sonya let his body slide to the floor and also let the blood-soaked towel drop on top of him.

Sonya quickly felt for a pulse at his neck, and then shrugged. "Too bad." She then ripped off his belt and placed his machete sheath on the belt around her own waist, and turned to Meena.

"Let's take our ship back."

* * *

Cate, Jack, and Carlos quickly moved out of the flooded bay area. They'd had to wade through the waist-deep water in darkness, lit only by the sparse red emergency spotlighting.

Carlos operated the manual releases for the bulkhead doors and then re-shut them. But the crack in the hull had obviously widened to move beyond the bay area and more sections of the ship were being flooded.

They made their way higher, and Carlos turned to whisper, "We need to find Meena. She will know what is happening."

The ship was oddly silent, and when Carlos reached another internal door he half turned. "This leads out to the cabin areas. From there we can make our way to the deck, bridge, or anywhere we want." He put his fingers to his lips and then pushed the door open.

The gunshot was brutally loud in the enclosed space and both Jack and Cate threw themselves backward.

A small hole appeared in one side of Carlos's head and blew out the other in a gout of thick, dark liquid that splashed against the wall.

The huge Russian swung the gun around, pointing it from Cate to Jack, and then back to Jack. "Who like to be next?"

Cate and Jack just stared, shock and disbelief still twisting their features.

"Hands up," the huge man growled.

Both raised their hands.

Jack seethed as he looked down at Carlos's body. "You bastard."

"Your fault. You surprised me." The Russian scowled at them. "I have not seen you before." He pointed his gun at the dead Carlos. "But I know this one. I threw him overboard a few hours ago."

He snorted his indifference. "Seems like this one had more lives than a cat. But last one used up now." He waved the gun. "Come, the captain will want to talk to you." He grinned. "Hope you brought your bathers." Then he looked down at their wetsuits and smirked. "I see you already did."

Jack and Cate were led up the stairs and onto the foredeck. The big man made Jack drag the dead body of Carlos with him.

Outside Jack and Cate could see the significant tilt of the deck and, with the ship continuing to fill with water, both knew it wouldn't be long until the warm sea reached them. Jack just hoped the vessel didn't tip before then.

At the side rail stood two men who looked to be in charge. Toward the front of the ship was the assembled *Sea Princess* crew. All looked nervous. It was tropical warm and humid in the cave, but many had their arms folded tightly across their body as if they were freezing. A few cried out or wept when they saw the body of their friend.

As Cate and Jack watched, a few more of the crew came up from below and were directed to join the group. Some of them were hunched over, cowed.

One of the Russians at the side rail stepped forward and hooked his thumbs in his belt. "My name is Yuri Zagreb, captain of the *Boris Yeltsin* anchored just outside of this accursed cave. My second in command is Mr. Anatoli Chekov." He grinned. "I think many of you have also met my crewman, Mr. Dardov, and somewhere below is my other man, Mr. Moshev."

He smiled and nodded. "We have enjoyed our brief stay with you. But now we have to go our separate ways." He turned and nodded and Chekov and Dardov began to lower one of the remaining boats over the side.

Yuri watched it for a moment, and Jack had the urge to run at them while they were distracted. For now, there were just three Russians, and if he rallied the crew, he bet at least a couple of them would be prepared to stand and fight with him.

But he felt Cate grip his arm, hard. He looked down and saw her shake her head slowly.

Yuri turned back, just as from the corner of Jack's eye he saw two more people from below deck hurriedly make their way to the assembled group at the bow of the ship. Both had shawls or towels over their heads.

"It is vitally important for me to make it out to the *Boris Yeltsin* so I can call for help for you poor people." Yuri's grin was theatrically broad. "And now, we need our distraction." He leaned closer to Dardov. "Throw the body over the side. And then kill two more. Make sure you give a few chops with the machete so there is plenty of blood in the water."

Cate heard every word of his deadly plan and also heard the one called Chekov begin arguing with him. She turned to Jack. "Okay, now we need to do something."

"Yeah, we do," Jack said. "Something big."

He slid his eyes to the huge Russian who walked toward the *Sea Princess* crew now all jumbled together at the bow of the boat. They all seemed to have their backs turned and were talking in a group.

The big man held a handgun in one hand and a machete in the other. The guy was solid, but slightly overweight. Jack bet if he could get him on the ground, the Russian would be like a turtle on its back.

Jack lowered his head, ready to take a run at the Russian and hit the back of his legs like a freaking cannonball.

But the captain, Yuri, had a gun as well so he would be exposed. His only hope was the crew would back him, and he hoped that their huddled discussion was along the same lines as his plans.

If they backed him, they might win. If they didn't, he'd be one of the first bodies going over the side.

When the big Russian was just thirty feet from the *Sea Princess* crew they all parted at once.

Jack's mouth dropped open – he realized they weren't just talking; they were planning, and more importantly being organized. And now he saw who had been organizing them.

Sonya was at their center, and she had powered up the deck laser, which had a power source independent of the ship's engines. Her eyes blazed with hatred.

"Hey, *mu-dak*," she yelled.

Dardov, taken by surprise, was rooted to the spot for a moment.

The laser beam shot out and touched the man in the center of the face. Sonya had opened the beam to about an inch wide, and she kept it there for a second or two and then switched it off.

"Fu-*uuuck*," Jack whispered.

There was a perfect inch-wide hole in Dardov's face. It went in at about the middle of his nose and exited the back. Smoke rose from both holes.

The Russian collapsed like a puppet who'd just had its strings cut.

Sonya wasn't finished and swung the laser toward Yuri.

"Throw down your gun," she yelled.

Yuri hesitated and quickly glanced over the side of the ship, perhaps judging his chance at keeping the weapon and also making it into the lifeboat.

"Oh, please try me," Sonya said, softer this time.

To emphasize her point, the laser powered up, and she shot a beam just past his ear. He held his hands up and grinned. "No problem." He tossed his gun onto the deck.

"Your weapons too," she told Chekov.

The man drew his long knife from its scabbard and threw it to the deck. Jack and Cate walked across to retrieve the weapons.

"We meant you no harm," Yuri said. "I just wanted to save my crew and get them home."

Sonya spoke through bared teeth. "My dead crew member doesn't believe you."

Yuri shook his head furiously. "No, my man – that man, Dardov – exceeded his orders." He made a dismissive movement with his hand. "It is good he is dead. He deserved it."

Sonya was unconvinced. "And now I think the time has come for us to part company, as you said. Time for you to leave us."

"You can't kill us in cold blood."

Jack and Cate joined the crew and stood beside Sonya. She half turned to nod at them, and then turned back to Yuri and Chekov.

"Your fate will be in your own hands." She half smiled. "Over the side you go."

Meena grabbed her arm. "Not Chekov. He helped us." She leaned closer to her boss. "We might need him."

Sonya seemed to think on it for a moment and then grunted. "Just you, Mr. *Kapitan*."

Yuri glanced at Chekov and frowned.

"Hurry now, or I'll burn you. Like your man who exceeded your orders." Sonya's short, sharp laugh was like a bark.

Yuri turned to Chekov. "We are in this together, comrade."

Chekov took two steps away from him. "I wish you good fortune, Captain Zagreb." He saluted.

"You bastard. I'll see you hang for this mutiny."

Chekov shook his head. "It's not a mutiny when it's not your ship."

Yuri glanced again over the side.

"If you think you can leap into the boat, I will cut you in half before you even start," Sonya said. "Move along ten paces."

Yuri kept his hands up and did as asked. He turned, his eyes glaring at her. "This isn't over."

"For you it is," Sonya said. "Jump."

Yuri gazed angrily at Chekov and then, without another word, he leaped over the side.

They heard the splash, and the entire crew rushed to the side of the boat to watch the man come to the surface and then swim strongly toward the rocks. It wasn't a huge distance, and already he was a third of the way there.

Sonya walked out from behind the laser and headed for Jack.

"Boy, are you ever a sight for sore eyes," he said.

Sonya grabbed the front of his shirt and dragged him forward to kiss him hard on the lips.

"*Hey!*" Cate objected.

Sonya let him go, and Jack spluttered for a moment.

"Meena told me you dived down in the darkness to save me." She gave him a small bow. "Thank you, Jack Monroe. I know you –" she turned to Cate "– and Cate, rightly hate me for bringing you here. But I'm glad I did."

Jack half smiled. "Hey, you can thank us by getting us all home."

"I will." She watched as Meena went to Chekov.

The man bowed deeply. "Thank you."

Meena shook her head. "You are not our friend. But you didn't deserve that fate. Behave, help us, and you can live."

Chekov put a fist over his heart. "You have my pledge."

They watched Yuri, who was making good progress and would climb up on the rocks any second.

Cate looked along the water – there wasn't a ripple or any sign of anything underneath the surface.

"Where's the Megalodon?" she asked. "It was just here."

"Maybe it's had its fill," Meena replied.

Now Yuri was clambering up onto the rocks. He wiped both hands down his face and then turned to yell obscenities and make a few Russian hand gestures for their benefit.

"Unbelievable. The bastard made it." Jack turned to Sonya who now stood by the railing, arms folded, staring out over the dark water. "And now, what do *we* do?"

Sonya ignored him and continued to stare for a moment more before finally responding. "The *Sea Princess* needs to be up in dry dock for major repairs. That isn't going to happen here. The engines are flooded, but some emergency operations can still be used. For a while."

She turned to them. "We're sinking. No way around it. We need to either take to the water, or the land. But we can't stay here."

Cate looked over the side. "You have two rafts . . ."

"And a mini submersible," Jack included.

Cate nodded. "Two rafts and a mini submersible that can take three people. If we overload them, we can take everyone. All we need to do is make it outside these caverns to your relay beacon."

"*If* we can make it outside," Meena said.

Sonya sucked in a deep breath, filling her lungs, and once again looked out over the ink-like water. "We're blind without our sonar. For all we know the Megalodon is under the ship right now."

"Yuri made it," Jack said. "But it's still too high risk. While the super predator is around, we'll get picked off." He ran his hand up through his wet hair as he thought it through. "I say we split the risk. One boat heads to the shore with some supplies. The other lighter boat tries for outside to hit the beacon."

He placed his hands on the railing. "Megalodon sharks have the same sensory abilities as great whites. They have excellent

smell, sensors for vibrations and electrical currents. They also
have good vision above and below water, *but* sight is not their
strongest sense." He turned. "And we can use that."

"We confuse it?" Sonya asked.

"Yes. Everything that can float goes over the side. We
create a storm of floating debris." He pointed out at the sea.
"We give the debris time to move away from the ship. Then
we take to the rafts, paddling, and, well . . ." He gave them a
crooked smile. "We hope for the best."

"And if the beacon boat fails?" Meena asked.

"Then we can either try again or just sit tight until someone
comes looking for the *Sea Princess*," Cate replied.

"My people will look for me. But it still could be days, a
week, longer . . ." Sonya said.

"Then the shore boat needs to have plenty of supplies."
Cate looked at the dark shoreline. "And weapons, because
I'm betting that Yuri asshole would love to get some revenge."

"And a boat," Jack added.

"We need more." Sonya turned. "The raft heading to shore
will only need to cover a few hundred feet and will be in the
water, including loading time, around ten minutes. But the raft
trying to make its way out has many miles to cover, and therefore will be moving over the surface for hours. And many more
hours if we only row."

Jack nodded. "I hear you. It'll be well outside the debris
cloud we create. The Megalodon needs to be drawn well
away. A long way away."

Sonya folded her arms and faced them. "We need something to attract it. Something irresistible." Her eyes were
clear. "Remember what the Russian captain was going to do
to Carlos? Well, we have two of their dead men right here."

"We use them as bait?" Jack's brows went up.

"Yes, and this is where I must call on you to help, Jack."
Sonya stared at him, unblinking.

"Hang on –" Cate began. "Can't someone else do it? Why Jack, again?"

Sonya turned to her. "Alina could pilot the sub. So could Miguel. But they're both dead. I can too, but I have other work to do."

"It's okay." Jack already knew where she was going. "You want a decoy run."

Sonya nodded. "We tie the dead men together. Attach a buoy to them to keep them at the surface. And you use the submersible to tow them away. Out to sea."

"That's suicide." Cate scowled. "Even if the Megalodon follows us, how are we supposed to outrun it in a mini submersible with a top speed of around five to six knots? There's no chance."

"I'm sorry, but it's the only chance my crew has. Look at them," Sonya replied.

Cate turned to the still-huddled crew – they looked frightened, and so young. She bet many of them were still in their twenties. She groaned. "Blackmail."

Sonya ignored her. "You need to step up again, Jack. You'll only have line of sight plus your intuition and experience. But we can rig a long towline, so you're not close to the lure."

"Step up? This is the guy that swam down to rescue you, solo," Cate said. "We were only supposed to be advisors. Now look where we are."

"The situation has changed," Sonya said. "Events not in our control have overtaken us. Now we just need to – how do you put it? Play the cards we're dealt."

Jack rubbed his chin and Cate's frown was so deep it creased her entire forehead.

Sonya swept an arm back toward her huddled crew again. "Help us save them."

Jack looked up. "I can do it," he said. "And you're right – there's no choice."

"Dammit." Cate sighed. "*We* can do it. Just make sure the rope attached to the dead Russians is detachable."

Sonya strode forward and put a hand on each of their shoulders. She looked at each of their faces. "People like you make the world a better place."

"Just . . ." Cate grimaced. "Just make it out to that communications buoy and bring help back. Fast."

"Count on it." Sonya let them go.

In fifteen more minutes, the two rafts were ready. Everything that could float had been hauled up from below deck and tossed over the sides of the ship. On the calm water, most items bobbed close by, but a few pieces sailed off into the blue twilight.

The ship was riding very low in the water now, and the tilt was pushing twenty degrees. Food supplies, weapons, some portable tents and sleeping mats, and even a pair of thermal vision goggles were placed on a small raft that the inflatable would tow. Eleven crew members would be in the landing craft, with Meena in charge.

The second boat heading to the entrance would just have Jorge and Sonya. There would be some cold weather gear, water, and minimal supplies.

Their priority on exiting was to find and initiate the beacon on the emergency buoy.

Hopefully the comms link would be intact and Sonya could inform her team of their predicament, get a timeline for rescue, and then retreat back inside the cave to wait with the others. But if entering the cave and crossing the dark sea again proved too high risk, then they were prepared to wait in the glacial cave mouth until help arrived, no matter how many days it took.

Cate and Jack would tow the meat wagon, as he called it, a few miles down the coast and further out. It was hoped if the meg was in the area it would follow them. But how long this could be maintained was anyone's guess.

Sonya, Jack, and Cate had no real plan for what happened if the Megalodon *did* take the bait. They just mentally leaped over this part for their peace of mind and went straight to what happened afterward – the plan was for the mini submersible to join Sonya and Jorge outside the cave. At least the sub had heaters against the potential cold.

"I wish you luck," Jack said to Sonya.

Sonya nodded. "And I wish I could bring my laser." She smiled. "But luck to you, Cate, and everyone. I think we will need plenty of it before this day is through."

* * *

Yuri watched the activity from the rocks. The shapes were dim and he wished he still had his binoculars, but he was sure he saw supplies being loaded onto one raft. He bet some were staying while the other boat would make a run at the cave mouth – after all, that had been his plan.

He only had the medium-sized knife at his belt. He had no guns. And he couldn't rely on surprise, as they knew he was here, even if not exactly where.

But the Russian had been brought up on the mean streets of Kyzyl, where murder was the city's main sport, and he had learned to be as rat cunning as they came.

He looked over his shoulder to the darkness closer to the cliff wall and thought he heard a familiar soft sliding sound. He stared for several moments but saw nothing.

Finally he turned away. No, he had no intention of staying here. He was prepared to die trying to get off this rocky shore and back to his ship waiting outside. And Yuri knew he had something else those pampered pleasure-cruisers did not – he had already spent time on the rocks, and he would use that experience to his advantage.

The Russian captain worked himself into a hiding position, to watch and wait.

* * *

Sonya grabbed the leg of the dead Dardov and dragged him to the center of the deck. She ordered two men to retrieve Moshev's corpse from Meena's cabin, and others to bring up some rope, release clips, and a large buoy from their stores.

She crouched, unbothered by the corpse with the large hole in its head, and with a crackling of tendons, took the gun from the Russian's rapidly stiffening fingers. She then called Meena from the group.

She handed the gun over and placed her hands on the small woman's shoulders, looking down into her eyes. Jack and Cate could hear her words in the twilight silence of the massive cavern.

"If you see this Yuri, or even glimpse him, kill him. Do not wait to judge his intentions." She dropped her hands and straightened. "Because I know his type and he will try to kill you, and take your boat and supplies, the first chance he gets."

Meena nodded.

Sonya looked down at the deck for a moment and shook her head. "I'm stupid. I should have killed him earlier." She half smiled. "I just never expected him to make it to shore."

Meena smiled back. "The devil takes care of its own."

"Me or him?" She chuckled and then turned to Chekov. "And what to do with you?" She walked forward until she was right in front of the man.

Chekov straightened his spine, but still wasn't as tall as Sonya. She narrowed her eyes. "If it was up to me, you'd be attached to the rope by your heels, as more bait for the shark."

"This was never my idea," Chekov said. "I'm a sailor, a fisherman, not a pirate or murderer."

"Meena has vouched for your life. But I still do not trust you. And so, I will keep an eye on you. You will come with me and Jorge as our oarsman. If our rescue comes, you are free to go back to your fishing ship." She nodded briefly to the dark shoreline. "But I would not return for that creature."

"Thank you." He nodded once, deeply. "I will leave with the ship immediately."

"And tell no one of what is in here." Sonya shook her head. "No rescues. Or I will ensure you all hang for piracy."

In ten more minutes, the grisly sight of the two dead Russian men tied by their ankles to a large white marker buoy sat on deck. Trailing from it was a few hundred feet of rope.

They had set it up so the "package", as they referred to it, could be released from the cabin. And as the small submersible had no significant sensors, one of the crew had rigged his own GoPro to the bottom of the buoy along with a strong lantern. He gave his phone to Cate and showed her how to swivel the camera, enlarge or retract, and even switch to an infrared lighting.

"How come I don't have his tech on my phone?" she asked.

Jack chuckled. "You probably do. But like most of us, you never need it so you never use it. I use them on my dives all the time."

Cate swiveled the camera and watched the small screen of the phone as it took in the deck, the railing, and then the twinkling blue lights above them. She enlarged and nodded. "I've got this."

"Ready?" Jack asked.

"As ready as I can be," she replied.

"I want that meat cart lowered over the side, and not dropped," Jack said. "And for everyone else who enters the rafts, just slow paddling. The less noise and vibrations we make the less chance we're going to attract attention from you-know-who."

"Don't worry, Jack. We know what to do," Sonya replied. "We'll give you five minutes, and then we'll start to disembark."

Sonya looked around. "She was a beautiful ship. And now she's about to vanish where no one will ever see her again."

She smiled tightly, and then gave them a small salute. "Hope I see you on the outside."

"Yeah, us too," Cate replied.

* * *

Cate and Jack headed down to the bay area, but the first deck was now awash. The only lights were the red dots of emergency lighting, casting a faint hellish glow along the dark corridor.

Water was rising rapidly by the minute, and Jack held a waterproof flashlight up high and shone it over the flooded corridor. The pair waded in and then began to breaststroke amid the debris.

Together they moved down the blood-red passage. At the hatch leading to the bay area, he turned.

"It's not far, but we're going to have to do the last of it underwater. And then exit via the open bay doors." He saw she looked pale, but resolute.

"I'm ready," she said as she started to draw breaths in and out. "On the count of three, two, one."

They both dived and swam down to the hatch door. They passed through the bay area, and Jack grabbed Cate's hand and held the light in the other. When they got to the ripped-open bay doors, he switched off the light. The overhead blue lights actually made the outside sea glow, and he didn't want to do anything that might attract any mega-predators.

Together they swam out into the underground sea. Jack felt nervous, but they quickly surfaced and made their way to the submersible.

Jack popped the hatch and climbed up and in. He turned and helped Cate over the side. When she slid in she sucked in a deep breath and nodded to him.

"Piece of cake." She grinned, her teeth showing white in the near darkness.

"Good," he said. "Because that was the easy part." He nodded to the two dead Russians being lowered to the waterline. "And here's our package."

"How do you want to do it?" Cate asked.

"Couple of options: we can attach the tow rope to one of the eye-hooks on the submersible's skin, and we drag it on the surface – the bodies will dangle a few feet below the waterline and be held up by the buoy. But that means the submersible will be vulnerable to attack from below." He bobbed his head. "Second option is we submerge, leaving the meat wagon on the surface. This might be a little safer, but it means we can't quickly release the package if it's grabbed by the Megalodon."

"We drag it on the surface," Cate said. "Then we release it when we're a couple of miles out. But we monitor the GoPro screen, and if there's any movement we jettison it immediately and dive. I don't want to be tied to this thing if it gets eaten by a seventy-five-ton meg. We'll be dragged like a tin can behind a bus."

"Okay." Jack glanced over the side to one of the tiny loops of steel he could tie the package onto.

He waved his arm for the bodies to be completely lowered. When they entered the water, the rope was thrown down to them. He tied it off and gave the thumbs-up.

Cate looked up to see Sonya and Meena leaning over the railing, both looked a lot closer than they should be as the boat had settled even lower in the water.

She nodded to them. "See you soon, friends," she said.

"Okay, let's get this party started." Jack steered the small submersible away from the hull of the ship and they felt the tug of the bodies drag on them. Cate looked over her shoulder to see the buoy following them two hundred feet back, which meant that about six feet below it the two bodies were trailing them, and undoubtedly leaving a highway of blood scent and other interesting fluids that should be irresistible to a large predator.

After a few minutes, Cate switched on the light underneath the buoy. It created a ball of illumination for about twenty feet below the surface. In the tiny camera screen she held she saw the boots of the two men trailing behind them as they were dragged along. She felt a shiver of revulsion.

Any other time she would have rejected desecrating a human being like this. But these were exceptional circumstances. And, as Jack had told her, Yuri had planned to do this to their crew, or at least kill them and throw them overboard.

She turned away from the screen to glance back at the sinking *Sea Princess* and the dark shoreline that was rapidly being left behind. She could still make out one of the rafts heading toward it.

"Do you think that Yuri guy is waiting for them?" she asked.

"You can count on it," Jack replied, and then exhaled through pressed lips. "I wouldn't like to be them, having to worry about that asshole creeping up on you in the dark."

"Oh yeah, we definitely got the pick of the jobs." Cate laughed.

Jack looked over his shoulder. "Laughing in the face of danger! I like that."

Cate turned back to where she thought the shoreline was and could only just see a pinprick of white light. "Yeah, he'll be there, watching them."

CHAPTER 26

Yuri watched and waited in the deeper shadows close to the cave wall.

He guessed the small boat would pull up on the rock platform, and then they would spend their time organizing their supplies and people. Maybe they'd even stay put for a while before seeking better shelter.

There were numerous hiding places, and even more danger spots. He thrilled at the thought of them encountering some of the strange and deadly things that had plagued his crew. But he had no sympathy for them.

I could have helped them, he thought. "Fools, any bad luck you have is on your own heads."

He edged back even more into a crevice as the raft bumped up on the rocks and people leaped out.

He was relieved to see that the *krutaya zhenshchina*, the tough woman, wasn't amongst them. His objective was to secure a gun. He needed to watch for who was in charge because they would hold the weapons. Once he knew that, then everything else they had would quickly belong to him.

* * *

Sonya and Jorge were the last to leave the *Sea Princess*, and Sonya stayed on deck for a few moments more.

She ran a hand lightly over the magnificent polished wood of the railing. "Sorry, darling Valery, I could not save your beautiful ship." She sighed, and then went over the side, sliding down the rope to land in between Jorge and Chekov.

Chekov carefully placed the oars in the water. "Ready?"

She nodded. "We take turns. You get first shift, Jorge next, me last."

Chekov began to carefully place the oars in the water, and then gently pulled back, dragging the small boat in a silent glide away from the sinking ship.

Sonya checked her weapons and Jorge had a large flashlight and a pair of binoculars he used to scan the pond-calm water.

In twenty minutes, Sonya looked back over her shoulder at the ever shrinking ship. It was sitting almost at railing level in the water now and wouldn't be above the surface for much longer.

She hoped the Megalodon shark was long gone. But if it did show up, she hoped it went after Jack and Cate's bait first. And she prayed that held the monster up long enough to give them time to get out of the cave, and its territory.

She turned back to face ahead. She knew that getting out was no guarantee of escape, as the creature had emerged before, and undoubtedly would again.

But she still had one huge trick up her sleeve – the explosives they had lodged in the entrance cave. If she detonated them as soon as they passed through the cave it would certainly stop them being attacked, and more importantly trap the rest of the monsters inside forever.

But it would doom her crew, as well as Jack and Cate.

Could she do that to them? Not if she could help it. But it was an option, and she needed to think clearly, pragmatically, and mercilessly, when the time came. Doom a few people, and save hundreds if not thousands.

Chekov stared straight back past them almost in a trance as he worked the oars like a machine, pulling them forward, carefully digging them into the water, and pulling them back along the side of the tiny craft.

It was slow, but silent, and fair progress was made. Sonya estimated they had only gone a little over two miles. So based on their current rate of three to four knots, it would take them three hours to get to the exit cave.

She wondered if her crew were okay, and she lifted her head. "Hey, Chekov."

The man looked up at her and his eyes focused.

"Will your captain try to attack my crew?" She waited.

"Of course he will," Chekov replied. "A scorpion does as a scorpion is."

* * *

Meena leaped out and stood back as several of the *Sea Princess* crew dragged the boat further up onto the rock platform.

She felt the burden of responsibility settle heavily on her slim shoulders as she now had eleven lives, including her own, in her hands. At least she was thankful they'd made it to shore in a single trip without incident.

Once the boat was secure, they'd need to find a spot that was dry and away from the water and the rising tides. She felt the gun at her hip, and looked along the rock platform, then at the tumble of boulders down the coast – there was no obvious sign of Yuri, but she had a crawling sensation in her gut that told he was there somewhere, watching.

Meena looked from the boat to the coastline. There might be somewhere further along where they could camp.

Her dilemma was how to investigate while also having some of her crew stay to look after the boat – there was safety in numbers, and she hated having to split them up. Meena shuddered at the thought of leading a team to a potential campsite and then seeing their only boat start to head off in the opposite direction.

She could just imagine that horrible Russian captain jeering and gesturing back at them.

Never, she thought, and turned back to the dark water to wonder how Sonya was faring. And also Jack and Cate. She felt sorry for the pair who had basically been kidnapped, and ended up in the middle of all *this*. And now, they were out risking their lives for them.

She turned away. The best-case scenario was that Sonya made it out of the cavern, initiated the beacon and then managed to contact home base. Then, a spotter plane would be deployed to drop supplies, followed by their own rescue ship.

Even if the weather was perfect and the rescue ship departed immediately, they were looking at around two days, maybe more. Add that to Sonya's travel time, it was probably a total of three, maybe four, days. That wasn't a huge problem as Meena's group had enough supplies to easily last that long. They just needed to find some sort of shelter, stay safe from that lurking Russian, and stay away from the water.

But Meena could not ignore the knot in her stomach. Because, even with those hardships, it would all be inconsequential if Sonya failed – if they never saw Sonya again, and no rescue was ever called. Then they could be stuck here for months. Or forever.

Meena sucked in a shuddering breath. *That was the worst-case scenario.*

"Welcome to your new home," she whispered, morosely.

She blinked before sucking in a deep breath all the way to the bottom of her lungs, inhaling the smell of brine and cave dankness.

"Okay, people, we need to scout for a secure place to camp for a few days until Ms. Borashev returns. We also need to protect the boat. As there are eleven of us, we'll have four people stay to keep it safe.

She already knew who she'd pick, and called them out: "Maria, Steven, Ormond, and Eric."

The group's eyes were round with trepidation as they looked at each other and then back to Meena. She smiled, trying to radiate control and confidence. "You get the easy job. Just make sure you stay back from the water. You will also need to keep watch for any intruders."

They all knew who she meant and a few of them turned one way then the other to scan along the rock ledge once again.

Once they had organized their supplies, she gathered up her team of six. She would have loved to leave the gun with the team staying behind to mind the raft, as she bet this would be Yuri's major target. But she had no idea what her own team might encounter, so she kept the weapon. She also loaded her backpack with the thermal vision goggles, safety matches, and anything else she might need in an emergency.

The remaining team had knives, from their personal stores and from the mess. She wondered whether any of them would use them if the circumstances demanded it. She hoped so, as the boat might be the difference between life or death for all of them.

She took one last look at each of their faces, nodded, and then placed her hands on her hips. "We'll be trekking down along the coastline to see if there are more secure places to camp, it –"

"Why don't we stay here?" Ormond asked. "I mean, we expect Sonya to be back in a few days, right? Why bother looking for somewhere more permanent?"

Meena didn't need to reply as Maria turned to him. "Because she might not return so soon." Her mouth turned down momentarily. "And that means we might be here longer – a lot longer – than we thought." She turned back. "Isn't that right, Meena?"

Meena nodded. "Unfortunately, yes, that's right. We hope everything goes to plan. But between us here, Ms. Borashev heading toward the cave entrance, and Cate and Jack dragging the lure, the odds of failing are extremely high."

"Well, that's just great." Eric made a disgusted sound in his throat. "But how long?" he scowled. "I mean, are we talking extra days, weeks, months? How long?"

Meena just stared back blankly for a moment or two, aware of the time stretching while she tried to think of an answer that might allay their fears. But she also didn't want to mislead them, in the event they were here a long time. Mistrust would kill their small group.

"I wish I had a good answer, Eric. We've given ourselves the best chance of success. But we're still going to need a lot of luck." She smiled, but it was only a fleeting curve of her lips. "We'll know in the next few days how things are going to play out. But remember, Ms. Borashev, Sonya, is a competent woman, and if anyone can make this all come together, she can."

Meena noticed most of the crew were nodding in agreement. Some kept their heads down. And a few stared back with a little mistrust in their eyes. She kept a straight face with a tiny hint of a smile. At least she could try to look confident, even if she didn't feel it.

There were no more questions, so she turned to Maria, Steven, Ormond, and Eric.

"Okay, you guys, stay close to each other and keep your eyes and ears open. We'll only travel a few miles to see around the headland, so just sit tight." She gave them a small salute and then turned. "Everyone else, let's go."

The larger group headed down along the rocky platform. No one spoke.

* * *

Yuri watched from several hundred feet back along the rock wall. He was lying flat on his belly, and in a crevice, making him impossible to see unless you stumbled right over him.

He saw the larger group leave, then watched the four remaining people mingle around the raft. It seemed they were not really sure what they were supposed to be doing.

They looked up and down the coast, so they had obviously been told to look out for him. But they were young, inexperienced, and had probably never known desperation in their lives. Or violence.

He, on the other hand, knew about taking deadly risks, and absorbing, and delivering violence. And, when need be, taking lives.

Yuri had little sympathy for them as they had all been happy to watch him go over the side of the ship, and none cared if he lived or died. He owed them nothing.

After another twenty minutes the group had obviously formulated a plan to safekeep the boat. Two sat on one side of the raft, and two on the other, and they all kept watch.

Yuri smiled. His opportunity had presented itself. Now it was up to him to take the risk.

He felt the thrill of anticipation and daring in his belly and steeled himself. He was close to a long rock pool that led to the sea and immediately saw the possibilities it offered.

Yuri eased slowly out of the crevice, crawled on his belly to the pool and, like an alligator, slid into the water. He then crawled, swam, and dived his way to the sea and, once there, clung to the rocks and edged along slowly.

The group never bothered looking to the sea – why would they? No one could possibly come from that direction unless by boat. And they would hear and see that.

And that was what Yuri was banking on.

He kept edging along the rocks, and in some places dived to swim below the dark water. Every second he was in that bath-warm sea, he felt his stomach flutter at the thought of the giant beast in there with him. He faced the rocks, and never once looked back at the sea. He remembered what the monster had done to his crew members, and prayed it was now far, far away.

Yuri took his time as he knew he'd only get one shot at this. But in another thirty minutes he stopped and eased his head up above the rock line. In the dim, blue light he could see he was just below the boat, only about twenty feet away, give or take a foot or two.

He moved a little way along until he felt a small platform of rocky growth and eased his legs up under himself, coiling his muscles as he counted down the seconds.

In his hand was his blade, and he gripped it tight. He ran through his action plan, who he would take out first, and then next.

He was sure his sudden appearance would shock them for a few seconds, and a few seconds was all he needed.

He chose the biggest and most formidable man as his first target and counted down: *three, two, one . . .*

The Russian captain exploded from the water and was halfway to the group before they were even aware he was there.

The biggest man was seated on the ground, had his back to the raft, and forearms resting on his knees. He looked up. His eyes went wide, and his mouth dropped open. But by the time his hand even began to go for the knife he had tucked into his belt, Yuri was on him.

He thrust his own blade deep into the center of the man's neck, making him gurgle wetly. Yuri never even slowed and pulled the blade out as a gout of blood flew six feet over the rocks. But he had already moved on and next delivered a backhanded sideways slash across the throat of the young, dumbfounded man seated beside him.

Two down, he thought, and jumped into the raft to cross

quickly to the other two. The woman turned with her knife up, held in both hands, and swiped it at him, but she was no expert, and as he leaped from the boat he only needed to dodge the stroke and let the blade cut empty air, before he thrust his own blade forward to stab into her heart. Her lips made a perfect circle just before her eyes rolled back in her head.

Yuri spun to see the final man had taken to the rocks, screaming as he went. Yuri ran for a moment, and then stopped. Who cared if he got away? He really just wanted them all away.

He began to laugh and then cupped his mouth. "*Maybe you are not the lucky one,*" he yelled after the retreating figure.

He walked back to the boat and looked down at the three bodies leaking their life's blood onto the cold, dark, wet stone.

He shook his head. "Maybe you are the lucky ones," he said.

Yuri looked up at the running man as he scrambled over some fallen boulders, never looking back for an instant. If what Zimchenko had said about some of the things that lived on the land was true, then Yuri doubted many of this pampered lot would be alive in a few days.

The Russian captain began to push the boat toward the water's edge. He stopped and went back to gather the supplies. He stacked everything in the raft, and then changed his mind and took half out. He needed speed more than food, and if everything went to plan, he would be back onboard the *Boris Yeltsin* in the next half day.

He slid the boat into the water, and jumped in. Then he carefully began to row away from the shore. He sat facing the shoreline and dug in and then slowly pulled the water back, trying to make as little noise as possible.

"Good luck," he yelled, and the words echoed down the coastline.

"And good luck to me too." He began to smile. "Today is a good day to be me."

* * *

The three dead crew members of the *Sea Princess* still bled out, heavily at first, until their hearts stopped. Then the blood ran in rivulets to the water, where it joined into a spreading cloud that emanated out into the dark, warm sea.

* * *

Eric sprinted across the rocks. He was nearly out of his mind with fear and shock.

Part of him, a small part, wanted to go back because the guilt of fleeing hung in his gut like a lead weight. But his logical mind said that if he went back he'd be dead as well. He was no fighter. He'd been the onboard chef's assistant. The most he could do was wield a knife to cut up fish for the bouillabaisse.

He tripped in the holes in the rocky platform, and scraped his knees and his elbows, but he didn't stop. He only slowed when he tried to leap over and skirt around the big holes. He'd break his leg if he fell into one of those.

He changed his angle and ran closer to the tidal edge of the rocks where the holes were smaller and easier to jump. He glanced back over his shoulder and saw the inflatable raft heading away from the rocks.

He stopped and put his hands to his head. "Oh no," he whimpered.

They had been given one job. And they couldn't do it. Now he was going to have to find Meena and the rest of the group and tell them they were all marooned. And his entire team was dead. And he had lost the boat. And every one of them would hate him. He hated himself.

He had to find Meena; she would know what to do.

He spun and started to run again. But he only took about half-a-dozen steps before his foot went into a pothole. The first thing he felt was a sensation of softness, as if he had stood on a rubber pillow. But then came the pain as something like a bear trap closed on his leg about mid-calf level.

He howled from the pain and looked down. Inside the pothole, below the water, there was something like a clam or giant barnacle and it had snapped shut on his leg, halfway between his ankle and knee.

Eric punched down at it, but it was like stone and all he did was hurt his knuckles. He reached below the water and tried to insert his fingers in either side of his leg and lever the thing open, but it must have had a huge muscle underneath as it refused to budge. In fact, it closed a little more.

Eric howled again as the bone in his leg began to compress. He dragged out his knife and stuck it into the shell. But, perhaps in response, the thing began to retreat, and pulled further down into its hole. Just a few inches, but it dragged his leg down. And worse, the creature didn't stop disappearing into its sinkhole lair.

"Help. He-*eeelp*!" he screamed.

The massive barnacle-like thing pulled down another few inches. The hole must have been becoming smaller, or the muscles attached to the shell's lips were just contracting more as it closed. The bones in his leg began to splinter.

The creature was too far down for him to try to stab it anymore, and he gripped the top of his thigh with both hands and howled. Tears ran down his cheeks, and he looked beseechingly along the rocks in forlorn hope that he might see a bobbing light returning. But there was nothing but darkness.

Down it went again, and his groin touched the cold rocks. Eric began to feel lightheaded, and the pain was making him feel like he was going to vomit.

Horribly, he knew there were two ways this was going to end if the creature kept retracting lower: one, the thing would compress enough to shear his foot off mid-calf. Or his entire leg at the hip would get separated.

And following that thought, he sunk down another few inches, with the thing tugging now, like a dog holding a rope, and jerking it away.

Just before Eric blacked out he noticed movement from the corner of his eye. Eric turned slowly to see a massive eel at the waterline, its head as big as a large dog's, and almost transparent dagger-like teeth all curving backward in its ugly mouth.

The eyes were round, unblinking, and focused on him. Perhaps this was a deal it had with the mollusk that had played out many times over the years – wait for something to become ensnared by the barnacles – the barnacle gets what it can drag into its burrow. But the eel gets the rest.

It slithered toward him, and the way its weird mouth was shaped made it look like it was smiling.

He pointed his small knife at it. "*Fuck off*," he screamed.

It didn't.

Eric began to cry and looked away as the long and glistening body snaked up out of the water.

* * *

The huge eel knotted and coiled on itself as it twisted the top half of Eric from the leg stuck in the hole. It then retreated quickly back below the water with its prize.

Eric's left leg to the hip, was then tugged down into the barnacle's burrow to be digested at its leisure. Now even more blood entered the water to add to the cloud seeping out into the dark depths.

CHAPTER 27

Jack and Cate sat in silence. Jack licked his dry lips and half turned. "How far do you think we've come?"

Cate looked up from the tiny screen. "Over a mile, easy. Maybe a mile and a half. That feel about right?"

He nodded. "Yeah, I guess."

Cate looked around slowly. In the semi-darkness of the blue-lit environment, they couldn't make out the shoreline, any shoreline, anymore, which was a risk as they had no navigational equipment onboard. Once they were out of sight of land, and with no landmarks or stars, they were sailing by intuition alone.

In addition, with no real sensory equipment, they had no idea how deep the water was beneath them. Or if there was anything bigger moving in the depths.

Perhaps that was a good thing, she thought. They were in a tiny, yellow tin can, in an underground sea, and they knew there were monsters here. Somewhere.

"Look," she said, "nine o'clock."

Jack turned to where she indicated and saw the small island. It was little more than a dark rocky growth rising about twenty feet from the water.

"Maybe the top of a mountain. Or even some sort of reef," he replied. "We'd better keep our eyes peeled, because there might be others just at or below the waterline. Our proximity alert sensor isn't long range, and I wouldn't want to run aground on one of those."

They continued for another thirty minutes and navigated around more of the rocky upthrustings.

"Wonder how big this place is?" she asked.

"Looks like it goes for miles and miles," he replied. He looked over his shoulder. "Bad water . . . remember?"

"I do." She nodded. "Now it makes sense. Where else are monsters going to hide, right?"

Jack nodded slowly. "Makes me wonder what else is in here."

"Thank you, Jack." She swatted the back of his head. "Thinking about that really settles my already frayed nerves."

"Let's have a quick look-see." Jack pressed the button on the control panel and the canopy retracted. Immediately the humid air rushed in at them, and they inhaled its briny warmth. Except for the tiny whine of their motors and the gentle lap of water, it was near silent.

"It feels . . . unreal," Cate said.

"A world within a world." Jack half turned. "Where have I heard that before?"

"Sounds like something from Verne."

"There's another island. Tide must be low, or going lower, and exposing more of them." Jack pointed. "Strange. Nothing on their surface at all."

They went past the rocky outcrop breaching the water surface, and they saw it was just water-slicked black rock.

"There's a bigger one, further out. Good place for us to beach for a while if we want to stretch our legs," he said.

"I think I'd be happy to keep my legs cramped and get this over with." Cate tilted her head back to look up at the twinkling blue lights in the dark ceiling, like sprays of tiny stars. "I feel like yelling to test the echo."

"Please don't."

She grinned. "Don't worry, I'm mad but not stupid."

"And that's why I love you." He laughed as Cate reached forward to rub the back of his neck.

They cruised on for another few minutes across the still seawater. Before them, the blue lights reflected on the surface like tiny decorations. Cate could almost have enjoyed the ambience, and seen the lights as romantic, if not for where they were. Even the warmth was comfortable, and she found herself being lulled into a trance-like state.

Jack tilted his head to the side. "Hey."

"What is it?" Cate blinked a few times, focusing again.

He eased back on the power and the small craft slowed. "Do you hear that?" He tilted his head again. "Listen."

Cate sat forward and concentrated. Then she heard it. "Yeah. What is that? It sounds like a baby crying."

Jack cut the engines and the submersible glided on in silence for a few moments. They were then able to judge where the noise was coming from.

"It's coming from over there. I can see another of those islands. That big one. Let's take a look." Jack powered up the sub again and headed toward it.

As he did, the wash of something pushed the submersible sideways. Both he and Cate looked out to the dark sea but saw nothing.

They soon arrived at the small outcrop that was barely above the water level. Jack went completely around it and then slowed even more.

"There's something on the island. Just up from the water." Jack lifted in his seat a little. "I think . . ." He let out a breath. "Oh my God. You know how you just said it sounded like a baby crying? I think you were right."

"I can't see. What is it?" Cate tried to lift in her rear seat.

"It's a baby, all right. But looks like a baby whale. A calf." He turned and grinned at her.

"A whale calf?" Cate fully stood in her seat. "Oh yeah, I see it. Oh my god, it's huge. It's somehow beached itself." She placed a hand on his shoulder. "Let's go take a look."

Jack glided the sub closer, and once again the wash of something gave them a little push in the dark water.

He looked over the side. "You know what usually follows whales and their calves? Especially when they're in distress?" he asked. "Predators."

"Yeah, and also their worried mothers," Cate replied. "We take a look anyway."

Jack eased the sub in closer to the rocks, and Cate jumped out onto a small, submerged ledge and walked up the rocks to the beached whale.

"It's still damp. Lucky the atmosphere is humid." She laid a hand on it. "Not been here long." She ran her hand up toward its head and crouched next to the large blue eye. "Hi, baby. Don't be scared."

The whale calf was dark, almost black, but had speckles of white over the hide. It made a moaning noise, followed by some clicks and squeaks. As if in answer there came the sound of something like a waterfall from out in the darkness.

"Yeah, I'm guessing mama is out there somewhere. Watching us," Jack said, looking out over the water. "Those pushes we felt. Maybe she wanted us to find her calf."

Cate walked around the stranded animal. "This is amazing. It looks like a sperm whale calf, but it's different. Very different. The jaw is huge. Look at the size of those teeth! And its musculature is very pronounced." She looked up. "This could be a throwback, or . . ."

"Or what?" Jack was standing in the submersible as he tried to keep it close to the rocks without running aground.

"Or an actual remnant species called Livyatan Melvillei." She placed both hands on it. "We've got to save it. And soon. It'll dry out in a few hours, no matter how humid it is in here."

"The calf must have tried to cross the reef and got itself beached by the tide." He sat down. "What's it lying on?"

Cate got lower. "Moss, thankfully. Soft."

"Slippery?" he asked.

"Yeah, it is." She stood. "Can we drag it?"

"We can try." He reached under the console to grab a spare rope, tied it to a metal ring on the submersible and then tossed it to her.

Cate came closer and grabbed it. She walked quickly up the rocks and tied it around the strong tail.

"Ready?" he asked.

She gave him a thumbs-up.

"I'll pull, you push." He started the engine and put it in reverse.

The line tightened, and then lifted the whale's tail out straight. The whale calf made a distressed noise like a sob, and from behind him out in the darkness, there came a thumping and waves buffeted the submersible.

"Easy, mama, just trying to help," Jack said. "I think that's what you wanted."

Cate got to the front and put both hands against the bulbous forehead of the whale, she braced her feet. "Count of three, and two, and . . . *onnnne!*"

Jack lifted the rotations of the propellor and the sub churned water, throwing it forward. The whale calf screamed some more, but it slid a few feet toward the water.

"That's it," Cate yelled. "And again. *Goooo!*"

She yelled through her gritted teeth as she put everything into it this time, and the whale slid several feet, until it got to a lower set of rocks and slid into the water.

Cate quickly ran into the water and, chest deep, undid the rope from the calf's tail. She then came to its front and threw water up over its head.

"There you go, baby." She pushed it, and it headed out backward.

It looked like it was going to sink for a moment, but the tail moved, and it slowly maneuvered itself away from them and vanished into the dark water.

"*Yes.*" Cate raised a fist. "Our good deed for the day is *done.*"

She climbed back out of the water and stood on the shore of the dark pile of rocks for a few more minutes, scanning the water, before Jack called her back into the sub. She waded back out and climbed in, grinning ear to ear.

He reversed and they headed back out. He turned in his seat. "Feel better now?"

She nodded. "Yep. Now we're assured of good luck. I can feel it."

"I'll take me a large serve of that luck stuff, thank you, ma'am," he said.

Cate sighed, leaning back into her seat headrest. "Now, let's get back to dragging a couple of dead bodies around a sunless sea at the bottom of the world."

Jack smiled. "You make it sound so romantic."

They continued dragging their lure for another twenty minutes then, all of a sudden, the submersible was gently pulled backward and turned slowly in the dark water.

"What. Was. That?" Jack whispered.

Cate snatched up the phone with the link to the camera. She swiveled the camera in its large bubble of light.

"Uh, nothing I can see." She stared, her face illuminated by the tiny screen. "Our bait boys are still hanging there as creepy as ever." She looked up. "If this is ever over –"

"*When* it's over," he interjected.

"When this is over, you can tell people we saved a rare species of whale. But let's never mention that we did this thing with the dead bodies as bait, okay?"

"You got it."

She was just lowering the device, when something went past the screen, and kept going past, and *still* kept going past.

Her eyes widened. And then the submersible stopped moving forward as it was pulled by the rope attached to the buoy and its package.

"Something's there," she whispered.

"What? You just said . . . C'mon, Cate, is something there or not?" Jack quickly looked left and right.

"I saw it pass by, I'm sure." She glanced up at him. "But I don't think it was a Megalodon. It was something else." She looked up. "Oh no, do you think it could be the mama?"

"Oh great. So much for doing a good deed and it brings us good luck," he said. "We've just dragged two dead bodies for miles, and instead of attracting one monster, we've caught the attention of another."

"I forgot to mention that the Livyatan whales were a raptorial species. And super predators, who probably even took on Megalodon." She grimaced.

From somewhere out on the dark sea there was the sound of water breaking, and then a wet huff, as if a geyser had erupted.

Both Cate and Jack turned to it but said nothing and just stared for several seconds.

"What do you want to do?" he asked softly.

"I don't know." She couldn't decide if it was best to drop the bait and head back, as they might not have accomplished their primary task – to attract the huge shark that had been attacking them.

And then it hit.

The rope behind them went wire tight, and Cate yelled her surprise and looked down to see the tiny GoPro screen filled with the image of a large, black, and enormously battle-scarred hide. The creature was enormous.

The submersible began to be pulled backward and the buoys had already been tugged under.

"Shit. *Release, release!*" Jack yelled.

The submersible began to pick up speed and, with the canopy open, the immediate risk was that whatever had hold of the line was going to take them down with it.

Cate leaned far out over the side of the submersible and tried to unpick the knot from the ring on the skin of the submersible, but there was no slack for her to get her fingers under.

"*Stupid,*" she yelled at herself for not thinking of this obvious eventuality.

They'd just assumed they'd have time to release the rope before the Megalodon ran with the bait.

Jack spun in his seat, holding the dive knife that he still had strapped to his leg.

"Cut it!" he yelled.

She grabbed it from his hand and leaned out again to saw through the rope.

They felt the sub tilt. "*It's going down!*" Jack yelled.

Cate sawed and cut furiously, and just as water started to come over the cabin compartment rim, she cut the rope enough for the rest to snap.

The line whipped away and vanished beneath the dark water, and the submersible immediately stopped its backslide.

"That's it, closing canopy," Jack said. Water already sloshed around their ankles as he punched the button, and the clear shield passed up and over their heads. "And getting the hell out of here. Diving now." He turned the craft, pushing the stick forward as he powered downward.

Cate eased back into her chair and leaned her head back, feeling her heart race, and waiting for her breathing to return to normal.

"You see anything back there?" he asked.

She sat forward and noticed that the small screen she held in her lap showed that the lights on the buoy were still on, even though it was now deep below the surface.

She frowned down at the screen. She could see movement. "Wait a minute, yeah, I think . . ."

"Got something?" Jack asked.

"Whatever it was that grabbed the bait is still there."

"There? Where is *there*?" He looked one way then the other. "Can't see anything. All clear behind us?"

Cate spun around and looked out into the dark water behind them, trying to spot the buoy lights.

"Nothing following." She lifted in her seat and tried to peer below them, looking over the edge at starboard, then changing to do the same at port.

Then she saw it.

"Oh shit, got something."

She saw a dot of light out in the void of darkness.

"There's either a tiny bio-lit creature out there below and to port side. Or that's our bait buoy keeping pace with us." She narrowed her eyes. "It's maybe several hundred yards out."

She looked back down at the screen. "Whatever has got our bait is big and dark, so not one of the corpse-pale Megalodons." She frowned. "The camera is too close and the creature is too big to get a good look at it."

"Well, if it took the bait, it's a carnivore. And the camera was about twenty feet from the bait, so if it can't capture any sort of perspective image, then that says to me it's way too big to fuck with." He turned the small u-shaped wheel. "If it's at port, then we're going to starboard."

The small submersible turned in an arc in the water, and Jack pushed its speed to the limit. Without the drag of the bodies, he immediately got it up to about six knots.

Cate crabbed around in her seat, and watched the dot of light, which was now directly behind them.

"Still there?" Jack asked.

"Yep. Can't tell yet whether it's receding or keeping pace with us."

"Keep watching it. And pray. I do not want that big sucker taking an interest in our little tin can," Jack said. "Because this is as fast as we can go."

"Will do." Cate stayed twisted in her seat. After a moment she rested her chin on her fist. The light stayed constant. "What's it doing? If the light is staying on, it means it's not eating its prize, it's just dragging it along."

Minutes went by, and the light stayed exactly the same size. It shouldn't have. By now, five minutes had passed, and they would have put a quarter mile between them and the thing. It should have been a speck, not that constant dot of light.

"Still there," she whispered.

"Damn," Jack said softly.

She frowned. Suddenly the light seemed to grow, and then it winked out.

She straightened. "Hey."

"What is it?" he asked.

"It just sort of, went out." She turned slowly trying to spot it.

"Did it fade, move suddenly, or did it just switch off?" Jack asked.

"Just went off. Suddenly," Cate replied. "That's good, right?"

Jack cursed under his breath. "Might mean we've lost it."

"But you don't think so." She turned to him.

"It might mean the buoy and lights finally broke free. Or the creature ate it." He sighed. "I've got everything crossed because, whatever it is, it's now invisible to us."

Cate groaned, and then after a few moments sat forward. "So what's the plan seeing we don't have the lure anymore, and might not have lured the Megalodon?"

"Our mission is over." Jack spoke over his shoulder. "We can't do a thing for the people that have been beached. We have no weapons and no way to pick up passengers, other than cramming one extra person into the rear of the sub."

Jack momentarily looked down at his controls. "So the plan is still the original plan. We head for the cave mouth leading out of here and we link up with Sonya."

"How's the energy level?" she asked.

Jack checked the battery storage. "Not as good as I'd like. We're not using the thermal systems for warmth so we're saving on that. In fact –" He pulled back on the wheel and the submersible gently rose in the water. "– we'll take it back to the surface and pop the lid. That way we can switch off the circulating air and save even more power."

"Is that wise?" Cate asked. "Means from below we're visible on the surface. And we'll generate a wake."

"If we had a full charge I wouldn't. But worst case is we run out of power before making land." He glanced back at the controls again. "As long as we don't need to push it we should be fine. However, we'll need to stop and let the batteries recharge soon."

Seconds later they breached, and Jack opened the canopy.

"Let's just get out of here. I want to see the sky again." Cate looked up at the blue glowing ceiling. She noticed that whatever was causing the luminescence was thicker in some places than others. She also thought she saw it moving and undulating, like seaweed in a gentle current. Or maybe because something was moving through it.

Her mind started to conjure images of living things launching themselves down from up there to try to land on them. She shivered and blew air through her pressed lips.

"Okay back there?" Jack asked.

"Yeah, no, I just . . ." She sighed loudly. "I just wanna go home."

"Me too," he replied. "And we will. Our job is done here."

From somewhere out in the darkness, there came that telltale whooshing noise and the sound of water falling.

"That's a whale spout," Cate said, "I'm sure of it now."

They sat in silence, just listening for the sound to repeat. Then the submersible moved sideways in the water, and Jack grabbed the wheel to stabilize them. "*Whoa* there."

"What was that?" she asked.

"Crosscurrent, I think. I'm shutting the canopy."

"A crosscurrent?" She gently pushed at the back of his head. "Really?"

"Probably. Maybe," he replied. "I just wish this baby had more electronic eyes and ears. I hate driving blind in the dark."

The submersible was moved in the water again, this time from the opposite side.

"I felt that," Cate said softly.

"Yep. Still there."

"Another crosscurrent?" she asked, already knowing it undoubtedly wasn't.

"Dive or no dive?" he asked.

"Take it down a hundred feet," Cate replied. "Might give us a little more protection from an ambush from below and we won't be outlined against the blue lights from overhead."

"Good a plan as any." He pushed the small wheel forward and they submerged.

Jack leveled off at a hundred feet and they moved through the underground sea like a tiny spaceship in the dark void of space. After a while he shook his head. "I can't keep flying blind. I've got to take a look now and then or we're liable to run into something when I'm traveling at top speed. I'm not even sure how deep it is here. We could bottom out."

"I don't like it," Cate replied. "But I don't see we have any choice. Maybe flick the beams on and off, strobe-like, to try to break up our pattern."

Jack flicked on the lights and Cate shrieked.

The proximity alert screamed in the small cockpit. Right beside them, so close they could have reached out and touched it, was an enormous body. It was dark, maybe blue-black, with a few speckles of white, and heavily scarred with a few crusted barnacles making it seem as ancient as time itself. As it moved past them the eye appeared and swiveled to look in at the tiny creatures inside the plastic and steel bubble.

"That's not a meg's eye," Jack whispered. "Or any sort of shark's eye."

"Whale. Livyatan," Cate said in little more than breaths. "I knew it."

The eye was the size of a manhole cover and was shaped more like a human's eye. It wasn't the soulless black orb of the Megalodon shark, but instead, there almost seemed intelligence there.

"What'll we do?" Cate said.

"Nothing. We just keep going forward and minding our own business." Jack slowly turned away from it. "This is probably the creature that took the bait, so . . ."

"I get it," she said. "Let's hope it's not looking for more of those tasty, soft human things."

It veered into them, and the sub jostled in the water. "Hey!" Jack wrestled with the controls until he got the submersible aligned again. "Come on, big fella, we're just a floating speck minding our own business here."

The creature began to rise beside them, and for a moment they were close to the mouth. It was long, huge, and the teeth were tusks – each around two and a half feet long.

"Yeah, that's our lost whale," Cate replied.

"Is it mama?" Jack asked.

"If it is, I hope it remembers what we did for junior."

Jack continued to stare. "I never knew the carnivorous whales got this big."

"Like I said, raptorial whales. And they're not this big now." Cate almost breathed the words as the massive creature lifted toward the surface to leave them behind. "But they were once."

"The Livyatan," Jack said.

"Correct." Cate craned her neck to watch it vanish in the darkness.

Their tiny submersible was buffeted by the turbulence from the sweep of its massive paddle-like rear fin.

"About nine million years ago a species of sperm whale evolved that was one of the largest predators to ever exist on our planet. *Livyatan melvillei*. The name was inspired by the Leviathan sea monster. It rivaled, and probably competed with, the Megalodon."

"It's a monster," he said. "And here it is, alive and kicking."

"Remember, we once thought Megalodons were extinct."

"There have always been monsters – you just have to know where to look." Jack half turned. "Maybe they've been out there the whole time. There are always stories of boats being attacked or sighting huge, oversized whales. They're probably smart enough to avoid us."

"The thing is, sure it was an apex predator that preyed on other whales, seals, and even Megalodon, but from what I remember of fossil remains, they only grew to about sixty-five feet. That creature looked bigger. A lot bigger." She sat back.

"I thought about eighty to ninety feet, give or take a few barnacles on the tail fluke," Jack said.

"Looked about right," Cate replied. "Maybe we were too small or uninteresting to eat."

"Here's hoping."

They continued in silence for another fifteen minutes before Jack half turned again.

"Why was it bigger?" he asked.

"Good question," she replied. "Probably gigantism, where a very large body size is an important trait to achieve or maintain competitive superiority."

She looked out the window at the dark water, but only saw her own reflection. She thought she looked pale. And frightened.

There was something else she remembered from her research days. "There's a biological rule applied to some aberrations, giants, called Foster's Rule, or Island Syndrome, whereby creatures trapped in a limited environment grow huge. It helps them compete more effectively. Also, territorialism can play a part. A study on islands determined that bird and reptile species that were territorial tended to be larger on the island compared to the mainland. In territorial species, larger size makes individuals better able to compete to defend their territory."

"Maybe somewhere there's a hidden island with giant humans." Jack briefly looked over his shoulder with raised eyebrows.

"After seeing this place, who knows. But the fact is, evolution favors the bigger, stronger species."

"Yep, and here we are, just a couple of unevolved, normal-sized human beings in a land of giants." He chuckled.

"Yeah, but we're the ones with the big brains." She grinned. "Most of us."

He laughed. "Flatterer."

"It makes me wonder though."

"Wonder what?" Jack asked.

"Makes me wonder what else down here has been subjected to the same rules of gigantism. Maybe the Megalodon and the Livyatan aren't even the biggest baddest things in here."

"I'm not even going to give that any thought." Jack exhaled. "I don't think my already tattered nerves could take it."

The propellor rotation slowed a little and their console lights dimmed. A warning light blinked.

"Ah, shit no," Jack said under his breath.

"That can't be good." She craned forward.

"It's not. Remember when I said we'd be fine as long as we didn't push it?" He half turned. "We just pushed it trying to outrun mama whale. The power is about to give up on us."

"How long will it take to recharge?"

Jack exhaled through puffed cheeks. "A full charge will take six to eight hours. But we should be fine with a half charge." He looked about. "Find me one of those little islands. That'll be perfect."

CHAPTER 28

Meena and her six crew members headed down along the coastline. The rock shelf had ended a few hundred yards back, and now they edged along a line of crumbled rock that had fallen from the cliff wall maybe thousands of years ago.

There were small waves here that moved differently – they were full and didn't break in any shallows, making her think the water was deeper. But it was impossible to tell as the sea remained as dark and ominous as ever.

The small group walked in a line, with one of their mechanics, Gino, out at the front by a few paces, then Meena, then came Kathleen and Benjamin, Aaron, and then Phillipa, and finally Rachel. *It was a good and spirited team*, she thought. Aaron was one of their best engineers, Kathleen was the ship's medical officer and a pragmatic thinker, and the rest were all positive personalities and physically fit.

Meena still had the thermal vision goggles in her pack and held her flashlight in her hand but hadn't switched it on. It was just light enough to see from the overhead blue glow, but there were shadows everywhere, which she didn't like.

She had told everyone to stay well back from the water, but now they needed to cross one last length of boulders that went right to the water's edge, and there seemed to be a surf running here.

"Stop," she said, and Gino turned.

Behind her the team caught up and also waited.

"What is it?" Gino asked. "Have we gone far enough?"

"No, not yet. There're no safe camping sites I can see here." Some of the group were already looking a little tired. "Let's take five."

A few people sat down and spoke among themselves, and a few wandered off, exploring. Kathleen seemed focused on the rock wall at the rear of the platform and after a few minutes headed toward it.

"Meena," she called out.

Meena looked to her, but the medical officer just motioned her closer. When Meena arrived she noticed that Kathleen's lips were pressed into a thin line.

"I think we have a problem." She pointed. "Check this out."

Meena looked from the woman to the wall. She walked along the rock face but saw nothing out of the ordinary – there were a few crustaceans clinging there, some seaweed, and a few tiny many-legged creatures that resembled long crabs.

"I don't get it." She turned. "What am I looking for?"

"Oh you're looking at it, all right, but you just don't see it." Kathleen stepped even closer. "See this here?" Her finger nearly touched a shellfish clinging to the rock like an eight-inch oyster. "That's a tidal bivalve. And right here is a form of seaweed that can tolerate drying for short periods but is usually in water."

"Oh, oh, oh." Meena shook her head.

"*Now* you're getting it." Kathleen lowered her hand.

"This is a tidal zone, and it's low tide." Meena stepped back. "Just how high will it go?"

Kathleen lifted her gaze. "I'm seeing discoloration up to about seven feet." She turned. "We need to find somewhere a lot higher, or we'll all be swimming in a few hours."

Meena stepped back, taking in the tide line. Kath was right, the entire rock shelf would be underwater. And her priority to keep them safe was to avoid the water.

"Okay, then we have no choice." She turned away. "We need to climb this pile of rubble and see what's around the headland."

"One more thing?" Kathleen said.

Meena turned. "Give me some good news this time."

Kathleen hiked her shoulders. "What about the others at the raft?"

Meena looked along the rock platform toward where she had left their four other crew members, as if she could see them from this distance. She shook her head. "We don't have time to check on them. At least they've got a boat. We don't."

"We might not be back until the next low tide," Kathleen added. "Should we send a runner to tell them?"

Meena thought it over. It would be good to give the other crew members a heads up. But the risks were starting to pile up.

"No, we can't split our teams further. Besides, that Russian guy is probably lurking somewhere, so I couldn't send a single person back, it'd need to be two or three people. And we don't know what we're yet to face."

"Yeah, I get that. I agree with all your decisions." Kathleen nodded and then walked away from the rock face. "That means we've got about six hours before the tide turns again."

Meena looked up. "I don't even know if it's night or day anymore."

"It's night, at least outside," Kathleen said. "No wonder we're all beat."

"Yeah, but we need to find somewhere safe before we break for camp – somewhere dry, sheltered, and defendable. How hard can that be?" Meena turned away and clapped her hands once. "Okay, people, we need to keep moving. This is a tidal zone, and if we stay here when the next high tide rolls in we're underwater."

"What about the others?" Gino stood.

"They have a boat, and four good brains. They'll be fine. They'll be able to float, we can't. So let's get going."

Gino gave a cheerful salute, turned, and moved quickly along the rocks.

They headed toward a huge rockfall cutting off their shelf from what was beyond, and Gino began to scale up some of the larger rocks. At the bottom of the pile the stones were slimy and made for a treacherous climb. The upside was that it glued the rocks together so there was no debris coming loose.

Gino was the best climber, but it still took him twenty minutes to reach the top. He stood there, hands on his hips, turning slowly.

In a few more minutes Meena and the others had joined him. He turned to her. "Am I dreaming? Is that what I think it is?" He began to laugh.

"A forest." Meena snorted in disbelief. "Underground."

Kathleen grabbed her arm. "It's big. We don't know what lives in there."

Meena nodded. "I know, I know. But we can't stay on top of these boulders, and the shoreline there looks above the tidal zone." She turned. "If things go to plan, then Sonya will be initiating the distress beacon anytime now. Then a day for a location plane, followed by a rescue ship in a few more days. All up, we've got to prepare for being stranded here for nearly a week."

"And if things don't go to plan?" Kathleen asked.

"Then we might be here until someone finds us." Meena half smiled. "Whenever that might be." She took a few steps and then paused to look back. "Coming?"

Kathleen nodded. "Sure. At least it's above the high-tide line."

* * *

Gino, Meena, and Kathleen leaped from the rocks onto dark, sandy soil. A few moments later they were followed by Benjamin, Aaron, Phillipa, and Rachel.

They continued for a few minutes more before finally stopping on a grassy plain just before the stand of tree-like growths.

"No one goes anywhere by themselves," Meena said. "Everyone stays in twos or threes."

"We aren't the first ones here." Rachel pointed to the ground where there were a couple of parallel drag marks.

"I'm betting that was the raft the Russians made to get to the *Sea Princess*." Kathleen followed the tracks with her eyes. "They cut the wood from in there."

"So what's the plan?" Gino said.

"Survival mode," Benjamin replied. "We have some supplies, but we need to find alternate food and water sources."

"Plus shelter." Aaron looked up. "Though I doubt cold or rain is going to be an issue here."

"Good suggestions," Meena said. "Anyone here know any forest-craft?"

There was silence for a few moments, before Phillipa raised a hand. "I used to go camping with my dad. We went hunting and fishing."

"Then you're it." Meena smiled. "We need to find the best places to hunt, gather food, find shelter, and make fires." She clicked her fingers. "Gino and Benjamin, you're collecting wood. Aaron and Phillipa, scout for possible best places to hunt or trap game. If you find a stream, then fish is good."

"Fish?" Gino thumbed over his shoulder. "We've got an entire sea behind us."

"I know." Meena gave him a half smile. "But I want to avoid going anywhere near that for now."

She looked over the brooding forest. Right now, it was dead silent. They were already in a blue-muted twilight, but the tall, weird-looking trees cast even more shadows.

"Kathleen, Rachel, and I will look for a camping spot. Twenty minutes and then back here. *No excuses.*" She was about to turn away, but then paused. "And leave a trail so you can remember which way you went."

The group split up.

Meena watched the other two groups head into the forest or along the shoreline. She had a knot in her stomach but reminded herself that at least they were dry, and the place looked promising for a campsite. Plus it wouldn't be inundated by the tide.

She headed into the forest, with Kathleen and Rachel behind her. The ground squashed wetly under their feet.

"It's like a bog. Must be a water source further in the forest," Rachel said. "We need to find somewhere higher or create a platform above the ground to stay dry."

"Let's head further in. I think it slopes upward there." Meena had switched on her flashlight and shone it into the darkest areas beneath the straight pole-like growths. She had at first thought they were trees, but the bark on some was more like fibrous cork, and others had long, brown fibers like hair or fur.

Walking past a small pool of stagnant water, she moved her light over the ground, and she saw foot-wide glistening trails. They ran throughout the forest but she had no idea what could have caused them.

In another fifteen minutes they found an area with a small hill at its center that had a ground cover like tightly woven clover. Meena crouched and touched the ground with her fingertips. "Good," she said as she stood. "Dry."

Over the hill there were more pools of standing water, and the trees were a little more stunted with thicker undergrowth.

"Weirdest forest I've ever seen," Kathleen said. "No birds, no insects, no nothing." She stepped closer to something that looked like a fern, but its fronds were bulbous like a seaweed.

"If I didn't know better, I'd say this was more like a fungus rather than a plant." She turned about. "In fact, everything here looks like some sort of ancient form of lichen or fungus."

Kathleen looked up at the leafless tops of the tree-like growths. "Could be a prototaxite. And everything around me looks like some sort of survivor species from the late Ordovician period." She half smiled. "When fungus ruled the lands."

"Old?" Rachel asked.

"Oh yeah, over four hundred million years old." Kathleen put her hands on her hips, still looking up. "These guys were the tallest things in the primordial moss forests; when there was just a single global landmass, which Antarctica was part of."

"Kinda makes sense," Rachel said. "What else but fungus would thrive in a humid, lightless environment?"

"Smells a bit like a drain. But we can deal with that," Meena said.

Kathleen went to the forest edge and found a stick and a fist-sized rock. She returned to the top of the hill and reached into her pocket for a small handkerchief. She tied it to one end of the stick then she hammered it into the ground with the rock. "I claim this land on behalf of the *Sea Princess* and all who sailed within her."

"And may all her bounty and good fortune come to us." Meena grinned and saluted. "Now that we've found our campsite, let's round up the others and bring them back here. I'd love to catch a few hours' sleep."

* * *

The trio headed back the way they'd come, and the silence and darkness returned. But from deeper inside the forest eyes watched them.

Lots of eyes.

* * *

"No fish, and no game we could find." Phillipa shrugged. "We didn't even see any sign of something living here." She looked over her shoulder at the dark sea momentarily. "If we are going to be here for a while, we might need to try the sea after all."

Meena nodded. "Okay, we'll hold that thought. We have supplies for now. We can check again tomorrow. At least now we have a site to use as a base camp."

Gino and Benjamin let a pile of fibrous-looking woody material fall at their feet. "Wasn't easy getting this. Lots of fallen debris, but most of it is too damp to burn. This is the best we could do."

"Then a smaller fire it is," Meena announced. "We've found a suitable campsite. We'll head there, maybe find some more dry stuff, and then rest a while. Then a few of us can head back for the others so they can bring the boat around, while the rest do another foraging expedition."

Meena, Rachel, and Kathleen led them back through the forest to the clearing on the small hill. It was about a hundred feet around – almost like an island in the sea of thick, marshy undergrowth.

"Smells like a swamp," Benjamin remarked.

"Yeah, methane, probably from rotting vegetation. Unlikely to be drinkable water around here," Gino said.

"That's also on our list for tomorrow." Meena sighed. Their task list for tomorrow was an arm and a leg long already.

"Task one: Gino and Benji, you head back and round up the others," she said.

"Will we sail the raft or carry it?" Gino asked.

"Good question." Meena thought quickly. "Carry it, so take Aaron as well."

Aaron groaned. "That thing weighs around three hundred pounds. Be a lot easier for us to push it into the water and motor it."

Meena slowly shook her head. "The monster is still out there. I know it'll get heavy and it'll be a struggle to carry it up the obstacles but humor me here."

The men sighed but nodded. Meena then pointed to the small stack of wood. They'd managed to find more dry material, but there'd be no big bonfire.

"Let's get that fire started."

Rachel gathered a small section of the dry, woody material together. She teased out some of the hairy fibers and used the lighter to start a flame on the edge of it. The material caught quickly, and she blew on it to give it more oxygen.

The flames got bigger, and she sat back and added larger and larger pieces until the fire had taken.

"What's for dinner?" Benjamin asked.

Gino opened the stores and sorted through some of the cans. "Tuna fish or sardines. Peaches or apple sauce. A-*aaand*, beans or asparagus." He grinned. "A feast."

Meena lifted a finger. "We're only opening a few tonight, and eating sparingly. We're all on a diet until we catch something."

"Asparagus, *yech*." Phillipa stuck out her tongue.

"Shark repellent," Benjamin said as he held the can. "Did you know they used to give Second World War pilots from aircraft carriers two tins of asparagus juice. If they were shot down over water, while waiting to be rescued, they were supposed to drink it. Then when they pissed out the asparagus pee, the scent was supposed to deter sharks."

"Is that *really* true?" Rachel asked.

"Scout's honor, go ahead and google it . . ." He held up two fingers by his ear in a scout salute and grinned. "Oops. I mean when you get back."

"One tin between two people. Try and pick something you both like," Meena said. "But if we get hungry enough, anything is going to be satisfying."

The group ate slowly, trying to savor the spartan meal. They sipped from bottled water, and then Gino managed to get the small blaze going again. The fire pushed back the shadows, and seemed to dry the humidity, at least on their faces.

After another few minutes of sitting in a circle, staring into the blaze, Meena felt her eyelids grow heavy. But there was one task left.

"We sleep for just four hours. I want a watch changing every hour. I'll go first shift with . . ." She looked along their weary faces. "Kath." Kathleen nodded. "Who wants to go next?"

It was Gino and Benjamin, then Aaron and Phillipa, followed by Rachel doing the last and shortest shift. She was happy to go solo, but promised to scream to high heaven if she even saw a mouse.

The group settled in, and Meena took the empty cans to the tree line and, using the toe of her boot, made a small depression in the wet earth and then tossed the cans in. She scraped the dirt back over them.

The group slept, and just Meena and Kathleen sat in silence, each lost in their own thoughts. Meena hoped the other group was okay, and she prayed they were on the rocks safe and sound when they went back for them tomorrow.

But she also prayed that Sonya managed to make it out and contact the outside world. There was no way she wanted this to be their new home.

She blinked her eyes, trying to moisten them. Her lids were heavy, but she refused to let them close, and pinched her thighs to sting herself into wakefulness.

After what seemed like an eternity, Gino sat up, and nodded to her.

The shift changed and in seconds Meena was asleep.

* * *

It followed the scent and soon found where the tins were buried. It slid into the loose soil to taste them. The oil in the tuna tins excited it, and it moved its broad, sticky tongue over every speck, drawing it all in.

It then lifted itself back out of the soil and its unblinking eyes watched the group of animals. More of its kind began to appear, and it knew if it waited too long the others would claim the feast.

It slid silently forward, picking which one to taste first.

* * *

Gino threw another handful of dry fibrous material onto the fire and it caught and began to burn. He saw that Benjamin's head was lolling forward and he laughed – *No staying power*, he thought.

He understood though. They were all tired, and he was looking forward to grabbing another hour's sleep when Aaron and Phillipa took over.

He checked his watch and saw he had another forty-five minutes to go, so he grabbed up the fire material, balled some of it up and tossed it onto the flames. He did this several times, watching the small balls of hairy bark catch fire, unfurl, and flare up briefly, to then crinkle down to nothing.

Over the other side of the fire he heard Rachel let out a muffled groan in her sleep. His eyes slid toward her and he tried to work out what he was seeing. Two eyes on long slimy stalks rose from her head. No, not her head. Her actual head was covered in something gray and muscular that glistened in the firelight.

Rachel made the muffled sound again, like someone had a hand over her mouth, and her body began to tremble. Then another slimy pad of flesh crept up over her waist and then two more eyes popped up, on stalks.

"Hey." Gino shot to his feet, feeling giddy from fear. "*Hey!*" he shouted and pointed.

"*Huh?*" Benjamin woke. "What?"

The others started to wake. And then Aaron screamed.

Gino was still pointing at Rachel, but he glanced at Aaron who also had something that looked like a crash helmet attached to his back.

"It fucking burns!" he yelled.

"*Ra-Ra-Rachel,*" Gino spluttered.

Meena, wide awake now, also screamed and then everyone was on their feet. Gino looked around and saw that, coming out of the forest from the swamp area, were things like giant snails.

Their pad feet were three foot long and left glistening trails behind them.

"Get off, you bastard." He stepped around the fire and launched a boot at the one clamped on Rachel's face. The boot connected with it, and with a sticky, sucking sound the creature was dislodged.

But Gino's eyes went wide, and he felt his gorge rise as he tasted his meal of tuna again. There was little skin left on one side of Rachel's face, and her eye socket was empty. The giant snail had been liquefying and digesting the skin off her face and sucking it up.

"Don't let them touch you." He reached down into the fire and picked up a burning stick then jammed it into the eye stalks of the other creature on her waist. The bulbs simply retracted down the stalks, and the fire sizzled when it touched the slimy body.

"*They're eating her.*" He sobbed as he jabbed at the thing again.

"Get them away," Meena shouted as she began to kick the things away from the group. Some pulled back into their shells and the kicks managed to roll them back down the slope. But others reared up, as if attempting to latch onto the legs of the people as they struck out at them.

Gino dragged more burning debris from the fire and scattered it around, creating a little circle of flames which repelled the slimy things immediately. After another moment, all that remained were the sticky sliding sounds retreating into the darkness.

They all stood breathing heavily, shoulders hiked and holding anything that could act as a weapon. Rachel was lying on the ground, unmoving, and Aaron writhed in pain.

"What, the fuck, were they?" Benjamin said through clenched jaws.

"What the fuck is right." Phillipa pointed, her face screwed in anger. "You were supposed to be on watch."

Gino held his hands up. "We were. Those things crept up on us out of the dark, from nowhere. We never saw or heard them coming."

"Not from nowhere." Meena pointed to the slimy trails all leading into the swampy area. She turned back to Phillipa, and then the rest. "No recriminations, everyone. We're in a dangerous and alien place, and strange and horrible things are going to happen. Things we can't be ready for."

"I fucking hate this place." Phillipa balled her fists and shut her eyes tight.

"Kathleen." Meena sighed. "You're a doctor and the closest thing we've got to a biology expert. What were they?"

"Gastropods," Kathleen said. "Like giant snails." She knelt by Aaron who was now pale and shivering.

She rolled him over and several of the group sucked in a breath or turned away. The back of his shirt was dripping in slime and mostly gone. As was much of the flesh. His back now showed the raw bones of his rib cage and a few strips of deteriorated muscle.

"They must exude some sort of toxin that numbs their prey." She gently lay him back down and felt the pulse in his neck. "Then, like most gastropods, they exude their stomachs through their mouths and start to digest their meal in situ."

"That's gross." Gino wiped his eyes.

Meena knelt by Rachel, and after a moment pulled the hood of her jacket closed over her face. "She's gone."

"Oh god, no." Gino crouched and put his face in his hands. After a moment he looked up. "I'm sorry."

Meena shook her head. "It's not your fault. I chose this campsite. We should have done a more thorough check."

"Rubbish," Kathleen shot back. "*We* chose this site. And who could have guessed that lurking in the swamp were giant carnivorous snails?" She looked about. "For all we know, everywhere down here is going to be like this. Like you just said, we're in a dangerous and alien place, and strange and horrible things are going to happen."

"The fire scared them off," Benjamin said.

"Then we need more fires," Meena declared.

"And more weapons," Phillipa said. "We can't be trying to kick things away that try and attack us."

"Spears," Gino suggested. "We can make some spears."

"Tomorrow," Meena said. "How's Aaron?" she asked.

"Still unconscious." Kathleen used a thumb to roll his eyelid back. "It's like he's been drugged, and for now it's numbing the pain." She stood. "And that's a good thing."

Meena nodded. "I think these snail things are gone for tonight. We need to get some rest."

"*Are you kidding?*" Phillipa's mouth dropped open. "I'm never sleeping again."

"That's fine because it's your watch," Meena said. She was exhausted, but with Rachel now dead, and Aaron out cold, she couldn't let Phillipa be on watch by herself.

Meena sucked in a deep breath. "And I'll watch with you. Two more hours until the tide starts to turn. Then we head back."

"Will this still be our base camp?" Benjamin asked.

"Maybe. We can scout for a better place when we've got all the team back together. For now we're not moving." She nodded toward the fire. "Stoke the flames up, it's going to be our best friend while we're down here."

Phillipa stared into the fire. "Monsters in the water, monsters on the land. I want out."

No shit, Meena thought and sat with her back to the fire as Gino and Benjamin threw more debris on it, causing the flames to grow.

Meena felt the comforting heat on her back and looked across to Aaron, whose breathing was deep but ragged. *We've been here less than a few hours, and I've lost one of our crew, and another one is severely injured. I'm not doing my job of keeping everyone safe*, she thought glumly.

"You okay?" Kathleen came and sat next to her.

"Not really." Meena shook her head. "How the hell are we supposed to last a week when this happens on the first day?"

"We will. And you're doing a great job holding us all together." Kathleen reached out to grip her forearm and squeezed it. "I'm not tired, so I'll do the watch with you," she said.

"Thank you." Meena's mouth twitched into a brief and fragile smile. "Each watcher take a section and face outward. Everyone else, try and get some rest. Tomorrow is going to be a big day."

CHAPTER 29

Sonya motioned with her hand for Jorge to steer them closer to the rock wall. Chekov looked back and over his shoulder at the cavern.

"We found ancient cave drawings back there. About the giant shark, whales, and something with many arms." He turned back. "So others were here before us."

"How long before?" Sonya asked.

Chekov shrugged. "They were very old. Looked to me like it was done by the first people in South America. So maybe a long time. Who knows, perhaps even before there was ice here."

"Or maybe when it was last open to the outside world." Sonya continued to stare out over the dark water. "We have to get across the deep area to get to the cave mouth." She turned to Chekov. "It was where we saw a wrecked boat. A Russian boat."

Chekov grunted. "I thought this. Two of our crewmen were meant to return to the ship and bring us back supplies. But no supplies came." He looked up with a flat smile. "I know, stupid question but was there . . . ?"

"No, no survivors." Sonya turned away. "But it tells me the Megalodon hunted them all the way here."

"Hopefully, Cate and Jack lured it away this time. If they did, then it would be miles from here by now," Jorge said.

"Unless there are more," Chekov replied.

"There will definitely be more," Sonya said. "I'm betting there's a healthy breeding population in here. But they're very territorial, so one large one will have a huge patch and keep the others away." She shrugged. "Anyway, this is why we came." She turned to the two men. "One more thing. If we do end up in the water, then best to try and swim out to the communication buoy. Priority is to make contact with home base, no matter what. Until then, we're invisible."

"And if it's just me left?" Chekov grinned.

"Then it's your lucky day," Sonya said.

"Should we stay close to the wall?" Jorge asked.

Sonya shook her head. "Not this time. There's breaking water and shallows. We're going to need to get around the cave rim – shortest route is a straight line."

"Slow and silent," Chekov said.

Jorge drew in a deep breath and started to row. Sonya was at the front of the raft and tried to look everywhere at once, but it was impossible to see even a single foot below the ink-black water.

Chekov looked behind and tried to spot anything on the surface – a splash, a fin, a V-shaped wave signaling an approach of something beneath the water, or a huge conical snout watching them. So far it was smooth except for a slight surge pouring in through the cave mouth creating a tidal current.

"All clear back here," Chekov said.

"Are we going backward?" Sonya asked.

"Hard . . . to row," Jorge replied.

"Let me help." Chekov took one of the oars and together both men rowed hard for around fifteen minutes. They got to the center of the open water area that they thought preceded the cave mouth.

"Where is it?" Sonya turned about.

She flicked on the powerful flashlight and shone it toward the cliff wall. She saw that the tidal flow coming in through the cave mouth was creating a significant surge. If she was in the *Sea Princess*, with its powerful engines running, it would barely have registered but in a small raft, especially as they weren't using their motor, it was going to be too hard to row against.

"Oh *no, no, no*." She exhaled. "Bastard."

"Have we gone past it?" Jorge asked, his face bathed in sweat.

"No, it's here." She nodded toward a section of the cliff wall. "But the rising high tide has covered it."

"That's a huge tide," Chekov remarked. "The cave might still open up further in, but we can't get under the lip now. Should we wait it out?" He looked around. "Wait for the turn of the tide?" He turned back to the dark interior of the massive cave for a moment before facing Sonya again.

Sonya rested her hands on the gunwale and looked down into the dark water. "Every minute we're in here, there's a chance more of my people will die." She looked toward the spot where the cave mouth once was. They were so close, and the tantalizing pull of freedom felt so strong it was like a physical force.

She finally turned to the two men. "We're in a small boat so we only need to wait until it drops enough to get under the rim."

"Look at the cave wall – the tidal mark. It's still coming in." Chekov stopped rowing, and then Jorge did the same. The small boat was pushed backward.

"We wait." She sighed. "We have no choice." She turned. "Let's hope the others found somewhere safe."

CHAPTER 30

"There." Cate pointed.

"Looking good," Jack replied. He edged the wheel around and headed toward the rocky outcrop.

He had already shut down many of their instruments, but with such a low remaining charge the submersible was barely moving in the water.

"Will we make it?" she asked.

"Just. I think we only have a few minutes of power left. So this is a just-in-time stop." He sat straight in his seat as he chose the best place to land. There was a flat surface on one side of the mini island, and he hoped the water was shallow enough for them to step out and not have to swim.

Then he'd need to secure the submersible, and switch on the self-charging systems for the battery.

When he was within fifty feet of the rocks the submersible simply powered itself down and they glided for another dozen feet until they were just a bobbing metal shell a dozen feet from the shoreline.

Jack looked over the side, then grabbed a flashlight and shone it down into the water. "It's too deep. This island must be like a pencil uplift from the bottom – a shaft of rock rising from the depths – and this is the top. Looks like we're going to have to paddle."

They had no oars, so with Cate on one side and Jack on the other, they dug their arms in and pulled the water back. It moved the craft forward about an inch a stroke until there was a thump from below and then a grating sound.

"On it," Jack said as the submersible started to bounce away. He leaped out, and onto the narrow rock shelf below the surface. He stretched and held on to the submersible and dragged it closer to the flat rocks, which were just under an inch or two of water. He held tight to the side and dragged it in.

Even though it wasn't a large sub, and was floating, it still weighed a few thousand pounds and needed to be gently held against the rocks.

"I've got it. Out you get," he said.

It scraped some paint, but Jack held tight as Cate jumped out.

"Nothing." Cate looked around. "Just a rock sticking out of deep water."

"I'll see to this." He half turned. "You put the coffee on."

"You brought some?" She grinned. "And what about some eggs and bacon, or perhaps lox and bagels?"

"Stop that." He laughed as he flipped open the recharging bay. "My stomach is growling just at the thought."

The submersible lifted a little and scraped against the rocks again.

"Easy on the paintwork, this is just a loaner, remember?" Cate said.

"I'm trying, but there are a few little waves coming in at us."

"Waves?" Cate frowned and looked past him. But there was nothing out on the calm sea.

The first thing Jack did was pull out a length of cord with a small grappling hook on it and hand it to Cate. She grabbed it as he fed out the line, and she found a jutting piece of sharp rock which she tied it off to.

The submersible had already powered itself down now that it was totally without charge, and all Jack needed to do was switch it to recharge mode – one of Sonya's little blue-sky technologies for energy generation that was based on a liquid graphene oxide that was able to harvest energy from the humidity in the air to self-charge.

He closed the small lid over the bay. There was nothing to do now but let it do its thing for the next few hours.

He looked beyond the submersible as another wave struck the craft, pushing it toward him until it once again ground against the lip of rock. He could see the submersible's base and his legs below the surface.

"Where the hell are those waves coming from?" He spoke over his shoulder. "Hey, you don't think mama whale followed us do you?"

He turned back to the water. And froze.

Just below the surface, and a little further out, was a vision from hell.

The massive shark hung there, a few feet down. It looked like some gigantic, pale alien creature hanging in a void of space.

Its black, glassy eye was impossible to read, but he knew it looked right up at him. Perhaps if the submersible wasn't between him and the Megalodon, it would have launched itself forward to pick him from the rocks, like ripe fruit from a tree.

He backed up. Fell on his ass in the shallows, and then scooted backward on all fours, keeping his now very wide eyes on the water as he went.

He finally got about twenty feet back and up onto another level of the rocky outcrop and beside Cate.

"What's the matter with you?" But then she must have seen his bleached complexion and the expression on his face.

She spun to the water, as the massive conical snout slowly lifted from it, not making a ripple or sound – higher, and then higher again, until it was about twelve feet from the surface and easily ten wide.

It simply hung there, watching them.

"Oh shit, shit, shit." She grabbed his arm and began to drag him even further away.

Jack managed to get to his feet, and they both watched as the Megalodon eased itself back into the water, perhaps satisfied with what it saw.

"Those waves I felt. That was it going past." He whispered. "It found us. Or maybe it was there the whole time?"

She shook her head. "Does it matter?" She grabbed his arm. "What do we do?"

"Nothing," he replied. "Just hope it loses interest and moves off. We've got to wait for around six hours before the sub is fully charged, and at least three for a half charge. I do not want to be sailing away from this rock and run out of juice on that black ocean."

"So we wait it out here?" She looked back at the craggy lump of dark rocks. The small island outcrop was about fifty feet around and only rose about six feet from the water's surface. For now it was still too big for the monster shark to try and snatch them from the rocks.

"There's a few things that look like oysters and mussels higher up," Cate said. "Maybe we can make a meal of them."

Jack looked at her. "What? Where?"

Cate scaled to the near top of the island. She pointed into a crevice. "In here."

Jack followed her. And looked down. "Oh, shit no. They're still alive."

"That's a good thing, isn't it?" She frowned up at him. "Means they'll be fresh, and edible."

"That's not the problem. It means they're alive, and for that to occur they need to be covered in fresh water, and often."

She shook her head. "So what? All that –" She stopped dead and turned about. "Oh shit, I get it. This place must get fully submerged every high tide." She looked up at him. "And the tide is coming in."

"Yeah, the tide." Jack turned back to the submersible. "We forgot about that because there was so much going on." He sighed. "It's coming in, fast. Look at the sub."

She turned and saw that, even in the short time they had been on the rocky outcrop, the water already looked higher down where they'd stepped off the submersible.

As if to compound their troubles, a huge dorsal fin broke the water, and about fifty or more feet back from that the tip of a tail also lifted. It glided past them about a hundred feet from their shore.

"Its fin," Jack said.

There was a notch missing from the dorsal fin. Where Alina's explosive-tipped harpoon had struck it.

"It's the same one. Territorial, as we expected," Cate said. "We need to find somewhere safer."

Jack nodded. "Yeah, but we need at least a half charge to be sure we can make it to somewhere else. Anything less and we risk getting stranded out there. And, believe me, we do not want to be trying to swim anywhere."

She folded her arms across her chest so tightly he saw the muscles in her arms strain. "If the water comes in high enough that monster is going to be able to grab us right off the rocks."

Jack put an arm around her shoulders and pulled her close. "It's never going to happen."

She had nestled in close to him and looked up from his chest. "Then what can we do?"

Jack watched the shark fin glide past again. "Sharks are attracted by scent, vibrations, and also movement. We need to buy a few hours, so the sub's batteries build up a charge. And then, when we're ready, leave without that monster following us. We need to stop it waiting for us."

She looked up, waiting.

"Sharks have three hundred million years of predatorial instinct. But they're not smart. They get bored quickly. So, we do nothing that interests it. We hide, and maybe in a few hours it'll take off to somewhere else."

"Maybe?"

"It's all I've got." He half smiled. "We need to stay here for a few hours anyway, waiting for the submersible to build up the semblance of a charge so we can either find a bigger island, or the coast. Unfortunately, we don't have many other choices."

"Will the tide give us that?" Cate asked.

"I . . . I don't know. I hope so." Jack shared a crooked smile with her.

Cate snorted. "Worst. Holiday. Ever."

He laughed. "That's the spirit. C'mon, let's go find somewhere to hunker down for a few hours."

* * *

The island wasn't really an island. It was just the tip of some sort of underwater mountain peak, or some other strange, long, and thin geological formation created in the weird and unique world beneath the Antarctic's frozen surface.

It would undoubtedly vanish on the rising tide. Luckily it was riven with cracks and boulders and, at the top, there was a rent running about twenty feet long and three deep. There was water at its base, and as Cate had discovered its sides were covered in oysters, mussels, and there were also small beds of seaweed at the bottom.

"In there?" she asked.

"Yep. It doesn't look all that comfortable. But we can try and grab some rest." Jack looked about. "There's nowhere else deep enough for us to stay out of the Megalodon's line of sight."

"Can we at least lie together?" She gave him a crooked sort of smile.

"That sounds romantic." He laughed, but then saw she

wasn't joking and knew why. "Of course, an excellent idea. I'm bigger than you so you can rest on me, and I'll keep you out of the water."

Jack put his foot down into the crack. As soon as he touched the weed-covered bottom, something like a three-foot-long eel shot out and slithered up and over the rocks, heading to the water.

"Holy hell, that just scared ten years out of me." He closed his eyes and shook his head. "Don't worry, I've got this." He lay down, facing upward and trying to wedge his shoulders so he stayed above the water. "Lie on top of me."

Jack felt the sharp rock and oysters digging into him but didn't care. If things did end badly, he at least wanted this time with her.

Cate lay on top of him, and he put his arm over her. She looked up at him and smiled.

He grinned back. "Not the worst holiday after all, right?"

"My eternal optimist." She lay her head on his chest. "I'm going to dream about us being back on the *Heceta*. Sitting in the sun."

"Me too." He stroked her damp hair. "Me too."

* * *

Jack lay there staring up at the cavern roof. In this place, this world, it was a sky, dotted with tiny blue stars that could have been in galaxies billions of light years away.

We're not on Earth anymore, he thought. We've landed on an alien planet and we tiny humans shouldn't be here at all.

He stared. Without any other lights, the blue dots seemed to magnify the ceiling's glow, and he was sure it moved up there, rustling and undulating like seaweed in a current. He also thought he saw things moving through it, like clown fish hiding among the stinging tentacles of a sea anemone.

Up there is a mirror world, he thought. He wondered if there were creatures up there, looking down, or looking up from their perspective, and seeing this world and wondering about the inhabitants as he did about them now?

As he lay there, letting his mind work, he tried to remember how long ago it was he had seen another of the small islands poking up out of the water. It had been hours. And none of them had been as big as this one so they would surely be inundated as well.

And that was what kept him awake. Should they return via the same path? Or should they strike out in a different direction to search for more land that was safer?

But if they did that, they'd need more than just half a charge. Otherwise he'd realize his biggest fear and they'd run out of power in the middle of nowhere.

They had little food and water, and he would have been terrified by the thought of swimming even if he *did* have a destination in sight. Swimming out with nothing but blackness and endless sea meant a certain death – either slow by finally tiring and slipping beneath the surface to drown; or fast by . . .

He closed his eyes for a moment and squeezed them tight. He didn't even want to think about that happening to Cate. He promised her he would never let that happen. But what could he do to stop it?

He prayed.

After a little more time had passed, he raised his hand and looked at the luminous numbers on his wristwatch; it had been two hours – they were climbing toward a half charge. Nearly enough, and not nearly enough.

He would have liked to have sat up and carefully peeked over the edge to see if the monster was still there. Or to know at least how far the ocean had risen. But he knew Megalodons were of the Otodus shark species, and their eyes were geared to spotting even the tiniest movement – if it was there, it would see him.

He drew in a deep breath and let it out real slow so as to not disturb Cate. He doubted she would have been able to sleep, but just resting was good enough for now.

Jack shifted a little to try to move away from a barnacle or something sharp that was digging into his shoulder, and as he did the water splashed the back of his head – odd, because he was about a foot above it before, and he doubted he had sunk down anymore.

The rocky outcrop was probably run through with cracks and holes, he thought. That meant the tide was coming in faster than he expected. He quickly checked his watch: just on two and a half hours gone.

He had no choice. "*Hey.*" He gently shook her.

"Hmm." Sleepily, and then. "What, *what*?" Cate launched herself upright on his chest.

Jack groaned as the pressure from her rapid movement forced him down harder on the oysters. "It's okay, I just need to check on something."

Cate didn't wait, and sprang up to see first. Her face dropped. "Oh no."

Those words and her tone scared the hell out of him. He eased her off him and levered himself up onto the rocky top and out of the crevice. His arms, shoulders and back ached liked hell, and stung from multiple mini-cuts, but he ignored them and spun to the shoreline.

As expected the tide was in and the water was high, real high. But that wasn't what Cate was reacting to.

The tide had come in so high and fast, it had somehow dislodged the anchor cord they had used to secure the submersible to the small island. It now floated a few dozen feet from shore.

"*You sonofa . . .*" He cursed, but then toned it down and let the rest out as a hissing breath. He didn't want to make any loud noises or sudden movement lest they undo all the good work they had done by hiding for the last few hours.

"What'll we do?" Her voice rose. "We can't swim out there."

"Just be cool," he said. "I . . ." He sighed. "I have to. Either we have a way to escape, or we don't." He looked over the surface, seeing nothing but an endless calm sea of darkness. "Let's get it before it drifts even further away."

Together, they crept down to the waterline.

"Look, there." He pointed.

Lying in the water was the long length of cord, although it was no longer attached to the sub. He picked it up and saw the end looked stretched. "It somehow came undone. The sub's beyond the length of the cord so I'll bring it closer. You hang onto the rope from shore. When I've secured it to the sub, you drag it in."

"It's suicide." She grabbed his arm.

"No, it's not. I can't see the Megalodon anymore. Like I said, they get bored quickly. It's probably long gone. When I'm closer you toss the rope, I grab it, tie it off, and you drag the sub in – there and back in under a minute, easy."

She looked from the floating submersible back to him. "Then I'm going –"

"*No.*" He cut her off. "You need to be here as my lookout. Remember, when I have it close enough, you throw the rope, and drag it back. Stay low, no movement, and wait for my signal. Okay? *Please.*"

She grimaced. But eventually Cate nodded. "I can do that."

"Good. Good." Jack turned back to the water and assessed exactly how many strokes he'd need. The submersible was floating on the glass smooth water about a hundred feet from them now.

It's weird, he thought. As the tide was coming in, the sub should have been pushed up on the rocks not drifting away from them. But perhaps the rushing water coming in so fast had created some sort of backwash. *Who knows, this is a crazy place.*

He took his shirt off and tossed it onto the rocks. The temperature was about eighty degrees and probably that in humidity, but he still shivered.

He felt a little sick in the pit of his stomach; he did *not* want to do this, and his body was letting him know that it also thought it was a bad idea. But he knew there was no option. Plus, the longer he left it, the more the damn thing might have moved away from them.

Cate stood with the looped rope in both her hands and Jack stepped into the water. "I'm going to drag it with me or at least nudge it toward us."

He reckoned a hundred feet meant just over a hundred strokes, breaststroke style so he wouldn't cause a ripple. He'd head out a little to the left of it, come around the –

Get on with it, he demanded of himself. He knew he was procrastinating now, putting it off for as long as possible.

"Okay." He took a step forward and was stopped by Cate getting in front of him and reaching up with both hands to grab his face. She pulled him closer, and kissed him.

She wouldn't let go, and she was pressing so hard she hurt his lips. He finally eased her back a step and he saw her streaming eyes. She tried to smile up at him, perhaps to give him courage, but it just looked like a grimace.

"Hey, come on. I'll be back in a few seconds. You watch." He grinned and turned away, lest she see the tremble in his own lips.

He got to the edge of the rock shelf, which had been dry when they had arrived but the water there was now chest deep. Beyond that it was over his head, so he began to swim.

The water was bath warm, but he felt everything shrivel and he focused on the submersible.

There was nothing he could do now except pray the giant Megalodon was gone. He was in its domain, and all the odds were in its favor. If it was here and wanted him, he would be gone.

He kept stroking, gently, slowly, quietly, and just focusing on the bright yellow submersible. He desperately wanted to look left and right, but forced himself to just look at the part of the miniature sub that was closest to him; which now was the rear.

It had turned slightly, but he'd felt no current.

The rear of the sub had the propulsion vent which would make a natural handle to grab onto. He saw it now at the waterline.

Easy, he thought as he closed in on it, *don't rush it now*.

And then his shaking hand was on it.

Okay, we've got this, he thought. Even though the sub was back to front, he knew he could tie the rope off to the rear, no problem.

He began to sidestroke back to the tiny island. He saw Cate there, right on the water's edge, on what was now little more than a couple of feet of black rock rising from the dark sea.

In the blue light, she almost glowed. *An angel*, he thought. That's what she looked like. *I'll have to remember to tell her that.*

He grunted, straining. Even though the submersible had excellent buoyancy, it wasn't easy to drag as it was a lot bigger and heavier than he was. Also, he wanted to be gentle and not cause any surface turbulence, so he wasn't using all his strength.

It was slow going and took him ten painstaking minutes to get the submersible just halfway back. Cate's eyes were on his and he raised a hand. *Now*, he whispered.

She held one end of the rope and swung the other in a circle to build momentum, and then tossed it. But it fell short. And unfortunately, it sunk.

Jack saw that the last bit of their island was rapidly vanishing beneath the dark water now.

"*Again,*" he urged.

Cate quickly wound the rope back in.

He dragged the submersible and scissor-kicked his legs hard, harder than he wanted. The kick created ripples on the surface this time. But he managed to bring the submersible a few feet closer, and her second toss landed near enough for him to grab the rope.

He tread water while he tied it off, tested the knot, and then gave her a thumbs-up. "*Go.*"

Cate tugged, but the sub only moved a fraction. She coiled the rope around her hand and forearm and tugged again, but it was hard going as the mass of the sub far outweighed her.

"I'm coming," he said and swam toward the shoreline. He knew that once he was beside her, both of them would be able to drag the craft back in seconds.

Jack breaststroked and made good headway. Without his shirt he felt the warm water move over his body – only fifty or so feet to go – and then a huge surge pushed him from the side.

Immediately his animal brain screamed danger and for him to flee. He stopped swimming, already feeling his heart begin to race.

From the surface the water seemed pitch black but that was deceiving – it wasn't stained an inky color, it was just that there was no strong overhead illumination from a sun or moon. In fact, it was near mountain lake clear.

So he ducked his head under the water, and opened his eyes. He saw it. And screamed, in the water, the breath boiling out in a stream of bubbles. Every one of them probably contained a small bit of his terrified voice.

Hanging in the water like a monstrous ghostly apparition was the huge, pale head of the Megalodon shark.

He knew it saw him. It looked right at him, and then veered away, leaving a swirl of agitated water below him.

It was going to come up underneath him like a freight train.

Jack lifted his head. "*Shark*!" he screamed.

Cate's head came up and her eyes and mouth formed into perfect circles.

Jack knew that if he could just get the submersible back to Cate, his job was done. So he used both his legs to push at it with all his strength and was also propelled back from it – just as the monstrous head breached, right under him, its train-tunnel-sized mouth opened wide, taking Jack and the submersible into the air.

But Jack's last move had caused the Megalodon to miscalculate, and both the sub and Jack went either side of the gaping jaws.

Jack felt himself flying, almost in slow motion, as he cartwheeled in the air to splash back down more than two dozen feet away. But the submersible's weight, coupled with its sudden and significant movement, jerked hard on the rope, the one that Cate had wound around her arm. And she was catapulted twenty feet from the shore and out into the water.

When Jack surfaced, he saw her come back up, spluttering. He quickly turned and saw the huge fin about fifty feet out but sailing past them. And worse, he saw it turning.

Not toward him, but toward Cate.

"Oh no." His heart sank.

* * *

Cate came back to the surface, stunned for a moment, and immediately felt the agony in her shoulder. Her mind tried to put together what had just happened. Then she realized where she was, and it all came back to her.

"*Jack*," she yelled as she tread water and looked one way then the other.

"Get out. *Swim*. Get out." She heard his voice, far away, and the words sounded frightened. That scared the hell out of her because Jack was never frightened.

She turned and the first thing she saw was the massive sail-like fin, front on, meaning the monster was coming straight at her.

Never before had she felt such an electric shock of fear run through her. She turned and started to swim back to the remains of the rocky shoreline. It was little more than a scab of rock rising about three feet above the waterline now.

Her elbow and shoulder hurt like fire, but they still worked so she figured nothing was broken or dislocated. But the shoreline seemed so far away – had she really been thrown that far?

"I love you." She heard Jack say, but his voice was distant.

What? Why did he . . . ? She turned in the water and saw Jack had swum back to the submersible and gave it an almighty kick toward the shore.

The shark was coming at her, rising now from the depths. It would have her soon, and for some reason, like a rabbit caught in the luminous night-glare of a wolf, she just froze, waiting for it.

And then Jack started to swim backward, yelling loudly, and splashing the water.

Don't do that, she thought, you'll attract the . . .

Oh no. She suddenly understood what he was doing.

"*Don't you –*" she screamed at him.

It worked. The shark veered away and went down; it couldn't resist the inbuilt programming that demanded it attack the thing that seemed in distress, like a wounded fish, or an animal flailing around on the surface.

"*Hey, hey!*" she yelled, trying to call the shark back.

But the tip of the fin came back up, and this time it was pointed at Jack.

He stopped swimming and just floated there. She could tell he wasn't looking at the shark anymore. But past it. At her.

Their eyes locked and time stopped. She reached out an arm to him, and just held it out.

Come back to me, she whispered as she stretched out her hand.

Jack was reaching for her hand too, even from that impossible distance. His face was calm. And he had that tiny smile of his that said everything was going to be okay.

And then the monster came up between her and Jack. Its mouth gaped open and it surged over the top of him.

"No-*ooo!*" She screwed her eyes shut for a second as she heard his scream, feeling his fear and pain stab right through her heart and soul.

And when she opened them, the shark was gone. And so was Jack.

She began to cry as she tread water.

The surface settled back into its glass-like stillness, and looking out at the vast underground sea she knew she was just a speck in a world of monsters.

And she was all alone now.

CHAPTER 31

The injured and comatose Aaron was carried on a make-shift stretcher between Gino and Benjamin. Meena had fleetingly thought about leaving him behind with one of the crew to guard him but disregarded the notion as she doubted anyone would want that job, and she wasn't about to order anyone to do something that might end up being a death sentence.

It was hard work scaling the tumble of boulders, but the tide was beginning to turn and had gone out enough for them to cross to the high point on the flat rock shelves again.

It took them several hours to return to the small hill of stone that led to where they'd arrived, and she remembered they needed to keep a look out for the damn Russian captain as well. At least the tide had gone further out and so gave them plenty of rock shelf to walk across.

Though Meena thought herself the kind of person who didn't want to wish ill on anyone, she'd make an exception for the murderous Russian, and hoped he was long dead.

At the top of yet another pile of fallen rock, she stood with hands on her hips as the group joined her, with Gino and Benjamin carrying their unconscious crewmate up the steep incline.

"Where is it?" Kathleen frowned. "Where are they?"

The rocks were empty – no boat, no Maria, Steven, Ormond, or Eric. Not even any sign of them.

"Oh shit," Phillipa exclaimed. "Sonya came and got them." She turned. "They left us behind."

Meena rounded on her. "Shut that crap down. You know it's not true. There is no way that our people would leave us behind. The first thing they'd do is come and get us."

Meena turned back to the empty rock shelf. "But I think maybe when the tide came in, they took to the boat and headed somewhere safer."

"They went out there?" Gino said.

The group slowly turned to the dark water.

"I don't get it," Benjamin said. "Why would they head off somewhere, and not just hug the rocks and come down the coast to find us?" He looked up. "I could understand if they tried to head to the cave mouth to find Ms. Borashev. But I know them. Eric is my friend. He'd never, ever just leave us."

Meena sighed. There was another possibility: that the group headed out but ran into a problem on the water. And she knew exactly what that problem might have been.

"Doesn't matter now," Meena said. "They're gone."

"Doesn't matter?" Phillipa's laugh was short and harsh. "It does goddamn matter, Meena. We're fucking stuck here now."

"Please calm down," Kathleen said. She turned to Phillipa. "This is not helping."

"What will?" Phillipa pointed at the comatose man on the stretcher. "Look at him. And remember what happened to Rachel? She had her damn face eaten off. And poor Aaron here has half his back gone and will die without medical care soon."

She raised a fist and shook it. "So going back to the godforsaken forest means being attacked by snails from hell. Staying here means being drowned. And, oh yeah, that's right, we don't have a boat anymore, so those are our only options."

"Then make a damn suggestion." Gino glared. "If you

don't like how things are – and who fucking does right now? – I suggest you stop trying to blame Meena, and share with us your brilliant ideas to improve the situation."

"That's enough," Meena said.

Phillipa leaned her head back and made a disgusted noise in the back of her throat. "I don't know. There is no plan. There's nothing we can do." She tilted her head forward again and her eyes were rimmed with fatigue. "We're all as good as dead."

"While we're alive, there is hope," Meena said. "I'm sure Ms. Borashev will have made it to the exit by now. And, for all we know, she has initiated the signal buoy's beacon and it's just a matter of time until rescue arrives."

"Yeah, sure, and . . ." Phillipa closed her eyes and let out a big breath. "Oh fuck it." She turned and walked away.

"*Phillipa*," Meena called.

"Let her go," Kathleen said. "We're all physically and emotionally exhausted." She turned to face Meena. "But we do need to work out what we do next. We can't stay here for long. And no one really wants to go back to that slimy forest."

Meena sighed. "Phillipa is right. I have no idea what to do." She walked closer to the water's edge. "Maybe the team from here went to find Sonya. And maybe they didn't. But we can't stay." She turned and held out an arm, pointing. "So, there are two options – we go back to the forest." She lowered her arm and raised the other arm pointing the opposite way. "Or we head further along the rock ledge. There were caves there; maybe they lead somewhere. Or at least will give us shelter for when the tide turns again."

There was silence for a moment.

"We take a vote," Kathleen said. "Raise your left arm to go back to the forest. Raise your right to go and check out the caves."

Everyone raised their right arm.

***

It took them a lot more hours than they expected to make their way across the rock ledge. And by the time they were closing in on the area where they had spotted the caves earlier, the tide had turned and once again the water was rising.

Time was against them, and they were tiring – carrying the man in the makeshift stretcher was taxing Gino and Benjamin.

Along the way, Kathleen had organized fossicking, mainly to collect anything that might be edible from the rock pools, and also to keep Phillipa occupied.

They had made small bags from their undershirts, and gathered seaweeds, shellfish, and things that looked like a cross between a crab and a brine shrimp. Plus a few tiny fish.

The fish were eaten almost immediately, and as the shellfish and crustaceans would stay alive out of the water for many hours they were taken with them. Some things spoiled rapidly in the heat and humidity and were quickly discarded. The last thing Meena wanted was a member of their group to be poisoned or fall ill.

In another hour, and with the water now beginning to submerge their ledge and lap at the cliff wall, they found the first of the caves.

There were three openings into the cliff, and after carefully placing Aaron on some high flat rocks, they quickly moved between each, trying to decide which one was worth their time and energy to investigate.

After a few moments, Gino called to them. "Here."

They gathered at the largest cave on the left side. He held his arms wide, lifted his chin and inhaled. After a moment he turned. "Feel that?"

Kathleen nodded. "Oh yeah, that's a breeze. A *cool* breeze." She smiled broadly. "This might lead to the surface."

There were cheers and a few claps.

"That's great." Meena clapped as well, but then stepped in front of them. "But what if someone comes when we're investigating? Should we give it a few days just to see if Sonya's mission was a success?"

"I don't think she's coming back," Phillipa said. "And this is the most encouraging news we've had since we've been marooned."

"Just a few days. Or even twenty-four hours." Meena pointed to the now submerged rock shelf. "There's food here. We can wait that long."

There was silence, and she knew that no one supported her suggestion. Not even Kathleen. She could understand – the thought of climbing out and seeing some sky again was irresistible.

Benjamin had been examining the entrances to the caves a little more. He kicked at something in the dirt. "Hey, check this out."

He pulled an object from the ground and wiped it clean. He brought it back to the group and Meena shone her flashlight onto it.

It was a short blade with a flat edge rather than finishing in a point. She thought it was called a tanto edge. And it had a name inscribed on one side: *Tank Lennox*.

Benjamin turned it over. There was an engraved picture of an eagle, and in its claws it held a sword on one side and a lightning bolt on the other.

"Looks sort of military . . . and it's new. Or at least not old. Someone lost this here I'm guessing not more than ten, fifteen years ago." He looked up. "And they dropped it as they headed into, or came from . . ." He turned and nodded to the cave mouth. ". . . this cave here."

The group turned to stare into the stygian blackness. There wasn't any of the luminescent blue glow from the greater cavern inside, so just a dozen feet in the dark was impenetrable.

"We'll need to use our flashlights, and lighters," Meena said.

"How far do you think we need to go?" Phillipa asked.

Kathleen shook her head and spoke without turning away from the darkness. "I don't think we're that far from the surface. And if it's a straight climb then maybe a few hours." She sighed. "But if it's a lot of twists and turns and slow going, then your guess is as good as mine."

"And we've got to drag this poor guy with us." Benjamin nodded toward the unconscious Aaron.

"You want to leave him here?" Kathleen rounded on him. "Maybe for the snails to finish off."

Benjamin didn't back down. "That's not what I damn meant. If we're climbing, it's going to be hard to bring him, and it increases the risk to all our safety. Maybe we should leave him here and someone stays with him."

"You?" Meena asked.

"Can't be me." Benjamin shook his head. "You'll need me for the climb."

"No, we need you to carry him," Meena said. "No one gets left behind." Her eyes were unblinking as she stared at Benjamin. "If it was you, I'm sure you wouldn't want to be left behind on the rocks, right?"

"I said *with* someone. Someone who volunteers," he complained.

No one did.

"Oh fine, forget it." He threw his hands up and stomped off.

Kathleen came up close to Meena. "What do you really think?"

"I think we need to plan on being in there for at least a day. And we need to remember how to get back." Meena looked up at the older woman. "One light on at a time. I do not want to be lost in a cave in total darkness."

Kathleen nodded.

"Wait." Meena held out her hand. "Ben, give me that knife you found."

Benjamin handed it over. Meena felt the blade – it was still strong and would do. She walked up to the wall, reached up high and began gouging long strokes into the moss-covered rock.

After several minutes she stood back. She had carved her name in foot-high letters and an arrow pointing into the cave.

"Just in case Sonya comes by."

"Good thinking." Kathleen patted her shoulder.

A small wave surged up over the rock ledge they were on, and Meena turned to the water. "Okay, people, the tide has caught up to us again." She flicked on her flashlight. "I'll lead us in, one light on at a time."

She turned back and lifted her head, feeling the breeze on her cheeks. There was also just the hint of an odd odor on the moving air. It reminded her of some sort of window cleaner. *Like ammonia*, she thought.

"Let's go home." She led them in.

* * *

Within an hour the humidity coupled with the nutrient rich rocks allowed the unique mosses and lichens in the massive cavern to slide down and inch across the new cuts in the cliff wall.

In a few hours more the wounds Meena had made in the stone had totally healed over and were gone.

CHAPTER 32

Hours passed, and more hours. Sonya sat like stone watching the rock wall beside her. The tide had risen dozens of feet, peaked, and was now dropping back.

Further and further, and finally she could just make out the top of the cave. She straightened.

"Soon. Get ready," she said.

Jorge sat upright. Chekov was already alert.

The receding tide was having the opposite effect on the sea currents at the cave mouth. Now it was streaming outward, and they could see the waves piling up against the sides as it rushed to be pulled out through the narrow cave mouth.

"We go near that now, we'll be sucked under or crushed along the cave roof," Chekov said.

"In another hour, it will have dropped enough for us to pass through." Sonya turned. "But yes, we'll need the motor to keep control of the boat and remain in the center of the channel or the tidal surge will overwhelm us."

"At least it'll be a fast trip," Jorge said.

She nodded. "And hopefully the surge noise will give us cover from any predators."

Jorge and Chekov waited for the order to start rowing out toward the cave mouth. Both men held one oar each and turned from watching the cave begin to show, to Sonya's face, which was like carved stone.

"We never talked about what happens when we get out," Chekov said.

Sonya didn't turn. "We head to the communication buoy, and I contact home base. They'll send a spotter airplane and then a rescue ship." She finally turned. "Then we go in and get my people."

"And before then, I can go back to my ship, yes?" Chekov asked.

"Once we've contacted my base and I have an understanding of timeframes." She smiled. "And if your ship is still there."

Minutes moved on, and the tide receded even more. Finally there was about five feet between the sea level and the cave roof – just enough if they ducked down on the way through.

"We've waited enough. Let's go," Sonya shouted over the roar of the rushing water.

Jorge started the motor, and Chekov sat down in the middle of the boat and gripped one of the oars to use in case they were buffeted too close to the cave wall. Sonya braced her arms each side of the boat's front and held an arm out guiding them.

The small inflatable raft swung around and headed into the central slipstream of the surge.

"Whoa, it's strong," Jorge said, as the boat fishtailed a little on the lumping water.

Jorge got them centered and the small inflatable boat lined up. "Ready?" he yelled.

"*Go, go, go.*" Sonya was almost over the edge of the boat, her head down and forward.

Jorge gave the engine a few extra revs and then they shot forward. With the engine at full throttle, combined with the moving current, the boat traveled at about twenty knots.

"Easy, easy," Chekov said.

They flew in under the lip of the cave, and immediately passed into near total darkness as the usual twilight blue illumination overhead disappeared.

"Can't see," Jorge yelled.

Sonya cursed and just pulled back in time as the boat came close to one of the walls. Chekov had to jam the oar into it to push them away.

"Slow the hell down then," she yelled over her shoulder.

Jorge eased back and traveled just enough to maintain control, but they still moved at close to twelve knots.

Sonya looked up. "There you are."

It was the explosive package she had set on their way in. She still wanted the option to use it.

"Light up ahead," she yelled over the sound of the engine.

Jorge accelerated, and then, in a few more moments, the dot of light became a beacon of frozen sunshine as they approached the glacial rim.

In just a few minutes Sonya felt the cold on her face and sucked in a deep breath of chilling and odorless air. After days of the humid and dank smells of the cave, it was a blessing. She shut her eyes for a moment to savor it.

The inflatable boat shot out from the cave and then from underneath the glacial overhang. Even though it seemed to be early morning, after the twilight dimness in the cave the light outside was blinding.

"Go straight ahead," Sonya said.

The water around them was still a warm current highway, but the air was dry and near freezing, and it bit as it sucked the perspiration from their skin. But not one of them complained.

Sonya craned forward and, finally, among the bobbing ice she saw the red, six-foot-tall buoy they'd dropped. It was bristling with antenna, lights, and electronics.

"There." She pointed.

Jorge made straight for it and, in minutes, pulled up close by. Sonya reached out and grabbed its edge and held on.

Chekov helped hold the boat steady as Sonya reached out for a plastic box stuck to the side. She opened it to display a bank of small lights, a satellite phone, and a large red button.

"It's working." She punched the button initiating the beacon, and then lifted the phone. She opened a communication link and cleared her throat.

"Mironov enterprise, this is Sonya Borashev, come in."

She only had to wait a few seconds as the response was returned.

"Markus Anderson here, Ms. Borashev, good to hear you. We see the beacon has been initiated and a support plane is being dispatched now. What is your status?" he asked.

She narrowed her eyes as she stared out over the frozen sea, but her mind was back in the cavern. "*Sea Princess* is destroyed. Crew trapped in cave system beneath the ice. Need rescue and medical care. Send *Sea Prince* immediately."

"Understood. *Sea Prince* was firing up its engines the moment the beacon was initiated. Will be leaving Tasmania within the next thirty minutes, and we estimate will be with you in six hours. Will there be anything else?"

Sonya lowered her head and exhaled. "Thank you." She lifted her head. "And yes, just stay on the line, Markus."

"Don't worry, I'll be here. We're on our way."

She smiled. "We'll be waiting."

Sonya eased back into the boat. "You heard?"

Jorge nodded, and Chekov turned to look back at the glacier and the blue glass-like interior that led to the hidden cave.

"I wish we'd never found that place. It is cursed." Chekov continued to stare. "It swallowed so many of our, and your, people."

"Cursed." Sonya followed his gaze and wondered about her crew. Were they still alive? She worried about Meena. The woman was competent, but a little fragile. And what of Jack and Cate? Were they still able to be rescued? Or even found?

Their mission to draw away the Megalodon must have been a success.

Knowing that pair, they would still be in there, laughing together, taking turns rescuing each other, and high-fiving their narrow escapes.

Yes, they would be in there waiting to be picked up. She hoped they were because they deserved their time in the sun now.

"See you soon," she said.

CHAPTER 33

On her hands and knees, Cate crawled up the rocks and felt the rope was still tied around her bruised wrist in a knot. She didn't know how long she sat there, numb, but she was roused by a metallic clanking noise and turned back to the water to see that the waves from the Megalodon attack had washed the submersible up onto the rocks. It now lay at an angle, facing her.

Get in, she thought she heard Jack say.

Almost trance-like she got inside it. Put her palms over her eyes and pulled her knees up to her chest. She had never felt so dead inside in her entire life.

Jack once told her that sharks couldn't count. So if two people hid, and one came out, it didn't know that the other was still there. Maybe that was true.

"I should have married you." She sobbed and felt the hot tears run down her cheeks.

Either the tide would lift the submersible free, or she would stay here until she went to sleep forever. She didn't care which one happened as her reason for living was now gone.

* * *

Over the hours, the tide came back in, and she barely felt the submersible lift. When the water was high enough the sub righted itself to sit squarely in the water. Cate Granger never moved, staying curled up and near comatose in her grief.

After a time the submersible was grabbed by the tide and moved off, caught in whatever currents operated within the colossal underground sea.

It was a tiny yellow steel and glass dot in a huge black ocean. And inside a grieving human being was lost in their own tortured mind.

CHAPTER 34

Captain Yuri Zagreb cursed again. The motor wasn't working and his hands were so blistered from rowing, they now left red streaks on the oars.

If that wasn't bad enough, he had headed away from the shoreline to ensure he didn't run into that mad Sonya woman, who he knew would shoot him dead the moment she spotted him.

But he had gone further than he had expected, and in the darkness he had become disorientated and now couldn't find the shore again.

He spat angrily into the water. It was a junior sailor's error, and what happens, he knew now, when sailors have no instruments, landmarks, or even stars to navigate by.

He rifled through the few bags left inside the boat and found a pair of binoculars and lifted them to his eyes, scanning a full 360 degrees. The featureless, black ocean was still with small vapor ghosts rising from its warm surface. He was about to lower the glasses, when he saw a speck of color in the distance – bright yellow. It didn't look all that big and it didn't look like a sea animal.

Yuri lowered the glasses. "What have we here?"

He spat on his palms to cool them and then tore a cloth he had found in half and wrapped it around his raw hands to cushion them. He gripped the oars once more and ignored the sting as he began to row.

In thirty minutes he was close enough to confirm it was what he hoped – the submersible from the *Sea Princess*. But it looked dead in the water. He rowed hard and then moved the last hundred feet as silent as a wraith until he came alongside it.

Yuri carefully knelt up to peer inside the clear canopy, and then craned forward as he held onto the clear cover – there was a small person in there. Maybe dead. Or maybe sleeping.

If they were sleeping, he didn't want to wake them. His priority was to take control of the vessel. And then to see if it was working.

He tied off his boat to the sub and then quickly searched until he found the button to manually retract the canopy. He ever so gently slid it back and lifted himself up and into the submersible.

Seconds later he had moved past the two seats and knelt by the woman – he had seen her before. He knew she had a partner. But where was he?

He lifted his head to scan the calm sea surface, but there was no one around. Maybe the man had drowned or been left behind. *Good for me, less trouble*, Yuri thought.

He touched her neck and felt a slight pulse – alive. He cursed. He would have preferred her dead.

He was about to throw her out and let the dark sea take her, but then he realised that she might come in handy.

He looked down at her figure, letting his eyes run over her athletic form. He grinned. "You are lucky I'm not a younger man."

Yuri rummaged around and found some soft rope and tied her hands together. Then he let her sleep.

He sat in the front pilot seat and looked over the controls – he was pleased to see they were very basic, and overjoyed to find the small craft had a sixty percent battery charge.

He started the motor, and it began with a soft whine. He engaged the drive and the small craft moved forward at about three knots. He tested the controls and found them working.

He stood, leaned out to where he had tied his raft off and undid it. "Thank you for all the blisters, you *Mudak*."

Yuri laughed as he retook his seat. He then found a half bottle of water and drained it.

He removed the bloody bandages from his hands and then flexed his fingers. "Better than rowing," he said and started to head to where he hoped the cave exit was, using little more than a sailor's intuition and a prayer for luck.

CHAPTER 35

Meena and Kathleen led Phillipa, followed by Gino, and finally Benjamin still dragging the comatose form of Aaron, through the narrowing caves until they entered a larger cavern space.

They were able to stand upright, and Benjamin carefully put Aaron down for Kathleen to check on him. The rest stretched their backs and sipped water.

"Good news is we're still heading upward," Meena said.

"But I can't feel the breeze anymore." Phillipa held a hand up to test the air.

"I think I can." Meena spoke the little white lie as they hadn't gone that far, and she needed them to stick with her. She was sure that as soon as they rounded the next bend they'd feel the breeze again.

"Hey, check this out." Gino pointed up at a large flat wall at the back of the cave.

They crowded around and a few more flashlights came on.

"*Whoa*. Very cool." Benjamin grinned. "Is this a good sign or bad?"

"Good sign," Kathleen replied. "It means people were here." She lifted her light.

The rear wall was decorated with ancient drawings depicting various forms of sea life, some they recognized and some they assumed were mythical. There was also a pair of warriors complete with spears and some sort of ceremonial headdress. And all done in magnificent detail.

"Can you read any of it?" Kathleen asked Meena.

She shook her head slowly. "Some of it looks like Aztec or Mayan, so I can guess at a word or phrase here and there. But mostly no." She stepped back a little. "From what I remember of my language studies, some of the ancient races used to place this type of artwork everywhere. They were a form of diary. And sometimes a warning."

"A warning?" Gino swore under her breath. "Yeah, I'm not going back in the water."

"Well, we can all read the drawings." Phillipa pointed. "That's the shark."

There was a drawing of the huge pale shark fighting with a dark whale of even greater size.

"Seems they had problems with the Megalodons as well," Benjamin observed.

"Or maybe they hunted them. This could have been a fishing expedition," Kathleen added.

"Then what's this?" Benjamin had walked further along the fresco and pointed at something at the far end of it.

They joined him and saw it was a picture of a huge, coiled tentacled mass. But the tip of each of the tentacles appeared to end as people, or four-legged animals, or sometimes, fish.

"*Qwotoan*?" Meena read the name underneath it. "Is that a word or a name?"

"A name, I think," Kathleen replied. "I've heard it before, or something like it. I just can't place it."

"*Qwotoan*." Gino snorted. "Well, if that thing is real, I really don't want to meet it."

Meena stepped back, feeling a little unsettled by the image. "If – *when* – the scientists ever make it down here, they're going to love this place." She lowered her light. "Come on, we're burning our batteries. Let's keep moving."

All the lights bar Meena's went out and Benjamin sighed loudly as he picked up the end of Aaron's stretcher and the team set off once again.

They were encouraged by the fact they were still headed upward. But the millions of tons of raw rock pressed in on them, and after a while they were relieved to find another opening into a larger space.

They fanned out and something on the ground rattled metallically and skittered out from under their feet.

Kathleen crouched down and scooped some up. "Hey, shell casings." She held them out.

Meena stared down at them, not knowing what it all meant. "There's so many. How?"

"And they're like the knife – old, but not that old," Gino remarked.

Benjamin eased Aaron down and came and looked over the cave floor. "There's hundreds. *Hundreds*. There were a lot of people, soldiers, shooting here. I bet the same team who dropped that knife." He frowned. "Something bad went down here." He looked up. "Why would they all be firing in a cave?"

"Why indeed." Kathleen let the shells drop. "And at what exactly?"

"I don't like this," Phillipa said in a small voice.

"*Qwotoan*," Gino said. "That's what they were firing at."

"Shut up, Gino. That's not funny." Phillipa glared at him.

"Go forward or turn back?" Meena asked, unsure of herself now.

"I think it's still on high tide." Kathleen remarked and then turned to look into the dark cave ahead of them. "We've only been climbing for a few hours. I say we give it a bit longer." She raised her hand. "Go forward. Just a bit more."

"All in favor?" Meena asked.

After a moment, the others raised their hands. All except Phillipa.

Phillipa shook her head. "It smells funny in here."

Meena sniffed and detected that window cleaner smell again. It was a faint ammonia smell. "Do you think whoever was in here before urinated or something?"

"It should have long dried and vanished by now." Kathleen bobbed her head. "But that's probably it."

Meena shrugged. "Or maybe a weird cave just smelling like a weird cave."

"Let's make a call again in another hour, okay?" Kathleen asked. "We'll know by then whether it's leading us out or not. Plus the tide will have turned more."

They continued and as they passed by a side cave, no larger than a foot-wide crack in the cave wall, Meena paused as she thought she heard something move deep inside. Like a wet sliding. But heavy.

"Weird cave just a being a weird cave," she muttered and hurried to catch up with her team.

CHAPTER 36

Yuri checked the submersible's energy levels and, after hours of powering ahead at three knots, saw he still had a fifty percent charge – *excellent.*

He worried now that if his crew from the *Boris Yeltsin* came for him, he would miss them. Or if the *Sea Princess* crew was rescued, he might also miss that boat out if he didn't hurry. Even after all the traumas he had inflicted on them, he gambled that, at the end of the day, they would play by the rules and give him safe passage. And that was why he'd kept the woman alive – she would be his bargaining chip, his show of good actions to buy his way onboard.

He pushed the throttle forward and lifted the small craft to its maximum speed of six knots. The whine of the engines became a little higher pitched, but the extra surge was comforting. The sooner he was gone from this hellish place the better.

The Russian captain hummed an old tune of his youth – even though he had seemed to have lost everything, he still felt confident he could profit handsomely from his misadventure. There were people all around the world who would be willing to pay big money to come to a unique place like this – big game fishermen, monster enthusiasts, trophy hunters, and even bored sports stars wanting to show off to their latest girlfriends.

Yes, he thought, *I will not be out of pocket for long.*

He glanced over his shoulder at the woman and saw her eyes were open, but they were glassy and still seemed dead.

"You have one job to do, American woman. You must stay alive for me a little longer." He nodded to himself. "You will be my ticket out of here. But if you misbehave . . ." His lips turned down for a moment. ". . . then I think not so good for you."

After another twenty minutes of maintaining his course in the inky black sea, he felt the submersible veer sideways in the water. It could have been a crosscurrent, but he had a feeling it wasn't.

He looked around outside but saw nothing on the water's surface, so tried to ignore his instinct. But a massive fin suddenly surfacing beside the sub made that impossible.

The ghostly, pale fin silently cut the dark water and glided past them. But then, when it was ahead of them, it turned to come all the way around.

"*No, no, no,* you don't want me." He knew that having a top speed of six knots was a death sentence. If the monster shark wanted him, then he was as good as dead.

Or was he?

He looked over his shoulder at Cate. "I have good news and bad news. The good news is that you are going to be very helpful to me sooner rather than later."

He popped the canopy and let it slide back. "The bad news is you are going for a little swim."

The small craft was buffeted again, and Yuri knew he had little time. He leaped from his seat and climbed back to drag Cate roughly up by the tied wrists. She began to fight, using her tied hands like a two-handed club and smashed down on his nose.

Blood spurted and Yuri cursed. He punched back, hitting her in the eye socket and rocking her head back. He went to backhand her but pulled the blow, not wanting to throw her out unconscious. He needed her to thrash around a little. She was groggy now, but he knew once she hit the water she would come to.

He pulled his knife and slit the ties holding her hands. Then, in one move, he lifted and flipped her out of the cockpit cabin and into the dark water.

"Now you can join your boyfriend," he yelled. He drew the canopy back over himself, and put the small craft into a dive.

* * *

Cate came back to the surface, alert, and sucked in a breath. She took in mostly seawater. She had no strength left but knew immediately where she was and what was happening – the Russian had thrown her to the lions.

She came back up again and, in the dim blue light, could just make out the massive sail-like fin as it glided past, and then sank.

Jack had told her what this meant – it was going to come up from underneath her and take her whole. Just like it had done to him.

She felt so weak, she could barely keep her head up.

I hope it's the Megalodon that took Jack, she wished insanely. *Then I'll be with him.*

Cate had nothing left, no will to live, so she just let go. She sunk down, her eyes open, knowing that the beast was rising below her.

She was dimly aware of the strange pops, squeaks, and clicks coming from somewhere, but her oxygen-starved brain began to shut down, and she drifted deeper in a twilight world of warm, dark water.

* * *

The massive Megalodon shark was rising toward the small warm creature. It knew them and had tasted them before. They were small, but blood-rich and it accelerated, eager to consume the morsel.

All its senses were focused on the food to come, but it became aware of the other. And it was near. And worse, coming right at it.

It was one of the only things in its territory it avoided. And it did so now.

The seventy-five-foot Megalodon shark veered away, and with a few powerful sweeps of its tail sped from the area. In a few minutes more, it knew it wasn't being followed and slowed.

It was still hungry. Always hungry. And it picked up the scent of the other thing that had been in the area before and followed that instead.

* * *

Cate coughed as she rose from the water. She was groggy and confused – somehow she was on land again, and she lay there drained of everything, still coughing and vomiting up the slimy seawater.

She looked up and saw the blurry stars high overhead. *This isn't heaven*, she thought.

Underneath her the rough ground seemed to move, and she turned her head to one side and saw the island she was on was black with dark blue stripes, and though the ground was an odd smooth texture, it was covered in barnacles and encrusted growths, and smelled like something from the bottom of the deepest oceans.

Livyatan, her brain whispered.

Fifty feet further out from her a much smaller version of the one she was carried upon surfaced, and stayed there, turning slightly so its large brown cow-like eye could regard her. It must have seen her movement as it veered closer, and she could even see the lashes over its eye.

Was that the calf she had saved earlier?

"Thank you," she said, and tried to sit up but instead exhaustion took her and her mind shut down again.

CHAPTER 37

Sonya stood in the small boat. The spotter plane had dropped another raft containing supplies and more clothing and relayed their exact position and status to the rescue ship.

The ship, the *Sea Prince*, was almost a duplicate of the *Sea Princess*, but had no onboard guns, lasers, or armaments.

Sonya raised her arm to wave to the ship but knew they had seen her and would have them in the next twenty minutes. She turned to smile at Jorge.

"Everything will work out," she said and then turned to Chekov.

"No sign of your boat. I think they have left you behind."

Chekov stared out over the frozen watery landscape. "I don't blame them. No contact for days, and they would have been running low on fuel and supplies." He turned back to the glacier. "Maybe Yuri got out. And then simply sailed them away."

Sonya stared at him for several seconds. "If he is alive, I will find him, no matter where he is in the world. And I will strangle him myself."

Chekov stared back with a blank expression. After a moment, he spoke. "So it seems I am in need of transportation. May I catch a ride with you?"

Sonya nodded. "Yes. But we're going back in first."

Jorge's face dropped.

Sonya looked back toward the blue glacier opening. "We have unfinished business."

CHAPTER 38

As he powered away, Yuri didn't give the woman a second thought. All he had done was perform an act of self-preservation. Besides, she was nearly dead anyway.

He continued his dive. His plan was to drop all the way to the bottom and scoot along the seabed. Anything that happened up top would be a long way from him.

He switched on the forward light, but the tunnel of illumination showed nothing but dark water.

How far had he gone down? Five hundred feet? Seven hundred? He knew he couldn't descend much further as this small submersible was more of a pleasure craft and not an industrial-strength deep-sea vessel built to sustain significant depth pressure.

He decided to give it another hundred feet, and continued his voyage following his light beam down into the impossibly dark water. But that was when the canopy popped and creaked.

"Ah no, don't you do that to me." He reached up to touch the toughened synthetic canopy and felt a small vibration against his fingertips.

Change of plan, he thought. He would level off and just keep going at his current depth. At least for a while.

Yuri felt the vessel yaw sharply to the side and he gripped the control shaft and corrected its sideways slide.

He cursed under his breath and tried not to think what might have caused the submersible's movement. "Lights," he said and switched the front beam off.

He traveled on for another few minutes in complete darkness but was frustrated by the lack of sensory equipment. He'd end up running into one of the cave walls, or an undersea island.

"*Cyka*, no choice." He switched on the lights.

And screamed.

The massive Megalodon shark's maw filled his world. The light illuminated all the way down its gullet, and the jaws clamped down on the small vessel.

The giant teeth, each the size of a shovel, at first met resistance from the toughened Perspex composite and steel, as even though the sub was not a deep-sea craft, it was still designed to deal with a high level of pressure.

The problem was the pressure was supposed to be applied on all parts of the craft at once.

Yuri's hands were locked on the controls, and he continued to scream as the small vessel now in the pale monster's mouth was pushed backward through the water. No matter what he tried, nothing was in his control anymore.

Then he could feel gravity pushing him down in his seat, so he knew the monster was also forcing him up into shallower water, and a small speck of hope bloomed in his chest.

A few of the teeth that were dug into the canopy above him were creating star cracks in the toughened glass. And then he heard it, the tiny splintering noise.

He could do nothing. He had no weapons and no way out. All he could do was sit there and stare at the glass. And wait.

Then it came again; the tiny plinking sound of the cracks spreading. His one hope was that if the glass broke and he was in survivable depths, he might just be able to swim to the surface. If the Megalodon continued to attack the bigger object – the submersible – he could get away.

Yuri almost vomited from fear as his lights showed him down the gullet of the massive mouth and he shook his head. "No, I'm not going in there."

He began to hyperventilate, saturating his lungs with air. He had no idea how long he'd need to hold his breath before he made it to the surface, but he was going to give himself the best chance possible.

Then the jaws finally came together, the glass exploded and the bubble of air, and Yuri, were ejected. He was still too deep, and his eardrums burst. But he ignored the pain and swam frantically as from behind he could feel the vibrations in the water as the massive shark continued to chew on the metal craft.

You can't kill Yuri Zagreb so easily. Go back to hell, stupid fish, he thought as he powered upward.

Every few seconds was two strokes and another six feet. Another six feet further away from the monster. Just a little more, he prayed.

Then the tearing of steel from behind ceased, and there came a moment of complete stillness in the dark water.

Swim, swim, swim, he repeated in his head like a mantra.

He knew it was coming now. He couldn't hear it, or see it, but his animal senses told him it was coming for him.

Swim, swim, sw . . .

He was hit, hard, and pushed through the water. He felt a red-hot vice of pain at his waist and punched down into a wall of rough muscle, and knew his bottom half was in the creature's mouth.

There was a brutal shaking and then he was free. The pain was gone and in its place was a freezing coldness deep in his belly. And strangely, he was spinning in the water, unable to stop.

He tried to swim again but it felt strange, wrong, and he stopped swimming to feel down his body – there was nothing below his waist, nothing but streamers of intestine, and flaps of ragged flesh.

Yuri let the last of his breath leak from his mouth as he sensed the monster coming back.

Stupid fish, he thought again as he went straight down that maw to hell.

CHAPTER 39

The female Livyatan whale and its calf continued on for hours with Cate sitting on the massive bulk of its head. She knew that it was aware she was there, and from time to time the calf would swim closer to roll a little so it could stare up at her with its huge cow-like eye.

She waved, not knowing what else to do.

Beneath her she could feel the clicks and squeaks as the mother must have been talking to its baby, and also sending out echo location signals to determine where it was.

And where was that?

She had no idea where she was going and hoped she wouldn't suddenly be deposited in the center of the sea once the whale got bored with its game. Or worse, it decided to eat her.

In another twenty minutes the whale changed course slightly, and it slowed and stopped, hanging in the water like a black and blue striped island.

She reached down to lay her hand on the skin – it was a solid mass and warm to touch. She knew the Livyatan whale was a mammal, but it had once been the largest predator in the world, on land or sea, and had only reigned for a few million years before completely vanishing.

Just like the Megalodon, she thought, and yet here they

were. She recalled what Jack had said to her once about monsters: *you just gotta know where to look.*

And then the whale started to sink, and the water rose around her.

"Hey, wait." She got up on her knees. "What are you doing?"

The whale continued to slowly vanish beneath the water until it was no more. Cate was at first worried that its slipstream would drag her under, or a single flick of the massive tail from the warm-blooded giant would crush her bones. But it seemed to have been very careful and gentle in avoiding her.

The calf remained on the surface a while longer, before she felt the vibrations of the squeaks and clicks right through her bones as it was called, and then it too vanished.

"Thanks for nothing," she called after them.

She didn't know what to expect. It was not as if it was going to carry her around, wearing her like a tiny hat, forever.

After another moment or two the silence returned, and the still, dark water was as smooth and impenetrable as ever.

She tread water, turning slowly in a full circle. There was nothing in any direction, and overhead the blue twinkling lights gave her little illumination. She decided she would focus on what was above her, as she refused to think about what was below her, seeing her tiny body there – she was just a mayfly on a river's surface waiting for a trout to pick it off.

Should she start swimming? she wondered. *But to where?*

She sighed, feeling tired, hungry, and thirsty.

But then she heard something in the far distance and turned in the water – there was the tiniest dot of light at the far edge of her vision. It looked like a tiny glowing star, and she knew it was coming closer.

Cate prayed. *Please don't be that Russian asshole,* she breathed as she watched it slowly approach.

It has to be a ship, she thought.

Cate was tired as hell, but the thought that rescue might be coming gave her a shot of energy, and she tread water, lifting a little higher.

"Keep coming, keep coming," she whispered.

"*Hey!*" she yelled.

Too soon, she chided herself.

That yell had made her heart beat faster. She needed to save every remaining ounce of energy for when whatever was coming came close enough to see and hear her. And she'd damn well make sure they heard her.

If they kept coming this way.

"*Please, please,*" she whispered as she tread water in the hidden sea somewhere deep beneath the dark ice of the Antarctic.

* * *

Sonya stood on the bridge with arms folded, dry and warm. If she felt at all tired, she didn't show it.

"Debris up ahead." The pilot, Blake Sanders, looked up from his instruments. "Check it out?"

"Absolutely," she said. "We'll check everything out on the water that might be one of our people. Then we'll come back along the rock ledge and see if anyone is still there waiting for us."

Anderson nodded, and then frowned down at the sonar before his head snapped up to peer out through the large windows. "*Whoa,* big signature just appeared on the scope. Coming in hot."

"Direction?" Sonya strode forward and folded her arms.

He looked back and then half turned. "Not at us, at the debris on the water."

"Seems the devil is back and has found one of our people – we need to get there first. Full speed ahead," she ordered.

The *Sea Prince* moved up to ten knots. It cut the water cleanly as it bore down on the small object somewhere out on the dark surface.

"Will we win?" Sonya asked.

Anderson exhaled through his nose. "It'll be close." He turned, grimacing. "But I think, no."

"Break out the arms and get some shooters on deck." Sonya knew it would make little difference, but it might buy them a few more minutes. She stared straight ahead, willing them on faster.

* * *

Cate felt the push of the current under her feet as something went past. "Hello again?" She turned expecting to see her whale come back to the surface, perhaps keeping an eye on her.

But there was nothing but the inky black ocean. She felt a prickle of fear run up her spine, which then made her scalp crawl.

For some reason she didn't think it was her friendly whale, but something far more ominous. And where were the friendly pops, squeaks, and clicks?

"Oh, no-*ooo*. Don't you dare." She turned in the water, suddenly cold.

It can see me, but I can't see it, she remembered Jack had told her. *It can sense my heartbeat, smell me, and feel my vibrations*, she remembered.

Shut up, she demanded of her panicking mind.

But her mind wouldn't.

The wash came again from her other side.

Found you, found you, found you, her mind screamed.

She spun to look toward the lights coming her way – bigger now, but still so far away. She knew it was a ship. All she wanted was to be on that deck, up high, and a long, long way from the water.

The light from above lifted the illumination around her to be just a little below twilight – not enough to see clearly, but just enough to see the shape of things.

And then she saw it – the massive pale snout came up and rode along the surface, circling her, not more than fifty feet from her. It was just staying high enough in the water for the wheel-sized black, soulless eye to look right at her. It was huge. So big, it didn't seem real.

Little flashes of light went off behind her eyes, and she knew how a small animal felt when a predator was stalking it, knowing that there was nothing it could do to escape its fate of being eaten alive.

"Stop playing with me, you fucking bastard!" she shouted.

It could take her right now, she knew. But she bet it wanted to see her, maybe even see her face, see the fear in her wide eyes.

This devil had been canceled out by evolution, but it had found a place to thrive in this hidden, primordial hell.

Cate desperately wanted to turn and see how far away the ship was, but she didn't dare turn her face away from the monster lest it come at her. For some reason, she thought that while she stared at it, it stared back, and that kept them both locked in place.

But that vain thought was dispelled as the massive twenty-foot-high and ten-foot-wide corpse-white snout finally sunk back below the water.

She guessed it had seen enough.

"I'm coming, Jack," she whispered.

CHAPTER 40

"It's a person, and the Megalodon is right underneath them," Anderson said. "Seventy to seventy-eight feet. A lot of mass." He watched the sonar with the intensity of a hawk.

"We've met." Sonya's jaws clenched as she held the powerful binoculars to her eyes. "The person is Cate Granger. I want her alive, no matter what."

Sonya slowly lowered the binoculars. "Where's Jack, Cate?"

"Megalodon is now moving out to the left side, range is about one hundred feet, depth at about fifty. It's coming around. Coming up."

"The devil rises." Sonya sighted the huge dorsal fin as it broke the water. She grabbed the mic. "Fire at will. But *do not* hit the woman."

Gunfire rang out, but she knew that, even if they hit the shark, the rounds would be like pinpricks to the massive creature.

They were still five hundred yards out and steaming in fast. But the Megalodon shark was too close.

Anderson grimaced. "Not going to make it. It's accelerating and coming up on her . . . *now.*"

Sonya punched her hand down on the console in front of her so hard she split a knuckle. She stared furiously at her nemesis as it was about to take another of her people.

Anderson's mouth dropped open. "What the . . .?"

The water exploded as something came up from underneath the shark. The blue-black mountain rose and rose, with the huge, pale shark in its mouth. It kept rising fifty feet into the air. A huge bulbous head, and jaws that must have been twenty feet long.

It eventually came down again in an explosion of water that swamped Cate, and even rocked the huge boat.

"*Find her, find her.*" Sonya's voice was high. "All external lights on. Get divers over the side, now." She dropped the mic and headed up on deck.

* * *

The whale took its hated adversary down, right to the bottom.

The Livyatan whale was larger and more powerful than this shark, who had been tormenting it for days, and trying to pick off its calf. It was the reason the young one had accidently beached itself. And though the whale was an air breather without gills, it could stay down for two hours without any trouble. Sharks could breathe water, but unlike other fishes, they had sensitive static gills, and needed to keep moving to ensure fresh oxygenated water passed over those gills. If not, the shark would drown.

When the Livyatan whale got to the bottom, it held the shark still against the mud, using its huge fluke to generate enough power to keep the monster pinned down.

But the Megalodon was like the great white shark in that its tail had caudal fins, unique amongst all the fishes, meaning the top half of the fin was far longer than the bottom half. This uneven design was common in many prehistoric fishes, but sharks are the only group to maintain the shape over a period of 350 million years.

What the tail allowed the shark to perfect was performing 'the spin', where the shark rolled, usually when it was tearing away massive amounts of food from a body, but also to get out of trouble.

And so, the Megalodon rolled, and its gigantic mass forced its way out of the Livyatan's mouth and in two sweeps of its tail, it was away.

But it didn't flee. Instead, its territorial instincts forced it to return for an attack. And as the huge whale began to come around, the Megalodon struck, clamping down on its flank with its spade-length, razor-sharp teeth.

The whale was pushed sideways in the water, and the jaws of the monster shark began to come together.

The Megalodon's bite pressure was around 40,000 pounds per square inch and the greatest bite force of any animal that ever lived on the planet. Its normal feeding and attack routine was to dig its jaws in, shake its head from side to side, and use its serrated blade teeth to cut right through the tough skin, muscle, and bone, and undoubtedly tear away several tons of meat. The whale would never recover.

The Livyatan used its fluke tail to shift the shark in the water, but with the Megalodon attached, all it could do was move the huge beast but not dislodge it.

The whale had lived for over a century and knew that if it couldn't remove the shark, the coming mortal wound would be devastating.

In the deep, black water, the scent of blood filled the area in a growing cloud, further exciting the Megalodon. Soon, more sharks would come.

The Livyatan groaned, the sound, a long, bass moan echoing out into the primordial depths of the hidden sea as the shark began to press its advantage.

The teeth were dug deep into the tough hide now, and the shark began its shake as it must have determined now was time to tear away the massive chunk of flesh.

At that moment, the Livyatan calf rocketed out of the

gloom. At just a few years old it was already the size of a truck, and came like a missile, directly at the gill slits of the shark.

It hit with an audible *thump*, and the Megalodon's sensitive gill fans, just inside the skin flaps, were damaged and started to leak blood.

Immediately, the shark's ability to breathe was compromised, and it let go – it was a mistake, as the Livyatan whale was not disabled.

The shark veered away, but came back fast, perhaps trying for easier prey as it began to hunt the whale calf instead. But the adult Livyatan, a raptorial whale, and the largest to ever exist on our planet, had already turned in the water.

Its echo location found the shark easily, and using every ounce of energy it turned its hundred-ton body into a battering ram of colossal proportions.

In the last hundred feet, it further accelerated to drive its solid, bulbous head into the Megalodon's exposed belly, bringing all of its hundred-ton mass and force together to crush cartilage, tear skin, and explode the Megalodon's gut from its gaping jaws.

The broken Megalodon twitched in the water, but its dying brain had no control over its body anymore. It sank to the bottom, where the calf followed it down to butt at its tail and fins, tormenting it, maybe taking some of its own revenge against the hated beast.

In twenty minutes, there was no movement and the giant carcass lay on the bottom, belly up. But the whale continued to circle the Megalodon shark's body for another fifteen minutes watching for any signs of life.

Blood seeped out in a cloud and the huge crustaceans that inhabited the stygian depths were already approaching in anticipation of the feast to come.

Satisfied, the huge female whale and her calf veered away.

This was its territory, and there would always be other challengers. But from this one, no more.

* * *

Cate was hauled up the side of the boat in the winch cage and held in place by one of the divers. At the top she was helped over the side rail. A blanket was thrown around her shoulders and a warm coffee thrust toward her. But she couldn't hold it as her hands refused to stop shaking.

Her head was down, and her hair hung forward over her bleached white face. Sonya rushed to her and grabbed her shoulders.

"I'm so glad, I thought . . ." She embraced her. "You were nearly taken by the devil."

Cate pushed her back and glared up at the tall woman for a second or two before punching her square on the jaw.

"*No*," Cate said through gritted teeth. "*You're* the devil."

She went to punch Sonya again but staggered as her legs began to buckle under her. She was held up by one of the crew.

She glared. "Everyone around you dies. You brought us here, and where is everyone? All your crew? And Jack, *my Jack* is dead because you took us from our paradise and brought us down to your own personal hell."

"Cate . . ." Sonya began.

"Your obsession with this monster has killed us all. I hate you." Cate backed away. "I hate you."

Sonya stood silently and watched her medical team take the woman below deck. Jorge came and stood beside her. "She's wrong about you. You did your best."

She sighed. "No, she's right. I'm like a disease infecting and killing everyone." She sucked in a huge breath and let it out with a slight groan. After a few moments she lifted her head and straightened her back.

"Let's find Meena and the rest of our people. Then we can all go home."

"And this place?" Jorge asked.

Sonya paused. "On the way out I blow the explosives and bring the cave roof down to seal it up. No one will ever find it again. Ever. I'll make sure of it." She looked back over her shoulder. "And nothing will ever get out again." She turned on her heel and headed back to the bridge.

CHAPTER 41

Meena huddled in the darkness, her back pressed to a cave wall and legs drawn up to her chest. Her eyes were wide, but she saw nothing in a darkness that was so complete if she held her hand a fraction of an inch from her face she still wouldn't see it.

On her forehead she had the heat vision goggles pushed up. When she had pulled them over her eyes she saw her own hands and feet, flaring red and orange, but little else in the cool cave. She had preferred the black nothingness over the red-orange ghost of herself and pushed them up again.

She took a shuddering breath and gripped her flashlight. It was long dead now and she held it as a club. It was the only defense she had, other than sitting silent and motionless and trying to make herself invisible in the darkness.

Meena's eyes were wide and blind as she strained to hear the slightest noise. But she knew she was alone, and her friends had all gone. The unconscious Aaron was taken first. He had been in a coma and Benjamin and Gino put him down in a corner on their trek up inside the winding caves so they could take a break and talk softly in the darkness.

When they went back, their makeshift stretcher was there, but the unconscious man wasn't. Their first thought was he had regained his senses and been disorientated and then simply wandered off in the darkness.

They gave up looking for him after an hour.

But then Benjamin stepped into a side cave following what he thought was the hint of a breeze. And he never came out. The weird thing was the cave was a dead-end after about fifty feet – there was nowhere for him to go.

Once again, they called and searched, but there was no trace. Kathleen founds puddles of something like jelly or mucous that had an acrid ammonia smell like a mix of window cleaner, bleach, and something organic.

Then Phillipa screamed. She was at the rear, and Kathleen, Gino and Meena had rushed back in time to see her wedging herself into a crevice in the cave wall – harder and harder – but it was impossible as it was no more than a few inches wide. In the beams of their wobbling flashlights her face was turned to them, and it was bleached bone-white from fear and pain.

When they got to her, following the brittle cracking sound of her skull, she vanished inside. She was still visible, or what was left of her, for a few moments before the blue shirt she wore was dragged so far in they lost sight of her.

No one said anything, until Kathleen spoke – Kathleen, the mature and sensible one, now sounded like a frightened child. "Something had hold of her."

"Smell that?" Gino asked. "That same damn stink of ammonia like when Benny went missing."

"I don't think . . ." Meena began.

"*Qwotoan,*" Gino said. "I told you. *I told you.*" He spun at her, his eyes wide with all the white showing around the pupils. "We're dead. We're all fucking *dead.*" His voice became a scream. "*It's going to get us all.*"

"*Stop it,*" Meena shouted.

Her words echoed away in the darkness, and just as they began to die away to silence, they all heard that horrifying, wet sliding noise again. It was getting closer.

They panicked then – running for their lives. Meena knew that Gino was right. Something in here was hunting them and taking them one by one.

"Fuck this. I'm going back down." Gino turned and sprinted back the way they'd come, moving fast, and quickly leaving Meena and Kathleen behind.

"Wai-*iiittt*," Meena yelled.

But both women stopped dead when, from far up ahead, Gino let out a bloodcurdling scream that made Meena feel like she received an electric shock.

Indecision momentarily tore at them, but Meena steeled herself and sprinted after her lost crewmate. Kathleen ran behind her.

They rounded a bend in time to see Gino in the embrace of what looked like Phillipa. But she was stuck to him. She wasn't holding him, but the length of her body where they touched seemed to have melted onto him, and the stink of ammonia made her eyes stream with acidic tears.

Gino cried out, and half turned his glued face all he could. "It hurts," he moaned, and lifted his free arm to them.

Meena went to step forward, but Kathleen grabbed her.

"Don't," she said.

Meena turned back in time to see the young man yanked away into the darkness.

They turned then, not even wanting to find out what happened, but instead to run back the other way. Deeper into the caves.

Meena and Kathleen ran blindly, and Meena, younger and faster, quickly outpaced the older woman. And of course, in the labyrinthine tunnels they ended up going in different directions.

And Meena became hopelessly lost.

And now she was here.

Whatever it was seemed to find them when they moved. Or

when they spoke or made a noise. So she wouldn't move and wouldn't make a sound.

Now it became clear to her what all those bullets meant. Whoever those soldiers were they were firing at the thing that hunted them in the dark caves.

Did their guns save them? she wondered.

A while ago, from somewhere far away, she heard what she thought was a distant explosion. She couldn't tell if it was minutes or hours ago as time meant nothing in here.

From the darkness she heard the wet sliding noise again, and then smelled the eye-watering ammonia stink. She felt she wasn't alone anymore in her tiny alcove, and she carefully reached up to pull the thermal goggles down over her eyes.

"Kathleen?" she whispered. "Is that you?"

The woman stood there. Not moving. But in the thermal vision she glowed a cold and lifeless blue and seemed to glisten as if covered in slime.

"Why are you so cold?" Meena's voice was little more than a squeak.

The figure glided closer – *glided* – because it didn't seem to use its legs.

Meena knew then it wasn't Kathleen and drew her knees back in even closer to herself. She put both hands over her mouth and nose and held her breath.

She wouldn't make a sound. Wouldn't even breathe. She would stay right here until someone came for here.

Sonya would come, Sonya would never leave her behind.

She closed her eyes and began to pray.

EPILOGUE

Forty-two years later, Nick's Cove, Marin County, California

The once beautiful boat, the *Heceta*, was on dry land, held upright in a wooden cradle. It had deteriorated to little more than warped decking, flaking paint, and rusting fixtures.

But the old boat still held one occupant, two if you counted Thompson, the permanently pissed-off, ginger cat who often visited the old lady who lived onboard.

The tiny woman sat watching a small screen linked to the internet as it telegraphed images from the drone above two research ships who were anchored just off the mouth of Thwaites Glacier at the Antarctic. Apparently, soundings had detected a void behind the newly exposed rock face, and they planned to open it. And then enter.

Catherine Jean Granger slowly shook her head. "Don't do it," she muttered.

Behind the two ships was another vessel, observing, and it was longer and sleeker, and far more modern. On its deck a lone person stood at the bow with binoculars to their eyes. Beside them there was something under a large tarpaulin.

As the drone's camera zoomed in, Cate could read the ship's name: *The Valery Mironov III.*

"Of course it's you." Cate's dry lips curved into a smile as Thompson leaped up and sat on the arm of the chair beside her. He looked up at her with his usual disinterested gaze for a moment, before turning to watch the images on the screen as if he understood what was about to happen.

Cate blinked red-rimmed eyes and watched as two smaller boats planted the explosive charges, and then retreated to a safe distance.

Her jaws clenched and her eyes slid to a picture frame on the shelf. Inside there was an old photograph that had been torn into four pieces, but then stuck back together with tape.

"We warned them," she muttered.

The picture was taken forty-two years ago and was of Jack, her, and a tall, fierce-looking Russian woman, Sonya Borashev, on the deck of the *Heceta.* It was taken just days before they went into the monster's cave.

Cate's eyes slid back to the screen; she knew it was an older Sonya who was now on the deck of the boat, watching and waiting. As she said she always would.

The narrator's voice was almost reverent as he told the audience that the scientists expected to find a body of water inside that may have been locked away for millions of years. They even postulated that they may find lifeforms inside not seen since before human beings even stood on their hind legs.

Cate snorted with derision and her sun-spotted, gnarled hands gripped the arms of the chair as the countdown approached zero.

The explosion shook the drone's screen for a few seconds and when the debris finished splashing down, a huge dark cave was exposed.

As if had been waiting, it came.

The huge white form surged from the cave mouth just below the waterline. Even from a distance its size seemed impossible, and it headed straight for the largest research ship, and struck it dead center, like the battering ram of a god.

The huge ship broke in half, and the massive shark passed right through the burning debris and rounded on the next ship.

On the bow of the *Valery Mironov III* the lone figure ripped the covers from the hidden item revealing a large twin barreled deck cannon, and with long silver hair streaming behind her she jumped into the seat and commenced firing huge tracer rounds into the water.

Even without sound, Cate could imagine some sort of Russian war cry booming out over the frozen sea.

Then came a massive explosion as the second ship was hit, and sunk, and then the feed from the drone was cut and the screen went black.

Cate put a hand on Thompson's head, who allowed her, and only her, to pat him. Thompson looked up at her briefly with his usual flat gaze, and then turned away.

"I tried to warn them not to open that cave." Catherine Granger's eyes were dead as she whispered the words. "Because when the gates of hell open, the first beast through will be the Leviathan."

Printed in the USA
CPSIA information can be obtained
at www.ICGtesting.com
LVHW051112180823
755540LV00045B/425